Lou... ...hen she grew up, ... ...d.

Several years ago an accid... ...she began writing onc... ...compromised ... ...nan ... Louise loves creati... ...vorlds, dark characters, and twist... ...ots.

Loui... ...in Nort... ...shire with ...r husband, sons, a dog an... ...er naughty cat, and also teaches mindfulness.

www.louisejensen.co.uk

# *The* Surrogate

## LOUISE JENSEN

sphere

SPHERE

First published in 2017 by Bookouture, an imprint of StoryFire Ltd.
This paperback edition published in 2018 by Sphere

1 3 5 7 9 10 8 6 4 2

Copyright © Louise Jensen 2017

A CIP catalogue record for this book
is available from the British Library.

ISBN 978-0-7515-7059-5

Printed and bound in Great Britain by
Clays Ltd, Elcograf S.p.A.

Papers used by Sphere are from well-managed forests
and other responsible sources.

Sphere
An imprint of
Little, Brown Book Group
Carmelite House
50 Victoria Embankment
London EC4Y 0DZ

An Hachette UK Company

www.hachette.co.uk
www.littlebrown.co.uk

*For my sister, Karen Appleby,*
*the strongest woman I know.*

*If you prick us, do we not bleed?*
*If you tickle us, do we not laugh? If you poison us,*
*do we not die? And if you wrong us, shall we not revenge?*
*—William Shakespeare*

# LATER

There is a rising sense of panic; horror hanging in the air like smoke.

'They're such a lovely couple. Do you think they're okay?' says the woman, but the flurry of emergency service vehicles crammed into the quiet cul-de-sac, the blue and white crime scene tape stretched around the perimeter of the property, indicate things are anything but okay. She wraps her arms around herself as though she is cold, despite this being the warmest May on record for years. Cherry blossom twirls around her ankles like confetti, but there will be no happily ever after for the occupants of this house, the sense of tragedy already seeping into its red bricks.

Her voice shakes as she speaks into the microphone. It is difficult to hear her over the thrum of an engine, the slamming of van doors as a rival news crew clatters a camera into its tripod.

He thrusts the microphone closer to her mouth.

She hooks her red hair behind her ears; raises her head. Her eyes are bright with tears.

TV gold.

'You don't expect anything bad… Not here. This is a *nice* area.'

Disdain slides across the reporter's face before he rearranges his features into the perfect blend of sympathy and shock. He hadn't spent three years having drama lessons for nothing.

He tugs the knot in his tie to loosen it a little as he waits for the woman to finish noisily blowing her nose. The heat is insufferable; shadows long under the blazing sun. Body odour exudes from his armpits, fighting against the sweet scent of the freshly cut grass. The smell is cloying, sticking in the back of his throat.

He can't wait to get home and have an ice-cold lager. Put on his shorts like the postman sitting on the edge of the kerb, his head between his knees. He wonders if he is the one who found them. There will be plenty of angry people waiting for their post today. 'Late Letter Shock!' is the sort of inane local story he usually gets to cover, but this… this could go national. His big break. He couldn't get here fast enough when his boss called to say what he thought he'd heard on the police scanner.

He shields his eyes against the sun with one hand as he scouts the area. Across the road, a woman rests against her doorframe, toddler in her arms. He can't quite read her expression and wonders why she doesn't come closer like the rest of them. At the edge of the garden, as close as the police will allow, a small crowd is huddled together: friends and neighbours, he expects. The sight of their shocked faces is such a contrast to the neat borders nursing orange marigolds and lilac pansies. He thinks this juxtaposition would make a great shot. The joy of spring tempered by tragedy. New life highlighting the rawness of loss of life. God, he's good; he really should be an anchor.

There is movement behind him, and he signals to the cameraman to turn around. The camera pans down the path towards the open front door. It's flanked by an officer standing to attention in front of a silver pot containing a miniature tree. On the step are specks of what looks like blood. His heart lifts at the sight of it. Whatever has happened here is big. Career defining.

Coming out of the house are two sombre paramedics pushing empty trolleys, wheels crunching in the gravel.

The woman beside him clutches his arm, her fingertips pressed hard against his suit jacket. Silly cow will wrinkle the fabric. He fights the urge to shake her free; instead, swallowing down his agitation. He might need to interview her again later.

'Does this mean they're okay?' asks the woman, confusion lining her face.

The trolleys are clattered into the back of the waiting ambulance. The doors slam shut, the blue lights stop flashing and slowly it pulls away.

From behind the immaculately trimmed hedge, hidden from view, he hears the crackle of a walkie-talkie. A low voice. Words drift lazily towards him, along with the buzz of bumblebees and the stifled sound of sobbing.

'Two bodies. It's a murder enquiry.'

# CHAPTER ONE
## Now

*Don't turn around.*

Behind me, the laughter rings out again. I tell myself it can't be her, but I know, even after all this time, it is. The world falls away from me and I grip the counter so hard my knuckles bleach white.

*Don't turn around.*

In front of me, Clare's mouth forms the question: 'whipped cream?', but I can't hear anything above the thrumming in my ears. I shake my head as though I can dislodge the buzzing that's growing louder and louder. Clare lowers her arm; the nozzle to the cream had been poised over my mug. I always have the same drink every time I come here, but today the sound of laughter has thrust me back into the past. The smell of the hot chocolate I usually find so tantalising is causing my stomach to roll.

'Are you okay, Kat?'

I'm hot, tugging at my scarf as though it is choking me. White frost still patterns the pavement outside, but in here it is stifling; the coffee machine hisses and spits and steam rises towards the oak beam ceiling.

An impatient cough from the man shuffling his feet behind reminds me I have not yet answered Clare.

'I'm fine,' I say but my mouth is dry. My voice a strange croak. Pushing coins over the counter with one hand, I pick up my drink with the other. Hot liquid slithers down the side of the mug, trickling over my fingers, scalding my skin. Reluctantly I turn around. There it is again.

Laughter.

*Her laughter.*

My eyes dart around the café, and when I see her, everything else fades into the distance. She has her back towards me but I'd recognise that glossy black bob anywhere. She runs her fingers through her hair as she speaks animatedly to the elderly lady sat opposite her; tilting her head to the side she listens to the response. It seems like I saw her only yesterday, but of course I didn't.

*Lisa.*

My palms feel hot as they start to tingle. I haven't had a panic attack for such a long time, but underneath the mounting anxiety is an inevitability about it all, a resignation almost.

I'm unsure what to do at first; my feet roasting in my UGG boots. My scalp prickling. The room around me tilts and sways. I move to lean against the wall and it bears my weight while the lunchtime crowd stream in for their bowls of home-made soup and paninis dripping with melted cheese. There's no way I can leave without her seeing me and I can't face the confrontation. Already, I am emotionally drained and longing to check my mobile once again for news. Focusing all my attention on placing one foot in front of the other, I inch my way towards the round table in the corner, all the time feeling as though I might faint. Sinking into a tub chair, I plonk my shopping bags on the floor as I try to make myself as small as possible. My drink remains untouched in front of me, a thick skin forming on the top. My throat is tight and I cannot swallow. *What is she doing here?* We are sixty miles from home, and as I think this, it jars me I still automatically refer to *that* place as home, and not here, where I have made a new life. Fingering the gold cross hanging around my neck, memories crash and tumble around my mind: our first day at school; Lisa crouching to tie up my shoelaces as I hadn't yet learned; cross-legged in my garden in the hot summer sun, threading daisies into chains, and later, stuffing toilet tissue in our bras, and practising kissing on the backs of our hands. I have missed her so much but I don't know what to say to make amends. What I can possibly do to make it right. I can pretend I don't need her, but that doesn't stop the aching inside my chest when I think of the friendship we once had.

A loud clearing of the throat draws my gaze sideward. A couple glower at me as they wait for an empty table, their tray laden with steaming coffee and slabs of cake with cream cheese icing. Apologies spill from my lips as I pull on my coat, gather my bags. Taking a deep breath I stand and march towards the exit, head down, eyes fixed firmly on the floor. I have almost reached the door, my fingers brushing the cool metal handle, when a voice calls, 'Kat.' I can't help turning around.

'Lisa.' I study the face of my ex best friend, expecting to see anger, hurt, at the very least, but a smile creeps across her face. Her eyes crinkling at the edges. You would think the blazing row we had the last time we were together never happened. Or what came after. Especially what came after.

'I thought it was you!' She looks genuinely pleased to see me.

'What are you doing here?' My tone comes out more accusatory than I mean it to, and I soften my words with a tentative smile.

'I'm on a week's placement at St Thomas's Hospital. I'm a nurse now.'

'Like your mum?' I blurt out. I never usually allow myself to think of her family. Or of my own.

*The here and now.*

'What about you?' she asks.

'I've lived here for a few years.'

'What a coincidence.'

*Is it?* I hate the sense of mistrust creeping its way into my being. After all, Lisa is not the one who did anything wrong, is she? Before I can respond she has enveloped me in a huge hug. 'I've missed you so much,' she says, and despite my misgivings, I find myself hugging her back.

'You're not leaving already, are you?' she asks.

I glance out into the street. At the grey skies laden with swollen clouds. At the people rushing by, heads down, pushing against the biting wind. I know I have hesitated for a moment too long when she asks me if I have eaten lunch and my stomach growls in response.

'Aren't you with?…' I gesture towards the old lady at the table.

'No. I was just passing the time.'

Lisa always did have the ability to chat to anyone, to fit in anywhere, and I feel the dull weight of the loneliness I always carry.

A quick bite to eat. It can't do any harm, can it?

'I think we've lost your table.' Two teenage girls are slipping into the empty seats.

'I vote we find a pub.' Lisa grins, and the years fall away. Tears inexplicably spring to my eyes as I find myself pleased she is here. Not a chance to recreate the past; I shudder when I think of the past, but there is comfort in the familiarity: the way she links her arm through mine; the floral perfume she still wears. Icy air gusts into the coffee shop as she shoulders open the door.

'We can walk to the pub over there.' I nod towards the building opposite: warm honey lamps glowing in the window, sign creaking in the wind. Nick and I often eat there.

A light snow has begun to fall, and as we pick our way across the icy road to The Fox and Hounds, I taste frost and hope on my tongue. Almost ten years. And just when we are approaching the anniversary, fate has brought us back together. That has to be a good thing, doesn't it?

\*

'Here's the local celebrity.' Mitch puts down the glass he is polishing and slings the gingham tea towel over his shoulder. 'The usual?' He pours a shot and fizzes open a bottle of tonic.

I take a sip. The vodka heats me from the inside out, thawing my chilled bones. Leading the way across the pub, I ignore the seats by the open fire that crackles and spits. Instead, we slide into my favourite booth in the corner.

'This is nice.' Lisa looks around. 'Not exactly The Three Fishes, is it?'

'Thank God!' We spent too much time there as teenagers, perching on bar stools with long chrome legs and faux leather pads. Sipping overpriced wine tasting of vinegar. 'Do you remember how often we used to slide off those stools?'

'Yes! I permanently had one foot ready to break my fall.'

'So, how are you?' I ask. There's a drawn-out pause.

Lisa tucks her hair behind her ears. 'Fine,' she says, eventually, with a smile that disappears before it is fully formed, and I get a sense there was something else she wanted to say, but instead, she asks: 'What was that about? "Local celebrity"?'

'It's nothing.' I pick at the beer mat on the table, peeling back the cardboard on the corner.

'It's hardly nothing.' Mitch rests a chalkboard on the corner of our table with the specials scrawled in his spidery handwriting.

Today's soup is carrot and coriander. I wrinkle my nose. I don't eat carrots unless they're in a cake.

'Kat and her husband were in one of those glossy Sunday supplements, at a posh charity dinner, mingling with the rich and famous. Wasn't as good as the food you get here though, was it, Kat?'

'Nothing quite beats your sticky toffee pudding.' I sense Lisa's eyes on me as I study the menu, my long hair falling forward, shielding my cheeks. I know they must be flaming.

'Roast turkey.' Lisa rubs her hands together.

It's only the 1st of December but Mitch has had a ridiculously tall tree in the corner for weeks now. Red and silver tinsel twisted around its plastic branches. Cheesy Christmas songs drift out of discreetly positioned speakers. The Pogues sing 'Fairytale of New York'.

'Pasta for me.'

Mitch bustles towards the kitchen. A heavy silence descends, pushing me back into my seat. I could stretch out my fingers and touch Lisa but the gulf between us seems impossible to breach. And for once, she seems nervous, fiddling with her cutlery.

'Lisa…' I trail off, sifting through my mind for the words I know I should say. Trying to put them in some sort of order before they spill from my lips, self-pitying and damaging.

'Shh. It's ok.'

'I hit you.' Even now my palm still stings when I think about it.

'We both made mistakes. Did things we regret, didn't we?'

'Yes, but your mistakes didn't kill anybody,' I whisper.

There is a pained expression on Lisa's face, and I feel compelled to carry on.

'About that night…' A hard lump lodges in my throat and I drain the dregs in my glass trying to wash it down.

'Kat.'

Lisa covers my hand with hers. Her skin soft and familiar. Tears rise and I bite them back, remembering the way we used to link fingers as we'd dash out into the playground, eager to get to the hopscotch before anybody else.

'You must hate me?' The hate I have for myself is ever present, smouldering away in the pit of my stomach. It would be a relief, almost, if she slapped me, screamed, at the very least.

'I did hate you,' she admits, and although not unexpected, her words still spear me, 'for a long time, but not so much for what happened – that wasn't your fault – but because you ran away, I suppose. We could have got through it together, and I have got through it.' Her voice is strong and determined.

'I had to leave. It wasn't my choice…' My voice cracks.

'We don't have to talk about it. Not right now anyway. Let me get some more drinks. Same again?'

'Please,' I say, even though I'm such a lightweight I should have a lemonade. But although the hot flush of panic has cooled, my heart is still racing a little faster. My breath is still coming a little quicker. The warm bloom of alcohol will calm me, I know.

Lisa slides out of her seat, and I take the opportunity to check my mobile again. Instead of a text alert, a picture of me and Nick kissing on our wedding day fills the screen. My mood dips when I see there is still no news. While Lisa is ordering our drinks, I slip into the toilets and splash cold water onto my face. Patting my skin dry with a rough paper towel I catch sight of my reflection in the mirror, my pale face framed by dark poker straight hair, the deep purple bags that shadow my eyes.

Back at the table I tip tonic into my glass, watching as tiny bubbles shimmy amongst the ice cubes.

'I don't know how you can still drink vodka,' Lisa says. 'Do you remember Perry Evans's party? We must have drunk nearly a whole bottle between us.' She pulls a face as though it was yesterday.

I haven't partied like that in over ten years. Nick keeps trying to persuade me to have a big celebration for my birthday next year, but I keep putting off thinking about turning thirty.

'I remember holding your hair back while you were sick all over the washing-up in the sink.'

I laugh at the memory and the sound momentarily startles me.

'I've never touched the stuff since.' Lisa shudders theatrically. 'Jake was there that night too, wasn't he?' Her question is casual, as if she can't quite remember, but I know she can. I see my own hurt reflected in her eyes.

Before I can answer, Mitch sets down a bowl of steaming carbonara and buttery garlic bread in front of me. As I lean forward to reach the salt, the gold cross around my neck hangs down, and Lisa lightly touches it with two fingers.

'You still wear this?'

I don't answer. I don't need to. I know we are both remembering, and I wonder whether, even after all this time, Lisa thinks she should be the one wearing this cross, but as usual, I'm connecting dots that aren't there. She's been nothing but friendly.

We fall silent for a few minutes as I twirl pasta around my fork. Lisa tackles one of Mitch's legendary roast potatoes which Nick and I always joke should come with a chainsaw.

'Tell me about this husband of yours then. Nick, isn't it? He's the patron of a charity?'

I've a mouthful of food so I nod my response, and at first, I am grateful for the change of subject but, just as I begin to swallow, I realise Mitch never referred to Nick by his name and neither did he say Nick was the patron of a charity. The bread sticks in my throat. Is it really a coincidence she is here or has she purposefully tracked me down? And if so, why?

*Revenge* whispers the voice inside my head.

I drain my drink to silence it.

# CHAPTER TWO
## Now

'Is everything okay with your food?' Mitch asks.

'It's gorgeous,' Lisa says. 'I was just asking Kat about Nick.' Lisa turns to look at me. 'Mitch was telling me a little about his charity work while I ordered drinks at the bar. He sounds a lovely man.'

That's how Lisa knows about Nick, there's nothing more sinister than that. Relieved, I order a bottle of red.

Lisa eats as I push food around my plate, filling up my glass twice as often as I do hers. She is barely drinking, sipping water instead.

'Why did you move here? We came on a school trip once, didn't we? The castle on the hill?'

'The rubble more like,' I say. 'Crappy Craneshill we called it, didn't we?' I suppose that was what drew me. The memories. The fact I'd been here with Jake. 'It seemed as good a place as any.'

'How long have you been married?' Lisa asks.

I twist my ring around my finger. The diamonds glint as they catch the light.

'Eight years.'

Lisa grasps my hand and runs her thumb lightly over my wedding band. 'Very nice! White gold?'

'Platinum.' I feel defensive although I'm not quite sure why. We both work so hard. Nick came from nothing, just like me. It's testament to how strong he is that he left school without any qualifications but he's made a success of his life anyway. He is determined to provide for our family. *Our family*. My mouth can't help stretching into a smile. Soon we will be three.

'It obviously suits you. Being married.' Lisa jars me out of my thoughts. 'How did you meet?'

'Sorry, I was miles away. I was temping and was sent to Stroke Support, a charity Nick was setting up with his best friend, Richard, after Richard's grandmother had a stroke.' I can still remember first meeting Nick in the greasy spoon – the charity still doesn't have an office, even now. Our outgoings are minimal, most of our staff volunteers. I was expecting him to be ancient, but he was the same age as me, brilliant blue eyes, and black curls. Gorgeous, although I was blind to it at that time, still recovering emotionally and physically. Despite my numbness, I felt a flicker of interest listening to his plans. He was so passionate. 'People can change so much after a stroke. I want to help sufferers and their families come to terms with both the possible physical and mental impairments.' I found myself becoming more and more animated as we brainstormed fundraising ideas, perched on hard orange plastic chairs, bacon sandwiches in thick sliced bread for lunch, melted butter running down my chin. Nick had wiped it away with his thumb, and I felt a spark. He brought me back to life.

'And you still work for them, Mitch said?'

'Yes, I run everything. Richard is busy with his law firm, and Nick has a property development company. That keeps us afloat financially.' I don't draw a salary from the charity. I feel humbled to be able to help. Before I met Nick, I'd assumed strokes were something that only affected the elderly but this isn't the case at all. The stories I've heard over the years have been both harrowing and heart-warming. Triumph and tragedy. As well as the admin, I arrange counselling sessions and also take my turn to man the phone line. Each and every day I think how lucky I am to have good health.

'And Nick swept you off your feet?'

'I suppose so.' Initially, I was in no state to have a relationship and turned him down time and time again, but his kindness softened the hard shell I had encased myself in. One date led to two, to three, until before I knew it he was slipping the ring on my finger, and I promised I would love him for eternity, ignoring the gnawing feeling in the pit of my stomach telling me I should know nothing lasts forever. I was ready for my happily ever after. Even after eight years my heart skips a beat when he walks into a room. My nerve endings throb whenever he touches me. I'd be lost without him.

'How is your mum?' I study Lisa's face trying to gauge her reaction, but I can't read her expression.

'She's doing okay. You know what she's like,' she says, as if that should tell me all I need to know. It doesn't. I don't ask about her dad. There's little point but suddenly I feel compelled to talk about what happened.

'Lisa, I'm so sorry. About leaving. About everything.' The fuzziness from the alcohol is starting to fade away. A headache forming behind my eyes. Mitch walks past the table with plates laden with chips, the smell of oil makes me feel nauseous.

'You've nothing to be sorry for.'

But I have. I was involved in a car accident that rocked our small town and then ran away, leaving Lisa to deal with the questions. The speculation. But I couldn't talk about the horror that led to the crash, I just couldn't. Only two of us know the truth and it must stay that way.

'Sorry,' I say again. It doesn't seem enough. 'I still feel so ashamed. I haven't even told Nick about the crash.' He has no idea. I have hurt people.

'Why haven't you told him?'

'I don't know.' I pick at the beer mat again. 'At first it was just too raw, and then when I thought I could share, so much time had passed it seemed wrong to bring it up, as though I'd deliberately deceived him. I didn't want him to think less of me.'

'Please, Kat. Stop blaming yourself. It was ruled an accident. The police didn't press charges. It was one of those things. You've always been the same. Do you remember when Miss Masters gave you the part of Mary in the Nativity and Shelley Evans cried? You couldn't stop apologising, although it wasn't your fault.'

'I remember picking up the Baby Jesus and his head falling off and rolling into the audience.' Even now, I can picture the front row. The sniggering, the sympathetic looks, the mortification on the faces of my parents. Lisa comforted me afterwards. It always seemed odd me longing to perform on stage when in real life I hate to be the centre of attention.

'I still think Shelley sabotaged the doll – silly cow.'

'Lisa, we were only eight! I'm sure she didn't.'

'You've always been too trusting, Kat.'

'Still, I don't suppose it matters now. It was hardly a West End production.' That had always been my dream, singing and dancing in musicals. To play Maria in *West Side Story*. I so very nearly did once.

'Do you still act?'

I hesitate before I answer. I suppose you could say I pretend every day but I know that's not what Lisa means.

'No.'

'That's a shame – you were really good. So what do you do in your spare time? You have kids?' She gestures towards the Mothercare bags heaped on the floor.

'Let me show you.' I fish my phone from my handbag and swipe through the photos.

'This is Mai.'

Lisa's brow furrows in confusion as she studies the photo of the baby girl.

'She's yours?'

'Yes,' I say firmly. I'm staying positive, getting ready for her arrival, refusing to believe anything can go wrong this time.

'But she's…' Lisa trails off before voicing what I know I'll be asked a million times.

'Chinese. We're adopting her.'

'From China?'

'Yes. There are so many children in the world needing good homes we thought adoption was the right thing to do.' The words I've practised in front of the mirror for months while I've waited for the paperwork to be finalised sound stilted and forced. In truth, we'd been trying to conceive for almost two years before finding out we couldn't, and even today it still feels raw. I take another glug of wine. It shouldn't be long now. Nick thinks we'll hear this week and then our house will become a home, and all of a sudden I can't wait to get back there. To unpack the tiny pink dresses and warm fleecy Babygros into the glossy white drawers in the nursery. *The nursery!* I rummage in my handbag for my purse and gesture to Mitch for the bill. Inside my purse is the note Nick tucked there this morning.

*Stop worrying – I love you!*

It's going to work out this time. It has to. Outside the window, day has turned to night although it is only four o'clock. Snowflakes swirl past orange street lamps.

'How exciting. When do you get her?'

I puff out air. Not quite sure what to say. 'Soon. I hope. We should find out this week.' My voice is small. 'We tried before: it was a boy, but it all fell through, almost at the last minute. It's such a precarious process, adopting from a different country.' I'd been looking into the process here, but Richard, Nick's childhood friend and our solicitor, suggested we look further afield. He said we had far more chance of getting a newborn, and he was right.

Dewei was only six weeks old. 'We had to start from scratch when Dewei was given to another couple without explanation. I don't think I could face it all over again if it happens with Mai; I really don't know what we'd do but I have a good feeling this time.' I force a smile and don't tell Lisa I still wake in the night dreaming of Dewei, feeling the weight of him in my arms. The smell of his hair. I'd been utterly desolate.

'I can't say I blame you. Adopting. Having a baby without ending up with a pot belly.' Lisa pats her stomach.

'You have children?' Shame washes over me as I realise just how little I have asked Lisa about herself. In my mind, it is hard to separate her from the 19-year-old girl I last saw who vowed she never wanted a family but, of course, she's grown up now. She's changed. We both have. 'Boys or girls?'

'A girl.'

'What's her name?'

There's a beat. A twisting feeling in my gut as I wonder whether something went wrong.

Emotion glistens in Lisa's eyes, and I find I've curled my fingers, nails digging into my palms, while I wait for her to speak.

Finally, she quietly says: 'Gabrielle.'

I open my mouth to comment on her name, and Lisa whispers: 'she is absolutely beautiful.'

'Do you have a photo?'

'She's not… I didn't…' Lisa studies the table, and I lean forward, covering her hand with mine, almost sensing she's about to say something terrible. 'Don't judge me, Kat.'

'I won't. Did you?…' I want to ask if she gave her up, but I can't bring myself to utter the words out loud. My body stiffens with the unfairness of it all.

'I was a surrogate,' Lisa says at last, and I pull away as though her hand is burning hot.

'"A surrogate"?' I repeat, even though I have heard her perfectly well.

'I had a baby for a couple who couldn't have one of their own.' Lisa's eyes lock onto mine and there's something almost challenging in her gaze, and I realise I had judged her. Unfairly so.

'Lisa, that's incredible.'

'I felt so privileged to do it. Acting as a surrogate is definitely something I'd consider again. Stella, the mother, she'd had so many miscarriages,' Lisa babbles, her face bright red, and I know she is embarrassed to be telling me, but I think it is amazing.

'It's such a selfless thing to do. I feel hopelessly guilty I can't conceive. Less of a woman, somehow.' I bite my lip. Know I'm over-sharing. My carefully fabricated pretence of adopting purely to give an unwanted child a home crumbles instantly.

'Did you ever think about surrogacy? Rather than adoption.'

'Not really, no. I read the headlines in the newspaper last week. That celebrity is looking for a surrogate but I don't know much about it. Tell me.'

'I met Stella at work. She was lovely but approaching forty and despairing she wouldn't ever have a family of her own. She'd tried everything to have a healthy pregnancy. You know that feeling? When you want something so badly you almost feel you'll kill for it.'

I inhale sharply.

'Sorry,' Lisa winces. 'Bad choice of words.'

We fall into silence.

An icy finger runs down my spine, and I look over my shoulder. The door to the pub is firmly shut and the fire is blazing but I can't stop shivering.

# CHAPTER THREE
## Now

It is winter dark as I step out of the cab. An icy wind biting my nose and ears. Whirling snow dances in front of my eyes. Instead of lowering my head and ploughing forward like I'd usually do, I turn my face towards the sky and stick out my tongue, catching the snowflakes and swallowing them down as they melt. I feel younger than I have in ages. Lighter. It was good to see Lisa. The more we drank, the more we laughed, until my stomach muscles ached and my paranoia was cleared away with our dirty plates. We have promised to keep in touch. I gaze up at the half-moon, my breath clouding in front of my mouth, and imagine I can see my hopes for the future soaring sky-high amongst the dotted stars.

I'm careful as I pick my way down our gravelled driveway past my Honda CRV. Nick thought the solidity of a 4 x 4 might help me feel a little more relaxed on the roads. It doesn't. It's inevitable that I have to drive sometimes, but I catch a cab, or the bus when I can. Nick knows I'm nervous, because I told him I was involved in a 'bump' before I met him. I said everyone walked away, and he's never pressed me for details. He was quiet for a few days before announcing he'd enrolled us both on an advanced driving course. He's a typical man in that respect, always wanting to fix things, find solutions, and while I was pleased he was trying to support me, some things just can't be fixed. The instructor told us 'advanced drivers are safer, more observant. Increasing awareness of potential hazards makes you statistically less likely to have an accident.' Nick had nodded along but even after the course I felt anything but safe.

The ice and alcohol collaborate, forcing me off balance and I splay my hands to the side, arms trembling under the weight of my shopping. It is a relief to put down my load on the doorstep and flex my fingers to get the blood flowing again. The miniature bay tree by the front door looks so pretty sprinkled with light snow. Its silver pot shimmering in the moonlight. I fish my keys out of my bag and let myself in to the red-brick house we are still settling into.

Nick started his property investment business purely as a way to fund the charity in its infancy days, wanting to match the money Richard was initially putting into it, but as the buy-to-let market boomed, profits soared. Nick bought this four-bedroom detached as an investment but couldn't wait to show me, and we linked hands and ran like excited children from room to room. The house isn't huge but it's in a lovely area. I had watched his face shine as we tumbled into the sunflower yellow kitchen, and I knew this would be our forever home.

'Look at the view.' He'd bounced on his toes as I'd wrapped my arms around his waist, my chin on his shoulder, and agreed it was stunning; beyond the quintessential garden are patchwork fields, sheep grazing.

Clare lives opposite. I already recognised her from the coffee shop and was delighted she'd be living so close. She's a single mum and only works part-time. It's nice having someone I can grab a quick drink with. Sometimes the stories I hear at work make me crave human contact. People assume working for a charity is all shaking a collection bucket and organising raffles, but there's so much more than that, and at times it is emotionally harrowing. I love it though.

My boots click on the shined-to-perfection laminate floor. I'd scrubbed the house before I left and a faint whiff of bleach emanates from the downstairs loo. Sitting at the bottom of the stairs, I tug off my suede boots and run my foot over the droplets of water dripping from the sole, dampening my sock. Nick won't be home for a while, and the house is still, silent, except for the tick-tick-tick of the grandfather clock.

Upstairs I put my shoulder against the white gloss door leading to the nursery and push my way inside. I'm about to become a mum. *A mum.* I roll the word around my mouth, tasting all the implications it brings. Dropping my bags, I sink into the chair I've bought for feeding and dig my toes into the soft digestive-coloured carpet, gently rocking back and forth, the lavender from the plug-in air freshener filling my lungs.

Today. We could hear today.

The room isn't ready. A border covered with sleeping bunnies wraps itself around all four baby blue walls. Nick had been reluctant to decorate; didn't want to tempt fate, I suppose, until Dewei was here and, in retrospect, he was right. After work one day, he had stuck his head around the door. I was balanced precariously on a ladder, feathering my brush against the ceiling, singing along to S Club 7's 'Reach for the Stars' blaring out of my Roberts Radio that, despite being digital, still sometimes crackled and hissed. He disappeared, and I thought he was annoyed, but returned minutes later, having replaced his suit with an old pair of jeans and a faded Levi's T-shirt. He crunched his way across the plastic sheeting covering the carpet, kissed me hard on the lips and picked up a paintbrush. We didn't talk as we worked but the silence was comfortable. Easy. An hour later we had finished but we couldn't bear to leave. Nick nipped out for a takeaway. We sat on the floor, avoiding leaning against the tacky walls, eating chips soaked in salt and vinegar, discussing what we thought Dewei would be when he grew up. We went from F1 driver (Nick) to actor (me) but in the end we both settled on happy, and although he is now not ours, that is exactly what I still wish for him.

Now, as I look around, I think tomorrow I'll buy some pink paint and decorate for Mai and, as much as I am looking forward to her arrival, regret lodges in my throat as I think I will be painting over Dewei. Saying goodbye to the family we never got to be. I swallow back my tears. I've had a good day and won't spoil it now. Instead, I kneel in front of the white wardrobe and begin to unpack my shopping. Cream Babygros with pink butterflies, tiny white socks with a lacy trim, a bib with 'Daddy's girl', pastel vests with metal poppers and the softest fleecy lemon blanket with a giraffe in the corner. I fold everything carefully and pull open a drawer. My heart skitters at the sight of baby blue clothing. I lift everything out as carefully as I can, holding each item to my nose, breathing in deeply as though I can smell the baby that was never really mine to love. That didn't stop me loving him anyway. My emotions rage against each other. I could cry at the injustice of it all and yet, as I cradle the stuffed rabbit I've bought for Mai, with ears that crinkle, and a bell in the tail that tings, I can't help but feel hopeful.

A mum.

I'm going to be a mum, and the enormity of it overwhelms me. I'll have a tiny person to protect, and panic twists in my gut. What if I can't protect her? What if I let her down too? But I tell myself it isn't the same. I'm not the same person I was then.

I am so lost in my thoughts I don't hear Nick as he comes home, and it isn't until he crouches beside me and takes my hand in his I know something is wrong. His cornflower eyes are filled with regret, and the scar on his forehead he's always so self-conscious about shifts as he frowns. Somehow, I know what he's about to say before he speaks and I pull back almost as though I can stop the words coming.

'Kat. I'm so sorry,' he says, and I try to stand but he doesn't let me go. 'Richard has called. There was an issue with the paperwork. Secretly he thinks someone has slipped a back hander. Mai has gone.'

And just like that my world crumbles. He holds me as my grief soaks his shoulder, his shirt darkening with the force of my tears.

'We shouldn't have instructed Richard. What were we thinking? He's a commercial lawyer.' I am desperate for someone to blame. 'We should have used an international adoption solicitor. A specialist.'

'Richard wouldn't have agreed to help if he was out of his depth. I trust him. He has consulted with the other partners. There was nothing anybody could have done differently.'

'Can we offer more money?' Anger begins to bubble. I won't take this lying down. I can't.

'It's too late,' Nicks whispers into my hair. He sounds as wretched as I feel.

'What about if we fly out there?'

'Kat.' He speaks slowly. Patiently. And I catch a glimpse of the father he could be. 'She's been given to someone else.'

'But…' I want to say they won't love her like we would. Like I do. But I don't know that, do I? There are other women whose desire to hold a baby burns hot and bright. Why should I be more deserving? *You're not* whispers that little voice, and all at once it feels like karma. Payback. I've moved away but I haven't been able to escape myself – the things I've done.

'What are we going to do? Should we try the UK? At least this sort of thing won't happen.' I raise my tear-stained face to Nick's but he can't look me in the eye.

'I don't think so. Remember the orphanages, the conditions? It's much better to offer a home to one of those babies but we need to think very carefully about whether we can go through it again. It's traumatic. For both of us.' He envelops me in his arms, and I slump against him, numb and mute.

The moon shines through the window illuminating the nursery rhyme mobile that's hanging over the crib, Humpty fat and round, spinning slowly. *All the king's horses and all the king's men.*

*

Much later, Nick is gently snoring. Sleep hovers in front of me and every time I snatch at it, it is whisked away from my grasp. My eyes are gritty with tiredness as I pad into the nursery. The rabbits stare down at me from the border on the walls judging me: *how could you let another baby go?* The wood creaks as I lower myself in the chair. I rock back and forth. Seconds, minutes, hours tick by. Dawn breaks and it's impossible to keep my eyes open any longer. Just before I slip into blackness, I remember Lisa's words: 'acting as a surrogate is definitely something I'd consider again.' Hope begins to unfurl once more. After all, she doesn't seem to hold a grudge at all, does she?

# CHAPTER FOUR
## Now

'This isn't legal,' Richard says as I try not to squirm under his disapproving gaze, or say anything stupid. There is a lot riding on this meeting.

My fingertips flutter to the gold cross around my neck, the way they always do when I'm anxious. The wait seems endless as Richard shuffles through papers on his desk. My mouth is dry but my palms are slick with sweat. I discreetly wipe them against my trousers before I stretch out my hand towards Nick. He links his fingers through mine.

'I must say I was surprised to get your phone call but I've done some research and had a chat with the chap who specialises in family law here. The laws for surrogacy are sketchy at the very least. You won't be protected if anything goes wrong.'

It's so hot in the office. A too large executive desk fills the space, sucking the air out of the room. Richard's aftershave is always overpowering: something expensive, no doubt. I half-wish I hadn't worn my cashmere jumper as I feel another trickle of sweat snake between my shoulder blades but I had wanted to appear confident and in control, but in control is the last thing I feel.

'Nicholas?' Richard asks in that tone of his which always makes me painfully aware he has never really approved of his best friend's choice of wife. I'm not sure why he has never warmed to me. In our wedding photos, he stands expressionless next to Nick, not even a hint of a smile on his too-handsome-for-his-own-good face. Neither Nick nor I have family to speak of, or that we really speak to, and it had meant a lot to me we had friends who could join us. But as Nick and I swayed to Jason Mraz's 'I'm Yours' in the tiny venue that was still only half-full, I was aware of Richard's cold, hard stare following me around the meagre dance floor lit with flashing blue and green lights. The taste of the garlic mushrooms we'd eaten for our wedding breakfast kept rising in my throat.

I glance out of the window and wish Richard would crack it open. A pigeon rests on the sill; his wings glint silver and purple in the weak winter sun.

'This is what I want.' I sense rather than see Nick look at me. 'This is what we both want.' He gives my hand a reassuring squeeze, and I am grateful we both want to build a family. Early on, he told me his parents were dead, and he didn't want to talk about them. I told him mine weren't but I didn't want to talk about them either, and it brought us closer. Bound by our loneliness. Our secrets, some might say, but I don't think there is anything wrong in a fresh start. Looking towards the future instead of the past. I had asked Nick, of course, about his childhood and he'd said there was nothing to talk about, but the tell-tale tic in his jaw, the vein that throbs at the side of his head, told a different story, as did the scar that streaks across his forehead. He hasn't had it easy, I know, but that only makes me love him more. Over time I have stopped asking questions because it's never one-sided, is it? Finding out information. If we have that conversation, sooner or later I'll be the one expected to talk about my parents, my past, and that's the last thing I want to do. Anyway, ultimately, we are all the same, aren't we? Skin and bones. Truth and lies. We all have our stories to tell. Regret we bury. Hope we try to tether lest we begin to think we can be something we're not.

My hand trembles as I lift my glass and water sloshes over the edge, soaking my knees. It is cold and uncomfortable but it will dry quickly here. The radiator next to me blasts out heat. I am beginning to feel dizzy.

'Surrogacy is a very grey area,' Richard says. 'We can certainly draw up an agreement to protect your interests, as much as it can, and ask the surrogate to sign a letter of intent, but neither is legally binding if she changes her mind during the process. There is no law that can force a mother to give away her child, no matter what she has promised.' Richard steeples his fingers together and stares directly at me. 'It's a shame the adoption fell through again. I did all I could but that's the way it goes sometimes. You win some, you lose some.' He doesn't sound sorry, or look sorry, and for an instant I wonder if he has sabotaged the process, but why would he? I dig my nails into my palm. If I ever found out he was responsible for me losing Dewei and Mai I'd kill him with my bare hands.

I try to keep my features neutral; I won't let him get to me. I won't.

'The surrogate we want, Lisa, she's done it before. I trust her.'

The napkin with Lisa's mobile number on it had been stuffed into the bottom of my bag, and I'd smoothed it out, carefully practising my speech. I would explain the adoption had fallen through and we were interested in learning more about surrogacy, but as soon as I heard her voice, the bond we'd shared as teenagers tugged the words from my lips, the emotion from my chest. I'd sobbed and sobbed down the phone. 'I've lost Mai, Lis. It's happened again.' She'd soothed and sympathised, and we had talked for hours. In the following days she had rung me every afternoon, and I was grateful for her support. For the chance to chat. Sometimes about our school days. My obsession with *Desperate Housewives*, her obsession with Justin Timberlake. Sometimes about nothing. But our conversations always circled back to Mai and the loss I felt and, in the end, it was her who brought up surrogacy first.

'Look, Kat,' she had said. 'I don't want to push you into anything, but… surrogacy?'

The pause seemed endless as I had silently urged her on. Was she really going to offer? Somehow, I didn't feel I could ask. My hand gripped the telephone receiver, fingers tightly crossed.

'You know I'd do it again. For you.'

'But you don't even know Nick.' I left my weak protest hanging in the air, waiting for her to bat it away.

'I didn't know Stella's husband, at first. I didn't even know Stella that well, but you and me, we have a history, don't we?'

'Yes.' The word came out with a rush of relief. I was saying yes to everything.

I'd held her offer tightly in my hands like a gift and, later, unwrapped every last detail of our conversation before recounting it to Nick.

He wasn't sure, at first. As we sat at the kitchen table I had spread out page after page of information I'd printed off the internet: beaming couples holding tiny bundles, surrogates standing behind them, smiling serenely like proud aunts.

'The chance of a surrogate getting pregnant...' Nick rifled through the papers. 'You've looked for all the success stories but what about the ones that go wrong? The couples who are still left childless. I can't face it again. Seeing you so upset. I can't put myself through it. Is it really so important to have a baby? We're okay, aren't we? We're happy?'

'Yes, but...' I bit my lip. Sifted through my mind for the words to communicate the huge gaping hole inside of me. It was like a wound almost. Sometimes I thought I was healing until I'd walk past a mum pushing a pram proudly through town, stand in a queue behind an expectant mother stroking her belly, and I'd feel the scab being ripped off. It hurt every single time. It never lessened, the searing pain; if anything, it was only getting worse. Sometimes it seemed the whole world had what I so desperately wanted. How could I convey that to Nick? That longing. But somehow, I must have because he said yes.

'And you're happy with this Lisa, Nick?' Richard asks.

'I'm happy if Kat is,' Nick says. 'But before meeting her I wanted to discuss the legalities. Hear your thoughts.'

'You could always buy a kitten or a puppy,' Richard says.

My breath catches in my throat. 'It's not quite the same, is it?' I try to make my tone sarcastic but my words are shaky. I don't know how much longer I can hold it together. It's all right for him. He's so focused on his career he doesn't want kids, but he must have some compassion: he wouldn't have wanted to set up Stroke Support otherwise.

'No, I suppose it isn't,' he relents. 'If you want to go ahead it won't take long for me to do the paperwork. We just need to agree on the finer points. Reasonable expenses can be paid to Lisa—'

'We don't mind what it costs,' I jump in.

'*You* probably don't,' says Richard, and I sit back, feeling my spine press against the wooden chair, as though I have been pushed. There's a part of me that wants to retort we wouldn't have to worry about money if I drew a salary from the charity set up for Richard's grandmother and we didn't rely solely on Nick's property business for our income, but today, I want to keep us all focused on the baby.

'You do want to stay on the right side of the law, don't you?' Richard's stare is unwavering, and I squirm uncomfortably. Sometimes I feel he can see right through me.

'What's the legal amount to pay?' Nick asks.

'This is where it all gets rather murky.' Richard swivels from side to side in his chair. 'It's illegal to arrange a surrogacy for profit, but not illegal for a surrogate to profit.'

'So Lisa could charge what she wanted?'

'Not exactly. As I said, it's not cut and dry. Before the family court will issue the parental order, they must assess what payments have been made. If they believe more than "reasonable expenses" have changed hands then the court has to authorise each payment before the parental order can be granted.'

'So, we could get to the end of the process and the court could say no?' There is so much that could go wrong. Frustrated tears prick the back of my eyes as I stare down into my lap.

'It's extremely unlikely the court wouldn't approve – they do have to take into account the welfare and best interests of the child – but it would greatly complicate the process if inordinately large amounts of money had changed hands. Expenses can include any outlay while trying to conceive, during the pregnancy, and expenditure during the postnatal period,' Richard continued.

'What sort of things would we need to cover?' Nick asks.

'There's quite a range. Costs involved while you're getting to know each other, travelling. If Lisa feels she needs counselling that's your responsibility financially, as are maternity clothes, trips to the hospital, any loss of earnings. We call the payments "expenses" but there is of course a degree of unspoken "profit", as it were. After all, the surrogate is inconvenienced for a prolonged period of time.'

It irks me he can refer to a pregnancy as an 'inconvenience' but I do understand what he means. It's a huge sacrifice Lisa would be making. If it were up to me I'd give her every penny I could get my hands on.

'How much do you think?' Nick asks.

'It varies but the general rule of thumb is anything between £7,000 and £15,000. More than £20,000 would potentially trigger alarm bells to the court. Expenses prior to conception are usually covered as you go along, and then once the surrogate is pregnant it's up to you. You can hand over a lump sum or pay a monthly amount. There's no hard and fast rule.'

'Is that okay?' I turn to Nick. 'We can cover Lisa's expenses?' It will wipe our savings out.

'If you use a clinic it will cost more, of course,' Richard says.

'How much extra do you think a clinic might be?' I'm worried we can't afford it.

'I don't know,' Nick says. 'I don't really want to take out another loan; the repayments for the buy-to-let mortgages are so high.'

'Perhaps you should give it some more consideration,' Richard says.

I almost laugh. Nick and I had thought of and talked about nothing else these past few days and had finally made our decision yesterday. My mobile had rested on the kitchen table between us as I called Lisa. The relief in her voice as it drifted out of the tinny speaker was palpable, and I had been touched to realise how much she must want to do this for me.

'Thank you.' Tears had shimmered in Nick's eyes. 'I can't believe you'd do this for a complete stranger.'

'Oh, you won't be a stranger for long,' Lisa said. 'We'll be getting to know each other *very* well, Nick.'

After we had ended the call we remained sitting at the table, grinning like idiots, until the sun lost its grip on the sky and I could no longer make out Nick's features. We'd gone to The Fox and Hounds and giggled as we ordered champagne from Mitch. We kept reminding each other it was early days and we should be cautious, but we couldn't help racing into the future. Wondering whether Lisa would fall pregnant quickly. Whether we might have a boy or girl.

'We've thought it through properly. Lisa is coming around tomorrow to confirm the finer details. Nick and I can talk again afterwards,' I say. Nick agrees with me, and it feels like a small victory, but Richard hasn't finished yet.

'You do understand if this is successful the child will remain legally Lisa's until the parental order has been issued after the baby is born? Lisa could keep the baby if she wanted to.'

'She won't,' I say.

'And how much do you know about her family? There are conditions that can be inherited,' Richard asks.

I answer immediately. 'They're all healthy. I've known them for years but we'll ask her.'

'It's not just the physical. There could be mental health issues? Personality traits that can sometimes skip generations?'

'It's all going to be fine. You don't need to worry. Besides, half the baby's genes will be Nick's, don't forget. There's nothing in your history I should know about, is there?'

Nick pulls a tissue from the box on Richard's desk and wipes beads of sweat from his forehead as he gazes out of the window. 'No.'

'There we go then.' I rest my palm on his back. 'Everything's fine. You'll be such a good dad, Nick.'

'I hope so.' He turns to me. His skin ashen.

'You're a natural. I've watched you with Ada.' Clare's daughter adores Nick. 'Anyway, it's not all about nature. There's nurture too, isn't there?'

Nick screws his face as though he is in pain. I call his name, but he doesn't seem to hear me. I stare helplessly as he slumps forward. His head cracking hard against the corner of the desk.

# CHAPTER FIVE
## Then

Nick sat cross-legged on the threadbare carpet. His dad, Kevin, stretched out on the worn sofa, fag in one hand, ash falling onto the floor. There wasn't anywhere else to sit. It wasn't like Nick had a bedroom to retreat to. Cigarette smoke spiralled around the page of Nick's colouring book. He pressed his crayon harder onto the page, turning the dragon from white to green, and tried not to think about the time they lived in a proper house, like a proper family. That was before his dad put his back out and couldn't work. Now, he couldn't even be bothered to shave. The odd can of Foster's he drank to 'unwind' at the end of the day became a lunchtime drink to 'ease the pain' until the snapping of the ring pull and the fizzing of lager was the sound Nick woke up to. His dad looked different. Smelled different. Was different. With all of his small heart, Nick missed the dad who used to helicopter him around the garden, as well as his grandad, Basil, who had recently died. He had loved staying in his tumbledown cottage, waking to the crashing sound of waves, the smell of salt on the air. Endless summers playing with the local kids on the beach.

Mum took on extra cleaning and looked permanently exhausted, and she probably was despite her reassurances that she was fine. Nick might only be seven but he was aware that her hair, that once looked like spun gold from Sleeping Beauty, was now dark at the roots, and there were lines etched onto her face that hadn't been there this time last year.

'It's only temporary,' she had said as they moved their meagre belongings into the tiny flat. She showed him where he could keep his things in the battered old sideboard the previous occupants had left behind, with its door hanging from a single hinge. Most of his toys had already been sold at a car boot sale, and their solid wooden furniture was long gone.

Nick's dad had groaned as he shuffled into the lounge and flopped down on the sofa that mum explained folded out into a bed. It was where Nick would sleep. Dad had drunk can after can of lager as Mum scrubbed the kitchen and washed the windows until they sparkled but the flat still smelled sour. Despite the patchwork rug and the bright cushions Mum carefully arranged, it didn't look like home. It didn't feel like home.

Nick yawned. He couldn't go to bed until Dad did, and Dad would wait until Mum finished her shift at the pub. Once home, Nick's mum would always find time to tell Nick a story and kiss him good night. Afterwards, Nick would lie on the sofa, his thin, itchy grey blanket pulled up around his shoulders, and cuddle Teddy Edward, his bear, running the red ribbon tied in a bow around his neck through his fingers, listening to the voices drifting through the paper-thin walls. His dad's voice low and angry, his mum's soft and soothing, and later, the squeaking of bedsprings. Nick would clasp his small hands over his ears.

Nick had nearly finished colouring in the dragon, as green as the ring his mum always wore that once belonged to his grandma. His tongue protruded from the tip of his teeth as he concentrated hard. For once, he had stayed in all the lines. Now for the knight. Nick didn't have many colours to choose from. 'Father Christmas doesn't have much money this year,' his mum had said, 'although you've been really, really good.'

'Stop fucking babying him,' his dad had bit back.

But when Nick woke on Christmas morning, the pillowcase he had left out was bulging with sweets, a new jumper that was Nick's favourite blue – although when Nick pulled it over his head it smelled a bit funny and there was a small hole in the elbow – and the colouring book and crayons. Nick's fingers hovered over the box as he deliberated between red and yellow but they had learned about St George in class last week so he picked out the red. He had tried his hardest to listen as Miss Watson's soft voice had told the class about swords and shields, but he had drifted off, waking as his friend Richard kicked him under the desk, whispering the answer to the question he had been asked. Richard always covered for him. Nick had sat bolt upright and wiped the trail of drool from his mouth, embarrassment heating his face as he'd caught the sympathetic glance of his favourite teacher. After class Miss Watson had held him back and asked him if everything was all right at home, tilting her head to the side the way mum did when she wasn't too tired to listen to him. He'd told Miss Watson everything was fine, and she'd told him to run along to the canteen. Nick said he'd forgotten his lunch, ashamed to admit his dad usually ate the sandwiches Mum made before she went to work. It didn't matter much though. He never got that hungry and Richard was always happy to share. Miss Watson had pulled open her drawer and silently handed him a Mars Bar, and he thought she was pretty, like the princess in the story.

Nick's eyes were heavy with sleep now. The ten o'clock news was on so it shouldn't be too much longer before his mum came home. In a bid to stay awake Nick pinched the red crayon harder between his fingers and pressed down on the page. There was a crack as the crayon split into two, and his head snapped forward as Nick's dad slapped him. Hard. 'Do you think your mum works all these bleedin' hours so you can break things?'

Nick shook his head as he tried to stop his lip from trembling. His dad hated it when he cried.

Dad's eyes had glinted in the light of the flickering TV as he ripped the dragon picture out of the colouring book and tore it in two.

'That was for mum. For the fridge.' Nick drew his knees up to his chest and tried to stop trembling.

'I'll let you into a secret. Mum hates your pictures and tacky fridge magnets. Says they make the place look untidy. Let's not tell her I told you; I'm trusting you to keep your mouth shut. Deal?'

His dad held out his hand and Nick slipped his small one inside and tried not to wince as his dad shook it so hard his shoulder felt like it was being wrenched from the socket.

That was the last time Nick ever coloured and the first time he had to keep a secret, but it wasn't the last time.

And it was far, far, from being the worst.

# CHAPTER SIX
## Now

I jump as I feel the weight of Nick's hand rest on my shoulder. I hadn't heard him come into the kitchen.

'Are you okay?' I twist my head around. My eyes drawn to the bruise on Nick's forehead. It was blue yesterday, today it's purple, and somehow that looks worse.

'I'm fine. Stop fussing. I've told you it was hot in Richard's office and I was a bit stressed that's all. I fainted. There's nothing wrong.' He nuzzles my neck.

Reassured, I dip my cloth into the bowl filled with warm water and lemon multi-surface cleaner, wringing it out, wiping the worktops until they are so clean they squeak. Lisa is coming and I want everything to be perfect. The air is citrus fresh, and my hands are pink and raw. The copper pans hanging over the Aga shine as the sun streams through the trifold doors. Swinging open the fridge, I pull out peppers and celery, and after shutting the door I wipe my fingermarks off the handle.

'Just think,' I say to Nick as I rub the stainless steel until it shines, 'one day this could be covered in drawings from our child. What do you think? A fridge covered in gaudy magnets?'

Nick doesn't answer, and as I turn around I am shocked to see the anger plastered over his face. 'Nick?'

'Sorry, I was miles away. Let me help.' Nick rinses the vegetables under the tap before I shake them dry, cool droplets of water speckling my forearms. I'll chop them into crudités to have with humus. Spotify streams a pop playlist; Little Mix threaten 'Black Magic'.

Nick usually laughs and tells me I'm too old to like them, but we all have them, don't we? Guilty pleasures. And although he says he hates pop music, often we bop around the kitchen together while we wait for dinner to cook. Stupid, over-the-top dance moves from an era that doesn't fit with the music at all: The Mashed Potato; The Twist. Today, though, there is no singing or dancing. We are both on edge.

'Are you getting changed?' I ask Nick. 'You look too casual.'

He's wearing jeans and a white T-shirt, his hair shower-wet. His bare feet have left dull marks on the floor I've mopped twice.

'It won't make any difference what I wear. I wish you'd just—'

I step forward and silence him with a kiss. His stubble grazes my chin, and I taste peppermint.

'I'm sorry.' I wrap my arms around his waist. 'You must be nervous too.' I snuggle into him. Sometimes I forget how hard it must be for him and, once again, I am grateful he chose to stay with me and didn't leave me for someone who could give him babies. I never could understand why Nick chose me in the first place. Why he pursued me so hard, with my hair that hangs limp and my bottom that strains my jeans at the seams. As he holds me, my mind drifts to the memory of the night he proposed.

He had taken me out to dinner but he barely ate; fiddling with the corner of his napkin, refilling his glass more often than usual. I had convinced myself he was going to break up with me as I pushed my chicken breast, oozing with garlic butter, miserably around my plate. Over the strains of classical music, I'd drunk in every last detail of his handsome face over the flickering candle. The black curls I loved to run my fingers through. The scar on his forehead.

'Marry me, Katherine.' His words sprang out of nowhere, and my hands rose to my chest to hold his question close to my heart. 'I'll look after you. I'll be a good husband. I promise.'

'Yes!' I didn't take a second to think about it. I loved him, I did, although it wasn't with the all-consuming, flame-hot love I'd felt before, it was real. Solid.

We had toasted: bubbling champagne tickling my nostrils. Later, we'd lain in bed, sheets tangled around our legs, his fingers rhythmically stroking my hair; I had thought I had never been so happy. But as I was nodding off my subconscious whispered I had been this happy once before, and the last thought I had, before sleep tugged me under, was of Jake.

*There's a squeal of brakes. The crunch of metal. It's dark. So dark. I cannot see and panic tornadoes through me.*

*It's hot. Unbearably hot. Acrid smoke seals off my throat. I cough and cough, my lungs burning with the effort of trying to drag in air. My ribs feel as though they will shatter. 'Jake'. I'm calling his name over and over but I think it must be in my head because I can't hear. Just for one solitary moment there is perfect, perfect silence before my senses roar back to life. Someone is screaming, anguished cries my ears will never forget but I don't think it's me. I can't move. I can't think. I'm trapped and I'm scared. So scared. There is something warm and sticky running down my face and, as it trickles down my nose, I can smell the blood. Every cell in my body urges me to move. To run. But I can't. Jake!*

I was drifting on the edge of consciousness. One foot in the past, one foot in the present, not able to step fully into either, not entirely sure where I wanted to be. When the roaring in my ears began to subside and my pulse rate started to slow, I became aware of Nick's steady breathing as he slept beside me. The sheets were damp with sweat, my pillow damp with tears. I scrubbed at my cheeks with the sleeve of my pyjamas, mopping up my guilt. Even in sleep I couldn't reach Jake. Even in sleep, it was too late. And it was always, always, my fault.

The sound of the doorbell breaks Nick and I apart. Lisa must be here. Feeling sick, excited, scared, I rush down the hallway, skidding to a halt in front of the telephone table, tugging a brown, curling leaf from the pale yellow roses Nick bought me yesterday. I hope Lisa can sense this is a happy home, despite the increasing strain we've been under trying to expand our family. A perfect home for a child. Strip away the polish, the bleach, the lemon cream cleaner and underneath there's love and laughter, and that's what matters the most really, isn't it?

'Lisa.' My voice is an octave too high as I step back and welcome her inside. We hug and my clothes dampen as I press against her wet coat. We've spent hours chatting on the phone every day but it feels odd to have her here.

'Come through,' I say gesturing towards the lounge.

'Kat, this is gorgeous.' Lisa shrugs off her mac and spins around on tiptoes. I have a flashback to our ballet classes. Pirouettes and tutus. Hair brushed into buns. 'And you have a piano now. I'm so pleased. You always wanted to learn.'

I had begged my parents for music lessons but Dad thought the arts were a waste of time, though I got the feeling Mum would let me if she could. Dad only tolerated me being in the drama group in sixth form because I got extra credit towards my extended project, and the points would count towards uni.

'I'm trying to teach myself but it's not as easy as it looks.' In truth, I have probably spent more time dusting it, imagining the row of silver picture frames that would display photos of our happy smiling family. Dewei, head thrown back, roaring with laughter, in a swing; tossing bread at the ducks; baking cookies together, steam rising from gingerbread men, the tips of our noses dusted with icing sugar. I could imagine Dewei balancing on the piano stool when he was old enough, banging out 'Twinkle, Twinkle Little Star' while I smiled and clapped. Then the adoption fell through, and the image in my mind had to change to Mai, and it was never quite the same. I think, even when we first signed the paperwork Richard had filled in for her, I half expected something to go wrong. And now the picture frames in my mind remain blank and empty.

The sound of a throat clearing causes us both to look up. Nick hovers in the doorway looking like a guest in his own home. I cross the room and take his hand. His palm is as sweaty as mine.

'Lisa, this is my husband, Nick.'

'Hello, Nick. You look even more handsome in the flesh.' Lisa shakes his hand. His face milk-white. He's as nervous as me.

'You two haven't met?…'

'I saw his photo in the Sunday magazine,' Lisa says, and I frown. She hadn't mentioned she'd seen a copy when we first met the other day. 'Mitch showed it to me. In the pub?'

'Of course,' I say. 'I'll make some tea.' It isn't until I am leaning against the worktop as the kettle gurgles and splutters, I realise it was Mitch who first showed me the photo in the Sunday supplement, and he gave his copy to me to keep. How could he have shown Lisa? But he could have bought another one, I suppose. I lift the tea tray and rattle down the hallway. Approaching the lounge I hear Nick exclaim: 'I can't believe it! Not Kat?'

They both turn to me as I enter the room.

'I'm so sorry.' Lisa's eyes are wide. 'I thought, being married, you'd have told Nick *everything*.'

# CHAPTER SEVEN
## Now

'Why didn't you tell me you used to be on stage?' Nick takes the tea tray from me, and I wipe my palms on my tunic top, feeling horribly exposed. But, of all the things Lisa could have revealed about my past, this is hardly the worst; still, when I find her gaze, I see a flicker of something in her eyes, and I feel a cold lurch of fear. Have I made a mistake inviting her into my home, into my life?

'It was only school productions and all such a long time ago now. I was hardly Jennifer Lawrence.'

'She's being too modest.' Lisa is smiling warmly now, Nick too, and I think it must only be me who can feel the atmosphere spitting and crackling with secrets. 'Kat was really good, always the starring role. And you loved it, didn't you?'

'I loved a lot of things then but it doesn't mean I do any more,' I say, and a flash of something crosses Lisa's face and I know she's thinking of Jake too. Thinking she loved him more than me. That she loved him first.



The clock in the hallway chimes. The crudités sit untouched on the coffee table, the cucumber drying, the peppers shrivelling. Lisa has told Nick how she tried to lighten my hair with Sun-in and it went orange, and I've shared that Lisa used to copy out song lyrics and use them for her English homework, but we still haven't talked about babies.

'More tea?' As I stretch my arms forward to lift the tray I catch a faint whiff of sweat and I draw my elbows in tightly to the sides of my body.

'Shall we talk about the real reason I'm here?' Lisa's eyes lock onto mine, and panic pinballs in my chest. For an instant, I am back in that night with the pain and the blood and the endless screaming, until she says: 'The surrogacy?' And I empty my lungs of air and urge myself to calm down. The smell of sweat is stronger now, and I excuse myself.

Upstairs, I strip off my jumper and wipe my underarms with baby wipes before spraying deodorant and pulling on a clean top.

Back in the lounge, Lisa has moved from the armchair into the spot I vacated next to Nick. Their heads are close together, thighs touching, and I feel a stab of jealousy remembering how we fought for Jake's affection – until I realise she is showing Nick something on her phone.

'Look.' Lisa stands and crosses towards me. She shows me a photo on her mobile of a tiny baby in a pink polka dot sleepsuit, rosebud mouth, fists clenched together as she starfishes in her cot. 'This is Gabrielle, Stella's baby,' Lisa explains.

As I look at the picture any doubts I have disappear. 'She's adorable, Lisa.' The fact she called Gabrielle 'Stella's baby' and not her own really brings it home to me the magnitude of what Lisa has done. What she is offering to do again. My sight is fuzzy with tears as I raise my finger to swipe the screen to look for more photos.

'That's the only one on there.' Lisa stuffs her handset into her pocket. 'The rest are on my computer. I don't need to see her every day. She's not mine. She never was. Stella sends me emails every now and then, updating me on her progress and sending through photos. I feel like a proud aunt, I suppose. I love her… but Stella's her mum.'

'How did you? You know…' I can't believe I feel so awkward asking.

'Want a sketch? Got any crayons?' Our shared memory of Lisa explaining sex to me with a diagram, scribbling on the back of her maths book with an orange Crayola, causes us both to burst out laughing, dissolving the tension in my muscles.

'We went through a clinic,' Lisa says, serious once more. 'You have to pay a fee. It was really expensive. They started with a semen analysis of Stella's husband's sperm.'

'The fault isn't with Nick,' I cut in. 'We've had tests.'

'You'll want my eggs then?' Lisa says as though we are discussing a shopping list. 'We should still get Nick checked for STIs, unless you've been checked before?'

'Yes. Before Kat,' Nick says, and I turn to him in surprise, but he doesn't meet my eye.

I wonder if that was with Natasha. She is another part of his past he doesn't like to talk about. Nick used to be plagued by texts and calls from his ex when we first got together.

'We also had a Peer Support Worker through the clinic who oversaw the process, and they helped with the parental order. The baby has to be living with you at the time for that to go through.'

'Richard will handle that,' says Nick. 'My friend's a solicitor,' he explains to Lisa. 'But, look, I've been trying to tell Kat not to get her hopes up. The success rates can't be high with this sort of thing.'

'It's not any different to trying to conceive naturally.'

'Even so, the chances of you falling pregnant must be slim? There are fertile couples who try for months, years sometimes, before they are successful.'

I stiffen at his words, and he puts his hand on my knee and squeezes. 'We both want to be parents,' he continues, 'but it hasn't been an easy couple of years trying to adopt from another country. Emotionally, we're exhausted. Both of us.'

'All the more reason not to try to adopt again,' says Lisa.

'So how does it actually happen… the insemination?' I can feel the heat radiating from Nick as he speaks, and I reach for his hand.

Lisa opens her handbag and pulls out a small package. 'I've brought a home kit with me in case you wanted to see how it would work without a clinic. It's all very above board. No physical contact needed between me and Nick.'

'And you'd try this more than once around ovulation?' I stare at the syringe. It's incredible to think a piece of plastic could help me become a mum.

'Yes. I know I'm ovulating today so I've worked out the dates for January, but I'm on a work course that week so the timing wouldn't fit. I could come and stay in February if you choose to go ahead.'

Although we are forming plans, my immediate reaction is one of disappointment. February seems so far away. When I look at Nick he is rubbing his scar on his forehead and I know he is thinking. I wait, wondering if he feels frustrated by the delay too.

'I can see the benefits of a clinic,' he says. 'Particularly when dealing with a stranger, but with you and Kat going back such a long way, I'm not sure it's necessary.'

'It's certainly an advantage to know each other so well. It's unbelievable to think I can be the one to change your life completely, Kat. I'm very much looking forward to it.'

I can feel Lisa's eyes on me but I can't tear my pleading gaze away from Nick; I'm willing him to read my thoughts.

The silence is unbearable. Dozens of words swim around my mind and I fish out the phrase I am looking for. 'No time like the present?' I say but my voice is small and uncertain.

'I think so too,' Nick says, and I fling my arms around him.

'Today?' says Lisa, and for one split second I think she's going to say no, but she shrugs 'why not', and she slips into our hug, and somehow we feel like a family already.

Lisa wriggles free of our embrace and passes a pot to Nick. 'If we're doing this you need to—'

'I know.' Nick's tone is terse and his muscles tighten, and as excited as I am, I can't imagine the embarrassment he must feel.

Part of me wonders whether we should wait for a clinic – if a sterile environment and nurses would make this situation that is anything but normal slightly easier for him to bear.

'Look, Nick.' I drop my arms and step back so I can read the expression on his face. 'We don't have to try today. There is no rush really.' The words almost stick in my throat, and my heart is hammering a tattoo inside my ribcage. My hopes are floating like a helium balloon and I can't tug them back down. 'Do you want to wait until February?'

Nick taps on the lid of the pot with his fingertips and it seems an age before he answers. 'No, it makes sense to start now while Lisa is here.' He takes a step towards the door, and Lisa says: 'Wait.' And there is a horrible moment where I think she's going to tell us she won't do it. Nerves writhe in my stomach.

'I hate to bring this up.' She bites her lip. 'But it is usual to pay some of the expenses before conception. I did travel here and buy the kit, not that I dreamt for a second we'd be using it today.'

'Of course.' I feel terrible she had to mention this first. I'd hate her to think we're not grateful. I glance at Nick. 'We could do a bank transfer, now, couldn't we?'

I know he doesn't want to delay any more than I do when he says: 'How about £1k now as a goodwill gesture and we'll draw up an agreement for the rest?'

'Perfect. But only if you're both sure?'

We reassure her we are. Lisa hands Nick her bank card and he transfers the money on the iPad, and when it's done he stands, the pot in his hand.

'Do you want me to come with you?' My face reddens as I feel Lisa's gaze on me.

'It's okay.' Nick kisses the top of my head.

'Just leave the pot by the side of the bed when you're done, and I'll go up and do my bit,' Lisa says, and as Nick paces across the room I can hardly believe we could be creating a baby today.

Nick's heavy tread mounts the stairs, and I spring from the sofa and envelop Lisa into a hug. 'Thank you for this chance,' I whisper into her hair. 'I never thought I'd be a mum. I never thought I deserved it.'

Lisa squeezes me tightly. 'Kat,' she says softly, 'we *always* get what we deserve.'

'Do you think Lisa could be pregnant?' It's ridiculous, I know. She only left three hours ago but already I can't stop thinking about it.

I'm half-lying on Nick on the sofa, my head resting on his shoulder; each time he exhales warm air kisses my ear. Stacked on the coffee table are the remains of a takeaway, plates stained yellow with turmeric, the smell of spices hanging in the air. I love evenings like these. Our stay-at-at-home date nights.

In the background, Spotify streams. Mumford & Sons promise 'I Will Wait'. I run my hand under his shirt, his skin soft and warm, heart slow and steady beneath my palm.

'I doubt it darling.' Nick's fingertips caress my forehead. 'Please try not to get your hopes up.'

'Was it awful? You know…' I reach for his hand and feather kisses on his fingertips. 'Into the pot.'

Lisa and I had sat in awkward silence on the sofa, both painfully aware of what my husband was doing upstairs. Time was long and slow until Nick shuffled back into the room, not looking either of us in the eye.

'I've had better experiences.'

'Thank you.' I tilt my face so I can see his expression 'And…' I swallow hard. 'I'm sorry.'

'You've nothing to be sorry for.'

'If I could conceive—'

'Kat.' Nick hitches himself up on his elbow so he can look at me properly. 'I love you. You know that, don't you?'

'Yes.'

'And I'd do anything to make you happy.'

'Even if it makes you unhappy?' I trace his jawline feeling the faint stubble under my fingertips. 'Nick.' I clamp my lips together in a bid to contain the words that I don't want to say, but they seep from my mouth all the same. 'You do want children, don't you?' If it wasn't for the wine, the emotions of the day, I wouldn't ask.

'You know I do. We've tried to adopt twice.' He leans over me and picks up his wine glass from the floor but rather than his usual sip, he takes a large gulp. I fiddle with the buttons on the front of his shirt, undoing the top one. Black hair coarse on his chest. It would be easy to become distracted. To forget he hasn't actually answered my question.

'You're not just doing it for me?' I prod.

Nick sits up and tops up both our glasses before handing me mine, and as I drink, the alcohol slides through my veins, leaving courage in its wake.

'Talk to me. Please,' I ask.

'I didn't have the best childhood, Kat. You know that.' I nod, although I don't, not really, but I know it isn't only the scars on the outside he carries. 'I don't want a child to go through what I did.' His voice cracks.

'It's important to me we both want this,' I say. 'My parents…' I drain my glass too quickly and hold it for refilling. Dutch courage. I think it is Lisa coming back into my life that has stirred up the past, and for once I feel the need to share. 'I never felt loved as a child, but I've been thinking about them a lot lately. Maybe not them specifically, but aunts and uncles. Cousins. Our child won't have a family other than us. Don't you think that's sad?' I'd loved my grandma when I was small. She was warm, funny, and kind. Everything my own mother wasn't. Apple crumble and custard. Pound coins pushed into my hand each visit.

'It is what it is, Kat.' Nick puts his glass down. 'We have enough love to go around. Look. Let's have a holiday. Get away. We've always fancied Italy, haven't we? It's been nothing but babies for the past couple of years, and I don't want to lose sight of us.'

Rather than having big holidays, we prefer long weekends. It's easier workwise and always seems more romantic somehow. I'm reluctant to make plans though. 'Let's wait and see if the surrogacy works.'

'I want this as much as you do.' Nick takes my empty glass. 'But we must be cautiously optimistic.' The scar on his forehead crinkles.

I lean over and lightly kiss away his doubts. He takes my face between his hands and his lips brush mine, electricity sparks as his tongue snakes inside my mouth. The sofa creaks as we shift until he's lying on top of me. We tug at each other's clothes, and we touch each other, properly touch each other, our ragged breath audible over 'The Sound of Silence' drifting from the speakers. This isn't the perfunctory Friday night fumble that has somehow become part of our routine. As Nick runs his hand up the inside of my thighs, I part my legs wider, feeling his touch in each and every nerve ending in my body. This is love. Real, solid, and tangible. *The way babies should be made* goads the voice in my head, and immediately I feel less of a woman. The touch that was making me moan with pleasure now brings tears to my eyes and I bury my face in Nick's shoulder so he cannot see them.

Lisa's words grow louder in my mind.

*We **always** get what we deserve.*

# CHAPTER EIGHT
## Then

'Stop moving.' Lisa tilted my chin, sponging foundation onto my skin but I couldn't help twisting my head again. Couldn't tear my eyes away from the TV. Eva Longoria was the most beautiful woman I had ever seen. 'I'll switch it off if you can't keep still.'

'Don't you dare. It's nearly finished.' I wanted to see the end of *Desperate Housewives*. I couldn't watch it at home if my parents were around. Dad only liked educational programmes, but to me, this was far more relevant to the future I dreamed of. I had wanted to be an actress since I was small. I loved the school productions, the smell of face powder and lipstick, the sound of applause. It was almost like stepping into another skin, I supposed. A more confident skin, a chance to become someone else, and even then, I wanted to be someone I was not.

'Do you think her hair is naturally wavy?'

'God knows. Bet she's got a team of stylists. Who looks like that in the mornings?'

Eva sashayed across the screen in a short silk robe, legs toned and tanned.

'Who looks like that at any time?'

'You'll look better than that tonight, Kat. I'm going to give you smokey eyes.'

'That sounds like a disease.'

'Very funny.' Lisa swirled a brush into eyeshadow. 'I saw it on an online tutorial. You'd be amazed at what you can learn on that new YouTube.'

'I'm not sure Dad would approve of me spending valuable revision time watching home-made videos.' I had asked my parents for a make-up set for Christmas but instead had been handed an A4 brown envelope. Inside was an annual online subscription to *Encyclopaedia Britannica*. It made a change from the hardback versions that stood stiff and proud, spines uncreased, on my bookcase.

Later, in the kitchen, mum had slipped me a small tin of Vaseline and told me I could highlight my cheekbones, use it on my lips and eyelashes. I had clutched the tin of possibilities tightly in my hand like the secret it was, as Dad's heavy footfall grew nearer and Mum turned her attention back to peeling sprouts.

'Does your dad ever approve of anything?' Lisa asked but it was a rhetorical question.

Dad thought I should spend every waking second studying. Every morning when I stumbled bleary-eyed into the kitchen and pulled cornflakes from the cupboard I couldn't help seeing the university brochure Dad had left on top of the microwave. My offer letter pinned to the corkboard above the fridge. As I splashed cold milk over my cereal, my stomach would churn. It wasn't as though I didn't want to go to university. I had been doing some research of my own and there were some fabulous courses offering degrees in Performing Arts, but to appease Dad I'd applied for English and History. Dad always wanted to be a teacher. 'It's a good, solid career, Katherine,' he said, but he had dropped out of uni. He called himself a 'financial advisor' when he was trying to impress people, but when it was just me and Mum he complained he was nothing but a 'glorified salesman'. But just because he wasn't clever enough to finish his course, it shouldn't mean I was forced to follow his dreams. I had my own.

Lisa checked her watch. 'If we're ready in fifteen minutes, Mum said she'd give us a lift on her way to bingo. Dad's working late again so she's making the most of it.' Lisa's mum, Nancy, was lovely.

'She'll pick us up after, too, and as you're staying here tonight, we won't have to leave at some ridiculous time for your curfew. Almost done.' Lisa swept bronzer over my cheeks.

'I nearly wasn't allowed to stay over. There was a problem when I told dad we were revising together.'

'What?'

'He knows you too well.'

'You're hilarious.' Lisa stepped back and studied me. 'And I'm a genius. Take a look.'

My reflection was stunning. Unbidden my fingers fluttered to my face as if checking it was really me.

'I look—'

'Oh God, don't start singing 'I Feel Pretty' again. I've heard it so many times I swear I could be your understudy.'

I was constantly practising for Maria in the sixth form production of *West Side Story*.

'I was going to say, I look like my mum.' I must take after her more than I had thought. I had never noticed a resemblance before but I had seen a photo once of her on stage when she was about my age. She looked so alive. When I had asked her if she ever wanted to be an actress instead of a secretary, she had said it was a one-off, but there had been a wistful look in her eyes. I had hoped that would be the moment she would open up, but she hadn't, and she remained a stranger to me. This woman who gave me life but came home exhausted, her trouser suit and faded dreams hanging from her tiny frame. Occasionally there were flashes of kindness, like when she gave me the Vaseline, but mostly we felt like three entities under one roof, not like a family at all.

'Don't get all mushy.' Lisa eased open her drawer. 'You might have crap parents but you know I love you.' She handed me a bottle of perfume.

'Lisa!' I'd coveted Sarah Jessica Parker's 'Lovely' fragrance for ages. I sprayed it onto my pulse points; rosewood and lavender danced around my nostrils. 'What do you think?' I held up my wrist.

'It'll do until Eva Longoria gets her arse into gear and brings one out. Let's get dressed.' Lisa shrugged off her dressing gown and slipped into a turquoise dress that sparkled like the sea. 'Fuck.' She tugged the zip. 'I'm getting so fat.'

'You're not,' I said, but actually she was, a bit.

'God. I'll never pull tonight.' She turned sideward in the mirror and sucked in her stomach. 'It's no wonder I can't get a boyfriend.'

'I thought there wasn't anybody you liked?'

'There isn't,' she said a little too quickly but there was a flush coating her chest.

'There is! Who?'

'It doesn't matter. I'm going to look awful.' She yanked off her dress, close to tears. 'Nothing fits me any more.'

'Wear the stretchy black one. It looks better anyway.'

'It's boring and it will cling to my belly.'

'You can wear my necklace to bling it up and draw the attention to your amazing cleavage instead.' I took off my thick silver chain with the diamanté heart and looped it over her neck.

'Are you sure?' Her mood instantly brightened. 'It's your favourite.'

'What's mine is yours,' I said.

'Really? I'll remember that,' Lisa said, and in that moment neither of us could envisage a time we wouldn't want to share.

How things changed.


Perry's enormous lounge was a throng of hot, swaying bodies; cheap perfume and aftershave. On the shelf above the TV, cat ornaments rattled as the bass pulsed from oversized speakers. Red and green flashing lights lit discarded paper plates heaped with crumbling sausage rolls and drying sandwich crusts. The 'Happy

18th' banner had become unstuck at one end, and Perry wrenched it down before wrapping it around himself like a cape.

I squeezed my way into the hallway looking for Lisa. She'd gone to the loo ages ago but the queue was still snaking down the stairs. Instead of waiting I headed through the kitchen and out of the open patio doors, into the garden. Multicoloured lanterns glowed; they were strung from the fence, hanging from the washing line. Even outside the music was still pounding.

Sitting on the picnic table, feet resting on the bench seat, were Aaron and Jake. I had to gulp my vodka – liquid courage – before I could join them. I saw them at school every day but this felt different somehow, with my short dress, heels sinking into the lawn. The wood creaked as I sat next to them.

'Hey, Kat.' Aaron offered me the spliff he held between thumb and index finger, and when I shook my head he shrugged and placed it between his lips. For someone who was intent on being a doctor Aaron didn't take his own health very seriously. As he took a drag the end crackled red before he exhaled, and the warm night air was heavy with cannabis and tobacco.

'Aaron!' Perry swayed in front of us, clutching a beer, still wrapped in the banner. 'It's my birthday. Got me a pressie?'

Aaron jumped off the table, and it wobbled with the sudden shift in weight. I stretched out my arms to steady myself, my left hand resting on Jake's knee. Aaron supported Perry as he led him back inside.

'Think we should help?' I asked reluctantly. I didn't know Aaron very well. We didn't share any lessons.

'Nah,' said Jake. 'I like it here.'

He turned to face me, and I realised my palm was still pressing against his knee. Underneath the denim was heat. I started to draw away, but he placed his hand on top of mine. Our fingers linked together, and my mouth went dry. It was crazy. I'd known him forever. He was like a brother almost, but since he'd been cast as

Tony in the end of year production of *West Side Story*, to my Maria, something between us had shifted. There was a confidence about him both on stage and off that made my pulse flutter. He didn't dress like the other boys, in his white T-shirt and skinny jeans, black pork-pie hat, the gold cross he always wore.

At rehearsals yesterday he'd cupped my face between his palms as we sang 'Somewhere', and when he took his hands away I felt like he had taken a piece of me with him too.

'Dance with me, Kat.' He pulled me to my feet and alone, under the endless indigo sky, it felt like we were the only two people left in the world. As my body gyrated with the beat of Paul Weller's 'It's Written in the Stars' Jake didn't once let go of my hand, and instead he pulled me closer. His lips brushed my ear, and I melted like butter as he whispered: 'you and me Kat, we're written in the stars'. As he pulled back, I studied his face to see if he was joking, this boy I had known most of my life, but his eyes were full of longing.

'This,' he whispered, 'is what I wanted to do at rehearsals yesterday.' His mouth skimmed mine, lips warm and smooth. I began to close my eyes. The last thing I saw was the utter disbelief and hurt on Lisa's face as she stood framed in the patio doors. Perhaps I should have pushed Jake away but as his kiss grew more urgent, I knew I was lost.

Rightly or wrongly I didn't let Lisa's reaction stop me slipping my hand into Jake's back pocket, pressing my body hard against his. I wanted him and, at that time, it seemed so simple.

If only I knew then the lengths that Lisa and I would both go to, to get what we wanted. The hurt we would cause.

The lives that would be lost.

If I'd know that then, I like to think I'd have pushed Jake away because, otherwise, what sort of person did that make me?

And I'm not a monster.

I'm not.

# CHAPTER NINE

The week since we saw Lisa seems endless.

'How was your day?' Nick bites into his pizza – spicy pepperoni – a string of cheese stretches thinner and thinner until he snaps it with his fingers.

Before dinner my arms had been sprinkled with gooseflesh, but now, jalapeños heat me from the inside out.

'Good,' I say taking a sip of water to soothe my burning tongue. 'I spoke to a guy, Alex, who runs a theatre group. We had a chat about them donating the profits of their next production to Stroke Support. He seemed quite keen.'

'Lisa got you thinking about the past, has she?'

Despite the fire in my mouth, a chill snakes down my spine. 'Sorry?'

'Acting. I still can't believe I didn't know that about you.'

'Yes. I suppose so. I'm going to meet him tonight at rehearsal. Do you want to come?' Outside a storm is raging. I loathe driving in the dark and rain.

'Sorry, I'm meeting Richard to discuss the expenses for a new project.'

'Speaking of expenses, have you transferred the money to Lisa?' I ask Nick. We've agreed on £3,000 up front and when she falls pregnant, for I have to believe it is a when: £1,250 each month.

'Yes. She's probably out now spending it all on drink and drugs.' He laughs to show he is joking but a knot of anxiety twists itself tightly in my stomach. After Lisa first offered to be a surrogate, I'd had a long conversation with her about her health and lifestyle. I grilled her, I suppose. She assured me she eats healthily, will take all her prenatal supplements and won't drink, but still, it's a lot of trust in someone to keep my baby as safe as I would, if I were the one carrying them. It occurred to me I could find a different surrogate. Someone who drank those gloopy green juices, performed yoga on the lawn each morning, whatever the weather, and avoided sugar and processed food. I went round and round in circles, trying to decide whether Lisa was the right person, and whether our shared history was a help or a hindrance but had concluded at least I know everything there is to know. Who knows what a stranger might keep hidden? Better the devil, I suppose you could say. The fact that we've grown up together is a positive thing, I think. We'll both be able to be honest if there's anything we're unhappy with.

'Great. She's hiring a relaxation coach.' I was so relieved when she told me. She really was taking her health as seriously as she promised. Any lingering doubts had evaporated. 'Lisa said when she was pregnant with Stella she had high blood pressure so it will help with conception, if she's not already pregnant.'

'What on earth is a relaxation coach?'

'They teach you meditation and stuff. She's going to see her once a week and can ring her up when she's feeling stressed as well. It must be incredibly pressured working at the hospital. It's horribly expensive but worth every penny, I think.'

'It's up to her, I guess. Richard put in the agreement she can use the expenses for anything relating to her well-being. We should be glad she's not drinking a bottle of wine a night to relax.'

My eyes flick over to our empty bottles waiting to be recycled.

'Maybe we should try meditation…' I grin.

'I can think of better ways to relax.' Nick lifts his eyebrows suggestively, and I suddenly wish I was staying in but, if I were,

Nick would likely become engrossed in paperwork while I'll be glued to social media on my phone. I only use Twitter and Facebook for the charity though that in itself could almost be a full-time job. Perhaps we should go to Italy before the baby comes, while it's still just the two of us.

We finish eating and I clear the table, popping the pieces of crust on the worktop near the back door to give to the birds in the morning. Nick rinses the plates while I lick my fingers before slipping on my shoes and buttoning my coat.

'See you later.' I do a jazz hands goodbye and high kick out of the room.


The community centre is freezing cold. There's a proper stage in a huge room. Grey folded chairs are stacked around the edge of the shiny parquet flooring. It smells of my old school. Rubber plimsolls and boiled cabbage. But it isn't the smell that causes my breath to hitch in my throat. On the stage, feet pounding, arms swinging, a group of men of different ages, belt out 'Gee, Officer Krupke'. The song strikes me with such force I lean heavily against the wall as though I would fall without its support. They are performing *West Side Story*. A film of tears coats my eyes. I can almost see Jake on the stage.

It takes me a second to realise the music has stopped and a couple are standing in front of me.

'Hello.' My voice sounds distant and hollow, as though it belongs to someone else. I shake the hand that is offered. 'Kat, from Stroke Support. You must be Alex?'

'Yes, and this is Tamara.'

'Hello.' She beams a smile. Glossy pink lips framing impossibly white teeth.

'Take five, everyone,' Alex shouts. 'Shall we?' He gestures over to the chairs and the three of us sit in a triangle. 'So, as I said on the phone, our next performance will be June. We won't start advertising it until the new year, although we've been rehearsing for a few weeks. Most of the cast work full-time and we don't get together quite as often as we'd like. We've had a chat, haven't we, Tam, and we'd be happy to donate the proceeds to Stroke Support.'

'Yes,' Tamara says. 'And you'd help us with advertising?'

'Yes. We'll print the posters; we'll need to put our logo on, and put out some leaflets. We can probably get the local paper to run a feature, and the radio. They're normally really good with things like this. We'd provide the programmes as well and get some volunteers to sell them on the night, as well as doing a raffle in the interval.'

'Sounds fabulous. We can firm up the details later if that's okay? We've only got the hall booked for another hour. Do you want to stay and watch us rehearse?' Alex checks his watch.

I don't want to stay. I've never been able to watch *West Side Story* since. It's too painful. Too raw. But I find myself saying yes.

'Who's playing Tony?' I ask.

'That's me,' says Alex. 'Tam is Maria. We're not hogging the best parts, honest. But other members have busier lives. This is our life. A bit sad really.'

'At least we know we're reliable,' Tam says. 'We lost our Anita this week. She found out she was pregnant. She's gutted. She's already got three kids and doesn't want another.'

My stomach clenches like a fist at the unfairness of it.

'Don't suppose you act?' Alex raises his eyebrows.

'Yes. Well, I mean, I used to. At school. I was never…' The words are coming out in a gibbering rush and I can't stop them. 'I was Maria once…' Again, I feel that contraction in the pit of my belly. Despite the hours of rehearsals, I never got to perform in front of an audience, did I?

'So you know the part?'

Too late, I realise what I have walked in to.

'It's been years…'

'It's like riding a bike. You never forget. What do you think, Tam? You practised for Anita a few years ago, didn't you? You know both parts really well so you could swap and Kat could be our Maria.'

'But I've *never* played Maria.' It seems only I can detect the faint note of desperation in Tamara's voice and that's probably because I've heard it in my own.

'It would save Kat playing catch up if she had a role she knew.'

'You're the boss,' Tam says. 'I'm happy if you are.' But the set of her jaw, the narrowing of her eyes, are a direct contrast to her words.

'Let's try you out and see if you fit. Everyone,' Alex claps his hands, 'Kat's going to sing us a song.'

As I stand centre stage, I have a sense of not being present in my own body. It feels as though a thousand eyes are burning into me. There's a thrumming in my ears and the room feels as though it's spinning. I don't have to do this, I know, but as sick as I feel, there must be a part of me deep down that wants to try, because as the backing track starts, I begin to sing. My voice is hesitant at first. My timing off. Something passes over Tamara's face and, as I deliberate whether it is annoyance or amusement, I forget my line.

'Sorry.' My whole body is trembling as though I am in shock.

The backing track starts again, and this time I close my eyes and I don't just hear the music, I feel it. The emotion rises as I remember singing 'I Feel Pretty' to Jake in his bedroom, powering my voice. My body starts to sway and my pitch is now perfect.

When I've finished I open my eyes, blinking furiously as the room comes back into focus. Taking in the expressions of the cast, the applause, I know, without a doubt that I am Maria. Again.

It could be a positive thing, I tell myself as I inch out of the car park. It will give me something else to talk about with Nick.

Something that isn't work or babies. Ever since he'd mentioned not wanting to lose sight of us I'd been worried, although we're just as affectionate as we ever were. Just as thoughtful. I still bring him a cup of tea in bed every morning, he still fills my car with fuel, but it would be good for him to see me in a different light. The romantic lead. Who'd have thought? My rising excitement is tempered by the fact I have to drive home in the dark. In the rain. The fear I feel in a car has never really left me, despite my GP referring me onto a course of Cognitive Behavioural Therapy. 'It's not unusual for the victim of an accident to feel anxious in a vehicle,' the therapist said, but despite her soothing tone, her use of the word 'victim' increased my agitation. When I'm behind the wheel I feel such a weight of responsibility, not just for me but for the other road users, as though I am the one that has to keep them safe, in a way I couldn't before.

The heater blasts out air and my toes begin to thaw as I leave behind the town and the street lamps, heading for home. The weather is atrocious. The radio station is playing Fifties music, and Elvis begins to sing 'Are You Lonesome Tonight?' I snap off my stereo, my breath coming a little faster. My shoulders hunched. Rain flings itself at the windscreen and the wipers swish at double speed but visibility is poor. My hands grip the steering wheel tight as I lean forward in my seat. Along with the woody smell of the air freshener swinging from the rear-view mirror, a sense of foreboding fills the air. I ease my foot off the accelerator. *It wasn't the car that hurt me*, I think in the way I'd been taught. *It was human error.* Knowing that is supposed to make me feel better. It never does.

The moon is hiding behind the rain clouds, and everywhere I look is black. Crushing. The sky blends in with the road and my full beam picks out the rain sheeting down. There's a particularly nasty bend coming up, and I slow down again, dropping into second gear. From behind there's a flash and the blast of a horn, and my underarms prickle, but I can't bring myself to drive faster.

The horn blares again. Intimidated, I speed up, trying to put some distance between us, but I can't help thinking of the other time I was in a car with the dark and the rain. The accident is sharp in my memory, clearer than it has been for years, and suddenly I am terrified. I drop my speed again hoping the other car will go around me. There's another blast of a horn, for longer this time. Headlights flash once, twice, three times. I tilt my rear-view mirror to stop myself from being dazzled. I'm arced over the wheel now. Every muscle in my body rigid. The car blasts its horn again, and I urge myself to calm down as I heave in a breath as though I am suffocating. There isn't a good place along this country track to overtake but I know there is a lay-by coming up, and I have seconds to make a decision whether to stop or carry on. It will be safer to let them pass. I indicate left and twist the wheel. My tyres scramble for traction and squeal, and the sound transports me back. My body is stone as I wait for the impact. The pain. But the car straightens and I am safe in the lay-by. The other car tears past me. I am hyperventilating as I rest my forehead on the steering wheel. Panic tearing my chest in two. I haven't felt like this for years. It's all starting again. Just like I always knew it would.

Lisa is back in my life.

I am Maria.

Oh God. I am slipping back into the past.

The good. The bad.

All of it.

# CHAPTER TEN
## Now

It's my first rehearsal and I'm terrified. Nick had left a 'good luck' message on the worktop spelled out in Cadbury's Buttons. Although I felt sick with nerves I still popped them onto my tongue, letting the chocolate dissolve as I dragged a brush through my hair and changed into clean leggings.

Alex has already ordered my costumes: 'you're committed now'. He passes me a gold dress that shimmers under the spotlight. 'Want to try it on? We're starting with the dance at the gym.'

'Talk about throwing me in at the deep end! I've no idea if I'll remember the steps,' I say as if every single move isn't still embedded into my memory. It's the scene where Tony first meets Maria, and is one of my favourite parts of the show. What I really mean, but cannot say, is that I've no idea whether I am still agile enough to carry it off. Not for the first time I wonder if I've made a mistake. If I'm too unfit. Too old. 'You're not thirty until next year!' Clare had laughed as I'd expressed my concerns over coffee. 'Go for it.' But now, under the harsh lights, with all the attention on me, I can almost see my confidence skittering across the stage, slipping down the trap door, swallowed by blackness, never to be seen again. The dress feels snug. I'd had to draw my navel to my spine to yank up the zip, pulling so hard the metal imprinted on my fingertips. I smooth the satin of the dress over my stomach, wishing I didn't mindlessly eat so many Hobnobs as I work at the kitchen table.

'We might as well go the whole hog and put the backdrop up?' Alex says. 'Any volunteers?'

'I can help.' I step forward.

'It needs securing properly,' Tamara says. 'We'll show you how another time.'

'I've done scenery before.' I'm eager to prove my worth. I still feel terrible about taking the part away from Tamara, although she has been really gracious about it.

My fingers are shaking as I secure the backdrop, looping rope around the rings. Muscle memory kicks in and I automatically tie knots as my mind wanders to the last time I did this. To the kisses I'd sneak with Jake backstage when we thought no one was looking – there was always a wolf whistle from another member of the group. Some secrets can't be kept.

The music blares, jolting me from my memories, and I hurry to take my place. Alex smiles reassuringly, and the stage vibrates with the clump of footsteps. All too soon the muscles in my legs are shaking. I hunch over, chest burning as I drag in air. 'Sorry,' I manage to rasp out.

'Not to worry,' Alex says. 'You've months to get your fitness up. This is only day one. Ready to go again?'

I nod as I straighten, trying to ignore the stitch burning in my side.

'Run!' Tamara screams, and at first, I can't understand what's going on but out of the corner of my eye I see the backdrop wobble. My heart leaps into my throat and I instinctively raise my arms, but it's too late as the scenery falls, falls, falls, crashing against my skull.

I'm sitting on the edge of the stage. Pressing a tea towel full of ice cubes to my temple but my head doesn't hurt as much as my pride.

'Are you sure you secured it properly?' Tamara asks for what feels like the hundredth time.

'Yes,' I say again but I am not sure. Not really. My mind is too full of Jake. Of Lisa. The past. The future. I realise how little headspace I am giving Nick and I feel sick with guilt.

'Kat!' Tamara shakes her head in exasperation, and I realise she had been talking to me.

'Sorry. What did you say?' I really have to pull myself together. I can't fall apart. Again.

The rest of December passes in a blur. It is the week before Christmas and I've been fundraising like crazy – everyone is so generous around this time of year. We're both so busy we only put the decorations up last night. As usual we've gone for a real tree, and drank hot chocolate laced with brandy, wearing Santa hats, as Nick wrapped the lights around the branches and I hung baubles.

It's hard to focus on the paperwork today. Thoughts of Lisa constantly creep in my mind. I rattle off yet another text, asking if she is okay when what I really mean is does she think she's pregnant, although she's assured me countless times she'll let me know as soon as there is news. Good or bad.

Lisa replies to say she'll call later. She's busy at work. Again.

'You need to slow down,' I had said the last time we spoke. 'You do so many hours. Can't you stop your overtime, for now?'

'That's what the relaxation coach says but I can't meet the rent without the extra cash.'

'But you have our first payment now. The £3,000. Isn't that enough? Do you need more?'

'No, you're already being generous, and you're right. That will cover the shortfall in rent. It's not just about money, I suppose. I enjoy keeping busy.'

'I know but it's not just about you now, is it?' I felt horrible, almost as though I was bullying her, but she sighed and agreed to turn down extra shifts.

Later, I'm jotting down a list of things we need from town, when my mobile rings. Lisa. My stomach flip-flops. I'm torn between wanting to hear what she has to say and being utterly terrified she'll tell me her period has started.

'Hello.' I am cautious as I answer.

'Hi. Sorry for the radio silence. I'm having a nightmare.'

'What's up?'

'Hang on a sec,' she says. I hear her speaking in hushed tones to someone else, and I want to scream down the handset 'are you pregnant or not', but at least this way I can have a few more minutes of pretending before she comes on the line again.

'Sorry, Kat. I'm really busy. You know what this time of year is like, and my car's broken down and garage says it will be £2k to fix. I can't afford it without my overtime so I've been taking the bus to work.'

'That must be inconvenient,' I say my mind racing to find a solution.

'I don't mind the bus usually, but—'

'But what?' While I wait for her to speak, I scribble tangerines onto my shopping list.

'I've been feeling a little queasy lately.'

The pen slips from my grasp and I watch it roll off the kitchen table and onto the floor. Everything is moving in slow motion. 'Do you think?' I trail off.

'Perhaps. I'll do a test if my period doesn't start on time but I just wanted to touch base. Explain why I haven't been in touch. The extra travelling time, you know.'

'You can't get the bus,' I blurt out.

'I don't have a choice.' Lisa's tone has cooled, and I am worried I have offended her.

'I just meant if you are pregnant. There'll be appointments, won't there? You have to be mobile. I'll transfer some money across.' Even as I speak, I have crossed the kitchen and am logging onto internet banking on the iPad.

'I can't let you—'

'Don't be silly. If you're pregnant, we will be starting the monthly payments anyway, won't we?' I brush aside her concerns. Lisa's account details have been stored from Nick transferring money before. 'There. Two thousand. It should be with you this afternoon.'

'Thanks so much, Kat. You're a star. I've got to fly.'

She hangs up before I can say 'you're welcome'.


The streets are crowded, everyone in a rush, bumping carrier bags and jagged elbows, but I'm in such a daze I barely notice. Lisa feels sick. *This really could be it.* I don't have much to buy. There will just be me and Nick on Christmas Day. I squeeze through M&S to buy Nick's favourite red onion chutney. I round a corner, bumping straight into a pram, jolting the handle, waking the baby snuggled in a navy padded snowsuit with Rudolph on the chest. Instantly, I look for the mother, to apologise, but there are so many people crowding around the shelves I don't know who she is. Despite 'Santa Baby' blaring out of the speakers, and the hum of voices, the baby's cry cuts through to my very core and, ever so gently, I start pushing the pram back and forth trying to soothe the infant back to sleep. His mouth is in a perfect 'O', beet red, chubby legs kicking angrily. Unsure, I look around before picking him up and making soft shushing noises in his ear. His wisps of hair are plastered to his damp scalp. It is unbearably warm. Too warm. After a moment of hesitation, I ease down the zipper on his snowsuit.

An angry voice shouts. 'What the fuck do you think you're doing with my baby?'

A woman snatches him from my arms, her ponytail swinging as she backs away from me as though I might try to grab him back.

'He was crying. And hot. I'm sorry.' I stutter my apologies while she glares at me.

'You're a fucking lunatic.' She spins the pram around and pushes her way down the aisle. My legs are boneless and I have to cling onto my trolley to support my weight but it isn't the woman's words that have upset me so. It is the shame in knowing that just for a split second I had been tempted to take the baby that was too hot. Too distressed. Too alone. Sometimes it scares me how far I'll go to have a baby to call my own. Sometimes I think there's nothing I wouldn't do.

It is nine when we wake on Christmas morning, and Nick lies spread-eagled in the bed while I pad downstairs to make tea. I can't wait for the day I'm woken up at 6 a.m., bleary-eyed from staying up late, filling stockings and dusting the patio with icing sugar reindeer prints.

'We said no presents!' I say as I return with our drinks to see a large gift, wrapped in sparkling purple paper, resting on my pillow. We're okay for money, for now, but we need to be careful. If Lisa falls pregnant, her expenses will wipe out the majority of our savings. Shaking my head as though I am cross I pull open the wardrobe and lift out a box that I hand to Nick. As usual when we both have something to open we count to three before simultaneously tearing off the paper.

'It's great!' In my peripheral vision I can see Nick wind the scarf I bought him around his neck. It's cashmere but it only came from TK Maxx and didn't cost the earth. The blue should match his eyes perfectly but I can't look at him. Can't stop staring at the framed poster of *West Side Story* in my hands.

'Thank you! Is it?…'

'Original, yes. All the autographs from the cast are real too.'

'It's incredible. I love you.' Finally, my eyes find his.

'I love you too.' Nick rests the picture on the floor, tugs at the belt of my dressing gown and it is another hour before we make it downstairs.

We play a logo quiz on the iPad while we wait for our M&S turkey to cook, and after lunch, Nick and I cuddle on the sofa, the fairy lights on the tree glowing muted cream, the scent of pine heavy in the air. Our mobiles rest on the coffee table along with a bottle of Baileys and two empty glasses. I am just scanning through the *Radio Times* deciding what we can watch next when Nick's phone flashes. It's a text message from Natasha.

'What does she want?' I ask, my words as sharp as the pine needles that lie scattered over the carpet. 'I didn't know you were still in touch?'

Before he can answer there's another beep for an incoming message but this time it comes from my phone. I crane my neck to peer at the screen, snatching at my handset when I see Lisa's name flash up.

The sofa seems to shift and sway as I read the message. I am floating towards the ceiling.

'What is it?' Nick asks but I cannot answer.

I cannot speak. I want to pass him the handset to show him, but I can't tear my eyes away from the message that reads:

*Happy Christmas Mummy*

Along with a photo of a positive pregnancy testing kit. All thoughts of Natasha vanish. I'm going to be a mum.

# CHAPTER ELEVEN
## Now

Usually I dread playing the hostess – perfect smile and perfect canapés – but I'm actually looking forward to our New Year's Eve party. This time next year, it will be a much quieter affair, night feeds and nappy changes, but tonight, I'm going to let my hair down. I wriggle into my bottle green sequinned dress.

Nick is subdued as he threads the brown leather belt I bought him for Christmas through his jeans, which are hanging looser than they used to.

'Hey.' I run my hand over his flat stomach, feel his muscles tighten. The soft roll of flesh he usually carries at his waist has shrunk. 'You're supposed to put on weight, not lose it, this time of year.' I'm worried about him. Ever since Christmas Day he's been quiet. Distracted. Spending too much time in the basement, feet pounding on the running machine. Lisa is pregnant and I can't stop talking about it; Nick, on the other hand, has little to say.

'Lisa's definitely coming tonight? I really want Richard to meet her.' Nick tips aftershave onto his palms and slaps it against his cheek. He smells of wood and spice.

'Yes.' I check my watch. It's almost eight. The guests will arrive soon, and I had hoped Lisa would come early, give us a chance to really catch up. These past couple of days I had tried to ring her several times but she hadn't picked up, sending a text instead, saying:

*I'm with my family.*

I know what that means. It means she is having to pretend I don't exist. She said she'd come to the party, though, and I can't wait to find out how she's feeling – really feeling – about it all.

Tonight will be mostly people connected to the charity or Nick's employees or clients, although I've invited the theatre group and, as an afterthought, I'd pulled on boots and gloves and thrust thick silver invitations through every letterbox in the cul-de-sac. We've haven't got to know our neighbours yet, not beyond raising our right hands in some sort of wave, like it's a code, whenever we pass them in our cars.

The doorbell chimes. I stand on tiptoe to kiss Nick before I brush my thumb over his lips removing the trace of pink lipstick. I pelt down to the hallway and fling open the front door.

'Happy New Year!' Alex hands me a bottle of champagne.

'We can't stop for long.' Tamara air kisses hello. 'We have another party to go to.'

I usher them inside, along with Clare who was standing behind them, balancing Ada on one hip.

'Hello, sweet girl,' I say to Ada. She's dressed as Snow White and looks adorable with her long dark ringlets, blue eyes, and porcelain skin. She's already stunning and she's not yet two.

'Hello, beautiful!' Nick clatters down the stairs.

'Hello, Nick!' Clare laughs.

'I wasn't talking about mummy, was I?' Nick holds out his arms, and Clare passes Ada over, and she wraps her legs around his waist like a baby monkey. 'Glad you made it.' Nick smiles at Clare.

'Not often I get the chance to go to parties nowadays. It'll be your big birthday bash next, won't it?' She jabs me with her elbow.

'Not a chance.' A look passes between them but I don't care. I really want something low-key. 'Let's get some drinks.'

In the kitchen, I introduce Nick to Tamara and Alex as Clare prises off lids from Tupperwares she has brought with her in a carrier bag. Her nails are impossibly long and embellished with Santa faces.

'These goodies are leftovers from the café yesterday.'

'You're a lifesaver.' I pull a plate from the cupboard, grateful for Clare's part-time job. It's beyond me how she can afford her big house on her wages from the café. We'd shared a bottle of wine before Christmas, and she'd let slip how tight money is. It didn't sound like Akhil, her ex, was paying maintenance, for some reason, but I didn't pry. Our friendship is too new.

I lift out vol-au-vents filled with creamy mushroom and prawns, cheese straws sprinkled with sesame seeds, and filo parcels. I bite into one and my taste buds tingle as cranberry explodes onto my tongue, drawing out the flavour of the Brie.

'Gorgeous,' I say. 'And speaking of gorgeous – check you out!'

'I hope you won't be the only one checking me out,' she says fluffing her long blonde hair and pouting with red lips. 'I'm single and I'm going to mingle.' She winks as she walks away, and I want to laugh but I'm on edge, constantly listening out for the doorbell, desperate for Lisa to arrive. Where is she?

Tamara helps me plate up the rest of the food.

'Are you really okay, Tam? With me playing Maria? I don't mind being Anita.'

'It's fine.' Her smile is warm. 'I'm just glad we're finally putting on *West Side Story*. We tried a few years ago but—'

'But?'

'The lady playing Maria died.'

The house is filling with people, with laughter. The smell of mulled wine wafting from the slow cooker. Alex and Richard are chatting in the corner. Clare is deep in conversation with Nick. Even the nosy woman with red hair from a few doors down has come. I should be happy but there's an uneasiness in the air and, as I take a deep gulp of my wine, I wonder whether anyone can feel it but me.

*

The starlight projector in the nursery hums as the motor rotates, casting a solar system on the ceiling. It is hypnotic rocking back and forth in the nursing chair, my head resting against a cushion. I'm transfixed by the moon and stars. The sense I could stretch out my fingers and touch them. Downstairs the party is loud; raucous laugher increasing in volume. The Rat Pack Christmas songs I'd been streaming earlier, has been replaced by an eclectic mix of pop songs. Mark Ronson's 'Uptown Funk' fades out and Brotherhood of Man urge 'Save your Kisses for Me'. Earlier, I had switched on the patio heater as the string of fairy lights glowed prettily around the pergola, and placed ashtrays on the garden table. I didn't want anyone smoking indoors. Now, the smell of cigarette smoke wafts up the stairs but I find I don't care whether there is ash over the carpet or fag burns on the sofa. I don't care about anything except the fact Lisa is not here.

'Kat?' Nick calls up the stairs, and I wipe my tear-stained cheeks on the ears of the floppy rabbit I've been cradling on my lap. 'It's nearly midnight.'

'Coming.' I stand and I am spinning with the stars, stumbling to the side, knocking over an empty wine bottle with my foot. Have I really drunk all that? No wonder I am emotional.

Gripping hold of the bannister tightly I slowly descend the stairs. Reaching the bottom, I hear a knocking sound over the music.

Throwing the door wide to a blast of freezing air, I lurch forward, enveloping Lisa in a hug.

'You came!'

'Sorry I'm so late – my car wouldn't start and I had to call a taxi. I don't suppose you've got some cash, have you? I asked the cabbie to stop at a cashpoint, but I don't think he understood me.'

'But I gave you the money for the garage?'

'I know. They must have been a bunch of cowboys.'

'Can't you?—' A sharp beep of the taxi's horn blasts. We'll have to talk about it later. 'Come in. I'll grab my purse.'

She steps onto the mat and pushes back her hood. She looks pale and I hope she's not going to suffer from morning sickness. I am overwhelmed with what she is doing for me. *For us*, I remind myself as I hear Nick's voice drifting out from the lounge followed by a peal of tinkling laughter. 'How much is it?' I unzip my handbag hanging on a hook by the door.

'It's £200.'

I know I don't have enough in my purse, and I'm over the limit and can't drive to the cashpoint but then I remember the safe. Nick keeps some cash in there. It's in his study. I don't usually open it, but with the meter on the cab ticking, I'm sure he won't mind. The numbers glow green as I punch in the combination, Nick's birthday, and pull out a bundle of notes. As I turn around, Lisa is leaning against the doorframe, pulling off her gloves.

'I'll take the money out.' She holds out her hand. 'I've still got my coat and shoes on. Make me a hot drink, would you?'

I hand over the cash.

In the kitchen, I am tipping boiling water onto coffee granules when the front door slams.

'All sorted.' Lisa wraps her hands around the mug as I add a splash of milk.

'Who's this then?' Richard scoops a handful of peanuts, dropping them into his mouth.

'This is Lisa, our surrogate. Lisa, this is Richard, Nick's friend and our solicitor.'

A frown furrows Lisa's forehead as she studies Richard. I look across at him and catch a flicker in his eyes. I think it's a sign of recognition, but it is too brief for me to be sure.

'Pleased to meet you, Lisa,' Richard says but his words are as cold as the icicles suspended from the guttering outside the window like daggers, and just as sharp.

# CHAPTER TWELVE
## Now

On New Year's Day, I wake, a sour taste in my mouth. The first resolution I make, and will probably break, is never to drink again. The smell of stale alcohol fills our bedroom. Next to me, Nick is lying on his back, mouth hanging open, arms spread above his head. We both overdid it last night, and my memories are hazy but I remember switching BBC on and, as Big Ben chimed the start of a brand new year, I had hugged Lisa tightly, feeling her heart beat against mine, and I imagined the baby's heart racing away too. At six weeks pregnant the heartbeat should be detectable. After Lisa's text came on Christmas Day, I'd ordered a pregnancy bible from Amazon, and I've memorised virtually every single stage of the first trimester already. I had tried to tell Nick that the baby's face is already taking shape and his circulatory system is developing, but he'd said it was impossible Lisa is that far gone despite the fact I had already told him the weeks of pregnancy are dated from the first day of the last menstrual period. As I explained for the second time, he glazed over. I'd pored over the pages, exclaiming in delight when I learned the baby would start to move at eight weeks and would be the size of a jelly bean. 'We should call him or her Beanie, until we know the sex. What do you think? A gender neutral nickname?' Nick didn't answer, and when I looked up, he had left the room. Thinking logically, I know some men aren't terribly interested in pregnancy, and it's not the fact it's Lisa carrying Nick's baby that makes him seem detached, but it still smarts all the same.

I swing my legs out of bed, and pad across to the en suite, almost tripping over the pile of clothes Nick had been wearing last night. I strip off my pyjamas, dumping them in the laundry basket, and bend to scoop Nick's clothes up from the floor. There is lipstick on the collar of his white shirt. I must put it in to soak. It's red so it's definitely not mine but everyone was hugging at midnight. I think I must have kissed everyone on the cul-de-sac. We had belted out 'Auld Lang Syne'. As we sang the line, 'Should auld acquaintance be forgot', Lisa had squeezed my fingers so tightly I feared my bones would shatter.

Under the water, I close my eyes and massage strawberry shampoo into my hair and try to picture the faces that swam out of focus as I sang and smiled, knowing this would be the year my dreams came true. I can't remember seeing Nick, and I know I was not the one to kiss him Happy New Year. A chasm has opened between us this past week, and I have no idea why. He's been off work but we have hardly spent any time together and although he is only in the next room, I have a horrible sense of missing him.

The underfloor heating is on an automatic timer. The tiles are warm under the soles of my feet as I pad into the kitchen. Lisa is perched on a stool at the breakfast bar, hunched over her mobile phone.

'Morning,' I call, although, as I glance at the clock, I see it is nearer to lunchtime. 'Did you sleep okay?'

'Fine,' she says, but the dark circles hanging below her eyes, the yawn she stifles, tell a different story. 'Thanks for the night light!'

We share a smile. Lisa was always terrified of the dark. Whenever we had sleepovers her bedside lamp would stay switched on until day seeped through the night.

'Breakfast?' I ask.

'I'm not hungry, thanks.'

'Lisa, you must eat!'

'I could stand to lose a few pounds.' She offers a weak smile. 'My stomach feels bigger already. My midwife told me about a woman who had a concealed pregnancy. I should be so lucky.'

'What's that?'

'The woman didn't know she was pregnant until she went into labour. Can you imagine that? She stayed in size 10 jeans throughout. Bitch. Apparently, some people never show at all and some end up like elephants. I can guess which way I'll go.'

'That's not important now.' But I know her too well. Know she will be worried.

'Why don't you use some of the expenses money to join a gym, not for the weights but you could use the pool? It would be good for relaxation too?'

'That's a good idea.'

I pull open the fridge door. 'Scrambled eggs?'

'No. Honestly, I'm feeling sick.'

She does look pale. I'm not feeling great myself, although my nausea is self-inflicted. I shut the fridge and flap open a bin bag and start to scrape cold pizza from plates stained with tomato sauce and congealed cheese. I pick up a half-full bottle of Newcastle Brown and tip the remnants down the sink. The ale froths and the yeasty smell rises. Lisa jumps up and runs out of the kitchen, hand clasped over her mouth. The door of the downstairs toilet bangs shut, and through the wall, the sound of Lisa retching causes my stomach to lurch. To mask the sound, I switch on the radio. Our local station is playing classic Number One hits. The Beatles sing 'All You Need Is Love'. Feeling helpless at the sounds drifting into the kitchen, I turn up the volume, and sit on a stool, my pounding head in my hands.


'This is such a lovely house,' Lisa says.

I've abandoned the clearing up and we are carrying our drinks out of the kitchen.

'I know. Nick bought it at a really good price to renovate. The previous owners, Mr and Mrs Whitmoore, had lived here for years until they went into a home. Their son, Paul, hoped to keep it but he couldn't afford the mortgage. Everything needed doing. Electrics, plumbing, bathrooms, kitchen. Nick fell in love with it and didn't want to sell.'

'You're so lucky to live here. My flat is tiny.'

'Do you live in the nurse's accommodation by the hospital?'

'No. They were all full when I started. You've so many books!' Lisa crouches on her haunches at the bottom of the hallway and runs her fingers over the spines. There's a mismatch of everything: the historical fiction I love; the crime Nick devours, and parenting books I've read so many times I could quote them verbatim. When we compared our book collection, I had told Nick I was the only teenager of our generation who had an encyclopaedia and I'd laughed when he said he had one too.

'What's behind there?' Lisa glances at a closed door.

'Nick's man cave! He has his exercise stuff down there. And a sofa.'

'Sounds cool.' Lisa looks impressed, and I remember her flashing me the same look when I finally mastered the perfect cartwheel.

'It is. And it's fully soundproofed, so I don't care how loud he plays his music as he runs, I don't hear it.'

Paul Whitmoore came around to collect some post a few months ago, after we'd moved here, and he'd stood on the step for so long sharing his memories I'd eventually invited him in for coffee. He told me his parents had renovated the small basement for him when he was learning the drums. They couldn't stand the noise. He'd left his drum kit down there when he moved out but always played whenever he came to visit them.

'You're lucky living here,' he'd said. 'I love this house. I wish we hadn't had to sell it when mum and dad needed to go into a home. I have such happy memories of growing up.'

I hope our child feels the same way.

'Can I have a look down there?' Lisa turns to me.

'Be my guest.' I open the door and flick on the light switch. There is a faint whiff of damp.

'Coming?' she asks.

I shake my head and take a step back. A look of sympathy flashes across her eyes before she turns and makes her way down the staircase. She knows why I won't put myself in a small, dark space. What she doesn't know is that I still wake up in the night sometimes, sheets soaked with my terror. The feeling of a bird flapping in my chest. Even now, the honeyed sunshine streaming through the glass in the front door can't keep my black thoughts at bay, and I fall back into a memory I don't think I'll ever escape.

*I was trapped. Alone. Scared. I bit down hard on my lip to stop myself from crying. There was no one to hear me. I couldn't allow myself to believe he would hurt me but panic welled again. I screwed my eyes tightly closed but when I opened them there was the same suffocating blackness and I worried I would run out of air in this tiny, confined space. I told myself not to scream, to preserve oxygen, but anxiety built and built until it burst, and I was banging against the door with my fists, begging to be set free, until, exhausted, I sank to my knees. There was nothing to be heard but the sound of my own cries ringing in my ears. I wondered how long I would spend here. It already felt like an eternity, but I thought about what might come after, when he came back, and I couldn't help myself. I began to cry and I didn't think I would ever stop.*

The clatter of Lisa's footsteps brings me back to now, where there is no locked door, no darkness, but the fear, it still lingers. I don't think I'll ever properly shake it.

# CHAPTER THIRTEEN
## Then

I replayed the events of Perry's party the night before on a loop until the memory became more colourful and vibrant than the present moment. The feel of Jake's hands entwined in my hair, the brush of his lips on mine, sweet apple cider on his tongue.

'Kat!' The irritation in Mum's voice snapped me back into kitchen where she was rolling stuffing into balls, roast pork spitting and crackling in the oven.

'Sorry. What did you?...'

'Set the table.'

I cleared away my revision books and laid out the cutlery. Not the weekday slightly tarnished knives and forks but the shiny silver wedding present set housed in a wooden case. Dad was so traditional. I couldn't remember a time we didn't have a roast lunch on a Sunday, even during the summer months when our terraced house became a furnace, the sun glaring furiously through the back windows.

The conversation at dinner was strained.

'What are your plans for this afternoon?' Mum asked Dad in a tone that indicated she knew exactly what he should be doing. It was the same every week. Dad would say he was reading the papers and Mum would remind him the fence remained half-painted, the loose stair carpet needed nailing down, the shelf in the lounge was still wonky.

'I'll get round to everything just as soon as I can,' Dad said, although we all knew he wouldn't. Sometimes I wondered whether he ignored Mum's lists as a matter of pride. A sense of needing to be the one who decided if and when things got done. Being in control, I suppose, in a way he hadn't been over his career. The way he tried to be over mine.

'Daphne's son—'

'Is a handyman. Yes, I know. Any more gravy?' Dad looked pointedly at the empty jug. For a split second, something flared behind Mum's eyes and I thought she might tell him to make it himself; I urged her on inside my head, but she scraped back her chair and flicked on the kettle. The sound of water boiling seemed deafening in the resentment-heavy silence. I tried to imagine my parents young and in love. It was impossible. They didn't even seem to like each other. Twenty years was a long time to be married but, still, I couldn't picture them ever feeling the way me and Jake had felt last night. I slipped back into my memories, wanting to be anywhere but here.

Later, wishing again I had a mobile phone, I sat by the landline like a lovesick teenager, and I suppose that's what I was. Jake didn't ring, although he never said he would. Lisa didn't either. It was unusual for us to go a day without talking, but each time I picked up the receiver, I'd remember her face as I kissed Jake, the shock and disbelief, and I couldn't bring myself to call. I told myself we spent so much time together it was always going to be awkward when one of us got a boyfriend, and her reaction wasn't specifically because it was Jake, but I wasn't sure and I hated to think I'd hurt her in any way. Still, I knew as I got ready for bed that tomorrow, at school, I'd be seeing them both.

I waited for Lisa on the corner of the main road, as usual, leaning against the postbox. It had gone quarter to nine by the time I realised she wasn't coming. The stop-start of the rush-hour traffic spitting fumes into my lungs, the incessant thrum of engines, sparked a throbbing behind my eyes, a queasiness in my belly. The bell had already rung by the time I fell through the classroom door, breathless and hot, inhaling the smell of sweaty feet and whiteboard markers. English was the only subject we had in common but, rather than sitting at the desk we always shared by the window, Lisa was sitting at the back, next to Jake, their heads close together. My jealousy was immediate and sharp, a stinging slap of envy. Jake raised his hand as he noticed me but Lisa's smile was tight, and it took every ounce of willpower to keep my eyes fixed on the board and not keep turning to look at them as the double lesson stretched on and on.

Finally, it was break, and I was swept out of the door where I hovered in the corridor, again the sick feeling in my stomach. Had Jake changed his mind about us?

He came out first and looped his arm over my shoulders and, just like that, we were a couple.

'Can you give me and Lisa a second?' I asked.

She was walking as slowly as she could towards the door, eyes fixed on the floor.

'Sure.' Jake briefly pressed his lips against mine. 'See you at lunch.'

'Lisa.' I caught her arm as she tried to walk past me.

'Kat, I didn't—'

'Don't pretend you didn't see me. What's going on? I waited for you for ages this morning.'

'Sorry. I—'

The bell rang shrill and loud.

'Everything's fine, Kat.' Lisa shook her arm free. 'I'll see you later.'

I watched her grow smaller and smaller as she hurried down the corridor. The distance between us felt vast.

\*

At lunchtime, I meandered towards Jake and Lisa across the overgrown grass that was yellowing with thirst and popping with buttercups and daisies. In the warmer weather, the sixth formers were allowed to eat their lunch on the sports field. I could feel the glare coming from the lower years, confined to the concrete playground, jostling for benches, knowing the hot tarmac would burn bare legs if they sat on the floor. I remembered feeling the same envy when I was younger.

'Hey.' I flopped next to Jake. Lisa averted her eyes as he kissed me hello. The gold cross glinted around his neck, and I wondered if the metal was hot against his skin.

'So you two are a thing?' Aaron chucked his bag on the grass next to us.

'They are,' Lisa said, her voice flat.

I unpacked my lunch. My sandwich was warm and unappealing, the bread soggy with sliced tomatoes, lettuce browning. Although I didn't have much of an appetite, anxiety over Lisa rolling around my stomach, I pulled open a packet of Walkers Smokey Bacon instead.

'Want one?' I offered the pack to Lisa. A peace offering, of sorts. She shook her head. She didn't have any food in front of her. Instead of eating she was plucking flowers from the grass and dropping them into her lap.

'Where's your lunch?' I asked.

'I'm on a diet,' she snapped.

'But still, you have to eat.'

'My sister has just lost loads of weight,' Aaron said. 'She ate proper food too. I could help you if you wanted?'

'I can't be arsed counting calories. I'd rather do something quick, like SlimFast.' Lisa stood and the tumble of buttercups on her skirt scattered over the grass. 'I'm going to the loo.'

'What's up with her?' Jake asked, shielding his eyes from the sun as we watched her stalk towards the school.

Without answering, I grabbed my bag and followed her.

The toilets were stifling. We stood in front of the cracked basins. The smell of bleach and stale cigarettes thick in the air.

'Are you pissed off about me and Jake?' I spoke to her reflection in the mirror as she dragged her brush through her hair. It seemed easier somehow than facing her directly.

'No. You're both free agents. You can do what you want.' She winced as the bristles of the brush caught in a tangle.

'So why didn't you meet me this morning? Sit with me in English?' I removed the brush from her hand and started to work the tangle free with my fingers. 'What was that about on the field?'

'Dunno.' I heard the catch in her voice. Could almost feel the tears burning hot at the back of her throat, transporting me back to a time she'd fallen over in the playground, chasing Reece Walker after he'd stolen my Kit Kat out of my hands. Her knee was bloodied, bits of gravel embedded in the skin but, although her bottom lip jutted out, still she didn't cry. She always found it difficult opening up, being honest about her feelings.

'Nothing will change, Lis.' I rested my chin on her shoulder, our eyes meeting in the mirror.

'It's not going to be a casual thing, is it?' Her voice was small. 'I could see that from the way you looked at each other.'

'I really like him, but if it's going to upset you…' I didn't finish my sentence. I didn't know how to. Really, I didn't want to choose. What would I do? It would have to be her, wouldn't it?

'Everything's changing.' She didn't elaborate but I knew what she meant. Soon we'd be leaving school. I'd be leaving town. She'd be staying. Lisa didn't want to go to uni; she didn't know what she wanted. Often, she was like that, ignoring decisions, unable to weigh up options, as if she hoped the future would never come. Me, my path had been mapped out for years.

'Nothing stays the same,' I said gently.

'I know. It's fine.' She sniffed. 'I'm just being silly.'

'I'll still spend lots of time with you. We won't leave you out.' I meant every word. 'You'll find someone too.'

'Who'd want me? Lardy Lisa.'

'No one calls you that!' I checked my watch as the bell rang. 'I've got to go. History.' I rolled my eyes.

'I'll miss you, Kat,' she blurted out as I tugged open the graffiti-covered door.

'I'll see you after school?'

'I meant when you're at uni.'

'I'll be back every holiday. It won't be that different.'

I didn't know then, of course, we weren't just approaching the end of school. In a way, it was the end of everything. None of us would ever be the same again.

# CHAPTER FOURTEEN
## Now

'Are you okay, Kat?'

Lisa touches my arm, and I start. I hadn't heard her come back up the stairs from the basement.

'It's really cool down there. I'd love a man cave!'

'Let's go and sit in my equivalent.'

I lead Lisa through the dining room and open the door to the conservatory. The difference in air temperature is startling. Bending, I flick on the fan heater, and it whirrs into life; the smell of hot dust is unpleasant.

'I thought I'd spend all my time out here when we moved in, but in the summer it was roasting and now it's freezing.'

'It's such a pretty view, though.' Lisa curls up in one of the two armchairs in front of the floor-to-ceiling glass that overlooks the winter-drab garden, covering her lap with the thick faux fur throw slung over the back of the chair. I sit in the other chair and do the same, drawing my feet under me and tucking my throw around my knees.

We sit in silence watching the birds swing on the feeder, pecking at the fat balls I'd made myself from pine cones, lard, and seed. Next door's cat slinks into the garden through a gap in the hedge and prowls over to the pond where he taps the thin layer of ice with his paw.

The fan heater clicks as it reaches temperature; the small space is soon heated, but it will quickly grow cold again. I sip my water. My head is throbbing.

'I'm sorry I drank so much last night.' I rub my temples.

'It was a great party.' Lisa turns to look at me. A wistful expression on her face. 'You have a good life, Kat. I chatted to Clare for ages. She seems lovely. I'm glad she's so close by.'

'It is convenient. She works part-time so I often pop over for coffee when I want a break. Her daughter, Ada, is gorgeous. It's such a shame her husband, Akhil, left.'

'He's Indian, isn't he, she said? I wonder why Ada's skin is so light?'

'I think it happens sometimes with mixed-race children. The genes of one parent are stronger than the other. It's so sad they split up. They don't seem to speak; she never mentions him to me, really. We're still forming our friendship, I suppose.'

'We were good friends, weren't we?' There's the smallest of nods as Lisa speaks as though trying to remind herself.

'We still are,' I say. 'Not many people would do what you're doing for me.'

A look of confusion flickers across her face for a second.

'The surrogacy,' I prompt.

'Of course. But that's not entirely for you. It's for me too.'

'How do you mean?'

'You remember when you used to stay behind after school to help the younger kids with maths club and I always thought it was because your dad made you?'

I nod. 'I enjoyed it. The feeling I might make a difference. Who knows what those kids have gone on to achieve.'

'Exactly. This is my difference.'

'A bit extreme though, isn't it? It's hardly the same thing.'

'But it is. I'm doing something for you but I also feel a sense of pride. Who knows who is in here.' Lisa places a hand over her belly. 'Or what they will be but I know I will have played a small part in that, and it feels good to do something selfless.'

'Do you think it's a boy or girl?' I ask the impossible question. 'We're calling him or her Beanie for now but I've been thinking of proper names.'

'Eva?'

I grin. I'd always said at school I'd name my daughter after my favourite actress. 'You've guessed it. I said Nick could pick a boy's name but he likes Basil.'

'Don't mention the war!' Lisa howls. Her mum had loved *Fawlty Towers,* and by the time we were 14 we could quote the scripts from memory.

'I know! Can you believe Nick's never seen it? His grandfather was called Basil, apparently. He used to love going to stay with him in Cornwall when he was young.'

'That's where Clare's from, right?'

'Yes. A different part, though. She wasn't near the sea like Basil.'

'Basil.' Lisa shakes her head. 'Perhaps I should have the final say on the name?' Lisa is still laughing, but I'm suddenly serious.

'Have you given much thought about how this will work?'

'How do you mean?' Lisa picks at a stray thread hanging from the throw and begins to twist it round and round her finger.

'With your appointments? I want to be as involved as I can. In six weeks you can have your first scan.'

'You've been reading up?'

'I've been driving Nick mad. Do you know, by the time you reach the end of the first trimester the baby will be the size of a peach?'

'You haven't changed much. Still studying.'

'I didn't have a lot of choice, did I?'

'You must go to university, Katherine. Don't disappoint us.' Lisa puts on a voice and looks down her nose like my dad used to. 'I'd forgotten how hard you'd had it too.'

'Do you ever see anyone? From school?' I didn't finish sixth form. I never went back after the accident.

'Not really.' Lisa shrugs.

'Not even Aaron?' Even saying his name makes me anxious.

'No.' Lisa shivers.

'Let's move somewhere warmer.' I lean over and a whoosh of warm air blasts my fingers as I switch off the fan heater.

As we pass through the hallway, Nick is at the front door saying goodbye to Richard. Their voices are low but urgent. 'You have to tell her,' Richard says.

'It's too late now,' Nick whispers, and I turn to Lisa and we share a look.

Richard catches sight of us. 'We'll talk properly later.' He turns and stalks down the driveway.

'Is everything okay?' I ask Nick.

'Fine,' he mumbles.

'What do you have to tell me? What's it too late for?'

'We'd planned to play golf but I slept in too late.' His eyes are fixed on a point behind my head. There's a stretched out beat while I'm aware of Lisa hovering awkwardly next to me.

'Don't you like Nick playing golf?' Lisa asks as we finally head upstairs but I don't answer. Reluctant to admit Nick rarely plays. I can't shake the image of the lipstick on his shirt.

At the top of the stairs I pause in front of the nursery.

'Ready?' I ask.

'For what?'

The door is stiff, it catches on the thick carpet, and as it slowly opens, I watch Lisa's face but I can't tell what she's thinking. She steps into the room and spins 360° taking in the shelves crammed with soft toys, the bookshelf full of the old-fashioned Ladybird books. The castle and knights I'd bought for Dewei stand on the floor next to the doll's house I'd ordered for Mai. I can't face parting with either of them, and my mind races ahead wondering if after this Lisa would do it again. I might have a boy and a girl, kneeling together, playing with the wooden farmyard I couldn't resist buying, with its handcrafted animals brightly painted, the smiling pink pig and the almost glow-in-the-dark orange chickens. Lisa stands still as she reads the 'Together We Make a Family' picture, the words shaped like a house.

'You really want this, don't you?' Her voice is thick with emotion as she crosses to the window and gazes out at the garden. Nestled under the pergola is the rose bush we had planted for Dewei. In the spring, we will plant one for Mai too.

'Yes. Even more than the adoptions, if that's possible. This will be Nick's baby. Part of him,' I say. Outside the sky is clear and bright but snow still clings to the branches of the skeletal trees standing like soldiers in front of our fence. 'If I had one wish, this would be it.'

Lisa turns to me, and I see the anguish in her eyes and I know at once I've said the wrong thing and, worse than that, I'm not sure if it is true. If I had one wish it would be for the events of that day never to have happened, and although I haven't seen Lisa for such a long time, I think she would wish for the same thing too.

'I hate to ask, Kat but I don't suppose you can cover the taxi fare home?'

'Of course.' The horn beeps again outside and I hurry into the study, open the safe and pull out two hundred pounds. It's a bank holiday so it should cost the same as last night, I reason. 'Are you going to get your car looked at again?'

'Yes. I think it's the cold. I'll get it checked out,' Lisa says, holding out her hand. 'I don't suppose you've a bit extra, have you? I wouldn't ask but once the sickness wears off mid-morning I'm ravenous. My food bill has doubled, and December's payday seemed to disappear over Christmas. I can pay you back end of the month.'

'Don't be silly. If it wasn't for us you wouldn't be eating more and turning down overtime. You must say if you're short. It's important you keep up the relaxation classes.' I push £20 notes into her hand.

At the taxi, we hug tightly.

'Thanks for coming,' I say. 'It means a lot. Everything means such a lot.'

'I know it does,' Lisa says. 'I know *exactly* how much this means to you.'

# CHAPTER FIFTEEN
## Now

January passes quickly. I check in with Lisa most days. You can't be too careful during the first trimester. I'm constantly on edge, worried something will go wrong, but the month passes, and I cross off each day on the calendar. Suddenly we are in February and I allow myself to relax a little as we inch past that magic twelve-week point. Now the baby's fingers can open and close, their toes can curl, and their mouth can make sucking movements. I read if Lisa prods her belly, the baby will squirm in response, although she can't feel it yet. It's all such a miracle.

Today is grey and dull. I feel I've made a million phone calls but nobody wants to discuss donating to charity at this time of year. There's an increase in the demand for counselling too, and I'm already shattered. I sing songs from *West Side Story* to keep myself alert as I sketch out my ideas for an Easter fundraiser. I can't decide on a theme and screw up yet another ball of paper, adding it to the others in a pile on the floor.

By late afternoon, the house smells of chilli; the light glows on the slow cooker on the worktop in the kitchen. I snuggle in the armchair by the kitchen window, engrossed in *Three Sisters, Three Queens*, by Philippa Gregory. It's sad when women don't trust each other.

It's hard to concentrate. I spoke to Lisa earlier and am so excited it will be her first scan next week. I was disappointed they didn't do it dead on twelve weeks, like I'd been expecting, but apparently, that's only a guideline. Anyway, babies are more developed at fourteen weeks. The size of an apple. Beanie's hearing abilities are growing so I'm going to speak to Lisa's bump at every opportunity so that when he or she is born there is a chance they might recognise my voice. I can't believe I'll get to see him or her, and I can't wait to tell Nick today I've learned Beanie has their own fingerprints and impulses from their brain enables them to make facial expressions. I wonder if I'll be able to see their face clearly on the scan? I do hope so.

Nick is late home and, as I look out of the window into the blackness, it doesn't seem possible it is only half past six. Rain lashes against the windowpane and thunder rumbles low and menacing. I've never liked storms. I pick at a grape from the fruit bowl next to me, biting it hard between my back teeth and letting the juice trickle down my throat. The rice is measured and in a pan; the water has boiled in the kettle. It will only take a few minutes to pull dinner together once Nick is here.

By seven thirty, Nick still hasn't arrived and I'm worried. The roads are treacherous. I try his mobile, but it goes straight to voicemail, and the office phone rings and rings. In my agitation, I tap my mobile against my leg. Nick definitely didn't say he was meeting Richard after work, as they sometimes do, but I call Richard anyway.

'Is Nick with you? He hasn't come home and I'm worried, it's so icy out there.'

'I haven't seen him today. Listen, Kat, we need to talk about this surrogate thing.'

'You mean my baby?' Instantly, I bristle. 'I can't talk now. I need to find Nick.'

Cutting the call, I close my eyes. It's not like Nick to switch his phone off. Even when he drives, he has it on the dashboard in a cradle and whenever it makes a sound he peers at the screen, taking his eyes off the road. I always scold him. 'It was just for a second,' he will say but I know a second is sometimes all it takes to change your life. Cars are dangerous, dangerous things. Panic ricochets around my mind and I try to tell myself I'm overreacting, but it's impossible to keep calm as I pace the kitchen, googling the numbers of local hospitals. I can't decide what to do. Nick's been so preoccupied these past few weeks, the last thing I want to do is cause a fuss about nothing.

I pick up my book thinking I'll try to settle by the window in the lounge instead. That way I'll see his car when he crunches into the driveway, and I can dash back to the kitchen, cook the rice and he'll never know how much I've worried. I don't immediately switch on the light in the lounge. I stare out the window. The blackness has turned the glass to a mirror and, at first, all I can see is my worried face reflected back at me, but my eyes gradually adjust until I can make out a shape at the end of the driveway. A car. Nick's car. My spirits lift as I wait for the click of the door, the interior light to glow, but there's no movement. The clock ticks. Minutes pass. I don't know how long he has been there but he must be waiting for the pelting rain to slow, I reason; my breath is coming faster, fogging up the glass. There's something about heavy rain that feels almost ominous. The atmosphere seems to thicken. I wish the thunder would come and lighten the air. The rain batters the window and through the cascading water I notice the light from Clare's hallway spilling out into the blackness as it switches on. Unable to wait any longer I hurry to the hallway and jab my feet into shoes, plucking the large umbrella from behind the coat stand. Opening the front door, I step outside. The wind whisks the umbrella inside out. Grappling to hang onto the handle I almost don't see the shadow moving across the street, stalking towards my house, and when I notice it's Nick I step back inside.

*

'I was waiting for you to get out of your car?' I turn my face away as he wipes his shoes on the doormat, shaking his head like a dog, droplets of freezing rain splashing my skin. 'Did you come from Clare's?'

'Yes. I saw her pull into her driveway. I went to tell her that her left brake light is out.'

'You're so good. And now you're soaked. Do you want to nip and get changed? Dinner's ready when you are.'

'Lovely. It smells great.' Nick is distracted as he shrugs off his jacket.

From the kitchen, my mobile starts to trill Justin Timberlake's 'Like I Love You', the tone I set specifically for Lisa as she used to love the song so much.

I hurry to answer the call before my voicemail kicks in.

'Hi, Lisa!' At first, I can't make out whether Lisa has pocket dialled me by mistake, all I can hear is background noise, but then I realise it is her sobbing. 'Lisa?' My stomach flips.

'Kat.' Lisa gulps air and her sobs turn to hiccups. It seems an age before she can speak. 'I slipped on the ice and… Kat… I'm bleeding. I think I'm losing the baby.'

And just like that my world shatters again.

# CHAPTER SIXTEEN
## Then

'You look so tired,' Mum said as she cleared away the breakfast things. It was always boiled eggs on a Saturday and, childishly, I still had the urge to turn the shell upside down in my eggcup and draw on a happy face.

I stifled a yawn. I was exhausted. The last month had been a frantic round of revision, play rehearsals and juggling Lisa and Jake, all without Dad finding out I had my first boyfriend. It wasn't purely Dad not giving me permission to date while I was still at school that had kept me single up until now. I had never had a boyfriend before because I had never wanted one. I'd never felt that pull other girls seemed to feel. That 'I fancy him,' or 'Isn't he hot?' For a brief time, I had wondered if I was a lesbian, but I'd never felt attracted to girls either. Was there something wrong with me? I would sit cross-legged on Lisa's bed, posters of Justin Timberlake covering her pale pink walls, and I'd imagined him kissing me, touching me, but I didn't feel anything other than slightly repulsed. Now it was different: every time Jake kissed me, touched me, I understood why love sometimes drove people to do terrible, terrible things. The rush of adrenaline, the out of control sensation. Jake was a craving; as vital to me as air and food.

'Take some time out today. It will do you good.' Mum clattered plates into the sink.

'It's nearly—' Dad jumped in.

'Exams. Yes. So it's almost study leave, and how much good is it doing Kat poring over and over the same pages? It's Saturday.'

'But her offer—'

'Is conditional,' Mum finished. 'We know but she's doing well. Let her have a break.' There was something firm and final in Mum's tone. It didn't happen often, this shift in power, but every now and then something would flash behind her eyes and she turned into a different person almost. Someone strong and assertive and not like Mum at all and, in those moments, Dad was different too. Smaller. Unsure. Not quite knowing how to cope when his authority was challenged. Panicking almost.

He cleared his throat. 'Get some fresh air but be back by dinner time, Katherine,' he said gruffly, as though it was his idea all along. He picked up his empty mug, and for once, he was the one to switch the kettle on.


Jake and I climbed into the back of Aaron's dad's van and, as Aaron slammed the door shut, it almost felt like the end of something. Instantly, it was hot and airless, a suffocating blackness. The stench of paint and turps was sharp. I held on to the carrier bags containing our picnic food with one hand; my other hand fumbled for Jake. From the front, Lisa's voice drifted until the ignition sparked and I was buffeted left to right as the van pulled away. The vibrations from the engine clattered my teeth. Although we weren't going far it seemed an age before the roar of passing traffic fell away and we were bumping along a country track. I was relieved we were nearly there. Although I'd never had a problem with confined spaces before my throat was stinging from inhaling chemicals; a headache burned behind my eyes.

The second the van was still and silent I leapt for the handle, rattling it furiously. Outside, I could hear the muted tones of Aaron and Lisa.

'Let us out.' I hammered on the door with both fists, a feeling of panic building when I realised it didn't open from the inside.

On the other side of the door I could hear Aaron laughing.

'What's the magic word?'

'Don't be a tosser,' shouted Jake, and there was a silence and a horrible, overwhelming feeling rose that we'd be stuck here forever.

'Lisa,' I shouted, and at last there was a click, a startling brightness, and I almost fell out of the open door as I gulped in fresh air. An impromptu picnic had seemed like fun, but the smell of paint coated my lungs, dissipating my earlier good mood. Aaron grinned at me, and I felt a pricking sensation at the back of my eyes and I willed myself not to cry. It was discomfiting that Lisa didn't seem to notice how upset I was: we'd always been so in tune with each other before, but more and more, I had been spending time with Jake, her with Aaron, and it occurred to me for the first time that, one day, we would no longer be the most important people in each other's lives. Perhaps that distance had already started growing. I glared at Aaron as though he was personally responsible for the hairline crack that had formed in our relationship.

We walked in a line, flattening undergrowth, ducking under branches. The woodland floor was dappled with shimmers of sunlight, a warm breeze rustling the leaves of the trees that bowed to greet us. I'd calmed down by the time we reached the clearing and was ready to make a concerted effort to get to know Aaron. He and Lisa weren't yet a couple but I had a feeling she wanted to be. She'd taken extra care with her appearance that day – a short, floral dress – it seemed like ages since I'd seen her socially – out of her school uniform.

'You've lost loads of weight, Lisa. You look great.'

'Thanks. Aaron's been helping.'

I raised my eyebrows before I remembered him saying something about his sister being on a diet. Lisa must have caught my expression because she said: 'he's been really supportive', in a tone suggesting I hadn't.

I ripped the cellophane off a packet of cheese straws and bit into one, shaking the flaky pastry off my skirt as I offered one to Aaron.

'These are good,' he said as he chewed.

'I get them from work,' Jake said. He put in early shifts at a bakery, packaging food for retailers.

'Do you have a job, Aaron?'

'Nah.'

'How are you going to afford uni?' I asked.

'I'll get by. How about you?'

'My dad's a financial advisor. Ever since I can remember he's been telling me there's a policy in place to fund my further education.'

'Let's not talk about uni.' Lisa feigned a yawn. 'Exciting news my end. I've won two tickets to a gig through Facebook.'

'That's fab.' We haven't had a night out since Perry's party. Already, I was excited.

'Do you want to come with me, Aaron?' As Lisa spoke, she glanced sideward at me, as though expecting me to be jealous, wanting it, almost.

I swigged from my can of Diet Coke, washing down my disappointment.

'If you can't get a real date—' Aaron said.

'Be nice,' Jake snapped.

'He was only joking.' Lisa rolled her eyes but looked secretly pleased.

I wondered whether Jake had always stuck up for her, and I wondered why it bothered me now. It was irrational to feel jealous when it was my hand Jake was holding, but I did.

Inexplicably I felt suddenly uncertain of my place in Jake's life, or Lisa's, as we danced around each other, trying to settle into our new relationships, balancing the old. The shifting dynamics as we pushed and we pulled was draining. I needed some space.

'I'm going for a walk,' I said.

'I don't fancy one.' Lisa barely looked up. I hadn't been asking her, I hadn't been asking anyone, but Jake stood too, and as we disappeared into the trees I could feel eyes burning into my back.

I'd always thought it was quiet here, peaceful, but as we strolled through the woods, my senses on high alert, everything seemed too loud; the birds chirping; the breeze rustling the leaves; my heart thumping. We were rarely properly alone.

'Want a rest?' Jake asked, and I fought to control my breath that came a little too quickly, breathing in slowly and deeply, the scent of pine, musky aftershave and anticipation.

'There's nowhere to sit.' I looked around the clearing. The ground was scattered with rabbit droppings.

'Then we'll stand.' Jake turned to face me, stepping forwards. His eyes locked onto mine, and I stepped backwards until my spine was pressed against a tree trunk. I swallowed hard.

'Kat.' He dipped his head and trailed warm kisses down my neck. 'What have you done to me?' he murmured, and I wanted to ask the same. Jake slipped his hand under my skirt and I felt the warmth in his fingers. I gasped and thrust my hips forward, urging him on.

'We don't have to do this,' he whispered in the way he always did but, this time, instead of asking him to stop I parted my legs.

'Are you sure, Kat?' His eyes were glazed, cheeks flushed, and I knew in that moment he wanted me as badly as I wanted him.

My body was tingling in a way it never had before, but there was a flicker of indecision as I realised what I was about to do. Should I? Although I knew I wanted Jake to be my first, I didn't know whether I wanted to do it here, where it was so open. Where we were so visible. His fingers brushed my inner thigh, and my doubts plummeted to the ground, where they tumbled with the dried and crispy leaves until they were out of sight, and I was out of my mind.

'I want to.'

I tugged his zip down but I was too scared to reach inside his jeans, unsure what I was supposed to do. I tried to pull back, but he took both my wrists in one of his hands, holding them high above my head, the rough bark grazing the skin on my forearms. His other hand ran over my body, pulling at my knickers, pushing into me until there was a sharp pain. I bit hard on his shoulder and he hesitated. 'Please,' I whispered, wrapping my legs around his waist, knowing however much this hurt there was nothing more I wanted.

Afterwards, we clung to each other, the weight of Jake slumped against me. Our breath hot and heavy. It was the sound of a snapping twig, as sharp as a gunshot, that jolted me back to awareness. Goosebumps chasing away the heat in my skin. I pushed Jake aside and tugged up my knickers, rearranged my skirt.

'What was that?' My eyes flitted around the trees, branches swayed, shadows shimmered. It came again. A snapping sound. The sensation of the whole world staring at me. Shame flooded the places lust had just vacated. 'Did somebody see us?' Panic wormed under my skin. If my Dad ever heard about this…

'Nobody saw us. Nobody's here.' Jake nuzzled my neck but he couldn't help jumping at the sudden noise that sliced through the silence. 'Christ.' He shielded his eyes, looking up into the blue cloudless sky as the birds rose above the treetops, cawing loudly, as though chastising us. As though someone had startled them. Despite Jake claiming there was no one there I felt uneasy, and as Jake said, 'Let's get out of here', I knew he felt it too. It was as though the moment, which had been so perfect, so private, was sullied somehow.

# CHAPTER SEVENTEEN
## Now

Exhaustion has blunted my emotions and I no longer have to fight to contain the tears that threatened to spill. I haven't cried. Not once. For if I cry, I'm giving up hope, and I am not doing that. Not yet. Once our call had been cut off, I had phoned Lisa over and over. Each time her answer service cut in and the words inviting me to speak after the tone sliced through me. I'd left an array of messages ranging from: 'Lisa, we're so worried about you, please call us back', to: 'Where the fuck are you?', and the last one was: 'Lisa, please tell me my baby is all right.' I repeated 'please, please, please', over and over until Nick gently unclasped my fingers, and put my phone on the coffee table. He pulled me into his arms but I couldn't allow myself to fall against him. I couldn't allow myself to fall apart.

'There's probably a problem with the mobile signals because of the storm but I think we have to prepare ourselves for the worst, Kat.' Nick had said, and I was screaming 'no, no, no,' over and over, though the room was silent, the words in my head. I clasped my hands over my ears as though I could somehow make the sound go away.

I had paced the room, a rat in a cage, trying to decide what to do. My mobile signal had vanished: Nick was right about the masts. I fetched the landline from the hallway, to ring the hospital.

The receptionist said: 'Hello, Farncaster General,' and just hearing the name of the town where I grew up made anxiety rocket through my veins, but Lisa hadn't been admitted.

'I can't believe this has happened to me.' I dropped my head in my hands.

'To us,' Nick said gently, rubbing my back as though I had been sick, and I had thought I might be.

'Sorry. This must be horrible for you too.'

'It is. You're not alone, Kat. I do understand.' Nick rested his chin on my head as I leaned back against him. 'I know what it's like to feel loss.'

We sat on the sofa, TV flickering in the corner, sound muted, flashes of lightning illuminating the room. Not knowing what else to say.

Nick refused to go to bed until I did and now, at 2 a.m., we slide under cold silk sheets but, instead of spooning Nick, linking my legs through his, warming my feet on his skin, as I usually would, I lie staring at the ceiling, waiting for Nick's light breathing to rasp light snores. He is finally asleep. I ease myself out of bed, conscious of the shift of the mattress, and slip my feet into the fleecy slippers with penguin faces on Clare had bought me for Christmas. Silently, I pad downstairs for a bottle of wine, which I carry, with a glass, into the nursery. The orange glow of the night light I always leave plugged in should make it warm and inviting, but it feels as cold and as empty as I do inside.

Twisting the clunky dial of the mobile, it jerks into life. 'Twinkle, twinkle little star.' But outside the window the sky is as black as my heart.

Another baby. How can I have lost another baby? This one didn't even have a name, but that doesn't make it any less real. Any less loved. I sink into the rocking chair and flex my toes against the carpet, rocking back and forth, back and forth. How much loss can one person take? Self-pity tightens its fingers around me and threads its way through my thoughts.

I'm not religious but, at times like these, I wonder whether God is real. Whether he is punishing me for the person I was, not seeing the person I am now. I wonder whether I deserve this but not once do I ever think about giving up. I hold the rabbit in my lap. Run my fingers across his ears, listening to the crinkle, and I know.

I don't quite know how but I know that I'm going to get a baby, even if it kills me.

I must have fallen asleep. The rising sun slicing through the window, casting stripes on the carpet through the bars of the cot, nudges me awake. I'm still rocking back and forth, and my calf muscles are aching but at least physically I am feeling something different from the numbness inside. Outside the storm is dying down, the rain a gentle patter against the window, the wind calmer now. The creak of our fence has subsided to a whisper as it gently sways. Reaching into the pocket of my dressing gown I pull out my phone. No missed calls. No messages. My thumb hovers over the 'contact' icon. Before I can dial Lisa, I wonder whether I should go and see her face-to-face. The thought fills me with dread. I have to decide whether my reluctance to go back to that place is greater than my desire to see her.

It isn't.

Although I had sworn never to go there again, I'm going to Farncaster. As I stand, my legs are jelly and I tell myself it's just because I've been in one position all night, but I know it's more than that. I'm scared.

Sleet gusts through the crack in the car window, dampening my fringe, but I daren't shut it: I'm relying on the freezing fume-filled air to keep me awake. I am anxious-hot anyway. Wet conditions are the worst conditions of all for driving. As I sit in traffic, engine thrumming, windscreen wipers swishing, a car crawls past, indicator flashing right, there is a heaviness in my chest as I notice the sunshine yellow 'Baby on Board' sign proudly displayed in the rear window.

My mobile buzzes and I glance at the screen, hoping it's Lisa, but it's Nick. He must have woken and read my scribbled note on his bedside cabinet telling him I'll be back in a couple of days. I only hope that's true.


It seems a long drive, although it's only an hour. I have stopped once for coffee, sipping the scalding liquid, welcoming the caffeine hit before I carry on. The slip road ahead tells me Farncaster is only ten miles away. I indicate left and as I twist the steering wheel my empty Starbucks cup rolls about in the passenger footwell. Ten years. It's been nearly ten years since I was last here, and my jaw locks as memories flit through my mind like stills from a film: the darkness, the sense of being trapped, the screaming, the pain. The terror I once felt floods back, pressing down on me, snatching my breath, and once more I have the feeling of being suffocated. The 'Farncaster' sign looms towards me, acting as a force field almost; my foot squeezes the brake and I screech to a halt. Somewhere to my right a horn blasts but everything is swimming in and out of focus, except my memories, which are clear and sharp. But it isn't the person I was then that is feeling so terrified, it's the person I am now.

'I know what it's like to feel loss,' Nick had said. If I cross into Farncaster, the place where I so very nearly died, the place I promised never to return to, is he going to lose me too? My fingers scratch against my throat as though trying to dislodge the hands that I can still sometimes feel there.

# CHAPTER EIGHTEEN
## Then

Nick kicked the scrunched up Coke can to Richard. It clattered as it skittered across the pavement. Richard deftly toed it back but Nick was hunched forward, hands pressed against a stitch in his side, gasping.

'They think it's all over, it is now!' Richard covered his head with his T-shirt and ran up the road, arms stretched high, chanting 'champion, champion', only stopping when he collided with the postbox. Nick couldn't help laughing as Richard crumpled to the ground.

'Serves you right.' Nick stood over his friend, offered his hand and pulled him to his feet. 'I don't know how you can run after that huge dinner. Your mum is an amazing cook.'

'Yours can't be that bad?'

'She is,' Nick said; as he spoke the lie, guilt seemed to increase the pain in his side. But it seemed easier to let Richard believe he never asked him to tea as his mum was a rubbish cook; rather that than telling him they couldn't afford the extra ingredients for guests. Besides which, there was no way he'd invite his friend into a lounge that reeked of stale lager and rotting dreams. He blanched at the image of Richard perched on the edge of the threadbare armchair, avoiding the spring poking through the seat.

Nick checked his watch, holding his wrist close to his eyes so he could see past the crack in the screen. 'I'd better go. See you at school tomorrow.'

'Not if I see you first, loser.' Richard slapped him on the back and jogged past him. If anyone else had called Nick a loser he'd have been upset, but not Richard. On the first day of school, Sammy Whilton had laughed at Nick's sandwiches wrapped in a plastic Tesco bag. Everyone else had swanky lunch boxes. Richard had stuck up for him, and at playtime he had sat on a bench in the playground, watching, as Nick raced around with a football, never once losing control. The next day, Richard had brought in a Power Rangers lunch box – 'it's old' he had shrugged – but it looked new. In return Richard asked Nick to teach him to play football; his family weren't big on sport. Nick had spent many hours in his small backyard, avoiding his dad, learning to dribble, shoot, head the ball. As he passed on what he had learned, he knew he and Richard would be friends for life.

Now, they were twelve and had just started secondary and were still as close as ever.

Nick jabbed his key into the lock and pushed open the front door. On the mat were his mum's shoes – as frayed and tired looking as she was.

'Mum?' She should be at work.

'In here, love.' There was a forced brightness in her tone, and the first thought that sprang into Nick's head was 'what has Dad done now?' Stepping into the lounge he saw his parents sitting together, and his hands furled into fists behind his back but then he noticed something he hadn't seen for years and he wasn't sure if he felt relieved or repulsed.

His mum and dad were holding hands. And this was more frightening than the usual shouting. Nick began to shake. He knew whatever his mum was about to tell him it would be bad. Very bad.


'Do you think Mum will be okay?' Nick and his father stood side by side scraping potatoes with blunt knives. Neither of them could work the peeler; Nick's knuckles were bleeding from trying. He couldn't remember the last time he had wanted reassurance from his dad and, for a moment, it had drawn them close together. Fear slithered into the darkest corners of his mind. Cancer. How can such a small word be the disease that was destroying his mum from the inside out?

''Course.' Dad tugged a box of fish fingers from the back of the freezer. 'Fuck's sake,' he shouted as they tumbled to the floor, packet splitting, golden breadcrumbs and clumps of ice slithering under the cooker. 'Loads of people survive breast cancer nowadays,' he said as he dropped to his knees and began cleaning up the mess. As he stood at the sink, rinsing the fish fingers he had picked off the floor under the tap, his shoulders shook. He looked as small and scared as Nick felt.

Later, they had cramped around the small kitchen table eating lumpy mash and charred fish fingers. A cool breeze filtered through the kitchen window, which was cracked open to release the smell of burned oil. The three of them had made stilted conversation the way people do when they are not used to each other's company. Dad didn't have a lager. His hand shook as he picked up his glass of water. Nick couldn't stop watching him, watching Mum. Dad loved her. He never would have thought.

After they had pushed food around their plates for ten uncomfortable minutes, Nick offered to wash up. He stuck his head around the lounge door when he had finished. Elvis crooned from the record player that was once his grandmother's. He didn't know how to feel as he watched his mum and dad in an awkward dance. Feet shuffling over the threadbare carpet that once was red but now sun-faded pink. Dad's arm was around Mum's waist, and she rested her hand on his shoulder. The naked bulb hanging from the ceiling picked out the diamonds in the emerald ring Mum always wore. After the song had finished there was the crackle and hiss as the needle circled empty grooves. Nick's parents didn't move.

Arms wrapped around each other. Once more the atmosphere was thick, not with bitterness this time, but with love.

They felt something akin to a family. Nick hoped it wasn't too late.

# CHAPTER NINETEEN
## Now

Farncaster is dingier than I remember. Without consciously thinking, I find myself indicating and turning into the estate I once called home. I crawl along, drinking everything in: the bright red postbox where I had posted applications to universities I didn't want to go to; Mrs Phillips's bungalow – she had always given me an apple as I walked past on my way to school; the cherry tree that coated the pavements with a pale pink blossom, obscuring my chalked out hopscotch. The house I grew up in appears to have shrunk. The engine hums while I study the front door, green paint peeling, the rotting wooden window frames, thick net curtains. Such a contrast to the rest of the road. What would happen if I knocked on the door? Who would answer? My gaze is drawn to the upper left window. I can almost picture my tiny childhood bedroom. The desk in the corner that wobbled if you leaned on the left-hand side; the bookshelf crammed with encyclopaedias; my long white nightgown, like something out of the Victorian era, smelling of Persil washing powder, neatly folded on my pillow. A movement catches my eye. The net curtain in the lounge billows as though it has been moved. I can make out a shadow. My pulse skyrockets. I can't tear my eyes away from the window as I release the handbrake and pull out without looking. A horn blares for the second time today, and I am shaking as I mouth my apology to the other driver. Squeezing the accelerator, I leave, looking in my rear-view mirror one last time. The shadow is still there.

I have been seen.


Lisa's old house looks exactly as I remembered. There is still a caravan in the driveway but it is yellow with age, the roof and windows covered with a thick green moss. Memories crowd from holidays with Lisa's family: stamping bingo cards with red markers; arms raised in the air as we rode a roller coaster; lips that stung with vinegar and sea-salt-air, and later, from being kissed. I think Nancy must still live here and, if she does, she must know where Lisa is, but although I cut the engine and grip the door handle tightly, I can't bring myself to leave the car.

*Coward.*

Even as I remind myself of what is at stake I find myself twisting the key and pulling away. I'll start with the hospital where Lisa works, but first, I want to freshen up, to buy some mints and water. I feel a state and wish I'd taken the time to shower and clean my teeth before I left, but I'd been hesitant of waking Nick.

Afraid he'd try to stop me.

*Afraid he'd want to come with me.*


There are plenty of spaces in the car park behind the old cinema, which was replaced with a multiplex on an industrial estate while I still lived here. It's sad to see the architecture crumble into ruin. I slot in between two smaller cars and squeeze my body out. I can never open the doors wide enough. I look longingly at the parent and child spaces. The High Street is half-empty but crammed full of nostalgia: HMV is now a Poundland; The Three Fishes is boarded up. It's all so different and yet feels exactly the same; it's as though I never left. *Step on a crack break your mother's back* – my adult veneer is slipping away and I feel horribly exposed. In the doorway of the newsagents is a man. Despite his beard, the hair that hangs in his eyes, I recognise him for the boy he was. Aaron. It is almost as if the ground shakes beneath my feet. I can't look up. Can't make eye contact. My skin crawls. I don't think he's seen me as he pulls out a mobile from his pocket, shoulders hunched, anger radiating from him.

I dart down an alleyway, passing a small café called The Coffee House, and I think caffeine is just what I need. To sit. Think. My legs feel shaky after seeing Aaron. The table is rickety, covered with a red-and-white plastic tablecloth, a folded piece of cardboard stuffed under one leg. I sit with my back to the window and, ignoring the bacon that hisses and spits, I order a cappuccino. My mobile is full of missed calls and frantic texts from Nick, and I send a message telling him I am fine, not to worry, I will explain everything tomorrow.

Idly I play with the salt and pepper pots, twisting them round and round in my fingers. Engrossed in thought, I don't look up when the bell rings again, and it isn't until my table falls into shadow, my head rises. I see who is there and my heart sinks.

# CHAPTER TWENTY
## Now

'Nancy!' I almost don't recognise Lisa's mum. Her face sunken, grey skin stretched over her skeleton.

'I can't believe you're here.' Her words spill out with a gasp, and I don't know if she means because of what's taking place now, or what took place then. The last time I saw her we sat on her sofa, and I remember the feel of her hand in mine. 'What's happened?' she had asked. 'Between you and Lisa? It breaks my heart you've fallen out. Tell me everything.' She didn't know then what I had done. Neither of us knew what the fallout would be. She was so kind to me once. My eyes search hers but I can't tell what she is thinking.

She sinks onto a chair and when she speaks again she sounds exhausted, not angry. 'I couldn't believe it when I saw you in that magazine. Katherine White, bit of a change from Kat Freeman, isn't it? You've obviously done well for yourself.' There's an edge as she speaks and it sounds like an accusation, and I want to tell her that however far I move away I haven't been able to forget.

'You're married then.' She nods at my ring. 'Family?'

She can't know about the surrogacy, and I hesitate. 'Not yet. I thought I was going to be a mum but—'

She raises her hand to silence me, and I press my lips together, keeping the words I want to say inside.

We stare at each other wordlessly, uncomfortably, until my drink is slopped in front of me, coffee thick and dark, and she speaks again.

'Treasure what you have, Kat. When you've lost everything like me…' She shakes her head, and I want to tell her she hasn't lost everything. She has a daughter.

More than anything I want to reach out to her, but I don't; instead, I start to ask: 'Lisa?…', but Nancy says: 'I can't do this, Kat…', and heaves herself to her feet as though she is far older than she is. As she reaches the door she turns and after a beat says: 'Take care.'

And I so want to believe that she means it, that she wishes me well, but it sounds like a threat all the same.

Seeing her has stirred up so many emotions. How stupid to think I could just come here to find Lisa. I need to say sorry. I need to make amends. I need to start with Jake.


The car park at the bottom of the hill is full of potholes. Weeds push through ground that was once covered with gravel. It's been so long since I last saw Jake. There are so many things I want to say. Things I want him to know, but now I'm here I don't know if I'll be able to speak. The black wrought iron gate creaks as I push it open and coax my reluctant feet to step forward. I'm feeling edgy now I'm here. Uneasy. Constantly looking over my shoulder. There's a sense of being watched. Clouds scud across the darkened sky and there are shadows everywhere. I tell myself the only thing following me is my own guilt. Still, I speed up my pace, striding up the incline, my feet sinking into damp, overgrown grass. I don't care my suede boots will probably be ruined now. I don't care about anything except finding Jake. Telling him how sorry I am.

By the time I reach the path at the top I am breathless. I hunch forwards, my hands on my thighs, waiting for my heart rate to settle. But it's not just the exertion that's making my pulse race. It's unfathomable I haven't been here before. My eyes scan the crematorium. Emotion ping-pongs around my chest. The wind chimes dangling from the tree above the children's section sway in the breeze, tinkling a lullaby that can never soothe. The headstones surrounding me are moss coloured, names and dates faded. I head to the back where the memorials become glossier, crosses replaced by angels and elaborate designs. The flowers here are freshly laid, the plots neatly maintained. I tiptoe between the rows, watching where I tread.

Seeing Jake's name on a black marble rectangle is like a punch in the gut. I sink to my knees as my bones turn to dust. My lungs tighten painfully as I rock back and forth in silent anguish, my 'sorry' stuck in my throat. Now I'm here I can't believe it's so real, so raw. I knew he was dead, of course I did. After all, I was there, but I was still in hospital when he was buried and, missing the funeral, never coming back here, made it easier to pretend somehow, that he was still here. Still happy.

The wind whips up and from behind me I hear the chimes in the tree, but other than that, there is silence – it's not a comfortable silence, the air feels thick. Threatening, almost. My fingers are numb with cold and I stuff my palms under my armpits to warm. Now I'm here I'm not sure what to do. I wish I'd stopped and bought flowers to lay, something bright and colourful, because no matter where he went, Jake was always the most vibrant one in the room. I look around at the other plots, the drying wreaths, the silk bouquets; there's even a helium balloon floating high with 'Happy 40th Dad' on it. The thought of a family crowding around a plaque, blowing candles, cutting cake, is devastating.

There's a movement to my right, and I twist my head. At first, I can't see what's caught my eye. I squint into the gloom looking for a rabbit. A twig snaps. The bushes rustle. I crane my neck. *What's there?* Shuffling, leaves move and there's a flash of pink, a shape – a hand? *Who's there?*

'Hello?' I call. The wind howls. The bush shakes. I can't see anything but dark green leaves and shadow, but there's a sense of eyes on me. Unease crawls under my skin.

'Hello?' I ease one foot forward, ready to run. There's a crash behind me, and I flinch, looking over my shoulder but there's nothing to see except the swinging gate.

I turn my attention back to the bush. There are shades of light now where dark patches were, and I think whoever was watching me has gone. I know there was somebody there. Unnerved, I reach out and trace Jake's name as though he can calm me. Simultaneously a twig snaps behind me, and I jerk my hand away, start to stand, but it's too late. A hand has already clasped my shoulder, forcing me back on my knees, and it all comes flooding back.

*Fingers dug into my shoulder and a hand lay heavy on the small of my back forcing me forward. I tried to dig my heels in, stretching out my arms for something to grab hold of but my fingertips closed around air.*

*'Please.' My voice was high and shrill. My skin slick with sweat. 'Don't do this. You don't have to do this.'*

*There was a grunt behind me, the sound of heavy breathing, and I did everything I could to make it harder for him. I stiffened my body and struggled. There was a second when he released his grip, when I was free, and just as my mind was processing there were no longer hands on me, there was pressure on the top of my arms and I was shaken, hard. My brain rattled around my skull. I bit my tongue and swallowed down my fear and the metallic taste of blood.*

*My vision grew hazy, the ground beneath my feet felt soft, as my body grew limp. I had the sensation of falling before I was yanked back and thrust forward, landing heavily on my hands and knees. My head banged against something hard and solid and rockets of pain shot through my arms and into my neck.*

*Dazed I almost didn't hear the slam behind me. The click of a lock.*

*'No! Wait!' I leapt to my feet. Nausea rose as the world seemed to rock. I blindly reached out, trying to find the door. The blackness was all-consuming. Suffocating. My hands shook as I slapped my palms*

*over the walls, spinning around until at last I found it. I gripped the*
*door handle but my hand was clammy and it took me three attempts*
*to twist it, and when I did, it confirmed what I already knew.*
   *I was trapped.*


The memory has gone in a flash and again I'm kneeling on the
damp grass, fingers pressing hard into my skin.

# CHAPTER TWENTY-ONE
## Now

Inhaling sharply, I smell her perfume, fresh and floral. I know who is here. Lisa. She removes her hand from my shoulder and I glance over as she kneels besides me. Bruising stains the side of her face where she slipped on the ice, but I don't ask any questions. Instead, I stretch out my hand. She threads her fingers through mine, and I know he is here with us. In the breeze that ruffles my hair, in the rain that kisses my skin.

Jake.

His name is carved in large, swirling, impossible-to-ignore letters and that was him all over. Impossible to ignore. Pulling people to him with his charm and charisma. I loved him. I swallow down the lump that endlessly rises in my throat. I still love him. I don't need to see the pain that will be etched over Lisa's face right now to know she still loves him too.

'I'm so sorry, Kat.' Lisa squeezes my fingers, and I feel how much she is trembling. I think it is too much for both of us being here but I can't bring myself to leave.

'I've so much I wish I could tell him,' I say.

'I talk to him all the time,' Lisa says, and I think for the first time, how it must have been for her, the one who stayed. I feel terrible I never came back before now. For her. It's stupid I thought I could wipe it all from my mind as though it never happened.

'It was my fault,' I say. My voice is flat. There is no unspoken question mark.

'It was an accident,' says Lisa. 'If I thought for one second it was your fault… It wasn't. Really.'

'But if I hadn't—'

'Stop!' As Lisa shouts, the branches rustle and a bird squawks as it flaps its wings, soaring high into the sky. 'Does it have to be someone's fault?'

She screws her face as though it hurts to talk, and it probably does. The skin on her cheek puffy and swollen; her eye half-closed and black. I wonder if she's talking about Jake or about her miscarriage.

'Are you okay?' I ask. 'I didn't come here to do anything other than check on you.' I realise as I speak I am telling the truth. I know Lisa has lost the baby but I don't want to lose her, not again. 'Should you be out of bed?'

'As long as I take it easy the doctor says. No lifting or running marathons. I've stomach cramps still, and this.' She touches her cheek. 'But I'll live and you've got to start living too. Stop blaming yourself. Think about the future. Think about your baby.'

'What baby?' I say dully.

'This one.' Lisa takes my hand and places it on her stomach.

'But I thought?'

'I was bleeding. But the doctor did a scan and I'm still pregnant.'

'But how?'

'The doctor thinks it is—' She stops herself. 'It was twins. They do run in the family, remember?' And we both instinctively turn to look at the headstone of the boy we both loved unconditionally. Her as a brother, me as a lover. And as I kneel, the dampness soaking through my leggings, the cold wind numbing my cheeks, you wouldn't think it was possible to feel heartbroken and hopeful at the same time, but somehow I do.

*

It only takes a couple of minutes to drive to the pub. My clothes are still soaking. Lisa's must be too.

'Are you sure you don't want to go home and change?' Already I feel the need to look after her.

'No, it's okay. Let's go in and celebrate.' Her voice is as flat as I feel. Celebrating feels wrong.

'Are you okay?' I am worried. Her complexion, always pale, is as white as flour.

'Tired but the doctor says there's no reason the remaining twin should be at risk. It's just…' She bites her bottom lip and stares out through the windscreen, fogging again now I have cut the engine. 'Going to the crematorium…' She shrugs miserably.

'Do you go often?' It's supposed to be comforting, isn't it? Having a place to visit. But as I'd knelt there before Lisa arrived, shivering with cold and the sensation of being watched, I felt anything but comforted.

'Not enough. I went today because I knew you'd come looking for me, and how could you not visit Jake? Usually, I feel terrible. I avoid it because being there, visiting Jake, it brings it all back. I feel so bloody guilty.'

'What do you have to feel guilty for?' I am surprised. I thought I carried the guilt alone.

Lisa picks at a thread hanging off the bottom of her jumper and I know she is choosing her words carefully.

'That night—'

We both jump as there is a thud. Somebody bumps into the car as they hurtle past.

'What the?' I pull my sleeve over the heel of my hand and rub the misted window but whoever was there has long gone.

'Probably kids,' says Lisa. 'They play in this car park all the time. Let's go inside. I'm freezing.'

'What were you going to say. About feeling guilty?'

'It's all the "what if's", isn't it? Even…' She gazes out of the window, unable to meet my eye. 'If I hadn't been friends with you, my brother would never have met you. Would he still be here? But we'll never know, will we?' She opens her door and steps outside. I can still see her. I could stretch out my hand and touch her, but she feels so far away.

Inside the pub, I ease off my coat, throwing it over a stool near a crackling open fire.

'Hot chocolate with cream and marshmallows?'

'My go-to rainy day drink.' Lisa attempts a smile. 'You remembered.'

At the bar, the barista heats the milk in a machine that spits and gurgles. The sight of champagne chilling in the fridge saddens me. I'm still going to be a mum and I should be shouting it from the rooftops but the thought of the baby Lisa has lost is at the forefront of my mind. I can't help wondering if it would have been a boy or girl. It is almost incomprehensible I could be feeling such a raw sense of loss for a baby I didn't know existed, but I can. I do. Tears are not far from the surface as I try to bring my thoughts back to the baby who is left, reassure myself it is okay to feel happy.

'Do you believe in fate?' Lisa asks before I have even sat back down with the drinks. 'Or karma. What goes around. I don't know. Do you believe some things are meant to be? Inevitable almost?'

*Written in the stars,* I think, but instead, I say: 'I'm not sure. I used to, but some things seem so senseless, don't they? So pointless? If it's all part of some grand plan I can't help wondering why.'

'What I said. Before. About Jake still being here if he hadn't met you, I don't believe that. Not really. Car accidents happen every day, and if it was his time, where and who he was with wouldn't have made a difference, would it?'

'It doesn't stop me feeling any less guilty though. If it wasn't for me he wouldn't have been in the car at all.'

'Do you think she still feels bad? The other driver?'

I shrug. I hadn't really thought about her. 'At least she didn't have any passengers in the car with her. No one else… got hurt.' I can't say the word 'died'. 'I don't know. Maybe it still haunts her.'

'That's what frustrates me, I think. The police ruled it a non-fault collision. Atrocious weather. A tragic accident. But Mum seems to need someone to blame. Craves it, almost. She can't seem to let go.'

I take hold of her hand.

'Sometimes…' Her voice quivers. 'I wonder if she wishes it were me who died instead? If Jake was her favourite?'

'That's not true. She didn't have a favourite.'

'I suppose we believe what we want to, don't we?' Lisa sighs. 'Anyway, this is for you.' She pulls a grainy black-and-white picture out of her bag.

At first, I can't make it out.

'Is that?'

'The baby. I'm so sorry you ended up missing the scan. It wasn't supposed to be this way, Kat.'

I trace the image, the tiny limbs, the out-of-proportion skull – alien-looking, almost.

Lisa rests her head on my shoulder. 'I'm scared Mum will find out but I'm too scared to tell her,' she almost whispers, and I don't blame her. I don't think Nancy will take the surrogacy well. Not when she knows the baby is coming to me. It's hard, as I study the photo, to equate the black-and-white blur to the baby growing inside Lisa I press my hand against her belly.

'Thanks.' It's such an innocuous word but dripping with everything I feel. Everything I want.

Lisa looks around the pub and shifts in her seat. She looks uncomfortable as she brushes my hand away.

'It feels really tender still.'

'God. I'm sorry.' I'd thought about the emotional pain we are both feeling over her loss but she must be feeling awful physically too. 'Can I do anything for you?'

'No. I think I'll go home and put my pyjamas on. Something looser. It doesn't help my waistbands are tight. I know it's early days but I think once you've been pregnant before your abdomen muscles are shot and you expand even quicker. Last time I didn't show for ages, but this time I can't do my jeans up already.'

'Have you got any maternity clothes?'

'No. I gave them to a charity shop. Didn't think I'd need them again. You know I've never wanted a baby of my own.' She fidgets again, eyes darting around the pub.

She's putting me on edge. I find myself looking over my shoulder, paranoia gnawing at me.

'Lisa, what's wrong?' I know her well enough to know something is, and it isn't only that her clothes are tight.

Lisa stares miserably into her drink, dunking marshmallows under the chocolaty liquid with her finger and then letting them bob up again. 'I'm worried somebody might see us here together and mention it to Mum.'

'I saw her earlier.'

'You didn't say anything about the baby, did you?' She looks stricken.

"Of course not – but she's going to notice.'

'I know. I'm going to tell her.'

'Do you want me to come? Explain?'

'Best if you don't. Actually, Kat.' Lisa loops her scarf around her neck. 'I'm going to do it on the way home. I'll walk. It will do me good. You don't mind if I leave, do you? Nothing worse than secrets, is there?' Something unspoken is left hanging in the air.

'Let me buy you some new clothes, at least.' A small offering under the circumstances, and it's questionable whether I'm doing this for her or to make myself feel better.

She shrugs on her coat. 'I can get them out of my expenses.'

'I'd like to treat you.' Our eyes meet, and I think she sees how much I need to do something. 'We could even go shopping together?'

'Thanks. I'm feeling so drained though. If you transfer the cash, I'll order some bits online.'

I nod my agreement, and after scribbling down her address for me so I can always find her if I need to, she's gone.

I use the loo before I head for my car, rooting around in my bag for my keys. Broken glass crunching under my feet stops me in my tracks. Raising my head, blood roars in my ears as I see my car window is smashed. A prickle of unease causes me to whip my head around. Is someone there? Hiding behind the van, waiting to see my reaction? Crouching behind the wall leading to the beer garden? Thoughts ricochet as I try to rationalise what might have happened. Could someone have accidentally fallen against my car? Their elbow penetrating the glass? I dismiss each idea as it comes. The window is thick.

I peer inside the car. There is a brick on the passenger seat. Someone has done this deliberately. There's a clattering sound behind me, and I gasp and spin around, but it's only the barman tipping empty bottles into a plastic bin. He heads back into the pub, and there is only me left in the car park, but somehow, I don't feel alone. Another sound springs at me, something I can't identify, and I scuttle back to the pub. Back to warmth. Back to safety.

My eyes are fixed on the floor as I swerve to avoid a broken bottle. But before I reach the door, I round the corner and run smack into someone. My eyes take in his dirty trainers, dark blue denims, white shirt, and finally settle on his face.

'I've been looking for you,' he says.

# CHAPTER TWENTY-TWO
## Now

I hadn't recognised the man who'd said he had been looking for me but he had introduced himself as the landlord of the pub.

'I'm so sorry. One of the regulars told me a 4 x 4 had been broken into. There's been a spate of it, I'm afraid. Do you want me to call the police?'

He had walked me over to my car, and I'd checked the contents – nothing had been stolen.

'No. Let me ring my husband.'

The landlord had checked the other cars as I called Nick. His phone was switched off, and I'd been overcome with a wave of needing him. To feel his arms around me. I was exhausted, unnerved and longing to be at home.

'Do you think you could patch it somehow?' I had asked the landlord. 'I can get it repaired properly tomorrow.'

Now, I crawl along the back roads, the wind buffeting the car; the thick layer of polythene taped to the window flaps loudly in my ear. I ease off the accelerator, even though I am only going 35 mph in a 60 zone. I rehearse telling Nick our news, but the words I practise sound too clunky, too convoluted. The constant stream of cold air seeping through a gap in the polythene stiffens my neck, making my head ache. My muscles are tension-tight. I'm going to have a baby. *We* are going to have a baby. I force myself to think of Nick because it has only now properly occurred to me this baby will have Jake's genes too. Possibly Jake's warm green eyes, his dazzling dimpled smile and, if so, every time I look at my child I will be reminded of the lover I lost. The more I think, the more uncomfortable I feel. Disloyal, almost, as though I am sullying my wedding vows to forsake all others. For the first time, I question whether this was a bad idea. Whether we should have tried adopting again. But it's too late now, and in spite of everything, I can't be sorry. We're going to be parents.

It is gloomy-dark despite it being only teatime, and as traffic pours out of a nearby industrial estate, we come to a standstill. On a whim, I text Nick.

*What are you up to this evening?*

*Missing you. Just leaving work. Going to eat toast in bed and watch NCIS*

Nick's a good cook but never bothers when I'm not there. I think it would be a nice surprise to pretend I'll still be gone overnight and arrive home in an hour with a curry.

*You back tomorrow? Are you okay?*

My thumb punches out *Yes*.

The traffic edges forward again. I start to plan what I'll pick up from the Indian and, as I think about the creamy sauces, fragrant spices and tender pieces of chicken, my stomach growls. Leaning over I open the glovebox and pull out a tube of Fruit Pastilles and pop one onto my tongue, glad it's a yellow one. The sugar begins to melt and my mouth tingles with a citrus zing that immediately makes me feel more awake than I am. Walking home from school, Nancy would often call into the newsagents and let us choose a treat. We'd always want Fruit Pastilles. I'd trade my red one for Lisa's orange ones, and Jake would always eat his black ones first. We'd count down from three before placing a sweet in our mouths, regularly sticking our tongues out to compare how small they were getting. Lisa could never resist chewing, and by the time we reached her house me and Jake would still have a slither of the jelly sweet on our tongues while Lisa would have eaten all her packet and want mine.

Usually I park on the driveway but, with the window missing on the CRV, tonight I bypass our cul-de-sac and trundle down the lane leading to our garage. I slot the car in amongst Nick's golf clubs, the Black & Decker Workbench, and the array of tools he never uses. Opening the door, the musty smell of the garage mingles with the aroma of korma drifting out of the takeout bag on my passenger seat.

I let myself into the house via the back door. The kitchen is gloomy except for the green glow of the clock on the hob. I flick on the light switch. The oven tick-tick-ticks before it ignites, and I place the foil containers of food on the bottom shelf to keep warm. The fridge whirrs in the corner, and jars of chutney chink together as I yank open the door. My hand reaches for the just-in-case bottle of M&S champagne we always keep in the salad drawer, but it seems wrong somehow to celebrate the life of one child when another has been lost. I'm exhausted from the day, from the drive. I bite back the urge to cry as I pull out a bottle of Pinot instead and lift two glasses from the cupboard.

I don't switch on the landing light as I creep past the empty lounge and up the stairs, I don't want to alert Nick to my presence. Before I reach our room, I slip into the nursery and, easing open a drawer, rummage through the pile of vests, holding each one up to the night light, before I find the white one with 'I love my Daddy' written in red.

Despite my sadness, excitement mounts as I pad across the landing, and it is only then do I notice the silence. No TV. No *NCIS*. Tucking the bottle under my arm, I picture a smile spreading across Nick's face as I tell him Lisa is still pregnant, and slowly I push open the door. The room is in darkness, and disappointment wells as I think Nick must have fallen asleep. I hesitate, unsure whether to wake him, but I can't hear the heaviness of his breathing. I can't hear anything at all. Flicking on the light, I wait a few moments for my eyes to adjust but I don't have to see to know that Nick isn't here.

Frustration bubbles as I put down the wine and glasses and tweezer open two slats of the blind with my thumb and index finger. Our driveway, the space where Nick's car should be, is empty. I call his mobile. I'm spoiling the surprise now but I don't care. It rings and rings until the voicemail clicks in. I cut the call before sinking on the bed, unsure what to do.

Seconds later my mobile beeps.

*Sorry babe. At a crucial point in NCIS. Can I call you later?*

My chest tightens but I tell myself I must have got it wrong. He must be watching it with Richard, but on the blank, silent TV screen I imagine I see images of the lipstick on Nick's shirt. I punch out a reply.

*Where are you?*
*Tucked up in bed. Wishing you were here.*

My phone slips from my grasp and on the feather-soft duvet I curl into a ball, knees to my chest, arms wrapped tightly around my legs, as though I can keep my sorrow inside. As though I can keep my marriage intact.

*

Later, I peel myself from the bed and every muscle screams in protest. Scenarios whip through my mind, hard and fast, and none of them are good. Nick. I can't believe he's having an affair, I just can't, and yet all the signs are there. He's forever checking his mobile, he's been distracted, snappy almost, and I can't remember the last time we had sex. Is it my imagination or has the distance between us grown since Christmas Day? Since Lisa's text to tell us she is pregnant, but hovering just outside my consciousness is another memory, and I pace the bedroom as I try to pull it to the forefront of my mind. Nick received a text Christmas Day. My stomach drops. Natasha.

In the mirror my reflection taunts me, my unwashed hair hanging limp, my face – pale and blotchy with tears – my body, a roll of flesh spilling over the elastic waistband of my leggings. Working from home I have stopped making an effort. I have let myself go. Loathing myself I stare at my image for so long my vision blurs, and I drift: Nick on our wedding day. His voice breaking with emotion as he took his vows. The way his hand shook as he slid on my ring. I dive into the memory. It is colourful and bright. Warm and comforting. Better than the here and now in each and every way. But reality pulls and pulls at me until, reluctantly, I am back in my cold and silent room, desperate to talk things through.

I pick up my phone, scroll through my contacts and press dial. It rings and rings. Come on. I urge Lisa to pick up but a robotic voice invites me to leave a message. I don't. Instead, I try Clare. With every unanswered ring my frustration builds.

As though it is about to explode I hurl my mobile onto my bed. The desire to text Nick is immense but I want to see the expression on his face as I confront him. Agitation keeps me on my toes, and I find myself pacing furiously until my adrenaline ebbs away, and I fold myself around Nick's pillow.

*

The sound of a baby crying wrenches me awake. I sit bolt upright. The lost baby? The bedroom is swathed in darkness, the shadow of my furniture eerie. The crying fades to an even louder silence, and I know, with certainty, I should not have gone to Farncaster today, walking around the town, shoulder to shoulder with the shoppers, as though I am one of them. As though I belong. Slowly, the ceiling seems to bear down, compacting the air in the room. I think of the rock through my window, the figure at the crematorium, eyes following my every move. I wrap my arms around myself. I can't stop shivering and I know it's with fear, not cold. It's all going to catch up with me. I don't know if I can keep it together any more.

Not again.

# CHAPTER TWENTY-THREE
## Now

The sky is streaked pink and orange when I wake, the sound of a baby crying sharp in my mind. I have been so restless in the night, the duvet has slithered onto the floor and I am cold and stiff. I stretch out my legs, flexing my feet, encouraging the blood to flow and chase the pins and needles away before I stamp over to the window on still too-numb-too-feel feet. The driveway is empty. I rub the sleep from my eyes, as though I can make Nick's car appear. It doesn't. My mobile skitters across my bedside cabinet trilling 'Like I Love You', and I know it's Lisa.

'Morning, Lisa.'

'Hello.' She sounds flat. 'I told my mum last night about the surrogacy.'

'How did she take it?'

'Not well. She didn't understand how I could give a child up. Not when she's lost one.'

'Did she come around last time? With Stella?'

There's a beat.

'She wasn't thrilled, but this time it's worse. This time—'

'It's me.'

Lisa sighs 'I didn't mean… Look, Jake was my twin and I loved him as much as her, if not more. It was an accident. I can see that. Why can't she?'

'It might have been an accident but it was still the wrong place at the wrong time, and if it wasn't for me, Jake wouldn't have been there, would he? It's human nature to look for someone to blame.'

'But…' Lisa is crying now. I wait while she gathers herself. 'You weren't driving. Jake was and they don't blame him. Does someone always have to be accountable, Kat? She's so busy being angry and hurt she's forgotten the good times.' Her breath hitches. 'Do you remember when we made that Easter cake? We must have been about thirteen?'

'Yes. It was terrible! It sank in the middle.'

'Jake said he could do better, and we told him boys couldn't bake—'

'And he locked himself in the kitchen and made that chocolate log. It was amazing!'

'It was shop-bought, you know.'

'It wasn't?'

'I found the box in the bin. It was at the back of the cupboard, left over from Christmas. He just took off the snowman and stuck mini eggs on the top. I told him I wouldn't tell if he let me eat the rest. No wonder I was fat.'

'How funny. I thought he was an amazing cook. He made us a romantic meal for two once. Pasta and—'

'Dolmio.'

'No!' I laugh, though it is slightly disconcerting that the person I thought I knew better than anyone managed to fool me. But I suppose we are all taken in sometimes, aren't we? We believe what we want to see.

'I miss him, Kat, and I haven't had anyone to talk to about him. To be honest, my mum is still so wrapped up in grief she barely talks to me any more.'

'You can always talk to me, Lis. I'm always here.'

'Sorry. I'm hormonal.'

'Don't apologise. You've just lost a baby. A twin. You're bound to be feeling awful.'

Lisa cries even harder. 'I'm sorry.'

'Stop apologising, Lis.'

She blows her nose. 'It never gets any easier. The loss. I don't think time does heal, do you? We just have to learn to live with it, but what if we can't? What then?'

I sift through platitudes I quickly discard, remaining silent until Lisa's sobs abate.

'Do you want me to come and see you?' My offer is genuine.

'No. It's probably best you don't visit Farncaster again. I don't think you'd get a very welcome reception.'

'What about your scan?'

'I know you wanted to be there, but, Kat—'

'Please. I don't mind so much about the midwife appointments, but actually seeing the baby… I could meet you at the hospital and leave afterwards. No one will know.'

'I don't know.'

'Please, Lis.' The online surrogacy group I'm part of says it's such a great bonding experience if you can be present for the scan. 'I really want to be as involved as I can.'

'OK.'

She still sounds reluctant but I'm already mentally planning my route, how I can drive around the outskirts and avoid the town centre.

'You'll let me know as soon as it's booked? I don't want to make anything harder for you, Lisa. I promise. I respect your mum doesn't want anything to do with me but I'm here to support you in whatever you need, and it doesn't have to be baby related. It's been good – talking about Jake.'

'I've missed you,' Lisa blurts out.

'Come and stay with us. Soon. Bring some old photos.'

'The ones of Jake in that crazy pork-pie hat he wore?'

'He was wearing that the night of Perry's party.' It had slipped backwards as we shared our first kiss, and he'd steadied it with one hand, his other massaging the back of my neck.

'I'd like to come and stay,' she says, 'and share memories of Jake. I'd like that a lot.'

A feeling of warmth wraps itself around me like a cloak, and I berate myself for the time I've wasted.

The shower spits and splutters. I scrub at my skin, as if I can wash away my tiredness. The water torrents along with my emotions. Of all the things I am feeling about Nick, underneath the suspicion, the disappointment, the worry, bubbles happiness that me and Lisa are okay. The baby is okay.

As I lather coconut shampoo, I practise the things I'll say to Nick but, even in my head, the words sound cold and accusing. It will be better to wait and see what he has to say for himself. Once dried and dressed, I paint on a brave face. My skin tight under a thick layer of foundation.

I have chopped vegetables, dissolved stock cubes and am pacing barefoot, from sink to cooker and back again, my soles sticking to the tiles, when Nick slinks into the kitchen.

'Hey.' He can't quite meet my eye. 'I didn't think you'd be home yet.' He dips his head to kiss me, and his stubble grazes my cheek.

I pull back as the rank smell of whisky stings my nostrils.

'I've not been back long.' My voice is jovial, giving him the chance to tell me the truth, but underneath my calm exterior, anger is simmering like the soup on the stove.

'Something smells good!' He lifts the lid on the pan and inhales deeply.

'Where have you been?' The question slips out before I can think it through.

'I nipped to the office to pick up some papers. I missed you last night.' Nick nuzzles my neck, wrapping his arms tightly around my waist, squeezing me so hard my lungs grapple for air. I try to wriggle from his grasp, but he clings on and I can't break free. Sliding my arms around him, I feel his shoulders shake and think he might be crying but I can't be sure. I half-expect to smell traces of perfume – there's nothing but stale alcohol. Nick puts his palm on the small of my back, drawing me closer until there isn't even a centimetre gap between our bodies, yet I've never felt so distant from him before.

'There's something I need to tell you,' I say, pulling back. I find his eyes before saying: 'I know.'

There is a flash of panic on his face. 'You know?' He speaks slowly. Carefully. As if buying himself time to form a proper answer in his head before he says it out loud.

'I know you weren't here last night.'

A sharp intake of breath tells me I have caught him by surprise.

'No. I wasn't.' He doesn't elaborate further.

'Where were you?' I cross my arms. I am afraid of his answer but, at the same time, I am desperate to hear it.

'Kat.' He whispers my name with such regret. 'I am so, so sorry but there is something I need to tell you.'

# CHAPTER TWENTY-FOUR
## Then

Nick was freezing when he woke. His duvet was thin and his too-small pyjamas hadn't kept him warm. They'd moved into a two-up two-down council house a few years before but it still wasn't a happy home. There was a time, when his mum had breast cancer, that Nick had seen a different side to his dad, but once Mum had been given the all clear, it was as though all the fear, all the worry his dad had felt, transcended into anger. He was worse now than he had ever been. Nick had begged his mum to leave – Dad was becoming more and more violent – but she'd say to Nick: 'He's still in there. The man I fell in love with. Remember when I was ill?' But Nick thought, if you had to be dying for someone to be nice to you, they probably didn't love you as much as you hoped. He wouldn't think about that today though. It was his birthday. Nineteen! Although there would be no party, no decent presents, he didn't care. He didn't want anything except for his mum to be away from his dad. Nick worked full-time at Tesco now and rarely spent any money on himself. Everything went into a savings account. One day he'd buy a big house like the one mum cooed over on the property programme last night, with the island in the kitchen and the copper pans hanging above the Aga. He'd paint the kitchen sunflower, his mum's favourite colour, and while he went to work, she could bake cakes. She would never have to work again.

Nick caught a whiff of something delicious, not the usual mildew smell that filled the house as the patches of mould climbed the walls, clung to the ceiling, but sausages. Nick jumped up and pulled on a pair of socks before padding downstairs towards the kitchen as quietly as he could. His dad liked to lie-in.

'Happy birthday, Nick!'

Mum crossed the kitchen and wrapped her arms around him; she smelled of oil and cleaning products. Nick hugged her fiercely.

'You must be shattered?' He stepped back and studied her face. She looked so much older than Richard's mum, although they must be around the same age. The wrinkles surrounding her eyes definitely weren't caused by laughter.

'I'm fine.' She smiled but it was only with her mouth.

Nick reached to switch on the kettle to make her a cup of tea, but she slapped his hand lightly.

'Sit down and open your presents.'

On the table were two gift-wrapped boxes. He picked them up one by one and shook them, trying to guess what was inside. He slid his fingers between the join in the wrapping paper on the one he thought might be a book and eased it open, wanting to savour the moment.

'Thanks, Mum.' He flipped open the cover on the encyclopaedia and ignored the 'Happy Christmas, Emma!' inscription on the inside.

'If you're going to find a better job than shelf stacking, you'll need to know all that stuff,' Mum said. She had wanted him to stay on at school, go to uni, but how could he? He needed to be a man. Contribute to the housekeeping. He'd left school as soon as he had turned sixteen, eager to be bringing in money, but without sitting his exams it had been hard to find anything decent and he'd taken the first job he'd been offered.

'Open the other one before the sausages burn.'

Nick picked up the other box. He had no idea what could be inside. Smoke began to rise from the frying pan so he tore the paper off quickly.

'Mum!' Nick stared at the Nokia box, almost too afraid to look inside in case it housed something other than a mobile phone. He'd wanted one for ages and, more than once, he'd been tempted to buy one out of his wages but they had an unspoken agreement almost, him and Mum. Every penny would go towards their future.

'I hope it's okay. It's nothing fancy but you can text and call. I've topped it up with £5 credit for you.'

Nick slid the packaging out of the box. It was nothing like the one Richard had. There was no Internet, not even a camera, but Nick turned it over in his hands as though it were a gold bar. 'It's brill. Thanks.'

'Tuck in or you'll be late for work.' Mum slid sausages from the pan onto a plate.

Nick forked baked beans into his mouth as he switched on his phone, and it wasn't until he was halfway through his breakfast he realised his mum wasn't eating.

'Where's yours?'

'I'll have mine later with Dad.'

Nick hesitated. His mum was getting so thin he often wondered whether she ate at all.

'Really. Hurry up before yours gets cold.'

Nick finished, and his mum took his plate to rinse, and as he stood he couldn't help but pull open the fridge door. There were only three sausages inside, and he knew his mum wouldn't be eating at all.

His phone felt hard and heavy in his bag as he walked to work, a constant reminder his mum had yet again gone without.


'Happy birthday, mate.' Richard pressed a box into Nick's hands when they met for lunch, and he sauntered into the chip shop to buy them both lunch, as though it wasn't a big deal he'd just given Nick an iPhone. Nick had only ever seen a picture of one – apparently, they were going to be huge but they were almost impossible to get.

'What the fuck? I can't accept this, mate.' Nick tried to give it back to Richard when he returned with bags of hot, salty chips and golden fish. It wasn't that he wasn't grateful, but Richard gave him so much and it didn't seem fair the only thing Nick had ever been able to do in return was teach Richard how to play football. Even if he was bloody good at it.

'I want you to have it.' Richard opened a sachet of ketchup with his teeth.

'I think—'

'You think too much,' Richard cut in. 'I think you want one. I think you should have one. Seriously.' He leaned closer to Nick and lowered his voice. 'I'll always do what I think is right for you. No arguing. We're mates. We've got each other's backs, right?'

'Always.' Nick felt his grin almost split his face in two as he opened the box and pulled out the handset. 'They've only just come out though. How did you manage to get one?'

Richard tapped the side of his nose. 'I've contacts. I can sort anything out. It's not what you know—'

'It's amazing!'

'It's nothing.' Richard shrugged.

But it was something. To Nick. 'I owe you one.'

'Oh, you do,' said Richard. 'I won't forget.'

Walking home after work Nick passed the pawn shop and a thought struck him. He didn't need two phones. He could sell one and buy his mum something nice without it affecting their savings. Some flowers, perhaps, or chocolates?

The bell trilled as he pushed open the door. The smell of coffee rushed towards him. The man behind the counter, comedy moustache, eyed Nick suspiciously.

'If it's nicked, I'm not interested.'

'No. It was a present. Honest.' Nick put his rucksack on the counter and unzipped his bag. He rummaged through his Tesco uniform until his hand connected with the chunky Nokia. As Nick began to pull it out of his bag, he remembered the radiance on Mum's face as she'd watched him unwrap it that morning, her hands raw and red from cleaning, as she served up the breakfast she couldn't afford to eat herself. Nick dropped the handset as though it had suddenly burned him. Instead, he pulled out the iPhone Richard had given him and tried to ignore the heavy feeling in his heart as he saw the man's eyes light up, and although he only offered Nick a fraction of what he knew it must have cost, he stuffed the notes into his pocket anyway.

The shouting was audible before Nick had even unlocked the front door.

'You spent the housekeeping on a fucking phone?'

He hesitated, as though his dad's anger was pushing him back. He stood on the front doormat, clutching the baby pink carnations he'd bought. Tucked inside his bag was a box of Terry's All Gold. There was still some cash left he'd give his mum.

'It's his birthday. Did you even remember? He deserves something nice.'

''Course I remembered. I'm not fucking stupid. Unlike him. Leaving school without any bloody qualifications.' The kind voice his dad had used when his mum was ill was just a distant memory. He seemed even angrier now she was better than before she got sick. Mum said it was because he'd been so scared she'd die, but that didn't make sense to Nick at all.

'He's not the stupid one,' Mum screamed.

The sound of the slap reverberated through the house. Nick dropped his bag and the flowers and flew through to the kitchen.

'Mum?'

Mum stood, back to him, hands on sink, leaning over the bowl as though she might be sick.

'It's all right, love. You go upstairs.'

'No.' Nick's voice wobbled but he was a man now. He worked full-time, and the days of hiding under his covers, hands pressed over his ears, were over. Never again would he pretend to believe the stories Mum had walked into a cupboard or slipped getting out of the bath. Besides he had one advantage over his dad now. He was taller. Fitter. Faster. He shouldn't be scared, but Nick felt his knees begin to shake as his dad took a step towards him, hand raised.

His mum cried: 'Leave him alone', and spun around, and Nick saw her swollen lip, the blood trickling down her chin.

He knew he had a fraction of a second to decide what to do. To walk away or hit back. There was a buzzing in his ears and his blood felt as though it was on fire as it crackled and steamed through his veins. His dad's hand connected with his cheek, causing his teeth to slam together, and Nick felt an invisible force pull his fist back and pound it into his dad's face again and again. His vision tunnelled. He was surrounded by blackness but he didn't stop. Couldn't stop. In the background, his mum screamed, bone crunched, and Nick grunted with each and every punch. The anger he felt over every past hurt his father had caused teemed with the anger he felt now. It wasn't until his dad fell limp and loose, Nick released his grip on the front of his dad's shirt, and Kevin, for Nick swore then and there he would never call him dad again, crumpled to the floor. Gradually the thrumming in his ears subsided, the black dots in front of his eyes faded away, and as Nick stared with horror at the bruised and bloodied face lying before him, he knew he'd gone too far.

# CHAPTER TWENTY-FIVE
## Now

What does Nick have to tell me? I search his face for clues as I second-guess what he might have to say.

'You look like someone has died.' It is me who breaks the silence.

Nick threads his fingers through mine. I feel a jolt of electricity and try to pull back but I see the utter desolation in his eyes. I will myself not to cry as I relax my hand into his and wait.

Seconds blur into minutes and still he doesn't speak.

'Is there someone else?' I ask.

'What? God, no. How could you think that?'

'You weren't here last night. You lied to me. You've been distant for weeks since—' My throat is constricted with emotion. My voice quieter. 'Since Natasha's text.'

'Kat—'

'And I heard you,' I cut in, 'talking to Richard on New Year's Day. He said something about getting found out and you said: 'it's too late'.

'I did say that.' Nick nods. 'And now we have. Been found out.'

'I don't understand?'

'There's a problem.' His voice sounds controlled but it is only because I know him so well I can detect a slight tremor. 'With work. But it's nothing for you to worry about.'

'Work?' I hiss out air in relief but his expression tells me this is more serious than he is letting on, and that despite his reassurances, I should worry.

'What's wrong?'

'We didn't get planning permission for a renovation on a listed building. It wasn't intentional but it slipped by Richard and, by the time he realised, we had already started and stupidly decided to carry on rather than come clean. It's a stately home and a huge site. Potentially we could lose a lot of money, not to mention our reputation, but it's in hand.'

'Why didn't you tell me?' Marriage is about sharing and I am hurt he has kept this to himself but I don't want to make it about us. About our relationship. He looks so miserable.

'You've had enough to deal with – the babies, moving house – I was hoping I could get it sorted without you finding out about it. I know how much you stress.' That bit, at least, is true.

'But still…'

'I know. You're stronger than you look.'

'So, is it? Sorted?'

'Not yet. I drove down to the site yesterday, and the meeting went on so long I stayed overnight. I'll probably have to go back at least once more.'

'Can I do anything to help?' I know I probably can't but I feel helpless seeing him so deflated.

'You can make me a cup of tea.' He drops a kiss on top of my head. 'I'm going to shower.'

'And that's really it?' I can't help asking just as he's leaving the room. 'There's nothing going on with Natasha.'

Nick turns. His eyes seek out mine. 'Please don't worry about her.'

'It's been hard not to in the last 24 hours.'

Nick pulls his mobile from his pocket and scrolls through his contacts. When he reaches Natasha's name he presses delete and scans my face for a reaction.

'I can promise you, Natasha and I having an affair is something you will *never* have to worry about.' He doesn't blink, or look away, and I do believe him but I still feel uneasy. I just don't know why.

*

Later, after Nick has changed into a tracksuit and we have eaten, I clear away the bowls of soup we've barely touched. Sweep the crumbs of crusty bread into the palm of my hand and sprinkle them into the bin. I'm tired but I can't settle. I'm longing to talk to Nick about Lisa, but he's shut himself in his study, said he had a few phone calls to make.

The laundry basket is overflowing and I start sorting coloureds, checking each pocket as I go. I'm stuffing Nick's trousers and the clothes I wore yesterday into the drum when I notice a piece of paper flutter to the floor. Scooping it up I see it's the receipt from The Farncaster Bean Café. Tiredness burns behind my eyes as I screw the receipt into a ball and lob it into the bin. After adding softener to the drawer and switching the machine on, I carry coffee through to the lounge, calling for Nick to join me.

He flops onto the sofa, looking exhausted. We've both aged these past couple of years. It's time to tell him Lisa's news. I kneel in front of Nick and take his hand. Heat passes between his palm and mine and a ball of longing begins to unravel. I press my lips against his, my fingers fumbling for the buttons on his shirt, but he clamps his hand over mine.

'Kat, I'm knackered.'

Hurt, I try to pull away but he pulls me closer and shuffles back on the sofa, making room for me. I lie next to him, my head on his chest, feeling the thump-thump-thump of his heart.

'Tell me what you've been up to?' His fingers idly play with my hair and I feel myself sink into him.

'The car window was smashed in a car park. Nothing was stolen though.'

'I'll get it repaired in the morning.' He twirls a strand of hair around his finger. 'Did you find her?' he asks softly. 'Lisa?'

There was never going to be anywhere else I was.

'I'm sorry it didn't work out, Kat,' he says, after a beat of silence. 'I don't want to give up on having a family, I know how much it means to you, but can we just take a break? Be *normal* for a bit?'

'Normal?' The word stings but I know what he means. I struggle to think of the last conversation we had that wasn't about adoption or surrogacy. Babies have become the forefront of our world and we don't even have one yet.

'I don't mean you're not normal because you can't conceive, you know I don't.' He brushes my fringe from my eyes. 'It's all-consuming, isn't it? The constant worry. The hope. The disappointment. I think we need a break, is all, and maybe resign ourselves to the fact we might not become parents.'

'August.'

'For a holiday? Italy?'

'No. For becoming parents.' I prop myself up on my elbow so I can see Nick's face. 'Lisa's still pregnant.'

'But she fell. Said she was bleeding. Had cramps.'

'The doctor thinks it was twins and she's lost one. She's had a scan. She's definitely still pregnant.'

'Is that even possible? It sounds unlikely.' His eyes search mine for reassurance.

'It isn't. I've googled it and it's not uncommon to miscarry one baby.'

'She's really still pregnant?' The expression on his face oscillates between disbelief and excitement.

'Really. Look.' I wave the picture of the scan in front of him, as though it's a magic wand that can make his doubts disappear. 'This is our baby.'

Nick can't help smiling as he studies the photo. 'You can tell he's well hung, he must take after—'

'Idiot.' I punch his arm. 'That's his leg you're looking at. Or her leg. It's too early to tell yet.'

'It *was* twins though?' Nick's face darkens once more.

'Yes. They do run in Lisa's family. Look. There's something I haven't told you.' It suddenly seems important I'm honest. 'Lisa had a twin, Jake – he died in a car accident.'

'Oh no.' Nick is shaking his head.

'And I was with him. In the car. It wasn't just a bump, like I told you. We were nineteen. Almost about to start uni. He was.' I swallow hard. 'My boyfriend. First love, I suppose.'

'Oh, Kat, I'm so, so sorry.' Nick looks horrified as he pulls me towards him and strokes my hair. His body is shaking, and I don't know if he's sad for me or Lisa. The boy who never got to live his life or the baby we have lost. I wait – giving him time to absorb everything while I mentally prepare for the inevitable questions, but when Nick does speak he says: 'Sorry, darling, I'm knackered. Do you want to talk some more or is it okay if I grab a couple of hours' sleep?'

'I don't mind if you're tired,' I say trying to keep the disappointment out of my voice.

Nick presses down on my hip as he climbs over me; our eyes meet for a moment before he averts his gaze, and I feel ashamed in so many different ways.

'I'm so sorry,' I say. 'I should have told you.'

'It's okay.'

'But what if the baby looks like Jake? I should have thought.'

'Then he or she will be a reminder. Some things can't be forgotten. They-they *shouldn't* be forgotten.' He stumbles over his words, and I don't know whether it's because of tiredness or emotion, but I do know, as I listen to his heavy tread climb the stairs, I have taken a step towards the truth, and I wonder what would happen if I revealed all of me to Nick. The floorboards creak above me, and I reach for the remote control and scan the channels looking for something mind-numbing. *Dirty Dancing* is showing again. It's one of my favourites but as Baby carries a watermelon, my eyelids grow heavy, and as sleep beckons me over, I willingly surrender.

\*

*The darkness was all-consuming, swallowing my ability to think straight. To stay calm. Panic welled and despite knowing I should keep quiet – I shouldn't make him angry – I couldn't contain the whimper in my throat that morphed into a cry. Into a scream.*

*'Please!' I fumbled in the dark, trying to locate the door handle, my heart skipping a beat when, for one horrible second, I thought the handle was gone, but then my fingers located the cool metal that warmed quickly under my clammy palm. I pulled and twisted and rattled knowing it wouldn't make any difference but I was unable to just do nothing.*

*'Please.' I smacked my palms against the door over and over but each slap only fuelled my fear. 'Let me out!' The words were ripped from me and, over the pounding of my hands, the whooshing of blood in my ears, at first, I almost don't hear it. The sound coming from outside. I rested my forehead against the door, trying to contain my juddering breath, imagining him doing the same on the other side. My panic transformed to sheer terror as menace seemed to seep through the wood, and I stepped backwards, stumbling over something I couldn't see. I fell hard. The last thing I remembered was banging my head.*

*I wasn't sure how long I was out but when I came around, throat dry and head woozy, my bladder was full to bursting. My muscles cramping. I tried to stretch out my legs but as I slid them forward my feet hit the wall. I reached out with my hands feeling the solidity beneath my fingertips and fought to calm my breathing before I stood, knees buckling, and paused, wriggling my toes as I tried to get my blood flowing freely again.*

*'Please,' I whispered now, as I touched the door. Hot tears of humiliation pricked the back of my eyes. As much as I was afraid of what was on the other side of the door, the thought of wetting myself was mortifying. My fingers brushed against the door handle and, without hope, I twisted it once more. It was still locked.*

*

I am disorientated as I wake, and cold with fear. I think I hear a baby crying but my cheeks are wet and I think it was me that was crying. Everything is getting so muddled. The nightmares I thought I'd left behind are coming more frequently again, and I think it must be Lisa coming back into my life, stirring up the past. Outside the lounge window the sky is dark, clouds obscuring the moon and stars. I must have slept for hours, although it's not surprising as last night I barely got any rest. On the TV, the forecaster is predicting the imminent arrival of a storm that will wash away the snow. What has startled me awake?

I aim the remote at the TV to silence it, listening instead for sounds of Nick. There is nothing to be heard except the ticking clock in the hallway, the sound amplified in the quiet. My skin prickles. Something isn't right. Slowly I swing my legs from the sofa.

I have such a strong sense of being watched the hairs on the back of my neck stand on end. I shiver involuntarily and wrap my arms around myself. There's a soft shuffling sound coming from outside, it's barely discernible, and if adrenaline wasn't flooding through every cell in my body, enhancing my senses, I might not have heard it.

Somebody is out there.

It's late for visitors but I wait for the doorbell to ring. Seconds tick by and nothing happens. I can't take my eyes off the window. There is a lightness radiating from the snow, but all I can see in the glass is the lounge furniture reflected back at me. I tell myself it's nothing, even though I know it's something. I have to psych myself up before I can stand and cross to the window, terrified a face might suddenly appear. There's a smack against the glass. The sound comes again and again, and I realise the predicted storm has arrived, hailstones are clattering against the windowpane. I force myself to calm but as I stretch both arms out and grasp the curtains I see it, just before I can swish them closed. A shadow. A movement.

Somebody is out there.

There is not much to see beyond my own reflection as I stare outside. Part of me wants to run and fetch Nick, but almost of their own accord my fingers release their grip on the curtains and my feet carry me to the hallway. I flick on the outside light. My hand stretches towards the front door handle. I press my ear against the wood. There's a crack of lightning, and I almost turn and run up the stairs, but instead, I slowly crack open the door. Light floods in. No one is there, and I step outside, the snow and the rain saturating my socks, numbing my toes. Since I've been sleeping, fresh snow has fallen and the driveway is a blanket of white, but to the side of the garden, by the fence, where somebody who didn't want to be seen would walk, are footsteps. They lead to the lounge window, where they stop, before circling back again, avoiding the front door.

There *was* somebody out here.

And they were watching me sleep.

It feels like a warning.

*You mustn't tell, Kat.*

# CHAPTER TWENTY-SIX
## Now

I've taken to skipping breakfast these past few weeks. Ever since I saw the footprints in the snow I've had a feeling of being watched. I'm not sleeping properly, and my appetite isn't what it was. Rationally, I know it's unlikely anyone followed me home from Farncaster, but my mind races, jumping to conclusions. After all, Nancy saw me in that magazine, didn't she? God knows who else did. I know it's most likely Lisa coming back that has set me on edge: the approach of the ten-year anniversary. But in the dead of night, when shadows loom, and floorboards creak, I'm surrounded by an aura of dread. The cold, bony fingers of the past are reaching out to me.

But today I will need my strength. I throw a couple of rashers of bacon in the pan, standing back as they sizzle and spit. Despite eating less, at our last rehearsal, my costumes would no longer zip up. Mortification heated me from my toes to my scalp as Tamara told me not to worry, she could easily order some more in a bigger size. That didn't stop me standing on the scales the second I got home. They still said I weighed the same. I think the steam must have affected the reading and made a note to buy some more. That's the trouble with working at home and living in leggings, isn't it? You don't notice the waistbands getting snug, and I may be skipping meals but I'm still eating chocolate Hobnobs as I work. Cramming them into my mouth as though the mindless chewing will keep my snarling memories at bay. It doesn't.

Outside the garden is a riot of colour. April showers have nourished the weeds tangled amongst the plants. Nick keeps promising to tidy the borders.

The radio plays Corinne Bailey Rae's 'Put Your Records On'. It's one of my favourites but I don't sing along, focusing instead on slicing crusty white bread. One piece is an inch thick and the other is virtually see-through, but I slather it in ketchup nevertheless. I eat standing up, a tea towel tucked into the neck of my top to protect it from the grease dripping from my chin. When I've finished I punch out a text to Lisa.

*What time is the scan today?*

*Still 3 o'clock!!*

The doctor didn't repeat the early scan they did when Lisa thought she had miscarried so this will be my first time seeing the baby. Beanie is twenty-two weeks now and I've been so impatient. I was reading online that some women have their twenty week scan at eighteen weeks – every NHS hospital is different, Lisa's midwife said – but that doesn't stop me wishing we were one of the ones who had it early. Beanie is about as heavy as a bag of sugar. With eyelids and eyebrows developed and tooth buds in place. A proper little person. A mini 'Jake', I think but I brush the thought away as Nick sticks his head around the door.

'I'm off.'

'Wait!' I hurry across the kitchen. 'Kiss?' I stand on tiptoe and he wipes the corner of my mouth with his thumb.

'Ketchup,' he says before dropping his lips onto mine.

'Hungry?' I ask.

'No.'

He's not sleeping properly either. Or eating. He tells me not to worry about the business, but it's hard not to when he so obviously is. I wish he'd talk to me properly.

I don't know how much trouble we are in. It's impossible not to fear the worst. It's selfish, I know, but I wonder whether we will have to move if Nick can't sort things out. If we'll lose the house. Where would we bring the baby up? I could get a full-time job, but what would happen to the charity? If I draw a salary, we'd have to cut down the counselling we offer and I'd hate for that to happen. It's so important to people.

'I wish you could come to the hospital today. I can't believe you're missing it.'

'I know. I'm sorry. I've so much on. You'll get a photo though, won't you, and I'll get to meet him or her in person soon.'

'I can't wait.'

'Me neither.' He rubs his nose against mine. 'It's getting real now, isn't it?'

'Very. I woke at 3 a.m. thinking I could hear a baby crying. My subconscious must be preparing me for sleepless nights.' I am trying to convince myself that almost every night I am dreaming of the baby we are about to have, rather than ones I have lost.

'Are you sure you will be okay today?' He tucks my hair behind my ear. 'It's a long drive. For you. And you've been… fraught lately.'

'I am not imagining things.' I step back.

'I know you think you saw footprints—'

'I did.' I can't help snapping.

'They weren't there when I looked.'

'The rain had washed them away.' By the time Nick ventured outside the lawn was a mass of sludge and there was nothing to be seen. If there ever was.

*Ten years.*

'I've told you there's been someone hanging around outside too.' There have been several times this past month I have tried to go out, and each time I opened the front door, there was someone stalking down the road, hands thrust into pockets, or a shadow crossing our driveway. It's not as though there are many houses in our cul-de-sac. It's rare to notice anything out of the ordinary. I am staying in more and more, unable to shake the slithering uneasiness in the pit of my stomach.

'Like the other night?'

'Do you have to bring that up again?' I had stood at our bedroom window, eyes fixed on the motionless figure half-hidden at the end of the driveway. My palms began to heat, my fingers tingled and, by the time Nick came out of the shower, I was gripping the windowsill, body rigid. 'He's watching me.' It had been an effort to speak through my shortness of breath, and Nick had looked at me, his blue eyes darkening with sympathy. 'Kat, it's just the black bin. I put it out earlier.' He had gently drawn the curtains and led me to the bed where I lay waiting for my heart rate to slow. The buzzing in my head to stop.

'What's going on with you lately?' Nick had asked, the mattress dipping as he curled himself around me.

*You mustn't tell, Kat.*

My lips were pinned together as I turned to the wall.

'Clare hasn't seen anyone lurking around,' Nick says now, as though that makes everything okay.

'You've been talking to Clare about me? When?' Yet again I have a cold feeling writhing around inside of me and I rub my arms as though I can warm myself.

'I don't have time for this.' Nick picks up his briefcase.

'You don't have time for me.' The words scorch my tongue.

As I watch him leave I want to call him back. Tell him I am sorry. I take a step forward but the outside world rushes in at me and, in my peripheral vision, I see movement. I twist my head but it's only the wind battering the cherry tree. Nick climbs into his car, but before I can catch his attention, there's a sound to my right. I jump. It's only an empty can of lager clanking across our driveway. Hurriedly, I slam the door closed and lean against it.

My mobile vibrates in my pocket and I pull it out. My heart sinks a little when I see it is Tamara.

'Morning, Tam.'

She skips the pleasantries altogether. 'You missed another rehearsal yesterday afternoon, Kat. What's going on?'

'Sorry.' I don't explain I was fully intending on coming, but I thought I saw someone crouching by the side of my car, and I had shrugged off my coat, slipped off my shoes and gone for a lie-down instead.

'We open soon. We've sold tickets already.'

'I know. I'll be ready. I will.' But we both know I won't be. I'm constantly forgetting the words. The dance steps. I can't seem to concentrate.

'You're going to die on stage if you're not careful. I could take over—'

'No,' I bite, sharper than intended.

'I only want what's best for the play.' I hear the desperation in her voice, and I feel a stab of guilt. I've grown quite fond of her these past few months and we've become friends, of sorts. Her life revolves around the company, and I should make more effort. I'm not being fair.

'I'll be at the next rehearsal. I promise. We can talk everything through properly then. Sorry, got to go.'

I cut the call. I've got hours before I have to leave to meet Lisa. I look out of the window. The street is quiet. Silent. Inside, the clock ticks. 'Die on stage.' It's a throwaway comment. Just a word. I am anxious and tense as I wait to see if I have another panic attack. Sometimes the fear of having one is the worst fear of all.

My breathing is shallow but I think I'm okay. There's a knocking as the washing machine starts to spin, startling me.

I stuff my feet into my shoes and open the front door. Clare is home. Her car is in the drive. My skin is tingling. I can just cross the road to Clare's and have a coffee. Something small. Something normal.

I can do this.

I can.


'You don't look fine.' Clare starts to pass me a mug, but she glances at my shaking hands and places it on the side table instead.

'I am.' Tucking my legs under me, I make myself as small as possible waiting for my pulse to slow.

Ada is building a tower on the rug in front of the fireplace. 'Look!' She widens her big blue eyes as she places another brick on the top.

'She's growing so quickly,' I say feeling calmer now. I reach forward for a custard cream.

'It will be your turn soon. How is Lisa?'

'She's good. It's the scan this afternoon.'

'You're going?' Clare asks.

'Yes. It will be a relief to see everything's okay.'

'Are you worried?'

'A little. It's been tougher than I'd thought. Not being in control, I suppose.' I don't know where Lisa is. What she's eating. If she's taking her folic acid. It's not how I imagined it would be. I place my hand across my middle, longing to feel the bubbling of a new life. Tiny kicking feet. Sharp elbows.

'It will be worth it though. When he's here. Or she.'

'Yes, not that long to go really. Next week Lisa will be twenty-three weeks, and the baby's lungs could be developed enough to survive if they were born early. Imagine that! Beanie will be the size of a large mango.'

Clare laughs.

'Sorry, I get a bit carried away. Nick doesn't seem interested in this stuff.' I feel disloyal voicing my concerns, and I stuff another biscuit in my mouth as though I can force the words back in with it.

'Men often aren't. Akhil practically rolled his eyes every time I asked him for a foot rub or if he'd massage Aveeno into my stretch marks. You'd think he had nothing to do with the conception.'

'And now?' I haven't seen him for a while.

'He hasn't seen Ada for ages. It's his mum, really. She never approved of me and was disappointed Ada was a girl, her skin was too light, we gave her a Western name. Mother-in-laws.' Clare rolls her eyes. 'Don't you worry though. Nick will be a great dad. You only have to look at him with Ada to know that. Did you bring the tickets? For the play?'

'No. Was I supposed to?'

'Last week I asked you for three. I'm bringing my parents.'

'God, sorry.' My mind is full of gaping holes – my memories slipping through the gaps. It's stress, I know. 'I've probably blanked it from my mind. Tamara has just rung to tell me I'm going to die on stage. I can't say I blame her. I'm rubbish.'

'I'm sure you're not. It's just her manner, isn't it? Try to relax. You'll be fantastic.'

'That's what Nick keeps saying.'

'You're lucky to have him.' Clare nods as she speaks. 'Most women would give anything to have a husband like yours.' Her eyes glisten as she watches Ada's tower wobble precariously. One false move and it will tumble to the ground.

Clare's mobile phone lights up. She practically dives on her handset and turns it over but not before I've seen the name on the display.

*Lisa Sullivan*

'Why is Lisa texting you?' They'd only met once at the party, I'd thought.

'Oh. I…' Clare looks away before she meets my eye again. 'We've just been comparing pregnancy notes. Exchanging experiences. I hope you don't mind?' Her cheeks are patched red.

It brings it home to me, once more, that no matter how many books I read, I will never fully understand how it feels to have a life growing inside me – acid reflux, swollen ankles, morning sickness – and all at once I want to weep into my coffee.

# CHAPTER TWENTY-SEVEN
## Now

Seeing Richard is the last thing I want to do but there's some charity paperwork that needs signing. It's on my way to Farncaster, and I've time before the scan. Normally I avoid seeing Richard on my own. The conversation is always strained and awkward.

'Can I leave this with you?' I ask the receptionist but the phone rings and, as she picks up the receiver, she gestures at me to go upstairs.

I tap on the door and push it open. Richard's office is stifling, as always. Aftershave thick in the air.

'Morning.' I keep my voice bright and breezy, hoping he doesn't realise I'm holding the envelope to my chest as though it's a shield.

'Kat.' Something flashes across his face, and I can't tell if it's irritation or panic as he stuffs papers into his drawer before slamming it shut. I wonder if they are to do with Nick's business and I feel a shift of discomfort that I don't fully know what's going on, how bad it is, and although I had intended to leave, I pull out a chair and sit.

'This is an unexpected pleasure.' Although, by the tone in his voice, Richard doesn't think it's a pleasure any more than I do.

'I've brought the proposal for the sponsorship. Could you look it over, please?'

'Now? I'm very busy.' There's a coldness to his voice that unnerves me and I suppress the urge to bite it was his idea to form the charity. For his grandma. At the very least, he could take more of an interest; he always acts as though it's such a chore, or perhaps it is only me he finds tiresome.

'I can leave it with you.'

'I wanted to talk to you anyway. About Lisa.' He steeples his fingers, his expression unreadable.

'I'm off to meet her. It's the scan today.'

'You've been authorising extra payments, Nick says? We had an agreement—'

'Nick and I are more than happy with our arrangements,' I say a little too forcefully, although I'm not too sure whether Nick is happy. A rush of heat sweeps over me. I'd tried to ask Nick whether I should be spending less with the trouble the business is in, and he'd told me not to be silly and my anger had flared that he wasn't treating me like an equal.

'I run the charity almost single-handed. I'm hardly some helpless female,' I had snapped.

'Funny. That's how you come across when you think you've seen someone skulking around outside and want protecting,' he had bit back, and although we had both quickly calmed down and apologised, the gap between us had widened that little bit more.

We never used to argue. We should be enjoying our last few weeks as a family of two, and I vow to make more of an effort.

'Perhaps it's time I drew a salary from the charity if it's that bad?' I ask Richard but I'm tentative. Reluctant to take the money I've worked so hard to raise.

Richard leans back in his chair and holds my gaze for so long I am reminded of the staring competitions we used to have: me, Lisa, and Jake. I'd always look away first. As I do now. Averting my eyes to the window and watching the sun bouncing off the rooftops outside.

'Is it you?' I ask as the silence becomes insufferable. 'Who's supposed to apply for planning permission for listed buildings?'

'Of course.'

'And yet you didn't?'

'Didn't I?'

'The stately home…' I root around in my memory. Where did Nick say it was? 'Is it in a lot of trouble? The business?'

'You can always find trouble, Kat. If you go looking for it.'

I wait for him to elaborate. He doesn't. I sigh. I know I am not going to get anything like a straight answer. 'I've got to go. Are we seeing you this weekend?'

'Not sure. I'll speak to Nick about it later.'

I nod. There's nothing more to say. I thought over the years Richard would soften towards me but, if anything, his disdain has grown. Nick can't see it; he says it's just the way Richard is; yet, if he cares so much about Nick, he should be more supportive about the surrogacy, shouldn't he? It feels like a constant tug of war for Nick's attention, and increasingly, I am wondering how much longer I can keep pulling. Something's got to give, I just hope it isn't me.

The hospital car park is full of vehicles circling like sharks, and it takes twenty-five minutes to claim a space. I clatter all my change into the parking machine and display the white ticket that cost almost as much as a pub meal on my dashboard.

I am late. I run towards the main entrance, almost turning my ankle as I swerve past a wheelchair, and am relieved to see Lisa is still there, shifting her weight from foot to foot, checking her watch.

'Sorry,' I pant. 'Couldn't park.'

'You needn't have rushed.' Lisa pulls a face. 'I've just been to check in and the sonographer is off sick today.'

'What? No!'

'Sorry. You've had the drive for nothing.'

'Let's go and talk to them. Explain I've come a long way. There must be someone else?'

'There isn't – it's a small department.'

'Have they offered you another appointment?'

'I've got to ring next week. See if he's back.'

My disappointment must show because Lisa squeezes my arm. 'If it's a long-term sickness they'll get cover or refer me to another hospital. They promised we won't have to wait too long: a couple of weeks at the very most.'

'Do you think you could call your midwife and ask if I can hear the heartbeat today?' My voice is small. Lisa's midwife sounds lovely, always setting her mind at rest. When Lisa was worried about stretch marks – she's so self-conscious when she speaks about them – her midwife gave her some bio oil to try. 'It's one of the most common things for expectant mums to worry about. The size of their bump,' she had told Lisa. 'Each woman grows and shows at her own rate. Stretch marks will fade.' She sounds nurturing and it brings me comfort to know she is taking care of Lisa.

'She's based at my doctors and she gets really booked up. I think you can buy the monitors to listen yourself.'

'Really?'

'You wouldn't believe half the stuff you can buy on eBay! I'll ask my midwife how effective they are. Let's go to the canteen. Have a mug of hot chocolate.'

As though the cream and sugar could make up for the loss I feel. I press my palm to Lisa's bump. 'I guess I'll see you another day?' I say but there is no wriggle to tell me the baby has heard, and even if he had, for I am thinking of him as a boy now, he wouldn't know I am his mum. Lisa's is the voice he hears every day. I am nothing but a stranger. Self-pity springs tears to my eyes, and Lisa gently draws my hand away from her belly.

'Come on.' She leads me into the hospital. Back into the place I was admitted after the accident. I grip her hand tightly as we weave through corridors, and it is only as we join the queue for drinks I release my grip, and she shakes her fingers as though they hurt as much as my heart.

'So this is where you work?' I ease the plastic lid off the cardboard cup and am hit with a cloud of chocolatey smelling steam.

'Yes. Well not in the canteen, obviously.'

'How can you bear it?' I am not talking about the constant noise, the rattle of trollies, the stench of neglect, but Lisa instinctively knows.

'I think of that night all the time. Did you see those black plastic chairs in A&E? That's where we sat. I felt sick as the nurse came over but I thought she must have good news. I thought if it was bad we'd be taken to a little room, like they do on TV, with shiny leaved pot plants and comfortable sofas, but it wasn't like that. When she told us Jake had died, we left the hospital, and I hoped I'd never come back. Even the smell of the disinfectant made my stomach churn for years. But not coming back...' She gives a small, sad shake of her head. 'It doesn't change what happened, and it's a good place to work. I'm helping people.'

I nod. As I raise my head to sip my drink I see someone outside the door, nose pressed against the glass like a dog begging to come inside.

'Is that—' I point. 'Aaron?'

Lisa turns her head but a family are crowding in, children whining for sweets, and the moment has passed.

'I can't believe I've seen him again.' I wrap my arms around myself.

'Again?' Lisa's brows knit together.

'I saw him in town the last time I came.'

'Did he say anything?' Her voice is shrill.

'No.' Aaron didn't have to speak. I could feel his hate, toxic and thick, and I had wished I could have hated him too but the emotion I felt, that I feel when I think of him, is always one of fear. 'Do you think that's him?' I crane my neck.

'Could be: he works here,' Lisa says.

'How can anyone employ him after?…' I'm not sure that I believe everyone deserves a second chance.

'I know. Let me use the loo and we'll get out of here.' Lisa hefts herself to her feet, and I watch her waddle towards the toilet in the corner, one hand cradling her bump.

My fluttering anxiety morphs into a fury that propels me to my feet. I don't want Aaron within spitting distance of Lisa, as though he might contaminate my baby somehow. I slip out into the corridor, and he's there. Studying the noticeboard as though it is the most interesting thing on the planet.

'I thought it was you,' I say quietly clenching my fists at my sides. 'What are you doing here?'

He spins around and he raises his hand. I flinch, but he scratches his head instead as he studies me in that way of his. I can't help noticing his wedding ring. Who in their right mind would marry him? Someone who doesn't know what he did.

Despite my earlier bravado, I find myself shaking. He takes a step forward. I take a step back. He steps forward again, and my heart hammers in my chest as the distance between us closes. I can smell tobacco on his breath. See the anger in his eyes. I back up until I am wedged in a corner, with nowhere to hide.

# CHAPTER TWENTY-EIGHT
## Then

The manager of The Three Fishes glared at us as he frothed lager into tall glasses, making yet another barbed comment about our school uniforms, but we didn't care. After final period our study leave would officially start and that was something we wanted to celebrate.

'I've got something for you,' Jake said, sliding a mobile phone across the bar. 'It's just a cheap one but I've topped it up with credit. Now we can text each other, and it won't seem so bad when you're grounded.'

I flung my arms around him, showering his face with kisses. It was utterly ridiculous to be grounded at my age. Last Sunday I had told my parents I would be at Lisa's studying and had gone to the cinema with Jake instead. Mum had rung Lisa's house to ask me to pick up some gravy granules on the way home. Lisa had tried her best to cover for me, telling Mum I had fallen asleep reading a textbook, but Mum didn't believe her, demanded she woke me up, and Lisa had to admit I wasn't there. Lisa tried to find me, to warn me, but had no idea where I was. After the film I had glided into the kitchen on a conveyor belt of happiness, with no idea I was walking into World War III.

'Where the hell have you been?' My dad sat at the table, his spine as stiff as the wood he rested his elbows on, hands pressed together as though in prayer, chin resting on index fingers.

'At Lisa's.' As soon as the words falteringly left my lips I wanted to snatch them back when I noticed Mum's shoulders stiffen as she chopped veg, the sound of the knife hitting the glass workshop saver. Liar-liar-liar.

'We know you haven't.' Dad's voice was measured and calm, and that was worse somehow than the shouting I had been expecting. 'And more fool you if you've been out with a boy. They only want one thing, you know.'

I couldn't keep the corners of my mouth from twitching as I thought about Jake unbuttoning my shirt, his fingers slipping inside my bra, his lips pressed hard against mine.

'You think this is funny, Katherine?'

'I'm nineteen,' I said, as though that would placate them. It didn't.

'Kat.' Mum wiped her hands on her apron. 'It's because you are nineteen that we worry. This is a real turning point for you. You'll leave school next month and it's important you do well in your exams. I want you to have the future—'

'She won't have a future at all if she's running about, God knows where,' Dad said.

'In a few weeks I'll be living away from home and you won't be able to keep me prisoner then. I can't wait. I hate you.' As the words spilled from my mouth I instantly knew it was the wrong thing to say.

'You're grounded,' Dad shouted.

'You can't ground me. I'm an adult!'

'I don't care how old you are. While you're living under my roof, you'll do as I say.'

'I can't wait until I'm not living under your roof. Mum...' But she was turning away from me. Back to the vegetables. Dad picked up the *Sunday Times* and held it like a barrier between us and, just like that, I was dismissed.

Now, I turned over the phone in my hands and it felt like I was holding independence.

'Shall we order food?' Aaron asked.

'I could eat a bowl of cheesy chips.' I hadn't fancied breakfast that morning and the smell of fried food drifting from the kitchen was making me ravenous.

'Me too.' Jake wrapped his arms around my waist and nuzzled my neck.

'Lis?'

'I'm not hungry.'

'Three bowls of cheesy chips please.' Aaron handed over a £20 note.

'Cheers mate.' Jake sipped his pint.

I wiped the foamy moustache from his top lip with my thumb.

'So this is it. Our last day at school,' Aaron said as we walked over to one of the high tables. The sun slicing through the window reflected off the stainless steel surface and I shaded my eyes as I climbed onto one of the tall stools, still listening to Aaron. 'I can't believe after this I'll have five years at uni. If my mum wasn't so proud of me I honestly think I'd be having second thoughts. She's told everyone I'm going to be a doctor.'

'What is it with parental pressure?' I said.

'Your dad picked your course, didn't he, Kat?' Aaron asked.

'He did but… No, you've got to guess.' My fingertips drummed suspense on the table top.

'You're not going to uni any more?' The hope in Lisa's voice was palpable, and I flattened my hand, deflated.

'I am going but I rang up admissions and there are places on the Performing Arts course, so I'm swapping.'

'Wow. What about your dad?'

I shrugged. 'What he doesn't know won't hurt him.' In truth I was terrified of him finding out before I went, but after he grounded me, I thought long and hard. He was always going to treat me like a child while I was still acting like one. It was time to take charge of my life.

'Hollywood, here you come.' Jake raised his glass.

'I'd be happy with a stage career.' We chinked.

'Are you okay?' I said to Lisa. She was jabbing at her soda water with her straw. Her half-moon of lemon bobbing up and down.

'It's all right for all of you. Off to uni.'

'You didn't want to? Mum did say—' Jake started.

'I know I didn't,' she snapped. 'I still don't but… I dunno. In a way I thought school would last forever. It's come round so quickly. You're all leaving me, and now dad's gone.' Lisa and Jake's dad had been having an affair and had run off with his 25-year-old mistress. Lisa vowed never to talk to him again. 'I don't want to leave Mum on her own,' she said. Nancy was spitting vitriol every time I went to visit. Spewing hatred against women who had affairs with married men.

'We're not leaving you.' I reached across and squeezed her hand.

'It's not like you'll never see me again, sis,' Jake said. 'I'll be home every holiday and some weekends.'

'Bet you won't,' Lisa said. 'Your uni isn't far from Kat's. You'll be spending all your time together.'

'We'll always have time for you,' I said.

'But it will be different. You'll all have exciting lives, and I'll be stuck here in some crap job in shitty Farncaster.'

'There's nothing wrong in staying in the same town,' I said, although I was itching to leave. 'By the time we finish uni, we'll be broke, with a mountain of debt and you'll probably have settled down with an amazing man and had a family.'

'God, no.' Lisa shuddered. 'You know how I feel about kids. Horrible, whiney things. Babies aren't for me.'

'You might feel differently in a few years. People change,' I said.

'That's what I'm scared of.' Lisa's eyes were glazed with tears.

'Stop being paranoid. I won't change. No matter how many new people I meet you'll always be my best friend, Lis.'

'Promise?'

'Promise.'

And at that time I meant it.


My euphoria regarding the future was tinged with sadness as I emptied my locker. It was the end of an era. The corridor was devoid of students but was jammed full of memories. Me and Lisa shuffling along, heads down, new school shoes squeaking on the lino during our first day at a place that felt a world apart from our small, safe, primary school. Later, sprinting to the canteen, knowing they always ran out of pizza, slowing, giggling, as Mr Lemmington barked 'walk, don't run!'

On my way to Lisa's locker I pressed the corner back down of the *West Side Story* poster that was hanging off the wall. Not long now until the performance.

'You nearly done?' I clapped Lisa on the shoulder. She jumped, her books clattering to the floor.

'Sorry.' I crouched down, gathering her strewn belongings.

'Leave them.' She shielded her possessions with her arms, as though they were precious gems rather than tatty textbooks.

'It's okay.' I picked up a folder. A packet fell out. Yellowish powder inside. 'What's this?'

'None of your business,' Aaron said.

I hadn't noticed him appear beside me. He tried to snatch the packet. I closed my fingers around it.

'Aaron, what are you?…' My eyes bounced between his face and Lisa's. The guilt and the shock. The anger. I stepped back. My hand a tight fist.

'What's going on, Lisa?'

'It's nothing.'

'If it's nothing, why are you hiding it?'

Lisa caught her lower lip between her teeth.

'If you don't tell me, I'll go to Mr Lemmington.' My voice rose with anger.

'It's an appetite suppressant,' Lisa snapped.

'What exactly is it? This appetite suppressant?'

'Stop fucking shouting, Kat,' Aaron hissed out his words.

I started to say there was no one in the corridor to overhear, but the expression on his face stopped me.

'It's harmless,' he said. 'My sister took it.'

'So they sell this in Boots, do they? If I took it in there, the pharmacist would know what it was?'

There was a beat.

'What. Is. It?' I demanded.

'It's mephedrone but—'

'Fuck, Lisa. We studied that in Health class. The effects—'

'If you take it in large amounts, yes, but I'm not taking it to get high. It's okay to use as an appetite suppressant in small amounts. Aaron says—'

'Aaron's not a bloody doctor, is he?'

'It's perfectly safe, Kat,' Aaron said.

'No drug is safe.' I don't know whether I was furious at Lisa for taking it, or furious with myself for not noticing. 'That's why you've been having mood swings. I can't believe you encouraged this,' I said to Aaron. He folded his arms and glared at me, and suddenly I understood. Why he always had money in the pub but didn't have a part-time job. How he'd 'get by' at uni. 'You're the one who gave her it. There was no "special diet" your sister was on. You're dealing?'

'I'm not "dealing". I'm helping teenage girls who want to lose weight. It's just a bit of cash for uni. No harm done. You've got to admit, Lisa looks great now she's thinner. I'm doing a public service.'

'You bastard.' Visions of the films we'd seen during drugs ed replayed in my mind. The long-term effects on mental health. The people who had died. How could he call himself Lisa's friend?

'I'm reporting you.' I had to, didn't I? I couldn't let him ruin lives.

'Don't, Kat. People will get the wrong idea. It's small quantities. A diet aid, that's all.'

I hesitated. Was that really all he was doing? Selling small amounts to girls? But then I remembered Perry approaching Aaron at his party: 'Got me a pressie?' he'd asked, clearly off his face.

'I don't believe you,' I said quietly.

It happened in an instant. My back slamming against the lockers; his hands around my throat. The smell of lager as he snarled: 'If you report me, I could get arrested. Lose my place at uni. I swear, Kat, if you tell, if you ruin my future, I'll fucking kill you if it's the last thing I do.'

# CHAPTER TWENTY-NINE
## Now

'Are you sure you have to go?' I perch on the edge of the bed as Nick pulls shirts from hangers, socks from drawers, folding them neatly into his overnight bag. He looks pale and exhausted, and I know I should be supporting him, packing for him, but the encounter with Aaron at the hospital has shaken me to the core, despite him slinking away when Lisa put herself between us and told him to 'fuck off'. There's something odd about that encounter that niggles at the back of my mind, but I can't put my finger on what it is. I've barely slept these past two weeks. I find myself constantly looking out of the window. Convinced I can hear footsteps crunching on the gravel. I've taken to leaving the curtains drawn all day. The footprints in the snow much on my mind again, and I try to recall the size of Aaron's feet. Was it him who was here? Paranoia has wrapped itself around me like ivy and, much to my shame, I have noticed Nick talks slower now, as though I might have trouble understanding, and I do. It often sounds as though he is speaking from far away. Even the weatherman predicting the fast-approaching May will be one of the warmest on record for years, doesn't lift my mood. Someone is trying to scare me, I know, and when I insist again someone is watching the house, Nick looks at me. His eyes full of concern. Full of pity.

'Sorry. I told you I'd have to go back to the site. It's unavoidable.' Nick closes the lid of the case, zipping it up. 'Please try and relax, Kat. I'm worried about you. You hardly seem fit to look after yourself. We could have a baby here in as little as three months.'

His words are bruising, but worse than that, is the feeling he is right.

'I'm trying.' I know he wants me to say I am fine, but I can't, so I say what I think I should be feeling. 'It's just Lisa's pregnancy seems endless and after Dewei and Mai… I'm so scared something will go wrong this time too.' With the words, tears come and I think perhaps I have inadvertently spoken the truth. I am scared I'll never become a mum so I am projecting my fear onto something else, something imagined, because if I stop to think about all the things that could go wrong with this baby, I would drive myself mad.

The mattress sags as Nick sits, wrapping his arm around me. I lean my head against his shoulder.

'Don't you think I feel the same way? It's hard to stay positive when you've been through what we have. I have those "what if" thoughts too. Something could go wrong with the birth. Lisa might bond with the baby and not sign the residency order; the court might not approve the payments, but we can't let our doubts shadow this experience.'

'I know. Sorry.' I sniff hard, feeling closer to him than I have in weeks. 'I could come with you?'

'To a building site? Not much fun. Besides, you've got your rehearsal, and Lisa's coming to stay, isn't she?'

Immediately my mood lifts. I'm so looking forward to spending time with Lisa, talking babies.

Nick carries on packing, throwing his toiletries into his washbag, and I try not to mind that he's taking the Boss aftershave I bought him for Christmas, not the Body Shop one he usually wears to work.

'I'll just use the loo and I'll be off.' The en-suite door clicks shut, and I sit on the bed, miserably picking at a hangnail. I hate goodbyes. I'm relieved as the landline starts to ring and I run downstairs.

I am puffed out as I pick up the handset; we really should get another one upstairs but we rarely use it. Even now I wait for the mechanical PPI tone to kick in, wondering why I ever bothered answering it at all. Instead there is silence, and I say hello several times before putting down the phone.

'That's odd,' I say to Nick as seconds later he hefts his bag downstairs. 'There was no one there.'

'Probably a call centre in India; they can't always connect.'

'I suppose.'

'Right, I'm off.' Nick pulls his coat out of the cloakroom. 'Have you seen my scarf?'

'The one I bought you for Christmas? No. Hopefully you won't need it. Hot weather is coming. Apparently.' We still have our heating on for now.

Nick is distracted as he kisses me goodbye. I pull him into a hug, burying my head in his chest, and he squeezes me tightly. 'Everything is fine,' he says, even though I haven't asked. It's as though he is trying to reassure himself.

The air is nippy as I stand in the doorway, watching him throw his things into the boot and, although the spring bulbs are breaking through the soil – the borders speckled with yellow, white, blue – my breath clouds in front of me. Nick climbs into his car and drives away. I wave until he disappears around the corner and close the door, walk towards the kitchen. Behind me, the phone starts to ring.

'Hello.' I speak as soon as I answer this time but there's silence again. I wait a second to see if it is a call centre trying to connect, and I hear it. A breath. I cover the mouthpiece with my hand. Was that my breathing I heard? And there it is again. A breath. Barely audible but someone is there. I slam down the receiver and rub my arms. Still chilled from the morning air, but my goosebumps linger.

I am walking into the kitchen to put the kettle on when the ringing starts again, and I snatch up the handset and shout: 'who's there?' I wait. The silence is thick. Heavy. There's a faint rustling sound and I think about all the people it could be. All the people I don't want it to be, and I slowly put the receiver down. It's nothing, I tell myself, but it does feel like something.

Tamara clicks her tongue as I mess up the dance routine again. My chest heaves and I know my face is as red as the T-shirt that is damp with exertion.

'You're not concentrating, Kat. Is something on your mind?' she asks.

'Sorry,' I say. Hunched over. Hands on knees. I almost wish I hadn't come, but if I miss another rehearsal, I know I'll be replaced, and I'm not quite ready to give up on my dream.

'It's okay. It takes time.' Alex stops the track.

'And a certain level of fitness,' Tamara mutters loud enough for me to hear.

I had been meaning to exercise each morning. Brisk walks around the block. Getting into a routine so that when the baby is here we can get out in the fresh air every day, but leaving the house is getting harder and harder. Every day I find a new excuse. The blackening sky. The threat of rain. Now a stitch burns a hole in my side, my heart is racing, and I wish I had made more effort. There are only the three of us here. We're trying to perfect the Tony and Maria parts before tomorrow's rehearsal when the rest of the cast will be present.

'I need some water.' I shuffle into the kitchen. My legs wobbly, muscles fatigued. I twist the tap and cup my hands under the cool water and splash my face before filling a tea-stained mug and gulping greedily.

'You're doing well.'

I start. I hadn't heard Alex come in and water dribbles down my chin. I wipe it with the back of my hand.

'I don't know if it's too much.' I say this at every rehearsal. 'It's not as easy as I remember.' In my head I'm still a teenager, but my body knows differently.

'I think you're capable. Very capable.' Alex always says this too. He steps forward and reaches out a hand, and his thumb brushes my cheek. 'An eyelash.' He blows the pad of his thumb. 'Make a wish.'

'I wish we could get on with the rehearsal,' mutters Tamara behind us.

'Sorry.' It's all I seem to have said today.

Alex heads out of the door. As I follow him Tamara calls me back.

'I've something for you anyway.' She pushes a leaflet into my hand. It's for Weight Watchers. 'A few of the group go,' she says. 'You don't have to but…' She shrugs. 'It isn't as straightforward getting the costumes changed as I had thought. Might be easier to lose a few pounds?'

Back on stage Alex and I gaze into each other's eyes as we sing 'Tonight'. My voice wobbles and falls off-key, and Tamara stops the backing CD.

'Can we call it a day?'

I grab my bag and my sense of failure and, as I hurry towards the exit, Tamara starts to sing 'Tonight', and it's so beautiful. So effortless. The tense feeling in my chest tightens.

The welcoming smell of tomato and basil soup greets me as I push open the front door. I'm glad I took the time to dig out the slow cooker and throw lunch together before I left for rehearsal. Despite the disaster it had been, I feel a sense of achievement just for getting out.

By the time I have showered and changed there is barely time to plump up the cushions before Lisa is knocking on the door, and I envelop her in a huge hug. Despite her loose-fitting T-shirt I can see her bump has grown considerably, and I am glad she must have her appetite back. I press my palm against it, feeling the solidity.

'It's hard, isn't it?' I think of my soft rolls of fat.

'It has to be to protect the little one. Like its own room, I guess.' She pulls back.

'Sorry. Didn't mean to manhandle you.' I take her huge overnight bag and usher her inside.

'It's okay. It's amazing how many people think they can touch my bump. In the queue at Tesco yesterday the cashier leant over and rubbed my belly, and I felt like saying "I'm not bloody Buddha. It won't bring you any luck." One woman wanted to see my bump – as though I'd want anyone looking at my stretch marked skin! Weirdo.'

'It must be intrusive,' I say but if it were me, I'd want everyone to share.

'The woman in the post office asked me how many weeks I was, and when I told her, she said my bump was huge and asked if I was having twins.'

We are both silent for a moment.

'People can be so fucking rude. My bump is too big. Too small. I'm carrying high so it's a girl, or I'm carrying low and it's a boy. Everyone has an opinion. Even my midwife says as the heartbeat is slow she thinks it's a boy.'

'Slow?'

'Yes, but normal. Nothing to worry about.'

I reach for her bag. 'Go and put your feet up. I'll nip upstairs with your things and unpack for you.'

'No!' Lisa almost shouts, and I let go of the handles of her bag as though they have scalded me.

'Sorry.' She offers a weak smile. 'I can do my own unpacking. But I've something to share with you first.' Lisa looks exhausted as she sinks into the sofa and pats the space next to her.

Intrigued I sit and watch as she pulls out her iPhone.

'Listen.' She presses play.

At first it sounds like the noise you hear when you hold a shell against your ear on the beach, whooshing and white noise, but then I hear it, a rapid thud-thud-thud.

'Is that?'

'This little one's heartbeat.' Lisa's hand rests on top of her bump.

'Can I?'

Lisa presses play again, and it's the sweetest thing I ever heard. The sound of life. Of hope. It doesn't sound in the slightest bit slow to me. Every protective instinct lying dormant in my cells springs into being.

'I'll send it to you as an MP3,' Lisa says, and I nod, not realising I am crying until Lisa brushes tears from my cheeks with her fingertips.

We sit, for the longest time, Lisa's head on my shoulder, our fingers laced together, as I play the recording again and again, and it is in this moment, perhaps for the first time, I am aware it is not just love I feel towards this baby. I *am* love.

I'm a mum.

I ladle soup into bowls and carry them carefully over to the table before I slip into the seat opposite Lisa.

'Bread?' I offer the basket of French stick.

Lisa stretches forward and her sleeve rides up. There are tiny bruises dotted over her forearm.

'Are you eating enough iron?'

'Do you mean meat? I think so. Why?'

'The bruises.' I gesture towards her arm. 'It's a sign of anaemia. Perhaps you should have a blood test. You do look pale.'

Lisa doesn't carry that glow some pregnant women seem to have. She looks washed out. Black half-moons fill the hollows under her eyes.

'I'll mention it when I next see the midwife.'

'Lisa, you are looking after yourself, aren't you?' She knows what I mean.

'Kat, we talked about this in depth before we started this surrogacy thing. I made one mistake as a teenager in a desperate bid to be thin. Please don't bring it up again. It was ten years ago. We've talked it through. I told you I've never taken anything since.'

'I know. I do believe you. Honest. It's just you don't look well.'

'Everything is fine. Anyway, I've another appointment for a scan. Next Friday. You'll come? You'll see for yourself baby is healthy.'

'It's not good enough, Lisa. I've been looking at the National Institute for Health and Care Excellence online. You really should have had the scan by now.'

'Ideally, yes. My midwife is cross but she's been keeping an extra eye on me. If there isn't a sonographer available what can they do? You know how overstretched the NHS is. I get people shouting at me almost daily for things that aren't my fault.'

'I guess. I read some women choose not to have a scan. I wonder why?'

'God knows. I definitely can't wait for mine. A chance to see your baby.' Lisa smiles as she looks at me. 'Do you want to know the sex?'

'I'm not sure.' I rest my spoon on the side of my bowl. 'With Mai and Dewei we knew, of course, and it helped with the nursery, the clothes.' I try not to think of the folded sleep suits they would never wear. 'But this time it might be nice to have a surprise. What do you think?'

Lisa studies me for a second before answering. 'I think you *should* have a surprise, Kat.'

I am puzzled by her tone for a moment until she slides a gift-wrapped box towards me.

'What's this?' I turn it over in my hands as though it might reveal itself to me.

'Open it.'

I tear off the candy-striped paper and laugh. It's a bottle of Eva perfume.

'Eva Longoria finally got her arse into gear.' Lisa smiles as I spray my wrists.

'You remembered,' I say as I inhale jasmine and lily of the valley.

Lisa looks me straight in the eye. 'I remember *everything*.'

Later, I have cleared away the lunch things and am on the sofa, my feet tucked under me, flicking through a copy of *Mother and Baby* I bought. I have sent Lisa for a lie-down. She looked tired and pinched.

The phone trills, and I hurry to the hallway and lift the receiver before it can wake Lisa. I lift it to my ear and hear the static coming down the line. 'Hello?' It's a question, not a greeting, and the air feels charged with tension and, all of a sudden, I feel angry, not afraid. Whoever is wasting my time, let's see how they like it. I stay on the line, silent, waiting for them to get bored. To hang up. But minutes tick by and I shift my weight from one foot to the other. Lisa will be down soon and now this seems childish. Fruitless. I slam the handset down but before I can return to the lounge, a shadow falls. There's a figure outside the frosted glass of the front door. I wait for the knock; instead, light illuminates the hall once more and there's scuffling, as though someone is crawling around the porch. I tiptoe into the lounge. Part the slats of the blind with my thumb and forefinger. The afternoon is bright. Quiet. There's no one there. No sound of a vehicle.

I go back to the front door and press my ear against it. There's nothing to be heard but birdsong. I fling open the door and a breeze washes over me. There's no one on the street. No mysterious figure, and I chide myself for my overactive imagination.

But that's before I look down.

Before I see it.

On the doorstep, is a wreath, a green ribbon stretched across the centre. 'RIP' written in blood red letters.

# CHAPTER THIRTY
## Now

Sunday sunshine streams through the window but it doesn't lighten my mood. I barely slept last night. The wreath and the phone calls had set me on edge, and even with Lisa here, without Nick the house seemed too cold. Too empty. Yesterday evening I went over to Clare's to see if she had noticed anyone hanging around the house, but she wasn't at home. I rang Nick to talk things through, but it had gone straight to voicemail, and in bed I had felt myself growing more and more agitated as I'd tossed and turned. The 'RIP' in blood red letters was etched onto my mind. I lay staring at the ceiling as the house creaked and settled around me, imagining each groan of the floorboard was someone creeping up the stairs. *RIP.* It was only when I slipped in my earbuds and played the recording of the baby's heart I began to relax.

My legs feel heavy as I climb out of bed this morning. I trudge over to the door and lift my fleecy dressing gown from its hook. It may be spring but the mornings are still chilly.

Lisa is already in the kitchen, nibbling on toast.

'Did you find everything you need?' The breakfast bar is bare save Lisa's plate, and I pull open the cupboard and lift out jars of local honey, apricot jam and marmite.

'Trying to make me throw up?'

'You still have morning sickness? Have you mentioned it to your midwife?' According to my book the nausea should have passed and she should be full of energy. She looks as exhausted as I feel.

'She said some women have it throughout. I'm just unlucky, I think.'

'But if you're not getting enough nutrients—'

'I'm hardly wasting away.' Lisa rubs her stomach. 'Anyway, you don't look the picture of health yourself this morning.'

I perch onto a stool next to Lisa and pluck a piece of toast from the rack. 'I didn't sleep well. That wreath—'

'You're not still thinking about that? It probably got delivered to the wrong address.'

'But why didn't the person who delivered it knock on the door? It seems odd to just leave it on the step, don't you think?'

'Not really. It's not like delivering a bouquet of red roses, is it? Something happy? Where there's a wreath, there's a loss and that makes people uncomfortable.'

'What if it *was* meant for me?'

'Why would it be?' Lisa asks.

'Punishment?'

'For what?' I can feel Lisa's eyes on me but I can't look at her. 'For Jake?'

I touch the cross around my neck. 'Someone is out to get me, I know.' Paranoia is as thick as the strawberry jam I spread on my toast. It looks like blood. I push it away.

'Lis.' I hate myself for asking. 'What was in your bag yesterday you didn't want me to see?' I can't help analysing her panic as I'd offered to unpack.

'The perfume. For fuck's sake, Kat. What are you implying?'

'Nothing. Sorry. It's just that it's almost the anniversary.' I always struggle at this time of year but somehow this year is worse. *Ten years.*

'Don't you think I don't know when the fucking anniversary is?' Lisa's eyes are blazing.

'Sorry, I—'

'So you bloody should be.'

'Jake wouldn't want us to—'

'Don't you think I know what Jake would and wouldn't have wanted? He was *my* brother, Kat.'

'I know. Sorry. Please can we forget this? Move on?'

Lisa is silent. Anger still radiating from her like heat.

'Lisa. Forgive me?'

''Course.' We lean forward and have an awkward one-armed hug. With forgiveness should come peace but the wreath by the back door seems to taunt us. *RIP*. There isn't always peace for the ones left behind, is there?

'Are you sure you won't be bored?' I say to Lisa, putting the car in reverse and backing off the drive, past Lisa's Fiat 500. I'm glad to see it's back on the road after the money I gave her for repairs. The thought of anyone watching me rehearse makes me feel faint. Goodness knows how I'll feel when I'm on stage in front of an audience.

'I'm looking forward to it,' she says, and I believe her. At school she'd always sit cross-legged on the hall floor as I practised, eyes following my every move, clapping, even when I forgot my lines.

I drive slowly past Clare's house looking for a sign she is awake. I want to ask her if she saw who delivered the wreath yesterday. Her bedroom curtains are still drawn and the post is still sticking out of her letterbox. Ada must be letting her have a lie-in.

In the community centre I introduce Lisa to everyone, and she is bombarded with questions from the women. She glances at me uncomfortably, unsure what to say. I watch the fuss everyone makes of her, the seat that is produced, the drink, the biscuits. I want to share that, at nearly twenty-six weeks, Beanie is the size of a spring onion and is inhaling and exhaling small amounts of amniotic fluid, developing their lungs, but no one ever thinks to ask me.

Tamara is friendlier today, smiling as she presses play on the backing track. Keeping my eyes trained on Lisa it is easy to imagine I am back in that school hall, shimmying and shaking away my adult insecurities, until I am once again the young girl full of hope, full of possibilities. I sidestep, twirl, and my voice has never soared so high, carrying my emotion up to the fluorescent strip lights buzzing and flickering on the ceiling. In front of me Lisa morphs into Jake, and all that I am, all that I want to be, goes into my performance until the last bars fade and I am crouching on the stage, chest heaving. Once again I am aware of Alex telling me I am magnificent. Lisa stands, clapping, and the harried expression she has been wearing is replaced by one of utter joy, and I know she feels it too. She feels Jake too.

My legs are trembling as I step off the stage. Alex proffers his hand, and I take it and when I am back on level ground he doesn't let it go but I am glad as I lean into him limply.

'You were marvellous.' Lisa hugs me. 'Maria! Finally!'

'Not quite as glamorous.' I pull at my T-shirt sticking to my skin. 'I'm just going to freshen up.'


The toilet is small and dingy. I tug blue paper towels from the dispenser and dab my skin dry before running a brush through my hair. Once dressed, I pull at the door but it is locked. It can't be. The caretaker opens it when he knows we are coming and locks it after we leave. I pull at the handle again. It's definitely locked. The room is hot and airless. There aren't any windows, and rationally I know that I won't be here forever. Someone will come and find me. But panic rises all the same, and I am sucking in air, feeling the chemicals of the toilet cleaner catch the back of my throat. I am trapped. I feel light-headed. My heart beating rapidly in my chest. And I bang on the doors with my fists, fighting the urge to scream. Fear bubbles and I don't know what is then and what is now.

*

*'Please help.'* It was almost a whisper. I had been alone for hours and my throat was sore from shouting. My hands stinging from banging on the door that rattled and reverberated every time I hit it. I have to believe he won't hurt me, but I'd seen the look in his eye and I wasn't sure.

'Please. I'll be good. Please.' My hands were clasped together, and I thought I was speaking to God but he didn't answer. No one answered. It was hot. The air stagnant with the smell of my own fear. My hands flew to my throat. I was drawing in oxygen through short, sharp bursts through my nose and there was a mounting pressure in my chest. I was going to suffocate. I was going to die here. 'Please!' I shouted this time, rattling the door as hard as I could. 'What do you want?' But even as I ask there's a horrible dawning realisation, and I know what he wants. I lie on the floor and curl into a ball. 'No. No. No. I won't do it. I won't.'


'Kat?'

'Lisa. Thank God. I can't get out.' I tug at the door.

'Hang on.' There's a pause. The handle turns and the air cools as the door falls open. 'It was stuck, that's all.'

'I thought…' My distress rises again.

'I know what you thought.' Lisa strokes my hair. 'I know.'

And I cling to her, grateful she is here.

# CHAPTER THIRTY-ONE
## Then

The handle to the locker was pressing hard against my spine but my body was turning numb, the feel of Aaron's hands squeezing my throat fading away. My fingers clawed at his grip. It felt as though my skull was expanding, a balloon inflating inside my head. I couldn't breathe. Couldn't swallow. My eyeballs ached, the edges of my vision blurred and darkened and I felt myself slipping, sliding. Just as I was surrendering to the feeling of nothingness, light and noise came rushing back. I slumped to the floor where I covered my throat with my hands as I sucked in air.

'For fuck's sake, Aaron.' Lisa was thumping him on the chest.

'I didn't…' I could feel his gaze on me. 'I wasn't…'

'Just fuck off.' Lisa shoved him. Hard.

'But if Kat—'

'I'll talk to Kat.'

Their words were muffled. My body shaking with shock.

Aaron ran his fingers through his hair and, for a second, I thought he wasn't going to leave, but he said: 'you'd better keep her quiet, Lis.' As his footsteps pounded down the corridor, I tried to stand, but my legs wouldn't support me.

'Let's go and talk.' Lisa gripped my hands to pull me up, and for the first time I noticed how frail she had become. How awful she looked. Huge purple shadows under her eyes. Skin pale. I'd thought it was the pressure of the exams – what sort of friend had I been?

'I said I'd meet Jake.' It hurt to talk. I brushed at my throat, still feeling a pressure there.

'Jake? It's always fucking Jake, isn't it?' Suddenly she was furious. 'This isn't about you, or Jake, or Aaron. It's about me. For once, it's about me.'

'You need help,' I said in a voice that sounded nothing like mine. The balloon inside my head was deflating, dizziness tilted the floor.

'For what? Wanting to be thinner? If that's the case most of the girls in our year need help too.'

'There are healthy ways…' I couldn't think straight, my head swimming.

'It's no different to SlimFast shakes or those herbal tablets that promise quick weight loss. You can buy those everywhere. If they were that unhealthy, they wouldn't sell them, would they?'

'It's not remotely the same as SlimFast. Why didn't you tell me, Lis? I'm here for you.'

'That makes a bloody change.' She turned and ran, and I stumbled as I tried to catch her, my shoulder crashing into the metal lockers.

'Lisa, wait.'


We were halfway to hers by the time I caught up with her. She spun around to face me.

'You mustn't tell, Kat.' It was the first time I was to hear those words that week. The second time… I try not to think about the second time. It's almost more than I can bear.

'Lisa, it isn't just you. What if someone has a bad reaction? Dies? Do you want that on your conscience?'

'No one is going to die. It's not heroin, Kat. So yeah, it gives me a bit of a buzz but not in a bad way. It feels good. Happy. You should try it and then you'd see it's not so bad.'

'Lisa, listen to yourself.'

'I have to! You never listen to me any more.'

'That's not fair, I—'

'It's all about my brother, isn't it? You don't care about me.'

'I do.' That much was true, but maybe I didn't care in the all-consuming-centre-of-my-world way I had before. The fabric of our relationship had become unravelled, knitting back together in an entirely different way. The edges no longer seamless. Sometimes it was dizzying keeping up with the ever-shifting dynamics. The vying for attention.

'Jake. Jake. Jake.' Lisa spun around slowly in a circle, hands clasped over her ears like a child. It was frightening. I almost didn't recognise her.

'Stop it.' I grabbed her wrists tightly and pulled her hands down.

'Jake. Jake—'

The slap I gave her stung my palm, cracked like a whip. To this day I don't know which of us was more shocked. I stood rooted to the pavement long after Lisa had disappeared around the corner, and as I turned and began to walk home, my hand still tingled.

That night I had told my parents I felt too sick to eat dinner. That was true, at least. I texted Jake to tell him that I had a headache and was having an early night. I didn't know what to say to him. Lisa was his sister and he had a right to know, but she was also my best friend, and my loyalty felt shredded. What should I do? It took me ages to make a decision as I tossed and turned in the heat, kicking the covers off before dragging them back up to my chin again when I felt cold.

At midnight my phone vibrated. Jake.

*Do you feel any better? Missing you.*

*Missing you too.*

*Fancy meeting in the park – it's too warm to sleep?*

I hesitated. I was going to have to face him some time. Talk things through.

*I'll meet you in 20.*

A clamp tightened around my chest as I silently crept across the landing, being careful to avoid the loose bit of carpet at the top of the stairs Dad still hadn't fixed. One step. Two. The third creaked, despite my carrying my shoes in my hand. I froze, waiting for the hallway to flood with light. For my parents to shout: 'Where do you think you are going?', but there was nothing. Somehow, the silence seemed the loudest thing of all. I pressed forward, descending the rest of the staircase as quickly as I could, holding my breath as though they might be able to hear me exhale, but I was unable to quieten the thudding of my heart which sounded terrifyingly loud. The hallway was shrouded in darkness. I caught my hip on the handle of the cupboard under the stairs, and the sharp pain tugged a cry from my lips. I clamped my teeth together and hobbled into the kitchen. It was lighter in there. Moonlight pouring through the window. My stomach rolled at the stale smell of the fried eggs mum had cooked for dinner. What was I doing? I reached for the back door, my fingertips gripped the key. Every instinct in me was telling me to go back to bed; I was bound to get caught. And yet I slipped on my shoes and turned the key. The back door creaked open.

I tiptoed down the side of the house. Paused as the latch on the gate squeaked open. It wasn't too late. I could go back to bed, but while my mind wavered, my feet didn't falter. I ran as fast as I could, not slowing until I reached the park.

\*

He was there, in shadows, slowly spinning on the roundabout that squeak, squeak, squeaked.

I suppose if I had slowed down, I might have realised the figure was too tall to be Jake. Too stocky. I suppose I might have noticed the white van parked outside the park gates. But as it was, it wasn't until I drew alongside him I realised it wasn't Jake at all.

It was Aaron.

The initial stab of betrayal I felt as I realised Lisa must have texted me from Jake's phone paled in comparison to the fear that rose as Aaron stood and loomed towards me. A twisted expression on his face.

# CHAPTER THIRTY-TWO
## Now

The community centre shrinks in my rear-view mirror. Lisa chats about the singing, the dancing, but all I hear is white noise. The terror I'd felt at being locked in the toilet still nestles beneath my skin, and I drive faster than I should. Desperate to be home. To feel safe.

'Shit.' I've pulled into the cul-de-sac too fast, almost in the path of an Interflora van. My brakes squeal as I screech to a halt.

As the van stops and cuts its engine, I put my car into neutral and pull on my handbrake. The delivery driver steps out, opening the back doors, and I am fearing the worst, but instead of a wreath, he pulls out a bouquet. Sunshine sunflowers and creamy roses. I puff out a sigh of relief. Sunflowers are my favourite, and Nick includes them in every bouquet he sends me. I think he must be feeling guilty about being away, although I see from his car on our driveway he is already back.

'Are they for me?' I step out of the car and flash a smile as I hold out my hands.

'Number eight?' the driver asks.

'No. I…' I glance over the road and gesture towards Clare's house. He thanks me and I stand, hand shading the sun, and watch as Clare opens the door. Even from this distance I can see the joy lighting up her face.

*

Inside, I call Nick's name, racing through the house. In the kitchen I hear the gurgle of water gushing through the pipes above me. Nick must be in the shower. I tell Lisa I'll be back in a sec and take the stairs two at a time, bursting into the en-suite.

'You're home!' I state the obvious.

'Are you okay?' Nick studies me, and I don't know what to say. How can I tell him I thought I was locked in a toilet? Someone delivered a wreath to the wrong address? Dialled the wrong number? It sounds ridiculous, and he's already looking at me with concern, the way he does when my panic attacks are fierce. Snatching my breath. Rendering me helpless. He wouldn't understand, and how could he unless I tell him the truth? The urge to be honest bites at me but the ramifications are enormous and I would crumble under the weight of them.

'How was your trip?' I deflect. Even in the steam of the bathroom Nick looks washed out.

The minty shower gel swirling in soapy suds at his feet clearly hasn't refreshed him. He has lost weight, his stomach almost flat. He twists off the dial and the showerhead drip-drip-drips. 'It was fine. Everything is close to being sorted. I might need to go away for another weekend though.' He yawns. 'An early night is in order.'

'I'm up for that.' I'll sleep easier with him next to me.

'I might sleep in the spare room tonight. I'm so knackered. You can stay up late with Lisa and not have to worry about waking me when you come up to bed.'

My protests gather and retreat. He's never slept in the spare room before but his eyes are rimmed red and he does look exhausted.

"I'll start dinner.'

'I'm not that hungry.' He steps out of the cubicle.

'You must eat with us. Lisa is here.'

'I don't know if I can cope with all the baby talk. The family stuff. Sorry,' he adds as my face falls. 'Of course I'll join you. I'm just shattered. I'll be down soon.'

I hesitate for a second before leaving the room but he doesn't speak again, scouring furiously at his skin with a rough white towel instead, as though he wishes he could rub himself away.

In the kitchen Lisa is lifting things out of the fridge. 'I thought I'd cook.' She sets a box of eggs on the side.

'I'm supposed to be looking after you.'

'I know it shook you up. What happened earlier.'

'Do you think someone deliberately locked me in?'

'Why would they do that?' Lisa tilts her head to one side as she waits for my answer.

'I don't know.' Outside the window the sky is darkening. Day dissolving into night. 'What are you cooking?'

'How about a frittata? Do you have a silicon dish?'

'No, but Clare probably does. I need to see if she's sold her raffle tickets yet for the bank holiday fundraiser.' I jam my feet back into my shoes.

Outside, the wind is whipping the cherry tree outside our house and it creaks and bends. I knock on Clare's door and wrap my arms around myself to keep out the biting chill as I wait.

'Kat!' Surprise crosses her face.

I shuffle from foot to foot trying to keep warm. 'Could I borrow a silicon baking dish?'

'Sure.' She hesitates, glances behind her before stepping backwards. 'Come in a sec.'

'Gorgeous flowers.' The bouquet delivered earlier stands on the coffee table in a cracked silver vase. 'Secret admirer?'

'Unfortunately not.' I wait for her to elaborate further, but she walks into the kitchen and calls over her shoulder: 'I'll just grab you the silicon dish.'

Her heels click-click-click against the tiles in the kitchen. I can't resist crossing the lounge and picking out the card that came with the flowers. Scribbled in blue biro is the letter 'N' and a single x but that is enough to make my heart twist. Clare's footsteps grow louder, and I drop the card and pick up a brochure for Italy and thumb through it, hardly taking in the images of brilliant blue sky and white sandy beaches. Nick and I never did book that holiday.

'It looks stunning doesn't it?' Clare peers over my shoulder. 'I fancy the coast but think I'm going to start with Rome.'

'Expensive?' The word slips out automatically but she is always complaining Akhil doesn't pay maintenance.

'We can dream.' She lifts the brochure from my hand and replaces it with a silicone dish. 'No hurry to bring it back.'

As she ushers me out to the hallway I start to ask about the raffle tickets but trail off mid-sentence as I notice a scarf hanging on a hook behind the front door: a blue cashmere scarf that looks just like Nick's. I turn to Clare. She busies herself unlocking the front door, head lowered, hair falling in front of her face, but she can't hide two pink spots, high on her cheeks.


Nick is speaking in muted tones and I hover outside his study, ear pressed to the door.

'It'll be longer next time,' he says and there's a pause before he continues. 'No, I haven't told her.' A sigh. 'I know, I know but it isn't easy. Too much water under the bridge.'

My heart quickens and there's a low humming noise in my ears.

I'm still standing in the hallway when the study door clicks open. I have one hand on the wall as though reassuring myself some things are solid. Reliable.

'Who were you talking to?'

'Richard,' Nick says without a beat.

'What were you talking about?'

'I rang to invite him for lunch. I hope that's okay?'

It would be if I believed him but I know my husband and the flush staining his neck tells me all I need to know. He is lying. Neither of us speak, conveying silent messages with our eyes. Eventually I say 'fine' and walk, head high, into the kitchen, where I clink open the fridge and pour a glass of wine, sipping it slowly while I try to put my thoughts into some sort of order. I need time to think things through properly, but if I don't challenge him about the bouquet and the scarf, am I accepting his lies? Does that make me as bad as him? It takes a liar to know a liar and right now I've never felt closer together, or further apart from my husband.

I drain my glass of Pinot and turn to face Nick as he enters the room. 'What time is Richard coming?' I ask, and Nick's face sags with relief. I've set the precedent. Pretended to believe him. Whatever happens now, I'll only have myself to blame.

I pour another glass of wine.


Richard arrives forty-five minutes later, and I swallow back my surprise as we air kiss our hellos. Perhaps Nick really was talking to him earlier. Perhaps it is solely the ten-year anniversary making me jumpy and paranoid. I try to recall the conversation but my memory is alcohol-hazy. Lisa serves the frittata, and I pass the salad bowl. This could be any other friends-for-lunch gathering but the atmosphere feels charged somehow and I'm not sure if it's the spark of suspicion warming my stomach, rendering me unable to eat, or if everyone feels it too. I watch Nick as he stabs his fork into a cherry tomato with more aggression than is necessary. Lisa stretches over and touches his hand.

'Are you okay, Nick?'

'Just tired.'

'I'm not surprised,' Richard says. He glances at Nick and something invisible passes between them.

I feel I could cry. Is Nick having an affair? Does everyone know? I push my plate away and draw my glass nearer, cradling it between two hands.

The doorbell rings, and Nick raises his hand to signal he'll get it. He pushes back his chair. Hushed voices drift into the kitchen and I strain to hear who he's talking to but Richard fills the silence with his booming voice.

'Lisa, I don't know much about you?'

'Not much to tell,' Lisa says. 'I'm a nurse.'

Nick sits back down, and I raise my eyebrows questioning.

'Clare,' he says. 'She's brought the raffle tickets stubs and cash over. I told her we're eating so she's scribbling you a note in the study. She'll let herself out. Oh, she brought my scarf over too. I must have left it there when we were over the other night for drinks.' He lowers his eyes and picks up his cutlery.

I try to remember if he wore his scarf when we went over. It was one of those rare spring evenings we could sit outside so I don't think it was warm enough, but I can't be certain. My head spins as metal clanks against china. I feel as though I'm at the Mad Hatter's Tea Party, swimming against an undercurrent I don't quite understand.

'And you enjoy it? Nursing?' Richard asks as though the interruption never happened.

'I love it. The hours are tough. Shifts. And sometimes.' Her brow furrows. 'People die.' She looks at me as she says this.

'I can imagine that's hard.' Richard tops up his glass, and I tilt mine towards him.

'And the money isn't very good, of course, for nurses. Speaking of money. I didn't want to bring this up but—'

'You need some more? What for?' Richard asks, and I think he should stay out of things that don't concern him.

'They've put the rent up on my flat.'

'We have to be mindful of the £20k... limit, for want of a better word. We don't want to complicate the court process when it comes to the parental order, do we?' Richard asks, although it isn't really a question.

'Of course not,' Lisa says. 'Normally, I'd be okay with my overtime, but with this little one, I promised Kat I'd cut down on my hours.' She pats her stomach. 'I'd hate to have to move back to my mum's house.' Her lip begins to tremble. 'I'd feel so trapped.'

As she says 'trapped,' her eyes meet mine and something skitters inside and I'm back in the community centre, back in the toilet, fighting to get out. There is the fleeting thought Lisa could have locked me in, but I dismiss it immediately. She's my friend, isn't she? But it suddenly strikes me what was odd about seeing Aaron. The fact that Lisa told me on New Year's Day that she never sees him. Surely if he works at the hospital too it's inevitable they'd run into each other occasionally? Why is it only now I am remembering the way she betrayed me before?

There's a sense the world is moving too fast. I feel disjointed. Disconnected. After lunch I tell everyone I have a migraine and slink up to the bedroom, seeking out ten minutes of peace. It's not exactly a lie. There's a headache creeping behind my eyes and I press my fingers into my temple to massage the pain.

On the bedside cabinet is Nick's phone and I can't help picking it up. It feels weighted with secrets. My thumb brushes the screen, and it illuminates and, even as I kid myself I'm only checking the time, I swipe right but it asks for a lock code, and I know he must be hiding something. Nick's never had security on his phone before. I try my birthday, his birthday, our house number, and I'm about to give up when I try the letters from his number plate, and I'm in. My hand starts to shake. Do I want to do this? Nothing good will come of it. Once I know, I can't not know, and yet curiosity burns and I find myself opening his emails.

I scan the list. Work. Spam. Amazon. Nothing suspicious there and I tell myself I should quit while I'm ahead, but that doesn't stop me from reading his texts. The top one is from a number, not a name:

*'So good to see you. Thanks for stopping the night x'*

Something akin to a scream builds and builds. Not now. Not Nick. We've finally got a baby on the way. Everything should be perfect but it's all crumbling around me, and I don't know how to stop it. There's a heavy tread of feet clumping up the stairs. Nick? I lock the phone and clatter it on the bedside table and dart over to the window as though I am just enjoying the view.

Outside, under the pergola the rose bushes are beginning to flower, cream for Dewei and lemon for Mai, but behind the pergola, almost hidden from view, are Richard and Lisa. Deep in conversation. He is waving his hands, and she is frowning and, even through the double glazing, I can hear the sounds of raised voices. Lisa turns, stalks back towards the kitchen and I see tears sliding down her cheeks.

I press one palm to the window, one against my chest. What has Richard done? What has he said? I think about Mai and Dewei. The babies I lost. The babies *he* lost us. He raises his face to the window. Our eyes lock and his face has a strange expression. Of hate? Of nervousness? I back away from the window. Exhausted with the emotion of everything. Trying not to overthink but knowing I will. I can. I do. Panic nestles under my skin, ready to break free.

The front door slams. An engine thrums. Tyres squeal.

I race down the stairs.

Lisa has gone.

# CHAPTER THIRTY-THREE
## Now

I wake with a jolt. The baby crying in my mind. I'm scrunched in the rocking chair in the nursery. Outside, the sun is slipping beneath the rooftops and the sky is streaked red and gold. My earbuds are still in and I press play on my phone to listen to the recording once more. Resting my head back on a cushion I begin to rock, staring at the ceiling for so long black specks swarm into my vision. I can't believe I have dozed. I had burst into the kitchen demanding to know where Lisa had gone; the silence did little to alleviate my panic and I asked again. Louder this time.

'Where is she?'

'On her way home, I expect,' Richard had said.

'But she was supposed to stay the night. She didn't even say goodbye?' I stared hard at him.

'You said you had a migraine. She probably thought it was the right thing to do.'

'Nick?' But his response was a shrug and, exasperated, I had huffed my way upstairs and punched out a text to Lisa asking her to call. But my phone lay still and silent. My eyelids grew heavy as I dug my toes into the carpet, pushing myself back and forth, the crinkly rabbit on my lap, listening for the burst of life on my phone. Sleep must have claimed me.

I massage my neck and tilt my head from left to right before padding over to the front window and peering out of the curtains. Richard's car is gone, and I am reassured to see Nick's car still there. Is he having an affair? What did Richard say to Lisa? Why did she leave? Thoughts crowd in on me. I feel I am standing on the brink but on the brink of what I do not know.

My forehead dips until it's resting on the cool glass.

Again.

It's all falling apart again.


Nick didn't come to bed last night and breakfast is strained. His eyes are glued to his mobile, thumbs tapping against the screen, and jealousy curdles as I wonder who he is talking to. My toast is overdone. Crunchy. I spread a thick layer of honey and bite into it, letting the sticky sweetness trickle down my throat, forming a barrier against the accusations that bubble and rise.

Nick leaves the table still fixated on his phone. He mumbles goodbye, and there's an empty space on the top of my head where his kiss should be. It seems incredible that only four months ago we were the happiest couple I know. I can't carry on like this. I think perhaps we should go for marriage counselling before we end up like Clare and Akhil. I don't know how she copes without a father for Ada.

The house feels too big. Too empty. Rain lashes against the windows. I pull my cardigan tighter around me. It's hard to believe that yesterday I was wearing shorts. Lisa's phone goes straight to voicemail when I ring again. She's probably at work. I can't shake the way her face seemed to hollow as she talked to Richard, the colour that drained from her lips. I rattle off a text:

*Please let me know you are okay*

And the second I put the handset down I snatch it up again to check for a reply, even though it hasn't beeped.

I'm edgy. Unsettled. I pace the kitchen. There's nothing to clean.

My mind is busy. I switch the radio on to Classic FM and soothing music fills the air, Vivaldi, I think. The raindrops seem to patter out the melody. I splay the charity's admin over the kitchen table. This is my favourite room. Usually I find it calming watching the birds swinging from the feeder outside the window, the light streaming through, turning the tiles a warm apricot. Sometimes I can almost imagine a dog snoozing by the French doors, body angled to warm in the sun. I always wanted a Labrador. Perhaps this is the right time. We could go on long walks, the wheels of the pram scrunching through orange autumn leaves, the smell of damp earth, the puppy straining at the lead. The image is so chocolate box perfect it takes a second to realise what has pulled me back to the kitchen. There are no muddy wellies and damp raincoats, collections of conkers in a bowl on the sideboard, just polished floors and uncluttered work surfaces.

The landline is ringing.

'Hello.' I am annoyed at the interruption. 'Hello?' My tone is sharper now. I wait. Listen. There's breath, soft and light.

'Who is this?' With the handset to my ear I stride to the front door. Pull the handle to make sure it's locked. It all speeds towards me. The phone calls. The wreath. The broken car window. I'm losing control again and everything I want seems so close and so far away.

*You mustn't tell, Kat.* I hear the words, sharp and clear, but I know they are part of the memories fighting to break free of the locked box I have kept them in for so long. I slam the handset back in its cradle as though I am slamming the lid of the box down, but when I try to seal it back up, it springs open again. There is the familiar tightening of my chest. The feeling of lightness. My knuckles are almost blue as I clutch the hall table while the world rocks around me. *I'm okay.* There's a noise. A text. It's Lisa.

*Sorry, Kat.*

I press dial but her phone is switched off. I sink to the bottom stair and drop my head onto my knees. What is she sorry for? For leaving yesterday? Or something else? Something worse? I text, asking her to call me and chew my lip so hard I wince.

I'm shaking now. I haul myself to my feet. I can't allow myself to think anything will go wrong. I can't lose another baby. I won't. I'm going to finish the books for the charity. I'm going to be normal. I know I sold some raffle tickets at the rehearsal yesterday and I lift my handbag from its hook, unzipping it to find the stubs. There's not much in my bag and immediately I see my purse is missing. I rummage through the make-up, tissue packet, throat sweets, hairbrush but I can't see the flash of purple leather. Kneeling on the carpet I tip the contents out but it's definitely not there. I close my eyes, retracing my steps. When did I last have it? I remember seeing it when we got to rehearsal and I dropped my keys into my bag, but was it there when I took them out again?

I call Nick to ask him whether I should cancel the credit cards, but his phone is off so I text instead. For a second I'm at a loss. I want to tally all the cash I collected, finish the balance sheets, and make a payment to the bank today. I remember the money in the safe. I'd sold four books so I'll take £20. I should wait for Nick to come home really; he was annoyed I'd taken out the money for the cab before and forgot to tell him, and I promised him I wouldn't go in there again. If I find my purse, though, he'll never know, and if I don't do this I'll only sit and think dark thoughts. I punch in Nick's birthday combination nevertheless and pull the door, my mouth falling open when I see what's inside. What isn't inside.

In place of the stack of notes is a teddy bear, and I lift him out and finger the red ribbon tight around his neck. He isn't new. There are thinning patches of fur, and his nose is hanging off. Where did he come from? Nick wouldn't be giving this to our baby. I sniff the top of the bear's head. Musty. At once I want to ring Nick and ask him about it but I spot a small black box in the corner of the safe. Inside, nestled on black velvet, is a ring. Emerald and diamonds sparkle. I run my fingers over the stones. It must be for my thirtieth birthday. That explains the missing money. We share a bank account and buying presents for each other is always awkward. I'd brought up my birthday last week, not wanting Nick to be extravagant but he was evasive and now I see why. He's already thinking about it. I can't help slipping the ring onto my index finger and holding my hand up to the light, watching the diamonds sparkle. It fits perfectly and I practice widening my eyes, loosening my jaw, the perfect 'surprised' face, but I can't even summon any fake enthusiasm. Where did the bear come from and why didn't Nick show him to me? I can't even ask him now or he'll know I've seen the ring. A hot flush sweeps over me and I bundle everything back into the safe exactly as I found it. The phone rings again. I won't answer it this time. I won't.

As I leave the study I catch a glimpse of a figure at the end of the driveway, staring at the house. Why would anyone be standing outside in the pouring rain? My panic rises quickly. Someone is out to get me. Nick won't believe me. I can't calm down. I don't know who I am morphing into. I don't even know my husband any more. Why isn't there enough air? I stretch the neck of my T-shirt.

The phone falls silent. Seconds later there is a banging on the front door, hard and relentless. The bulk of a man visible through the glass. I can't take this any more. Unbidden my fingertips twist the key, begin to turn the handle. My heart rate goes wild again as I prepare to face whoever is out there.

# CHAPTER THIRTY-FOUR

There was a horrible, horrible minute when Nick thought he'd beaten his dad to death, but he'd staggered to his feet. Neither Nick nor his mum made a move to stop him swaying down the hallway, shoulder bumping into the walls, hand pressed against his head. They had both flinched when the front door slammed shut.

Dusk fell, casting shadows across the kitchen, but neither Nick nor his mum flicked on the light switch. He didn't want to see the disappointment in her eyes, and he wished darkness would fall a little quicker, to cloak his shame.

'Do you think he'll come back?' Nick stared into his untouched coffee, a skin forming across the top. He kept his hands stuffed under the table where he couldn't see his swollen knuckles, although he could still feel them throbbing.

'I don't know where else he'd go.' Nick's mum sipped her tea now it had cooled, careful not to press the cup against the left side of her mouth.

'Mum. You should leave him. Kick him out. Something.'

'He wasn't always like this, you know. We met at a dance. Elvis was singing 'Are you Lonesome Tonight?' and he offered me his hand and twirled me around the floor. Afterwards we sat and talked for hours, and nobody had ever been so interested in what I had to say. We laughed so much.'

Nick didn't think his mum would see the slight raise of his eyebrows in the semi-darkness, but she said 'I know. I know. But he was funny and kind and he was a different person then. The accident changed him. Being in constant pain. Not being able to work. He felt less of a man, I suppose. Lost his purpose.'

'It doesn't excuse him hitting you,' Nick said quietly.

'I know but I kept hoping he would come back. That man I fell in love with. When I was ill it was the real him who brought me cups of tea and held my hand during chemo. Not this other version of him.' Her voice cracked.

They fell into silence. Nick was unsure what to say. Outside, a car alarm screamed. Nick gazed out of the window at the moon and, although he was an adult, he still wished he had a rocket sometimes and could zoom into space. The sky, popping with stars, always seemed so still. So peaceful.

'He could come back again, couldn't he?' Mum sniffed, and Nick's heart broke as he realised she was crying. 'He did it before and he must still be there somewhere. Under the pain, the anger, the frustration. The man who used to bring me a bunch of carnations after work every Friday, and a bacon sandwich in bed on a Sunday. Is it too late, Nick? For him to be the father he was? He doted on you once, you know. He'd make a coin appear from behind your ear and you'd look at him with such wonder. With such love.'

Nick screwed his eyes and searched through his memory. It sounded as though his mum was talking about someone else, but despite everything, he felt something inside him soften. He was about to ask her how old he was, and when it all went wrong, wanting to get to know this other father, this stranger, when there was a thumping at the front door.

'I bet he's forgotten his keys.' Mum scraped her chair back, but Nick stretched out his hand and touched her arm.

'Let me go.'

Nick felt strangely calm as he walked towards the front door, towards his father's apologies. He wondered whether this might be a new beginning for them all. A chance to sit down and talk. A fresh start. But as he opened the door his stomach dipped.

'Nicholas White?' said the policeman, a stern expression on his face. 'I'm arresting you on suspicion of assault.' And as the policeman read Nick his rights he couldn't hear anything except the click of the handcuffs. He twisted his neck and saw his mum hovering behind him, hands clapped over her mouth, but he couldn't feel anything except the cold steel of the metal and his icy, icy heart.

# CHAPTER THIRTY-FIVE
## Now

Hairy knees are the first thing I see as I crack open the front door.

'Morning, Mrs White.' Our postman, forever cheerful, forever in shorts no matter how bad the weather, hands me a rain-damp package. My eyes are drawn over his shoulder, and there's a dishevelled-looking man, salt-and-pepper beard, staring right at me, and instinctively I know he is the one who has been here before. Our eyes connect and he glances at the floor, but he doesn't move. I close the door quickly and lean against it, my spine uncomfortable against the ridged surface. The package feels heavy in my hands. Part of me wants to throw it away without opening it, knowing whatever is inside the package will be bad. The image of the wreath is burned onto the inside of my eyelids.

My fingers are shaking as I start to peel off the soggy cardboard which disintegrates as I touch it. Inside is a book.

*How to Cope with Death.*

It tumbles from my hand as fear slides me to my haunches. I can't. I can't cope with death.

*Ten years.*

*You mustn't tell, Kat.*

I am longing to tell, to atone, but I am frightened. Still too frightened. I cover my head with my arms as though I can make everything go away.

\*

The ringing phone slices through my wandering thoughts. I am still crouching on the doormat, the book lying at my feet. I have to get out of here. Be amongst people. Away from the house and the phone and the endlessly waiting for something awful to happen. I grab my car keys. My feet feel glued to the doormat. I grip the door handle tightly with both hands, urging my wrists to twist, but panic turns my body to stone. I fight to regain control. Waves of heat radiate from my toes to my scalp and I feel myself begin to sway.

It feels like hours but it is only minutes, seconds perhaps, when the anxiety pulsing around my body begins to subside. I am left feeling shaky and scared. My head throbs. I rattle out an aspirin and swallow it down with my guilt and my fear and tell myself I am not losing it again, but the words don't ring true, even to me.

I breathe in slowly and deeply as I step outside the door. The rain has slowed, the sun breaking through the clouds but there's still a breeze. Leaving the door ajar, I go back for my jacket. Cold. When I'm not hot with panic, I feel constantly cold.


The town is quiet. It always is on a Monday. I carry my handbag and a sense of disquiet. There are shadows everywhere. Each shop window becomes a hiding place. I shrink in on myself as an elderly lady brushes past. Like a beacon drawing me home I see the sign for Mothercare and hurry towards it. I feel open, exposed and long to be cocooned inside four walls.

I'm being followed. I know I am. There are footsteps behind me, matching me step for step, splashing through puddles I have just left behind. I grip the strap on my handbag a little tighter. As I speed up, so do they. Physically I can feel my heart is racing but my senses are dulled, dampened by exhaustion. I take a sharp left. There's still the sound, the slap of leather on wet concrete, and now an overpowering aftershave catching in my throat. I increase my pace. Too scared to stop. Too scared to turn. The door to the shop is ahead and I'm so nearly there with the smiling assistants and the soft honeyed light. In my haste I lose my footing on a paving slab and stumble, grazing my hand against a wall as I steady myself. Brick stinging my palm. Cologne stinging my nostrils. A shadow looms in my peripheral vision and a spotty teenager, eyes glued to his mobile, stalks past without noticing me.

Invisible. I am invisible.

There's no one else around. I remain propped against the wall until the beep of a horn slices through the silence causing my body to jerk like a marionette. I push myself to standing and, slower now, I carry on.


'Hello Kat!'

It crosses my mind I should feel a tinge of embarrassment that the staff in Mothercare all know me by name, feel obliged to tell them, like Dewei, Mai is no longer mine, but I feel almost numb as I lift a custard-yellow Babygro from the rail, rubbing the fleecy softness between both fingers, reminding myself I can still feel.

'Are you looking for anything in particular today?' I am asked. The bright strip lights glare overhead, and the colour drains from my vision as panic slams into me.

'No. Sorry…' I begin to back away. Feeling light-headed. I shouldn't have come here. It isn't safe outside. I need to be at home.

Something sharp digs into the small of my back and I spin around. A shelf wobbles but my reflexes are slow as I watch in alarm as a picture frame tumbles to the floor. The sound of shattering glass is piercing, and I apologise over and over as I pick up the silver frame and set it down. The stock image is a baby in a pink polka dot sleepsuit starfishing in her cot. A tug of familiarity pulls me, and I wonder if I've got the same frame at home. I've bought so much stuff over the last couple of years. There's a hand on my arm. A soft voice tells me not to worry about the breakage. I turn and flee.

The high street is busier now; the chip shop has its door propped open and the smell of hot oil mixes with exhaust fumes. My temples begin to throb. The newspaper stand is setting up and the headlines scream 'Murder', and remorse scratches at my skin.

By the time I reach my car my cheeks are wet with tears and I'm not sure if I'm crying for the things I've done, or the things I stand to lose. My hand is shaking as I hold my mobile to my ear, willing Lisa to answer. Willing her to tell me everything is all right. But it isn't, is it? Not really. The book this morning only confirmed what I already knew.

Someone is out for revenge.


There's a cacophony of horns. A squeal of brakes. I've run a red light. My skin turns boiling hot and then freezing cold. I mouth apologies at the driver of the car forced to screech to a halt. He opens his window and shouts: 'silly cow'. I ease forward, checking my mirrors constantly as though I am taking my driving test.

The rest of my journey is slow. Steady. All the time I mutter to myself as I drive. Reassuring words. I'm letting it all get on top of me and it's natural, I tell myself, to worry. Any prospective mum would have 'what if' doubts, and I may not be carrying my child but I'm emotionally invested all the same.

I climb out my car. Tension has made my muscles stiff and I think I'll have a bath, pour in some of the Jo Malone bath oil Nick bought me for Valentine's that looks so beautiful on the shelf I haven't yet opened it. Once I'm feeling calmer I'll ring Lisa, tell her how scared I am that something will go wrong and we can talk about it properly.

The front door feels harder to open. There's a breeze streaming down the hallway pushing it closed. I frown as I slip off my boots and carry them as I pad silently into the kitchen. I can't have left the backdoor unlocked, can I? I'm hesitant. Not sure what to expect. The door is closed but the window above the sink is open. I don't remember leaving it ajar. As I stretch to shut it, I notice footprints outside in the border, pressed into the mud. Large footprints. Footprints that are definitely not mine. And then there's a crash from upstairs.

# CHAPTER THIRTY-SIX
## Then

In the darkness, the whites of Aaron's eyes flashed dangerously. You would think the park would be still at night. Silent. Quiet. But the wind brought everything to life. The swing squeaked, an empty can rattled across the pavement, bushes swayed.

'What do you want?' Slowly, I backed away.

'Just to talk. Don't look so scared, Kat. We're friends, aren't we?'

'No.' I kicked myself as soon as I said it. I should have played along. There was a sense of things spinning wildly out of my control.

'Perfect, perfect, Kat. Have you never made a mistake? Done anything you're ashamed of?' A twig snapped under his footfall, and I thought of that day in the woods. Jake's hands on me. My half-naked body pressed against the tree. The horrible sense of being watched. I crossed my arms over my chest as I took another step back.

'Leave me alone.'

'I'm not going to touch you. Look, I've been stupid, I know. I didn't think about the consequences. To begin with I only wanted to help my sister lose weight. She was miserable. Being bullied. It really was small amounts.'

'Aaron, I—'

'Please, Kat. Don't tell anyone. I'll never be a doctor with a record for drug dealing and despite what you think I'm not a bad person. I'm not.'

'It's too late.' I licked my dry lips. 'I've already emailed Mr Lemmington.' Aaron stopped moving and, stupidly, I did too. 'He might not take it any further. I haven't mentioned Lisa, or your sister. I'm sure if you say sorry and—'

'You fucking bitch.' He lunged forward.

My glance flickered to the exit. It wasn't too far but Aaron was faster. Legs longer. He'd outrun me in an instant but I had to try. Fuelled by adrenaline, surprisingly, I did make it out of the gates, had almost passed the van before I was yanked backwards by my collar. I kicked out as hard as I could. Was pushed backwards, my body slamming against the van door.

'Stop!'

The cry caused us both to look around.

Under the hazy orange glow of the lamp post – Lisa.

# CHAPTER THIRTY-SEVEN
## Now

'There's someone in the house.' My whisper sounds too loud. I'm crouching in the utility room by the side of the tumble dryer clutching my boots to my chest as a child would clutch a teddy.

'We've been burgled?' Nick asks. 'You should leave.'

'Nothing is disturbed downstairs but the kitchen window was open. I'm sure I closed it before I left, and I heard something upstairs. Shall I call the police?'

'There's no sign anyone has been in?' Disbelief tinges Nick's voice. 'Is this like the bin thing again, where you imagined—'

'I'm not imagining this.' I hiss out my words.

'Just get out the house. I'm on my way.'

I stand. My thighs feel weak. Slowly I crack open the door leading to the kitchen. I can't see anyone. Can't hear anyone. But that doesn't mean no one is here. I take one astronaut stride at a time towards the back door. I count my steps. One. Two. Three. Sweat trickles between my breasts. Four. Five. Six. There's a scraping, a sharp pain in my hip. I'd been so fixed on the door I've bumped into a chair. I freeze. My instincts scream at me to get out of the house, but I'm nearer to the utility room and I don't know whether I should dart back in there. A creak. A floorboard? Seven. Eight. Nine. I'm faster now. Not caring if I make a sound. Desperate to be outside. Ten. Eleven. Twelve. Another creak. Louder this time. With a shaking hand I twist the key in the back door. It doesn't move. I wonder if I've turned it the wrong way.

If it's already unlocked. It isn't. The key slips from the keyhole and clatters on the tiles. My heart springs into my mouth. The creaking comes again and I snatch up the key and thrust it back in the lock, rotating my wrist, left, right, left. Why can't I remember how to unlock a bloody door? There's a click. A give. I tug open the door and step outside.

The fence sways in the wind, creak-creak-creaking. I cut across the garden, ignoring the damp grass soaking through my socks, the flowers I trample over. I almost fall through the back gate onto the driveway. The gravel crunches underfoot, sharp and jagged. My head is down as I run along the side of the house, arms pumping, hands gripping my boots. I wince as brick scrapes against my wrist. I slow. Look up. A man stands at the kerb. Dishevelled. Salt-and-pepper beard. Deep lines carved into his forehead. The same man that was here this morning. *What does he want?* Fearing the worst I throw my boots towards him. He sidesteps.

I sprint as fast as I can across the road towards Clare's and pummel at her front door with my fists, looking over my shoulder at the figure. He is standing stock-still, watching. The curtains twitch a few doors down from my house: the nosy woman with red hair peering out of her window. Why doesn't she help me? The front door opens and I simultaneously push Clare back with one hand as I step inside, slamming the door behind me. With a shaking hand I draw the chain across.

'Kat?' Clare's voice is steady as I swish closed the curtains in the lounge, but the way she tosses the iPad in her hand onto the sofa and crosses the room to where Ada is playing with a ragdoll in front of the fireplace, scooping her daughter into her arms, holding her protectively against her, betrays her concern.

'Are you okay? Where are your shoes?'

I chew my thumbnail, staring at the screen of the iPad, the picture of the Colosseum and the hotel room. Clare must be booking that holiday she wanted. I wish I were anywhere but here.

'Dark,' Ada says although there's a slither of sunshine pushing through the thin curtains.

Clare crosses to the light switch.

'Don't.' I stalk into the kitchen, to the back door, pulling the handle, once, twice, three times. The windows are closed. We're safe.

Electric light brightens the room behind me and I spin around but the look on Clare's face stops me telling her to switch it off.

'Mummy?' Ada's fingers play with the ends of Clare's pendant. Ada sounds so small. So uncertain.

'It's okay, Ada.' I ruffle her beautiful curls. 'We're playing a game. Hide-and-seek.'

Wordlessly Clare leaves the room, and as her footsteps thud up the stairs I allow myself a peek outside. There's nobody there. Who was that man? Was he in the house? Has somebody sent him? The last thought causes me to bite my lip and blood fills my mouth. In the kitchen I spit into the sink, turning on the taps, watching the water turn pink before being sucked down the plughole.

'What the hell is going on?' Clare speaks quietly but there is fury in each and every word. 'You scared Ada.'

'Is she all right?' I stand, wiping my chin with my sleeve.

'She's playing in her room. Who are you hiding from?'

'Someone has broken into the house.'

Clare's hands fly to her mouth and her eyes widen. I sink into a hard wooden chair and drop my head into my hands. She touches my shoulder.

'Have they taken much? Are the police coming?'

I shake my head. 'Everything downstairs was undisturbed but someone was upstairs. Nick's on his way.'

'Are you sure you've been burgled?' Her words are tinged with doubt, and I close my eyes. I had been sure. But now I question myself. What had I seen? Heard? An open window and a noise. 'You've been under so much strain lately. I'm worried about you.'

'There were footprints.' I remember. 'There was a man…' I trail off. It's all so cloudy but still. 'There was somebody there,' I insist as Clare fills the kettle, drops teabags into mugs. But I don't sound as convincing as I'd like.

'Here.' Clare spoons sugar into dark brown tea, and picks at the top of a packet of digestives with her nails as though this is a social call. I shake my head.

Clare slides into the seat opposite me and, as she moves, the sun glints against her pendant casting miniature rainbows on the duck egg walls.

'Tell me about the baby,' she says.

It's the distraction I need. 'Beanie is practically twenty-seven weeks and the size of a head of cauliflower. He gets hiccups. Sleeps and wakes at regular intervals, opening and closing his eyes. Lisa has another scan booked for Friday. I've been looking at those 4D ones – they look incredible, expensive though. I'm going to ask Nick whether we could afford one. We'd be able to see all his features. By now, his face is fully formed, with eyelashes, eyebrows and hair. There's no pigment yet so it will still be white but soon it will develop a colour.' I wonder if he will have black hair like Lisa. Like Jake. Like Nick. 'I say he but it might not be. I can't decide whether we should find out.'

Thinking of the baby helps me relax and we chit-chat until her mobile vibrates, skittering across the table between us. Clare grabs it and stuffs it onto her lap, her cheeks blazing, but not before I have seen Lisa's name flashing up on her screen. Their relationship must have progressed beyond the odd text. Before I can question Clare the doorbell rings. We glance warily at each other. Clare places her palms on the table and pushes herself to standing.

I follow her into the hallway, steeling myself for the worst as she unlocks the door. Shoulders sagging with relief when I see it's only Nick, my boots in his hand.

He looks pale, tired. I step forward and hug him, releasing my grip when I feel his body stiffen.

'What's happened?' I study him, expecting bad news. The upstairs trashed.

'Nothing. No one's been there.'

Frowning I push past him, striding towards home, almost not believing him.

'I definitely heard something,' I say but he doesn't answer, and I turn.

He's still standing on Clare's doorstep, and it hurts as I notice them hug. Notice he doesn't pull away from her.

'I don't understand.' I'm standing in the doorway of the nursery, reluctant to step forward wearing only socks. The 'Together We Make a Family' picture is lying on the floor, the frame splintered. Shards of glass imbedded in the carpet; there's some in the cot. I thank my lucky stars, for the first time, there wasn't a baby in it.

'The nail can't have been strong enough to hold it up,' Nick says. 'I should have used a picture hook.'

'But...' I look around the room. Nothing else has been disturbed. 'There were footprints outside the kitchen window.'

'I was weeding at the weekend around the rose bushes and thought I might as well do all the borders. It hasn't rained since. They were probably mine.'

'There *was* a man.' I cross my arms around my waist. 'Hanging around outside the house. I've seen him before.'

'Perhaps he's visiting someone. Look, Kat,' Nick places his hand on my shoulder, 'it's been a horribly stressful time, moving house, the adoptions and now the surrogacy.'

I shrug him off. 'I'm not cracking up.'

'I didn't say you were. I'm just… worried. Your boots were in the middle of the road, for Christ's sake.' He runs his fingers through his hair. His curls have got so long. He looks gaunt, and I feel terrible that I've only been thinking how this affects me. But I count the things that have gone wrong lately and paranoia pounces again.

'Nick, I think someone *has* been in the house. Yesterday, my purse—'

'There's a message on the answerphone,' Nick says before I can bring up the missing money from the safe. 'The community centre rang. A workman found your purse in the toilet. He was in there fixing the faulty lock.'

'But I didn't even open my bag,' I say, but even as I speak, I remember pulling my hairbrush from my handbag.

'What's going on, Kat? Talk to me.' He looks despairing and everything seems broken between us, and there's a big part of me that wants to fall against him, let it all pour out, but I remain silent.

*You mustn't tell, Kat.*

I'm a keeper of secrets, a guardian of the truth.

Nick crouches and begins to gather the large pieces of glass and, quietly, I leave the room.


My mind tick-tick-ticks as I stalk into our bedroom, my eyes scanning everything. Did I leave the decorative cushions on the bed at that angle? Didn't I smooth down the patchwork throw before I left? I'm perturbed. Something is off – I can sense it. The air feels thicker somehow. I slide open our storage unit, and lift out my jewellery box. Popping open the lid I run my finger over necklaces, rings, bracelets. Nothing is missing. My handbags are hanging where I left them. My shoes all lined up. I am sliding the door closed again when I notice Nick's leather messenger bag. I bought it for him on our first Christmas, and I feel wistful as I remember the turkey I cooked. Nick didn't complain once that it was dry and tasteless, or that the Brussels sprouts were like bullets.

He drenched the unappetising food with lumpy gravy and ate every single mouthful. How young we were. How hopeful. We thought we'd effortlessly have it all. The family. The happily ever after.

Emotion gathers inside as I lift the bag off the hanger and draw it to my nose, breathing in the leather. Almost smelling the fir tree that had stood in the corner of our lounge. The mulled wine that was warming in the kitchen. A family. That's all I ever wanted but at what cost? Lisa coming back into my life has been like uncorking a bottle of memories, and I can't jam the stopper back in. The truth is a black swirling mass with a pointed tail and snapping jaws. I'm tired of running. Permanently stressed and edgy. Nick looks exhausted and unhappy. He never really wanted children, did he? He wasn't bothered when I told him I couldn't have them. At once I feel the burden of everything heavy on my shoulders. Have I ruined us? Pushing. Wanting. A few more months and we'll be a three and yet, even now I'm looking further than that, wanting us to be a four. But in my mind a baby cries, needing a mum, and I know I cannot lose one again. I release my grip, the messenger bag thuds to the floor and a piece of paper flutters out. A bank statement. I frown. Nick keeps all the paperwork in his study but this account is in his name solely. Inside the bag are more statements. The same amount going in each month. The exact same amount being paid out to an account number I don't recognise.

I pace the room. Struggling to make sense of it. What is Nick paying for? What is he keeping from me? I reach the back window. Turn. A rat in a cage. The front window. I glance outside. Clare is closing her front door. Ada in her arms.

Ada.

I drink in her black curly hair, so like Nick's. Her fair skin. Think of the way Akhil disappeared. Not paying maintenance. The papers flutter from my hands. Clare manages in that big house all alone in this cul-de-sac Nick was so desperate for us to move to. Oh God. My stomach churns and churns. The flowers from

'N'. His scarf in her hall. The overnight trips. The text message. Could Ada be his daughter? Are these maintenance payments? Clare comes from Cornwall where Nick's grandad, Basil, lived. Could they have known each other as kids? Reconnected as adults? Had an affair? The carpet seems to sink below my feet as thoughts streak through my mind, and none of them are the things I want to be thinking. I have to be wrong, don't I?

All at once I don't know who to trust. Nick. Clare. I long to talk to Lisa. The person who knows me better than anyone. The person who won't tell me I'm going mad.

Lisa's phone rings and rings until reluctantly I cut the call. I pace the room, tapping the handset against my chin. I shouldn't ring her at work, I know. Hospitals are busy and she won't have time to chat, and yet just hearing a familiar voice, a friendly voice, would calm me. Perhaps I can arrange to meet her after her shift. I google the number for Farncaster General and ask to speak to Lisa Sullivan.

'I can't find her on the staff list. What ward?'

'Stonehill,' I say, and the ringing tone starts once more before I am connected to the right department.

'Lisa Sullivan,' I repeat for the second time.

'I am sorry,' says a harried voice. She sounds anything but sorry. 'No one works here with that name.'

'Are you?—' I begin but the call has been cut.

I dial again and this time I speak to a different receptionist who confirms what I've already been told. There is no record of a Lisa Sullivan.


Agitated I return to the nursery, as though to convince myself it's real. There is a baby coming. As the soft pile swallows my feet a slither of glass pierces the skin of my big toe and I crouch down and remove it. Under the changing table is a green box I store nick-knacks in and seeing it sparks a memory. With a sinking feeling I slide the box towards me. There's a thrumming in my ears growing louder and louder.

My hands rest on the lid. I don't want to open it. I don't want to see what I know is inside, but almost mechanically, I remove the lid. Lift out the contents slowly, reluctantly, until I find what I am looking for. A silver picture frame I'd bought from Mothercare last year; inside rests the stock photo of the baby in the pink polka dot sleepsuit starfishing in her cot. A baby familiar to me.

Gabrielle.

The baby Lisa showed me on her phone. The baby Lisa had for Stella. The tug I'd felt on my heart when I first saw it wasn't emotion. It was recognition.

This can't be Gabrielle.

The child Lisa said was her baby.

Stella's baby.

Except she isn't, is she?

She's a stock photograph.

Only as real as the baby that now cries in my mind louder and louder until I clasp my hands over my eyes and fold myself in two.

# CHAPTER THIRTY-EIGHT
## Now

In the shower I scrub at my body with lemon shower gel as though I can wash away the things I have learned. The things I now know. After seeing the photo I hadn't wanted to believe Lisa had lied. I had felt her bump. The first scan photo was on my fridge. I had heard the baby's heart. I googled and found a heartbeat on YouTube sounding exactly the same. My shaking fingers kept pressing the wrong keys as I googled again. 'You wouldn't believe half the stuff you can buy on eBay,' Lisa had said, and she was right, I thought, as I stared in disbelief at a prosthetic baby bump with the 'Buy Now' option.

Inside my head I hear the sound of laughter. Stupid. I'm so stupid.

There is no baby. *How could Lisa do this to me?* The water is too hot. The steam rises, and my hopes sink. I feel angry, betrayed, but overriding all of those things is a thought that this is what I deserve. Payback. I'm a terrible, terrible person. A wave of dizziness washes over me and I place my palms against the tiles to steady myself. *I'm not going to be a mum.* I'm dragging in short, sharp breaths through my nose. *I'm never going to be a mum.* My knees buckle and I sink to the floor. The water cascades over me. But I know no matter how long I stay in the shower I will never feel clean again. How could I not have known? The money she demanded. The appointments she kept me away from. The bump I never felt move. 'We believe what we want to,' Lisa had said. Oh, how she must have laughed at the way I sucked it all up.

The sun is dipping behind the rooftops and the sky looks like fire. I wrap myself in a towel, my damp hair tangled around my shoulders, and perch on the edge of the bed as though I don't belong here. As though this isn't where my husband and I made love. Made plans for our future. I don't know what to do. Say. How to act. I've lost everything. Nick is moving around downstairs, and it's almost as though I've been suddenly placed in some weird reality TV show, watching myself from high above. Waiting to see what I'll do.

Lisa.

She has broken my heart, just like I broke hers when I fell in love with her twin. How could I have thought she'd have forgiven me for loving him? For being the one who was there as his life ebbed away.

I need to speak to her. I find her in my favourites list; her smiling face transforms my sorrow to anger.

I need to see her. Face-to-face. I already know she will find another excuse to avoid having the scan this week. I think long and hard before I send the text.

*We need to talk about money.*

The reply is almost instant.

*I'm at work. Call you later? X*

Liar – I want to punch out, but instead I say:

*Would rather go through everything face-to-face. Know I'm meeting you on Friday anyway but I've been thinking and I'm not sure we're giving you enough for expenses. Feeling terrible.*

That last bit, at least, is true.

*You are sweet!*

Bile rises, stinging my throat.

*I could come over tomorrow – I'm off?*

*Look forward to it.*

I say, and I find that somehow I am.

# CHAPTER THIRTY-NINE
## Now

I'd drunk too much wine last night. Wanting to blunt the sharp edges of the truth. Nick and I had skirted around each other, pretending everything was fine as we'd prepared a lasagne neither of us could eat, draining a bottle and a half of Shiraz between us, as though this was normal Monday night behaviour. Nick was edgy. Distracted. We dined amongst the ruins of our marriage, staring at Nick's mobile, which sat between us, dark and silent, along with the Parmesan cheese and the secrets. A last supper, of sorts. As I was getting ready for bed the back garden was suddenly bright. Something had triggered the security light. Or someone. I had stared out of the window watching the bushes sway. A shadow move. But rather than fear I'd felt a certain inevitability. It was always going to fall apart. I was only surprised it had taken ten years.

'Morning.' Nick shuffles into the kitchen, smelling of stale alcohol, as I probably do, yawning although he seemed to sleep far better than me. Each time I drifted off, the sound of laughter, of a baby crying, grew louder and louder until I rolled over and pressed my mouth against the pillow and screamed. Nick didn't stir. Now, he runs a hand over his chin, as though he can't quite remember whether he has shaved. He hasn't.

'Morning. I feel rough.' That, perhaps, is the only truth I will speak today.

'Me too. Don't know what possessed us. On a school night, as well!' he says as he drops bread into the toaster.

His throwaway comment sets my teeth on edge. There will never be a school run for me. The early morning panic. Pulling together PE kits, locating homework.

Outside, a plane trails a frothy white tail across a clear blue sky, and in the cold light of day I'm beginning to doubt myself. Have I got it wrong? It seems incredible to think Lisa has lied. Growing up there were times she was mischievous, secretive, sometimes, but never malicious. Never cruel. And yet grief bends and breaks the people we were. Moulds us into the people we never wanted to be. Soon I will know, one way or the other, and if Lisa has lied, I don't know what I'll be driven to. After all, I'll have nothing to lose.

'What are your plans today?' Nick asks.

It's a perfectly innocent question but concern bubbles under every word, and I wonder if he wants me out of the way so he can see Clare. See Ada. It stings to think I am no longer the centre of his world, if I ever was. I need to confront him, I know, but I can only deal with one thing at a time.

'Lisa is coming.'

The toast pops and Nick spreads peanut butter on a slice, thick and crunchy. 'That's nice. I'll try and get home early. Look, I know I've been distracted lately but I'm happy about the baby, really. Excited even. It's getting nearer now. It seems more real somehow.' He turns to face me. 'I'm sorry I've not been as involved as I should have been. The problems with work… they're over now. It's over now.' He says it with such regret and, as he crosses the room and wraps his arms around me tightly, my resolve crumbles. I find myself hugging him back, hard, and our embrace shouldn't feel so full of love, but somehow it does.

My skin is pale, tired. I dab foundation on with a sponge. Colour my cheeks a little too pink. Make my lips a little too glossy. Painting on a veneer. The doorbell rings. This is it. *Don't let your mask slip.*

Lisa waddles through the door, and I hug her hello, trying not to recoil as I feel her bump hard and round. I can't believe it is real.

Fake.

Everything about her is fake, I think, as she recounts her journey, the renegade sheep that brought the traffic to a standstill. Her laughter peals as she tells me about the overweight businessman who tried to shoo it back into the field, face beet red, turning on his heels and running back to the safety of the car when the sheep started to chase him.

'Of course I couldn't help,' she says, and I nod my agreement as I fill the kettle. Spoon coffee into mugs.

I study her as we sip our drinks.

'How's work?' I ask, and she nods.

'Good.' But she doesn't elaborate further, and when I ask her to tell me about her favourite patient she changes the subject. Why have I never noticed how evasive she is? She shifts in her seat and the chair creaks.

'Hope the legs don't break.' She grimaces. 'I'm like a baby elephant now.' She tells me how she can't stop eating at the moment. Savoury things. Salty. I wait for her to slip up. Waiting for a sign. But she speaks about the pregnancy as though it is real, and it isn't until I mention money her eyes bounce around the room, as she looks at everything but me.

'Do you need more? Are you okay?' I lean forward. Rubbing her arm reassuringly.

She cups her bump, shaking away my touch. Wincing.

'He's kicking like mad!'

Quickly I move to her side. Place both hands on her bump, ignoring her attempts to brush me off. There's nothing to be felt. No movement. Just this solid, unnatural, mound.

We wait for a moment, trapped in this pretence, until she sighs and says: 'He's settled down again now.'

I jerk my hands away as though her words have hurt me, and in a way, they have.

She yawns. Rubs her eyes. 'Sorry. I'm shattered. Work is so busy. I need to get back this afternoon.'

'Can't you stay?' I pull a face. 'I miss you.' Something tugs at my heart as I say this and I know I miss the person she was. Not the person she is now. This Lisa I do not know.

'I wish I could…' She looks wistful, and something passes between us. An undercurrent. An understanding? A flicker of what might have been if things had turned out differently.

'Why don't you go and have a bath while I make some lunch. It will relax you after your drive.'

'Oh no. I couldn't—'

'Of course you could. I've got some Jo Malone bath oil and body lotion I've never used. We can catch up properly this afternoon.'

'It's tempting. Everything aches.'

'That's settled then.' I stand, urging her to do the same. 'There's plenty of hot water so keep topping it up. Lunch won't be ready for a couple of hours so take your time. You can get changed in the guest bedroom. There's a spare robe on the back of the door.'

'You might regret saying that. I could stay in there all day.' Her hands move to the small of her back as though it is sore. 'Thanks, Kat. You do spoil me.' She hefts herself to her feet.

'Oh, Lisa.' I smile warmth into my words. 'What was it you said to me? We *always* get what we deserve.'


My ear presses against the bathroom door and, once I hear the water slosh, Lisa's groan of relief as she lowers her body into the tub, I hurry into the spare room and locate her handbag amongst her discarded clothes and tip the contents out on the bed. Tissues, purse, brush, lipstick, car keys, phone. I press the button on the top of the handset and am invited to use touch ID or enter my password. Without consciously thinking I key in '0509' – her birthday – Jake's birthday – and for a second I am transported back to candle wax on paper plates, mouth crammed full of chocolate sponge with too-sweet-icing, the pass-the-parcel Lisa would always win.

Perching on the bed I open up Lisa's emails and type 'Stella' in the search bar. She'd said Stella sends her updates of Gabrielle and surely she wouldn't have deleted those. No results are found. My stomach sinks a little lower and I realise I'd still been holding on to a kernel of hope that I am wrong. I open up the photos and type baby in the search bar. The image springs up that Lisa first showed us. The baby in the pink polka dot sleepsuit, starfishing in her cot and there is not a smidgen of doubt in my mind she is the same baby as in the frame upstairs. Next, I scroll through her texts. Names I don't recognise. A name I do. Aaron. I open the message.

Lisa had texted:

*'I have to tell Kat. I can't do this any more.*

*You can't! Not now.*

Aaron's reply.

*I can't live with myself.*

*You haven't told the truth in 10 years. Don't fucking start now. You'll ruin everything.*

What has Lisa been lying about since Jake died? I know what she is lying about now: pretending to be pregnant. Her and Aaron must be in it together. How they must have laughed as I blindly handed money over each month, forking out for extras, never questioning what it was for. Or has Aaron forced her somehow? Blackmailed her? What has she been keeping a secret? I think back to these past few months. The times when Lisa has let her guard down and we have reminisced over *Desperate Housewives* and Curly Wurlys. Bacardi Breezers and Snow Patrol. I can't believe all this is borne of spite. If I ask her why, she's not likely to tell me, and I need to know. I need to know what was worth destroying me over, because the bottom has dropped out of my world and destroyed is what I feel. I must keep it together. I don't have much time.

I rattle off a text to Aaron.

*I need to see you!*

I pace as I wait, tallying the things that could go wrong. Aaron could refuse, if he even gets the texts at all. He could be at work. Not have his phone. There's a rigidity spreading through me, frustration turning my muscles to stone.

The minutes seem endless but at last the phone vibrates in my hand.

*We can't be seen together.*

*I'm not in Farncaster. Come here.*

I add my address.

The handset stays silent and dark. I think I've gone too far, but I can still claw it back, if he's desperate to keep Lisa quiet. I send another text.

*I'm barely holding it together. I'm scared I'm going to crack. Confess.*

From the bathroom next door I hear the running of taps as Lisa tops the water up. My heart pounds. I'm hot. Mouth dry. But at last a message comes through.

*OK.*

I hurry into my en suite and turn on the tap and, tipping out our toothbrushes, I fill a glass with water before removing Lisa's SIM card. I drop it into the glass and slowly swill it around before fishing it out, shaking off the droplets of water before patting it with a towel. Minutes later it feels dry. It looks normal. I slide it back inside the phone, press the power button and smile before I drop the handset back into Lisa's bag.

Aaron should be here in an hour.

And so it begins.

# CHAPTER FORTY
## Now

It is lunchtime when Lisa returns to the kitchen, skin bath-pink and clammy, hair damp. I close my laptop lid. I have learned all I need to know.

There's a quiche warming in the oven and I pull it out and slice it, turning my head away from the smell of cheese and onion. I couldn't possibly eat. The pastry crumbles as I lift quarters onto plates, drizzle olive oil over rocket.

'I can't help thinking about the time we ran into Aaron at the hospital,' I say to Lisa as we begin our game, if that's what this is to be.

'What do you want to think about him for?'

'It must be hard for you, with him working in the hospital too.'

'He's only a cleaner.' Lisa's voice changes pitch. She's uncomfortable. 'Our paths never really cross.'

I change my tack. Wanting to throw her off guard.

'I love the Eva Longoria perfume you bought me. You're too kind.'

'You're welcome.' She smiles. Relieved at the change of subject.

'It's funny, isn't it? Stella chose the name Gabrielle for her baby? That was Eva's character's name, wasn't it?' I spear rocket with my fork but I'm watching her reaction from under my lashes. The way she swallows hard. Reaches for her glass and gulps water as though something is stuck in her throat. The truth, perhaps?

'Was it?' Lisa's tone is too bright. Too high. But I know her so well I can detect the tremble. Notice the blush that wraps itself around her neck, and I imagine my fingers there in its place.

She places her knife and fork together at the side of her plate. 'I'm sorry, Kat.'

'Are you?' I lean forward. Almost urging her to be honest.

'Yes. It must have taken you ages to make this lunch. I get really full quickly now he's growing.'

Her hand strokes her belly, and I sink back into my seat, stuffing my hands under my thighs before I give in and sweep the contents of the table onto the cold tile floor, where shards of china will lay strewn amongst the pieces of my broken heart.

'I must go.' Lisa looks uncomfortable.

'But there's a lemon meringue in the oven.'

'Sorry.' She stands.

I expected nothing less.

'So you'll transfer the extra money?' She asks for confirmation, and I nod, not trusting my voice not to crack if I speak. 'I'll see you soon, Kat.'

She has no idea how soon.


I've scraped the leftover salad into the bin and crumbled the pastry onto the bird table when the doorbell rings and, before I even stride down the hallway, see the shadow in the opaque glass, I know who it is. Lisa. I couldn't just let her leave, could I?

'That was quick?' My voice trembles with nerves. With adrenaline. With excitement.

'My car won't start.'

'Oh no.' I feign surprise, and step backwards, letting her come inside, linking my hands behind my back. While Lisa was in the bath I had scrubbed at my skin with a nailbrush until my fingers were pink and raw but I can still detect the faint whiff of oil. A tinge of black under my fingernails. Lisa was right all those years ago. It's amazing what you can learn on YouTube.

'Nick's good with cars. I'll get him to have a look when he comes home.'

'It's okay,' Lisa says. 'I've got AA membership. There's something wrong with my mobile though. It's saying, 'no SIM', but I've looked and it's still there. I'll need to pop it into Carphone Warehouse, I think. Can I use your landline?'

'No!' I blurt out. This wasn't part of my plan. She was supposed to sit in the kitchen and wait for Nick, not knowing Aaron would arrive first. I wanted to confront them together. I can't let her leave. I just can't. What will I do if I'm alone when Aaron comes? What will *he* do? 'The phone's not working.' My words come out garbled. 'Remember those nuisance calls?' She nods. I'd confided to Lisa, and she'd showered me with sympathy. Little had I known then it was likely her ringing me. Or Aaron. Perhaps both. 'BT thinks it is a fault on the line. You'll have to use my mobile.'

I head towards the kitchen, but the basement door catches my eye. I hesitate. Turn to Lisa and frown as though I'm thinking.

'I haven't seen it all morning. I think I left it down there last night.' I nod towards the basement.

'What were you doing down there?'

'I'd been calling Nick for dinner and he didn't hear. I had to go and fetch him. He started talking to me while he was finishing his run.' She's not the only one who can lie. I tilt my head to one side. 'I remember putting my phone on the table as I sat on the sofa. Nip and check. I must rescue the lemon meringue from the oven before I burn the house down.'

I spin on my heel and hurry into the kitchen, where I stand with my back to the wall. My kneecaps feel as though they are made of rubber. There is laughter in my head but it is not mine and I fight against it. I can't do this, can I? I can't lock her in.

Her footsteps thud down the stairs. Slow. Even. No rushing for her with her fake bump, and her fake baby, and suddenly I am furious. My desire to know the truth is stronger than my desire to do the right thing. *What has she been lying about since Jake died?* I cross to the basement door and pull it closed. Lock it. Leaning my forehead against the door I imagine Lisa on the other side thudding her fists, screaming to be let out, and this image whirlwinds around my mind until it is me thudding on the door. Me crying for help.

I back away down the hallway but I can still feel my palms stinging, my throat raw from my screaming. I don't know what is me and what is her any more. I clasp my hands tightly over my ears and screw up my eyes, slumping to the floor. I only wanted a family. It wasn't too much to ask for, was it? Slicing through the pounding in my head, the screaming, is a baby's cry, shrill and desperate, and I begin to rock back and forth as though I am soothing an infant. Soothing myself. *Please, please make it stop. I don't think I can take any more.* But I have to move. Aaron will be here soon, and my plan has gone all wrong. I don't know what I am going to do.


He's not coming.

The clouds are heavy and swollen with the threat of rain. The sky battleship grey.

He's not coming.

If he'd left Farncaster after the text, he'd have been here by now and it's almost five. I can't check Lisa's phone to see if he has texted again to tell her he's changed his mind because I have broken it. Nick will be home in an hour. I pace the lounge. Back and forth. A caged lion. I imagine Lisa doing the same downstairs.

The tea light under the oil burner flickers in the corner but the smell of lavender does little to calm me. I don't think I'll ever feel calm again.

I hold Jake's gold cross between my fingers. What would he think if he could see me now? How would he feel? A rush of shame engulfs me. My belly a mass of writhing snakes. I've locked his sister up like an animal and no matter what she has lied about, the money she has conned from us, Jake wouldn't condone this. I can almost see the disappointment in his eyes that once looked at me with passion. With lust. With love.

Revenge.

It was never purely about money; I know that. Lisa still blames me for Jake's death. He shouldn't have been with me that night. He should have been with her, and it must eat at her, as corrosive as acid, burning her sense of right and wrong. Aaron still blames me for losing his place at university, his longed-for career in medicine. How degraded he must feel being a cleaner at the hospital he'd once thought he'd be a surgeon at. I begin to cry. Was it not enough to let me think I was going to be a mum and snatch my dreams away? Did they also have to lead me to believe I was going mad? The phone calls, the wreath, the book. The smashed picture. Locking me in the toilet. Breaking into my car. The man who has been watching the house – was that someone they roped in with the promise of easy money from a desperate woman? Because desperate is what I was.

Love.

I have so much love to give a child. Such a yearning to feel a baby in my arms, hear the soft snuffling against my neck, smell talcum powder, but it's finished.

I am finished.

There is such an inherent sadness inside of me. I am broken. The cross seems to warm between my fingers.

I have to let Lisa out. She is quiet now and I hope she is calm. I have to let her go. The answers I crave won't fill the cot upstairs. They won't miraculously make me a mum.

It's over.

My legs are heavy with sadness as I turn to face the lounge door, taking a step towards the basement. One. Two. Three.

A noise from outside. I freeze. But it's only the forecast storm. The rain has started lashing against the window, hammering to be let in as Lisa is likely hammering to be let out.

Four steps. Five.

The hallway is suddenly flooded with light. There's the thrum of a car engine. A silence. A door slamming.

Aaron.

*He is here.*

# CHAPTER FORTY-ONE
## Now

My feet are stuck to the carpet. I can't seem to remember how to move. I don't know if the banging I can hear is in my head, in the basement, or from the front door. A tidal wave of panic crashes over me, almost knocking me off my feet. I stumble backwards. Lean against the wall, not able to stand on my own. Footsteps thud-thud-thud along with my heart. My earlier courage, fuelled by anger, is slipping away, slithering down between the gaps in the wall and the skirting boards, never to return. What was I thinking asking Aaron here?

There's the jangling of keys and once again I am back in that night. Jake slipping his key into the ignition. The engine roaring to life. I shake my head, and the sound is replaced with a crying baby, or is it me that is crying? I touch my cheeks with my fingertips and they come away wet. Laughter. *Stop the laughter*. How can I make it stop?

The front door swings open and Nick steps inside, handkerchief pressed to his face, crimson with blood that is still dripping.

'I banged my nose on the car door…' He tails off as he notices the state I am in.

I am shaking and sobbing and he dashes towards me, his mouth opening and closing, but his voice sounds muffled and echoey and I can't make out his words. I stare past his shoulder at the basement door, wanting him to read my thoughts. Know what I have done. Make it all better, but instead, he slips his arm around my shoulders and leads me into the kitchen. The softness of his voice combats the scraping of the chair legs against the tiled floor. His tone soothes me, although I cannot understand what he is saying. He would have made such a good dad. The whooshing in my ears grows louder and louder and dizziness engulfs me every time I move my head.

I am back at Perry Evans's party. Red and green flashing lights bright in my mind. His mum's cat ornaments rattling on the shelf as the bass vibrates. Vodka relaxing my muscles as I sway to the music. Paul Weller sings, and Jake's hand heats the small of my back. His voice murmurs. He pulls me towards him. My eyelids flutter and my head tilts. Lips part. I lean in for his kiss but over Jake's shoulder I see Lisa's expression. The hurt. The anger.

Lisa.

I press the heels of my hands against my eyes, digging my fingertips into my scalp.

It is Nick's hand on the small of my back. Nick's voice murmuring. The thudding isn't the bass: it's my own guilty heart.

'Kat. Shhh. It's okay.'

I try to shake my head, clutching his hand, willing him to know what is wrong, but he doesn't ask, and I think of all the times he has come home lately. The times I had told him someone was watching the house, someone had been in the house. My almost hysterical outpourings, and I almost don't blame him for not asking. But I need to tell him about Lisa. I can't leave her for hours like I was left. Scared. Alone. In the dark. At least she has a light, I reason, a sofa; it's not so bad. But it is. It is very, very bad.

'Nick…' I snatch a breath while I try to put my words into some semblance of order. It's almost impossible to know where to start.

'What the?' There are deep grooves on Nick's brow as he stares over my shoulder at the window.

Lightning cracks, and I almost hold my breath as I wait for the rumble of thunder. What has he seen?

Or who?

Even though I am expecting it, I still jump in my chair as the thunder crashes. Nick straightens up.

'What is it?' I whisper.

Nick shakes his head, but he can't tear his eyes away from the window and, almost in slow motion, I turn. The kitchen lights are reflected in the panes of glass and all I can see are our kitchen units and our shadowy figures.

'Someone was out there,' Nick says, and my hand gropes thin air until I find his fingers. I grasp his hand tightly.

'Let's go upstairs.' There's an urgency in my words.

I catch sight of the scan photo on the fridge – God knows where Lisa got that from – and I realise how devastated Nick will be that yet again he won't be a father, and it's all my fault. There's a part of me that wants to usher Lisa out of the house. To tell Nick the surrogacy has fallen through, but there have been so many lies already. I glance at his profile. His curly hair flopping in his eyes. Hair so like Ada's. Is he already a father? Suddenly I feel weighted down with the past, and it is almost more than I can bear. It's time for us both to be honest. About everything. I draw a breath so deep my ribcage feels it will burst as my lungs expand, but before I can speak, Nick gasps, and this time I see it too. The face looking in. The eyes staring at us. I am powerless to react as Nick sprints across the kitchen and wrenches open the back door. My hands cover my mouth. The rain bounces off the skylight, fierce and loud.

A muffled cry.

Lightning.

The sound of a scuffle.

Thunder.

'Nick?' I rush to the back door, but before I can step outside, Nick almost falls into the kitchen, dripping wet and panting hard. He isn't alone. He is dragging someone with him and they crumble onto the kitchen floor. There is a sickening crack as their heads make contact with the tiles.

Nick is sprawled on his back, blinking furiously as he raises his hand to his forehead, and I offer silent thanks that he is okay. But what about Aaron?

He is still. Quiet. Lying face down.

And slowly I inch my foot forward and jab my toe into his side.

He doesn't move.

# CHAPTER FORTY-TWO
## Now

'Nick?' I drop to my knees. The tiles are pooled with pink and, at first, I don't understand but then there's a horrible realisation. The rainwater is mixing with blood.

'Nick!' I pull his hand away from his forehead. There's a gash running alongside his hairline. I lean over him and yank open the drawer, pulling out a clean tea towel. As I press it to his wound the stark white cotton turns crimson. I look over my shoulder, half-expecting my ankle to be grabbed, hands around my throat, but there is no movement.

Raindrops gust into my face, and the wind causes the backdoor to crash against the worktop. I skirt around Nick and push the door closed, my socked feet almost slipping on the water pooling on the floor. I pick my way, more carefully, back to Nick.

'Can you sit up?' I lever my hands under his armpits and pull him hard. As his upper body lifts the colour drains from his face and he sways slightly as he sits, swallowing hard.

'Sorry. I should have believed you. About the man hanging around. About everything.'

'Is he?' I look over my shoulder, I can't bring myself to say the word. But I notice the rise and fall of his ribcage. He's alive. 'Should we?' I am shaking so hard now I feel my body might break apart. We need to call the police, I know. An ambulance, at the very least, but first I need to tell Nick that Lisa is in the basement. How can I explain? I could go to prison. The very thought winds me and I can't move. Can't speak. I'm caught in a tangle of secrets and lies and I don't know how to unravel them.

'There are things I need to tell you, Kat.' Nick grips my hands so hard it hurts.

'Not now—'

'Yes. Now.' Nick's tone is as sharp as broken glass, and I flinch. 'It *has* to be now.'

'We can't talk with a body on the floor. He needs help. I'm going to call—' I pull myself free and start to stand.

'No!' Nick grabs my wrist with one hand, twisting the skin, yanking me back to the floor, and a bolt of pain shoots up my arm. 'Listen first.' The fingers on Nick's other hand flutter to his scar as he begins to speak.

At first his words are stilted, forced, his tongue not used to forming the truth. My head shakes 'no!' as the weight of Nick's past crushes down on me, as black and heavy as the swollen clouds that scud outside the kitchen window. He is crying as he speaks, the shoulders I thought were broad enough to carry us both seem to shrink before my eyes. His words trip over each other, desperate to be heard. I don't want to listen to what he has to say, and yet, at the same time, I know I have to. And unbidden my voice cuts through his and, sitting here, on the wet floor in our immaculate kitchen, we reveal ourselves to be the people we really are. I have never felt more vulnerable and exposed. I'm sharing me, all of me, and he is doing the same, and I'm utterly stricken as I realise the threads of our lives have been woven together in ways I could not possibly have imagined. Is it us? Was it always going to be us that were destined to be? Not Jake? Never Jake?

I try to pull my hand away, but he won't let me go until he reaches the end of his story, and I have told him mine. Once we are battered into silence by the truth I wrench my hand from his grasp. I don't want him to touch me. I don't want him to touch me ever again.

# CHAPTER FORTY-THREE
## Then

Nick hunkered down in the shop doorway, head dipped against the biting wind, freezing hands stuffed into his pockets. Richard was late, and Nick longed for the days he used to be able to call for his best friend and be invited into his home. That was in the days before he was arrested. Before he received a suspended sentence for ABH, for what happened with his dad. Richard said it didn't matter: his parents didn't judge him. He'd explained to them there were extenuating circumstances. At nineteen, Richard sounded like the solicitor he was determined to be. Still, Nick had felt the frosty disapproval of Richard's dad. He had noticed the way Richard's mum didn't quite make eye contact with him any more, and he'd wondered whether he would always be judged on that night. It hardly seemed fair. He'd told his boss at the supermarket about his conviction, and the very next day he'd been 'let go'. It was coincidental, apparently. Due to cutbacks, he said, but Nick didn't believe that. He didn't know how he'd ever be anything now except sad and angry. From the chip shop next door a whiff of vinegar drifted towards Nick, mingling with the smell of hot fat, and his stomach grumbled. He wished he could bite on crunchy batter, taste the soft white fish inside, the chip paper warming his lap, but he was skint.

The purr of an engine caused Nick to twist his neck and peer down the road but it wasn't Richard in the BMW he'd got for his birthday. Nick huffed out white air. His fingertips would be too cold to grip the steering wheel when Richard gave him another driving lesson around the old industrial estate. He could do three-point turns now and almost parallel park. Richard said he'd be ready for his test soon and that would be another step towards freedom. The atmosphere at home was thick with the things that were never talked about. Nick's dad's face had healed and his mum, thinner than ever, glided through the house like a ghost. You'd almost think that night had never happened if it weren't for the way Dad never quite looked him in the eye any more. It was a small victory.

At last headlights cut through the fog and Richard slowed to a halt in front of Nick. His car vibrated with the pounding bass from the dance music blasting out of the top-of-the-range speakers.

'Took your time.' Nick slid into the passenger seat and blew on his hands to warm them.

'Where's my jacket?' Richard asked.

'Shit. Sorry.' Nick had meant to bring back the jacket he'd borrowed for yet another interview for a job he'd never get once he declared he had a criminal record. He knew Richard needed it for a posh event he was going to that evening with his father. 'Networking,' he'd said. It sounded poncey. As Nick had been getting ready to leave the house his dad had come home and then he'd been in such a rush to get away he'd forgotten.

'Let's whizz over to yours and pick it up. I'll still have time to give you a driving lesson after, just a shorter one.'

Nick gnawed on the edge of his thumb as Richard eased the car forward.

Outside Nick's house he kept the engine running, the stereo blaring.

'Don't be long.' Richard pulled out his mobile and started tapping away at the screen as Nick jumped out the car and ran up the path, pushed open the front door.

*

Something was wrong.

He sensed it before he'd even stepped onto the doormat, and he paused, muscles tense, heart racing, as he tried to discern why the air was so thick. So heavy. It was laden with the smell of smoked haddock they'd eaten earlier, but that wasn't it.

Something wasn't right.

Nick didn't call out to his mum, as he usually would, as if he instinctively knew she wouldn't be able to answer him. He didn't switch on the lights.

Something bad had happened.

Nick was as certain of that as he was of his own name. He crept down the hallway, pushing open the door to the kitchen, blinking in the gloom. Nothing was where it should be. The table was upended. The chairs on their sides. He stepped forward. His feet splintered already broken crockery. There was a bang outside. The gate?

Fear.

Nick was scared. He stretched out his hand and fumbled for the light switch. The kitchen was awash with light but it wasn't warm or comforting as it shone a spotlight on the mess. The biscuit tin where mum kept her escape fund was lidless and empty, resting against the hob. On the floor was the large knife used to carve the Sunday meat, its stainless steel blade sharp and jagged. Nick's eyes trailed over the floor. He stopped as he spotted it. Breathed in sharply. Hand on chest as though in pain.

Blood.

Dark and dried on the grubby grey lino.

Blood.

It was then that the panic set in.

# CHAPTER FORTY-FOUR
## Then

'Is Lisa there?' I asked Nancy. I'd already tried her mobile but it was switched off again.

There was a beat. A muffled voice, as though someone was talking with their hand over the receiver. 'Sorry, Kat. You've just missed her,' Nancy said a little too brightly, and I knew she was lying.

That night, at the park, after Lisa had dragged me away from Aaron, I'd clung to her as we walked home, my legs shaking with shock. At my front door I'd started to say again: 'If you hadn't come...' but Lisa had held her hand up and taken a step back.

'You shouldn't have told Mr Lemmington, Kat.'

I was stunned. How was this my fault? 'I had to. Someone could have got hurt. Died even. What if you'd had a bad reaction? He needs stopping. Besides, did you see the look in his eyes? God knows what he's capable of. He'll try and get his own back. I know he will.' I was babbling. Fear pushing my words out in one gibbering rush.

'Stop thinking about yourself. What if he tells the police he was selling to me? Did you think of that?' She was shouting.

'He won't. Why would he? Don't worry,' I'd told her but she had walked away without answering.

I hadn't left the house in two days for fear of reprisals and now Lisa wouldn't return my calls. Still, I didn't think my dread of Aaron was the only thing making me feel sick.

I swung my legs out of bed and pulled on yesterday's sundress before sliding my drawer open. From underneath the tangle of bras and pants I pulled out the Boots paper bag. My period was late, and I couldn't keep pretending it was coincidental I never fancied breakfast any more and felt sick every day around dinner time. I had to find out for sure. I unfolded the paper that came in the box and read the words slowly and carefully, but despite my straight A grades at school, I had to read the instructions three times to try and make sense of them and I desperately wished Lisa was with me.

I hesitated before carrying the kit into the bathroom. Apart from the first time in the woods we had always used a condom, and no one gets pregnant their first time, do they? But the little voice in my head mocked *and you're supposed to be the clever one* and I knew if I wanted to find out, now was the time with the house to myself for the day. *If* I wanted to find out.

Perched on the toilet I scanned the instructions again just to make sure. My bladder was bursting, but I couldn't wee. I had to run the taps for ages before I could. I put the cap back on the test and rested it on the side of the basin before checking the time and washing my hands. The box said results could show in anything between sixty seconds and five minutes. To make sure the test had worked I was determined to wait for the full five minutes before I checked, but there were only so many times I could pace the small room, nerves slithering around my stomach, before I snatched up the stick, staring in disbelief at the + in the results window. Although I knew it meant positive, I studied the picture on the front of the box again, just to make sure. My knees turned to jelly and I sat heavily on the side of the bath. I couldn't be pregnant. I just couldn't. I was too young, but I was old enough to know better. *We* were old enough to know better, I reminded myself. I wasn't in this alone, but still we should have used a condom. My gaze darted between the box and the stick and the words '99%

accurate' leapt out at me. My shoulders sagged a little. Of course. There had to be a 1 per cent chance of failure.

I took out our toothbrushes from the glass on the windowsill and rubbed dried toothpaste from the rim before filling it with lukewarm water from the tap and gulping it down. It took four glasses and twenty minutes before I could produce a small amount of wee for the second test but I put the cap on the stick, hoping it was enough. This time I couldn't take my eyes off the small square box that would predict my future and as a cross began to appear, faintly at first but darkening with every passing second, bile bit the back of my throat. I shook the stick like a mercury thermometer and checked the window again, as though this may have altered the result, but it still showed positive. Positive. What an innocuous word but what implications it carried. My mind fast-forwarded to a time I'd be living in a grotty bedsit, fag hanging from the corner of my mouth – ridiculous as I'd never smoked – stirring a pan of beans at a one-ring hob, while a toddler in a stained T-shirt stamped his feet, screaming for attention. And yet there was another picture, nudging the first out of the way. Me crossing a kitchen, roast chicken browning in the oven, to kiss Jake hello as he came home from work and, as young as I was, I *liked* that picture. I'd always been drawn to babies. Always wanted to be a mum and it flitted across my mind that I might have done this subconsciously, found an escape from this house, my dad, but when I thought of my dad I felt sick. What was I going to tell him? What was I going to tell Jake?

The front door slammed, startling me. No one should be home. Heavy footsteps pounded up the stairs. The door rattled.

'Kat?'

'Dad. Thought you'd gone to work?'

'I forgot something. Need the loo now I'm here.'

Hurriedly I looked around. If I came out carrying the box and tests he would see them, and there was nowhere under my dress to hide them. In the corner was a stack of towels and I stuffed everything underneath the top one. I would move them as soon as he was done.

'Come on.' His impatience radiated through the wood.

I clicked open the lock and slipped through the door, not able to look him in the eye. In my bedroom I straightened my duvet and plumped up my pillows, waiting anxiously, listening for the flush of the chain, but it didn't come. A shadow fell behind me and as I spun around I was met by my dad's furious face. He raised his hand and slapped my cheek, hard. Falling back onto the bed I began to cry, but he yanked me to my feet and shook me like I was nothing. His eyes were wild, and I was scared. Really scared. As strict as he was, he had never laid a hand on me before.

'Slut.'

The word stuck like a spear. I opened my mouth but there was nothing I could say to make this better. 'Couldn't you keep your legs shut? We've time to get this sorted.'

I could see him mentally working out timescales, and I say: 'Sorted?' although I know perfectly well what he meant.

'You can't possibly keep it,' he said and, in that moment, I felt a burst of love for the baby. My baby. Jake's baby.

'I can.'

'You will bloody well have an abortion.'

'You can't tell me what to do. You're always telling me what to do!' Nineteen years of built up resentment came spewing out.

'While you're under my roof—'

'Then I won't stay under your roof.' I pushed past dad, knocking him with my shoulder, pulled open my drawer, flung clothes onto my bed.

'Don't be stupid,' he said. 'Where are you going to go?'

'Anywhere but here.'

'You'll stay in your room until I get back from my meeting.'

'I won't.' I was defiant.

'You bloody well will and we'll talk when your mum gets home.'

'I'll be gone by then.' I almost goaded him but I was too angry to tread carefully. I knew I had gone too far when his fingers dug into my shoulder and his hand lay heavy on the small of my back, forcing me forward.

'I'll make sure you're still here.'

I tried to dig my heels in, stretching out my arms for something to grab hold of, but my fingertips closed around air. Before I could properly catch my breath he was forcing me down the stairs. At the sight of the hall cupboard, with its lock on the door, I knew what he was going to do.

'Please.' My voice was high and shrill. My skin slick with sweat. 'Don't do this. You don't have to do this.'

There was a grunt behind me, the sound of heavy breathing, and I did everything I could to make it harder for him. I stiffened my body and struggled, and there was a second when he released his grip, when I was free, and just as my mind was processing there were no longer hands on me he opened the cupboard door. I tried to run but instantaneously there was pressure on the top of my arms and I was shaken, hard. My brain rattled around my skull. I bit my tongue and swallowed down my fear and the metallic taste of blood.

My vision grew hazy, the ground beneath my feet felt soft, as my body grew limp. I had the sensation of falling before I was yanked back and thrust forward, landing heavily on my hands and knees. My head banged against something hard and solid and slivers of pain shot through my arms and into my neck.

Dazed, I almost didn't hear the slam behind me. The click of a lock.

'No! Wait! Dad!' I leapt to my feet. Nausea rose as the world seemed to rock and I blindly reached out, trying to find the door. The blackness was all-consuming. Crushing. My hands shook as I slapped my palms over the walls, spinning around until at last I found it. I gripped the door handle but my hand was clammy and it took me three attempts to twist it, and when I did it confirmed what I already knew.

I was trapped.

# CHAPTER FORTY-FIVE
## Then

Something terrible had happened. Nick knew as he stared in horror at the trashed kitchen. He didn't know whether to call the police or search the rest of the house. He had never felt the blood whooshing through his body before but now he felt everything. His pulse throbbing in his ears, the heat in his veins, the prickling in his scalp. He picked up the knife and held it in front of him as he left the room. The lounge was empty. On its side, a crumpled can of lager on the coffee table, sticky liquid on the glass. Something else for his mum to clear up. *Mum*. The word filled his head, bouncing around his mind. He needed to find her, and yet he was almost scared to.

Something terrible had taken place here tonight.

There was a faint knocking noise and, at first, Nick thought it must be his mum, but it was only the fridge, and the house fell into an eerie silence once more. In the hallway, Nick switched on the light and his stomach contracted hard and fast as he noticed the blood trailing down the passage, up the stairs. He squeezed the knife handle. His palms were slippery now; his grip wasn't as tight as he would have liked.

Unbidden his feet began to climb the stairs. One, two, the third that creaked. His whole body tensed. As he reached the top he half expected a fist to slam into him, pushing him back down, but there was nothing there except the sense of foreboding sticking to him like a second skin. On the landing, Nick caught a whiff of the minty shower gel he had used before he went out. *Which way?* The bathroom to the left. His parent's room to the right.

His whole body was pulsing like it did in the car with Richard's dance music, and at the thought of his friend Nick wondered whether he should ask him to come in. Safety in numbers. *Coward* whispered the voice in his head. And Nick forced his feet forward.

*Mum.*

He crept into his parent's bedroom. Fearing the worst but hoping for the best.

He turned on the light and gasped.

# CHAPTER FORTY-SIX
## Then

I had lost all concept of time as I sat, knees drawn to my chest, arms wrapped around my shins. My eyes had grown accustomed to the blackness and I could make out shapes. Sometimes when I blinked I thought they moved but I knew that was impossible. I was alone.

To my shame I had peed in the corner like an animal, and the smell of ammonia stung almost as much as the humiliation I felt. Each time I swallowed my throat grew sorer. I had given up shouting. My face was streaked with dried tears, which made my skin dry and tight. I really needed a drink and I strained my eyes in the dark as though one might appear. I had long stopped believing in magic. But I still had hope. He couldn't keep me here forever. Someone would miss me – wouldn't they? Start asking questions soon.

Jake.

My mouth formed his name and my heart ached. There was a scraping sound outside. My head jerked up, eyes drawn to the door. I couldn't quite see and simultaneously I was praying for it to open, and equally longing for it to stay closed.

There was the soft click and light sliced through the blackness. I shielded my eyes, whimpering as a hand gripped my elbow, yanking me to my feet.

# CHAPTER FORTY-SEVEN
## Then

There was a mound on the bed, Nick had thought it was a body, but as he stood over it he saw it was just a bunched up duvet. The sour smell of his father and unhappiness tainted the air, and he spun around and left the room.

*Mum.*

The bathroom door began to creak open before it became jammed. Something heavy prevented it from fully opening. Nick rested his forehead against the door. He felt sick. *Coward.* He reached inside the gap, hands gripping air until he located the pull cord of the light switch. He yanked hard. There was a pop; light. Nick shook his head from side to side as he peered through the gap in the door and saw his mum's legs splayed out on the white tiles. The streak of blood by her side.

The knife slipped from his grasp as he gently pushed the door and squeezed through the gap, dropping to his knees in front of the too still, too silent body. *Mum.* He had found her – but he was filled with self-loathing as he pressed his fingers to her neck. He couldn't feel a pulse. He was too late. The front door slammed, and the stairs creaked under the weight of footsteps.

*Dad.*

White-hot anger seared through him, scorching his sense of good and bad. Right and wrong.

He picked up the knife and he waited.

# CHAPTER FORTY-EIGHT
## Then

'You stink.' Dad pulled me from the small cupboard under the stairs. My legs were stiff and I stumbled, too ashamed to admit I'd been unable to control my bladder, but the stench of urine gave me away. The look of disgust on his face made me feel smaller than I'd ever felt before. The rug in the hallway skidded on the floorboards and I lost my footing again, as Dad gripped my elbow, propelling me forward.

'Go and get cleaned up. Mum will be home soon and then we'll talk.'

'What's the point when you won't listen?' Every ounce of logic inside told me I should keep quiet but the words burst from me. 'I want Jake. Jake loves me.'

'Love,' Dad spat as he dragged me up the stairs. It was awkward with both of us squeezed between the two wooden bannisters. I slipped, my feet scrambled for traction, but he didn't once loosen his grip. In that moment I drank everything in, the yellowing gloss paint chipping from the rail, the way the carpet was darker at the edges, the wallpaper curling above the skirting boards. It was if I knew this would be the last time I would see them and I had to memorise every last detail.

'I'll tell you what love is. It's marrying the girl stupid enough to fall pregnant. The giving up on your own dreams to support a family you didn't want.'

We reached the top of the stairs, and I faced Dad; my eyes searched his face for some sign of affection.

'You're talking about Mum? About me?' I felt winded. I knew Dad wasn't exactly paternal but I never once thought he didn't want me. I thought his strictness was a sign of love, not fear of me repeating the same mistakes. 'You didn't want me?'

'Not just me. Mum had plans of her own but her parents were Catholic. She couldn't have an abortion.'

'And that's what you wish, I'd been aborted?' I couldn't quite believe what I was hearing.

'Oh don't look all wide-eyed, Kat. We made the best of it. We've been good parents, haven't we?'

'You locked me in a cupboard!'

'Only to stop you running off. We've encouraged you to work hard. Follow your dreams.'

'You've encouraged me to follow *your* dreams. I never wanted to be a doctor. I want to be an actress.' I was screaming.

'Well you had us fooled running around with that layabout.'

'Jake isn't a layabout, he's—'

'Not in your life any more is what he is. We can get you into a private clinic. Get this sorted out before uni starts.'

'*This*,' I placed my hands over my belly. '*This* is your grandchild.'

'It's nothing but a mass of cells.'

'It is my baby!' My throat was raw as the words were ripped from me.

'You will ruin your life.' Dad's voice raged over mine, and everything I knew I should do and say to calm him down, buy me some time, was eclipsed by one simple fact I could not contain.

'I love Jake.' My voice was quiet but firm and, even to me, my words rang true.

It was as though Dad aged as he ran his fingers through his thinning hair. I felt a pang of loss for the father who was slipping away from me, as well as for the father I wanted him to be, but summer-sunshine picnics and Sunday-afternoon-games-of-Monopoly were never part of our family. I vowed it would be different with my child. Behind Dad, through the landing window, I watched wisps of clouds float by, and I could almost see my ambition being swept away with them, but as strong as the pull of the stage was, the craving of applause, I couldn't imagine anything better than days spent making potato paint prints and moulding wild animals from Playdoh. The desire to hold my baby sparked a quiet determination in me that chased away my fear. My longing grew hotter and brighter.

'I won't have an abortion.' My eyes locked onto Dad's and I thought I saw sorrow but then his eyes grew cold and hard as he clutched my elbow once more.

'You'll do what I bloody well tell you.' He began to shake me. I tried to push him away but his grip was strong. A primal urge to protect my baby kicked in. I shook my arm free and placed both hands on his chest. My palms were burning hot and tingling as I pushed as hard as I could.

The world slowed and stopped. I became keenly aware of the thickness in the air, the terror on Dad's face as he began to fall backwards down the stairs, his arms windmilling. Automatically, I sidestepped so he couldn't drag me down with him. Each bump was sickening. His body bounced and twisted and, as he landed at the bottom, his head cracked against the hard wooden floor. I covered my face with both hands. The silence was weighted with guilt as I waited for a groan, the sound of movement, for redemption, but there was nothing except my heart punching my ribs. It took an age before I splayed my fingers and looked at my father lying face down on the floor below me, his leg at an awkward angle, a trickle of blood seeping from underneath his head.

There are so many things I could have done. So many things I should have done. But as I descended the stairs – my legs trembling, my palms still hot and tingling – and stepped over his motionless body, it wasn't to reach the phone and call for help. It was to reach the front door. I was numb to everything except the thought of reaching Jake. And it haunts me to this day that I didn't hesitate on the step for a single second.

I didn't look back.

I ran.

# CHAPTER FORTY-NINE
## Then

In my rush to leave the house I had left my bag and purse, but I couldn't go back. What if Dad was conscious? *What if he wasn't?* I jogged along our street. The bright red postbox where I had posted applications to universities I didn't want to go to; Mrs Phillips's bungalow – she had always given me an apple as I walked past on my way to school; the cherry tree that coated the pavements with a pale pink blossom, obscuring my chalked out hopscotch. Dad would never forgive me, neither would Mum once she knew. It looked like his leg was broken, sticking out at one of the odd angles we'd had to learn for GCSE maths that I thought I would never come across again. It would be incredibly painful when he woke. I slowed, thought I should go back, at least to call for help, sit with him until the ambulance arrived, but then Mum would know about the baby, and the inevitable tears, the guilt I felt over Dad's accident, might cloud my judgement. They might force me into an abortion just as they forced me onto a degree course I never wanted to do. It was best this way; but still my sense of right and wrong raged until the edges were blurred and I didn't know what the right thing was any more. I stood on the corner, lungs sucking in air. My palms hot and tingling as though they could still feel Dad's chest beneath them, the beating of his heart, before I pushed and he lay broken and bleeding on the floor. Mum would be home any minute; it wasn't like he would lie there for hours, in pain and alone, but I had never felt so conflicted before.

I lay my hands over the baby I could not yet feel, Jake's baby, and I carried on running.


By the time I reached Jake's house there was a stitch jabbing my side and, after I had banged on the door, I pressed both hands against my ribs trying to ease it.

'Hello, Kat love. Are you okay?' Nancy looked concerned. 'Of course you're not. Come in.'

In the lounge we sat on the sofa and I longed to pound upstairs and throw myself into Jake's arms but I couldn't stop trembling, didn't think my legs would make it. Nancy handed me a tissue, and I wiped my eyes, blew my nose.

'What's happened?' Nancy took my hands in hers. 'Between you and Lisa. It breaks my heart you've fallen out. Tell me everything.'

'It's not Lisa I'm crying about.' I fell silent. Where would I even start to tell her what's wrong?

'Whatever it is, I can help.'

I longed to tell her I was carrying her grandchild, but she couldn't be the first person I told.

'Is Jake here?'

'No. He's gone to The Three Fishes with Lisa.'

I stood. 'I'm going to find him.'

'I'd give you a lift but he took my car.'

'I'll be fine,' I said, but I could see by the concern in her eyes she didn't believe the words any more than I did.


'Jake.' My voice was too loud as I called across the wine bar. Heads swivelled but I didn't care my clothes were crumpled, my face streaked with tears. I flung myself into his arms.

'Do you mind? I'm *supposed* to be having a night out with my brother!' Lisa kept her voice light, as though she was joking, but her tone didn't quite coat the resentment festering underneath her words.

Stung, I tugged at Jake's hand. Now was not the time to start to repair my relationship with Lisa, although I wanted to. 'We have to go.'

'I don't think so.' Lisa sidestepped so she was standing between us and the door. 'The world doesn't revolve around you, Kat.'

'I know but…' The image of Dad, lying like a rag doll at the bottom of the stairs, was burned onto my conscience but I couldn't say what I had done in public. 'I need to talk to Jake, in private.'

'Private? I'm your best friend, or have you forgotten? But then you don't have any loyalty to me, do you? You could have got me into huge trouble.'

'What's she talking about?' Jake asked me but the hostility in Lisa's words had rendered me mute. His gaze shifted to Lisa 'What have you done?'

'Nothing as bad as she thinks.' She spat out the words. 'Nothing as bad as dating your best friend's twin without even talking to her about it first.' Lisa pushed her face towards mine. I could smell white wine, cheap and sour. 'My own fucking brother.' She was shouting now.

I could feel the curious gaze of the other customers and wanted to scream at them to mind their own business, but instead, I said quietly: 'My dad locked me in a cupboard.'

'What?' They both looked at me in disbelief.

'All day. I've been locked in a tiny cupboard all day. In the dark. I thought I was going to suffocate. I was so scared.' I started to cry again.

'Let's get out of here.' Jake put his arm around my shoulders. 'I've got the car outside.'

'No! You said you'd leave it here and we'd get a taxi back. You've been drinking, Jake.' Lisa held his arm.

'I've only had one pint and I feel fine.'

'We were going to talk. I have something to tell you. It's important.'

'You can see what a state Kat is in. You can tell me later.'

'Don't go.' She was pleading now, and I felt horrible for Jake as though he had to choose.

'I have to.' There was finality to Jake's words.

Lisa looked wretched as she said: 'Fine. I'll call you a cab.' She stalked outside, already punching numbers on her mobile.

'Are you okay?' Jake cupped my face between his palms.

'Not really. There's something else you need to know.'

'Come on.' Jake took my hand and led me out the back door to the car park.

'What about Lisa?' I climbed into the passenger seat.

'She'll be fine.' He eased the car out into the street, and sheltering in the front entrance Lisa turned, phone to her ear. 'Wait!' she shouted but Jake drove off, and as I looked in the side mirror I saw her standing there and she looked so distraught I felt terrible. *Is there anybody I haven't hurt today?*


We didn't speak as we drove for the short journey out of town. Jake's mobile rang, Lisa's name flashing up, and Jake switched it off. He slipped his mum's car into the lay-by outside the woods and silently we both opened our doors and stepped outside. Dusty earth rose, tickling my nose as I planted my feet on the ground. Wordlessly Jake took my hand in his and we fell into step together, both instinctively knowing where we were going. Jake hadn't asked any questions, as though he knew what I had to say would irrevocably alter our lives forever, and I hoped he would see it as a beginning and not an end. Splintered wood snagged my dress as I climbed over the wooden fence, goosebumps sprung up on my arms. It was colder under the canopy of trees and I hesitated, wondering whether we should turn back, but Jake rested his arm over my shoulders and I drew warmth from his presence.

Twigs cracked underfoot, and high above the treetops the moon shimmered its hello as the sun bid good night. It grew darker and darker until we reached the clearing where Jake first made love to me. It felt fitting I would tell him here. Jake shrugged off his jacket and spread it on the ground and we both sat, bodies pressed tight against each other. I could feel the heat from his skin. His forehead was damp with sweat. He looked scared.

'I know,' he said.

My stomach plummeted. 'What do you know?'

He took my hand, gently rubbing my knuckles with his thumb. 'You're pregnant,' he said, and he didn't sound sad, or angry, or any of the things I thought he might. He stated the fact as though it were inevitable.

'Yes.'

Time was suspended as I waited for him to speak. The wind stopped blowing, the leaves stopped rustling. I crossed the fingers on the hand that was hanging by my side, praying he would tell me it would all be okay. Instead he let go of me and stumbled as he stood. The first step he took away from me almost broke my heart.

# CHAPTER FIFTY
## Then

Jake took another step forward and it felt as though everything was being ripped away, but then he turned and dropped to one knee.

'Marry me, Kat.'

'Don't be stupid.' I looked into the eyes of the boy I loved and I knew I'd have to tell him what I'd done to my dad. He'd probably never look at me the same way again.

'Stupid?' He began to tickle me. 'Handsome, funny and oh so sexy but stupid? No. Madly in love with you. Yes. We can make this work.'

'Can we?' More than anything I wanted to believe him.

'We can.'

'But—'

'But nothing. It may be sooner than we'd hoped but you and me, Kat, we're written in the stars.' His arm arced towards the sky, a big, sweeping gesture. 'A baby! A family of three. It would have happened eventually anyway. You can still act. I can still be an architect. It will be fine. Better than fine. You'll see.' His words tumbled out, one mad rush, and his euphoria crashed over me, washing away my doubts. 'Here.' He unclasped the gold cross he always wore. I lifted my hair as he fastened it around my neck. 'I'll get you a ring, of course. We may be young but we'll do it all properly,' he said, and this time, when he made love to me, it wasn't against the tree, hard and fast, but on the floor of the forest, soft and sweet. I didn't care if we never made it to a bed as long as I spent the rest of my life in Jake's arms. If it wasn't for the drizzle I'd have been happy lying, limbs entwined, for hours, but as the cold drops of rain fell heavier, we ran to the car, holding Jake's jacket over our heads, and I felt as though we were running into our future.

'I can't go home.' I chewed my thumb nervously as I sat in the passenger seat.

'You can stay at mine. Mum will be cool.'

On the verges, rabbits ventured out now darkness had fallen, despite the rain bouncing off the car roof, making the road look even darker. Jake was driving faster than usual. The radio was tuned to the old-fashioned station Nancy loved. The Monkees sang 'I'm a Believer'. I glanced at his profile – the sheen covering his skin, his torso hunched over the wheel as if he could make the car go even faster.

'Are you okay?' Part of me wondered whether he'd gone into shock. Whether the news was too much. He turned to me, his eyes glinting in the gloom.

'I'm feeling a bit sick actually. My head's spinning. You're sure, aren't you? About the baby? I'm really going to be a dad?'

'Yes. Pull over and get some air. You're going too fast anyway.' I placed a hand over my stomach. The heater was blasting out warm air but the windscreen was fogging. I fished a tissue out of my bag and tried to wipe it clean, but I spread the dampness, making it worse.

'I just want to get home. Process it all properly. Parents! Us!' The car lurched forward as he speeded up and there was a squealing of tyres as we hared around the bend.

The Monkees faded to 'Are You Lonesome Tonight?', and Elvis Presley's voice was so wistful it almost seemed like a sign. Something bad was going to happen.

'Jake.'

'Chill. It's okay.'

His eyes locked onto mine. One of his hands left the wheel and he tucked my hair behind my ear, and his touch was so tender. The music filled the car, and it felt like the perfect, perfect moment, until lights dazzled me through the windscreen. My head jerked towards the road. I was transfixed by the headlights of the other car approaching us, on the wrong side of the road, far, far too fast.

Everything seemed to slow: I do not know whether I screamed first or raised both arms in front of my face. Metal crunched; the seatbelt sliced into me as I was thrown forward and then pushed back as the airbag inflated. My head pounded against the window and blackness sucked me under.

I don't know how long I was out for but the first thing I was aware of was the crushing darkness. It was dark. So dark. I couldn't see and panic tornadoed through me. It took every ounce of energy to prise open my eyes and I blinked furiously as they began to water.

It was hot. Unbearably hot. Acrid smoke sealed off my throat, and as I coughed and coughed, my lungs burned with the effort of trying to drag in air, my ribs felt like they would shatter. 'Jake.' I was screaming his name over and over but I think it must have been in my head because I couldn't hear. Just for one solitary moment there was perfect, perfect silence before my senses roared back to life. Someone was screaming, anguished cries that my ears would never forget. I didn't think it was me. I couldn't move. Couldn't think. Where was I? I was trapped, and I was scared. So scared. Somehow Elvis was still singing but I wasn't sure if it was real. I wasn't sure if I was real. There was something warm and sticky running down my face and as it trickled down my nose I could smell the blood. Every cell in my body screamed at me to move. To run. But I couldn't. Jake! *I must reach him* but I couldn't undo my seatbelt. I couldn't feel my body properly. There was no pain. Why wasn't there any pain? 'Jake!' I tried to shift in my seat. I was weak but I put my palms under me and raised myself up slightly before dropping again, and as I sank back into the seat I felt a dampness between my thighs. I was so scared I thought I must have wet myself.

'Jake!'

He didn't answer. I looked to my right. His eyes were open, a crimson river gushing from his temple. He was waxy, still, and his stillness conjured the image of my dad, bleeding and broken at the bottom of the stairs.

Momentarily I raised my fingers, touching the gold cross around my neck and it crossed my mind this was some divine punishment for what I'd done.

# CHAPTER FIFTY-ONE
## Then

Nick stood, hand gripping the knife handle. The steel blade glinting in the light. The footsteps reached the top of the landing and a voice called 'Nick? You found my jacket?' Nick stepped out of the bathroom and opened and closed his mouth, silently watching confusion, worry, and then an awful realisation flit across Richard's face as he noticed Nick's mum lying on the floor.

'Angela?' Richard's voice was loud. Firm. In control. Nick sagged against the doorframe, thankful Richard had done his Duke of Edinburgh Award. Nick silently promised he'd learn first aid so he'd never feel this helpless again. He covered his mouth with both hands, watching as Richard pressed his fingers against mum's neck; he hadn't felt a pulse, but Richard knew exactly where to touch. He nodded before saying: 'she's alive'.

'I'll go and phone for an ambulance,' Nick said but before he had reached the top of the stairs he heard his mum whimper and then moan. He rushed to her side.

'Mum.' Nick's voice cracked. 'I thought you were…'

'Where is he?' Mum's voice was raspy, her eyes glazed. As she struggled to sitting she pressed a hand against the side of her head; scarlet drops of blood trickled through her fingers.

'He's not here.' Nick exchanged a worried glance with Richard, keenly aware his dad could return at any time. 'Mum, I'm going to fetch a doctor.'

'No! I'm fine.' But his mum winced as she moved. 'He found out.' She tore off toilet tissue and dabbed at the cut on her mouth. 'The money. He knew I was going to leave. I thought,' she whimpered, 'I thought he was going to kill me.'

'I'll call the police, Angela.' Richard squeezed her arm. 'He won't come near you again.'

'No! Not safe.' Mum stood and stumbled. Nick caught her around the waist and she fell into him, and he remembered the time he used to press his small body against her legs, bury his head into her stomach to block out the shouting. 'I want to leave. I have to leave.' Hysteria crept into her voice and Nick soothed her, as she used to him.

'Shhh. It's okay.'

'It's not okay.' But her tone was lower. Calmer. 'We *have* to leave. When we're safe we can call the police.'

'Where will we go?'

'My sister. Your aunt. She'll take us in.'

'Is she local, Angela? I can drop you off.' Richard checked his watch. Nick knew he was thinking of the function he needed to go to; the icy disapproval of his father if he missed it.

'It's about an hour's drive,' Mum said.

Nick exchanged a glance with Richard. It would cost a fortune by taxi. Cash they didn't have.

'Richard? Could you lend me some money, please?' Nick hated asking.

Richard swallowed hard and tapped his keys against his thigh; the way he always did when he was thinking.

'Take these.' He pressed the car keys into Nick's hands. 'I don't have much cash on me and I must go. I'm nearly late as it is. I'll grab my jacket and catch the bus on the corner. You get your mum out of here. Away from…' Richard's gaze swept over the blood on the floor, the knife.

'But I haven't passed my test,' Nick said, though he curled his fingers against the key fob anyway.

'No, but you're good enough. You had a great instructor.' Richard offered a faint smile and there was so much Nick wanted to say but his head was full of things they needed to pack, the thought his dad might come back, and instead he patted Richard on the shoulder. Sometimes there was no need for words.

'Why haven't I ever heard of this aunt?' Nick said. The rain was torrential. Nick knew he should focus all of his attention on the road but he'd grown up watching *Casualty*, and knew from the egg-sized bump on Mum's forehead he should keep her talking. He was terrified she would fall asleep before he got there. It wasn't like he knew where he was going anyway.

'We were close, as sisters, growing up.' Mum started to speak, her words unclear as they spilled from her split lip, and Nick turned down the radio so he could properly hear her. He didn't want to listen to songs about being a believer. As he looked at his mum's battered face he thought he would never believe in anything again. 'After I married your dad he insisted we moved away, and every time she came to visit he'd be rude and he'd always twist it around to make it look like she was the one who didn't like him. It was awkward, I suppose, having her in the house. I'd still visit her though, at first, but each time I arranged to go, something always came up. Your dad wasn't feeling well, or there wasn't enough money for the train fare. I don't know.' Mum pressed her hands against her ribs, wincing as she shifted on her seat. Nick tried to smile reassuringly as he glanced over at her but his teeth were gritted, his hands clenched hard around the steering wheel. He almost wished they were round his dad's neck.

'It was an impossible situation for me caught in the middle. She thought he was a bully, and he thought she was trying to turn me against him. We were so close once.' Mum sniffed hard and Nick thought she might be talking about Dad until she spoke again. 'Lots of my friends had siblings they fought with but it wasn't like that with us. Our birthdays were close together and we always had a joint party; Mum couldn't afford to splash out for two, but we never minded. One year our mum tried to make it two different themes, mermaids and princesses, but we wanted to be the same and ended up mixing up the costumes so we could look identical. I had a fishtail and a tiara. I'll never forget that party…' Mum's voice grew fainter before her words were indistinguishable, and Nick felt a tight knot of tension in his neck as he twisted his head to look at her. Even in the darkness of the car he could see how deathly pale she was. How her eyelids fluttered as she tried to keep them open.

'Tell me about the last time you spoke to her?' Nick felt terrible firing questions at her, but he didn't want her drifting off. Not yet.

'She'd bought a house and asked us to move in with her. You and me.' She reached out a hand and touched Nick's arms. 'Dad was furious and then *someone* anonymously rang her boss and told him she had been bragging about stealing things from work. A complete lie but she lost her job, lost the house. Dad never admitted it but I knew it was him. He's always been too scared to confront people directly.'

Nick indicated left. He wasn't too sure this was the right turning. 'What a bastard.'

'Yes. But at the time I made excuses for him. I thought about how hard it must be for him, losing a career, money, being dependent on me. No wonder he lost his pride.'

'You can dress it up how you want, but the bottom line is he's a coward.' Nick leaned forward. Visibility was poor and he didn't know the roads.

'Why didn't you leave dad? If you had somewhere to go?'

'I don't know.' The distress in Mum's voice sliced Nick to the core. 'She was furious, telling me I had to choose between them. He was sweet, saying she was jealous; I had a husband when she didn't. He can be very persuasive when he wants to be. Divorce would have seemed almost shameful, I suppose. My parents wouldn't have been around to see it but they believed marriage vows were for life. And so did I.'

In his peripheral vision Nick noticed his mum twist her wedding ring around her finger, he hoped she'd tug it off and lob it out of the window into the blackness and the sheets of rain.

'It's not too late for you, Mum.' Nick believed this to be true. 'You can be happy again. Away from *him*.'

'I'm not going back. Not this time.' And under her exhaustion, her fear, her words were coated in steel. 'I'm going to spend some quality time with my sister and then I'm going to travel. See all the places I've never been. Try new foods. Experience new cultures. I want to *live*.' She exhaled sharply as though blowing her desire to travel out into the world she so wanted to see.

On the radio, Elvis began to croon 'Are You Lonesome Tonight?' Mum leaned forward to turn up the volume.

'This is my favourite song,' she said.

'Do you know where we are?' It felt as though they had been on the road forever and, with the lack of street lights, the open countryside, Nick hadn't seen a street sign for what seemed like miles. 'There's a sign for Shillacre – do you know it?'

But his mum didn't answer; her eyes were closed and she swayed slightly in her seat, lost to the music. Lost to a happier time past, or dreaming of the ones yet to come.

Nick twisted around and picked up the map he'd looked at earlier. He shook it out on his lap, glanced down as he looked for Farncaster, the town his Aunt Natasha lived in, but it was too dark to properly see. He popped on the interior light – for a second – and he eased his foot off the accelerator. He'd marked Farncaster on the map before they'd left. He ran his finger along the tangle of lines and saw he'd missed the turning. He'd have to find a gateway or something to spin the car around.

Everything seemed to happen at once: his mum's voice rose in pitch, singing out clear and strong; his foot squeezed the accelerator, energised now he knew they were almost there; the glare of the approaching headlights; the awful sinking feeling in his stomach as his head jerked upright. The realisation that he had – for a split second – drifted onto the wrong side of the road. Everything seemed to slow, and by the time his reactions kicked in, it was too late. There was the squealing of brakes, the look of horror on the face of the passenger in the other car before she raised her arms in front of her face. Her eyes screwed shut, mouth open in a scream, was something Nick had never been able to forget. There was the crunching sound of metal. He and his mum were thrust forward before being yanked back. Nick's reflexes roared back to life.

'Mum.' He was almost too scared to look. Too scared not to look. But as he turned, tears of relief fought their way free as his mum's eyes locked on to his. Despite the shock on her face, the sliver of blood trickling down her cheek, she looked okay.

'I'll call for help,' he said. He clicked open his door and, as he got out, he almost didn't hear his mum speaking above the wailing coming from the other car as a woman screamed 'Jake' over and over again.

'Wait,' Mum said. 'You shouldn't be here. You shouldn't be driving. You've no license and, with your suspended sentence, you'll go to prison.' With small jerky movements she dragged herself over to the driver's seat. 'I'll say I was alone. You have to go.'

'I won't leave you.' There was a gash above Nick's eyebrow; he wiped blood from his eye. Nick knew he should stay; he wanted to stay. But was his mum right? Should he flee? The sound of Elvis was drowned out by a roaring in Nick's ears that grew louder and louder, the word 'prison' spinning round and round his head.

The last thing he heard was his mum saying 'Run.' And to his eternal shame he did.

# CHAPTER FIFTY-TWO
## Then

There were shadows on the ceiling as consciousness tugged me awake. Dark, malevolent creatures with snapping jaws and flaring nostrils. My hospital gown was scratchy, tiny spiders skittering over my skin. I placed my hands over my belly as though I could keep the monsters at bay, keep my baby safe, but I knew, while I was sleeping, one of them had slipped inside of my head and they'd whispered it was too late for Jake. The image of him slumped in the seat, eyes wide and unseeing, was almost too much to bear but sleep was waiting and I stepped into its arms where it cradled me, warm and soft.

When I woke again, mum was sitting beside me, fiddling with the hem of her dress.

'How are you?' she asked but I couldn't answer her, fixing my eyes instead on the clear plastic jug next to my bed. She sloshed water into a beaker and gently propped up my pillows so I could sip, and her touch was so tender, so unexpected it brought with it a memory of lying on the sofa as a child. Throat raw. Fever raging. She had cradled my head in her lap and stroked my forehead. Time slipped past as I drifted between sleep and wakefulness and we must have stayed like that for hours until Dad's key had turned in the lock and she'd hurried to the kitchen to start dinner. And it hit me, for the first time: she loved me.

'Mum.' I didn't know what I wanted to say. I didn't know what I wanted her to say but she said nothing, fussing instead with water that had spilled. Mopping up with tissues.

'Mum,' I said again. This time louder.

There was another painful pause until Mum said, slowly, carefully: 'There's been an accident.' The whites of her eyes were streaked with tiny blood vessels as though she had been crying for a long time.

'But I'll be okay?' I shifted in my bed. My body felt heavy.

'I was talking about Dad. He had a fall. Down the stairs. While you were out with Jake. That loose carpet he never fixed, I expect.' She looked at everything but me.

'But he's okay?'

Wordlessly she shook her head, and I fumbled for her hand but she pulled it out of reach. I didn't feel guilt or regret or any of the things I thought I might. Not then anyway. Then all I felt was numbness.

'The police want to talk to you,' she said. 'They'll likely be in later. They'll want to talk to you about the car accident too. But I've told them about the loose stair carpet. Told them you were out at the time.' She stood.

'Don't go!' I cried as she headed for the exit, but I had no words to pull her back as she hovered, fingertips brushing the door handle.

She lowered her head, and her voice was barely audible over the clattering trolleys in the corridor outside. 'I think it's better if you don't come home, Kat. When you leave here. I've brought you in some clothes.'

'Why?'

'You know why.' She turned and held me in her gaze and it burned white-hot, and this time it was me that couldn't look at her. 'You mustn't tell, Kat.'

As the door swung shut behind her I realised she knew what I'd done, and that if I left we'd be the only ones who did. She was setting me free, and I was certain, for the second time that day, she loved me. But it was a small comfort.

*

The doctor stood in front of the window. A shaft of sunlight cast him in bronze, almost as though he was a god. He was speaking but it was like watching a foreign film without subtitles.

'We performed a D&C, of course, when we brought you in—'

'A what?'

'A Dilation and Curettage. It's where we scrape away the contents of the uterus. The scan showed there was still some tissue there.'

The dawning, when it came, was slow and sickening. My hospital bed spinning and spinning and I gripped the sides so I didn't fly away.

'You do understand what has happened, Miss White?'

'No,' I said without hesitation because if I pretended not to understand it could not be real. It could not be true. But it was.

My baby was gone, along with Jake.

I was all alone.

He explained once more before checking his watch and hurrying away, leaving me in the cold, sterile room with the monsters on my ceiling and my dark, dark, thoughts.

I curled into myself remaining dry-eyed and mute with grief as the hours blurred and stretched. I turned away from the kind nurse with the curly blonde hair, who murmured comforting words I did not want to hear. Phrases such as 'complete recovery' and 'future pregnancies' sprung at me with sharpened claws but still I could not feel.

Eventually, the sound of an infant wailing on a distant ward was my undoing. An onslaught of tears, and regret and shame, while the monster in my head laughed and laughed and told me I would always hear it. The lost baby. My baby. That I deserved no less.

*

Days later, as I dressed to leave I found an envelope in the bag of clothes Mum left: £5,000. Enough to start again. As I left the hospital, the bright sunlight bouncing off the row of ambulances, the world felt too large. I was too small. I was misshapen with grief and knew I still had it with me, the darkness. What I didn't know was the scar tissue left over from the D&C would prevent me from ever conceiving again. If I had known then, my unravelling might have been complete.

# CHAPTER FIFTY-THREE
## Now

It is the dripping of the kitchen tap that brings me back to the present moment. Nick and I slumped on the kitchen floor as though shedding the lies we've been carrying have made us heavier, not lighter. Eventually, it is me who speaks first.

'You killed Jake. My baby.' I hiss out my words, my anger catching in my throat

Nick rubs his scar and this causes my fury to erupt.

'You expect *me* to feel fucking sorry for *you* because you cut your fucking head? That accident left Jake dead. It left me infertile.'

'I am so sorry.' His useless apology claws at my chest, burrows into my racing heart that feels in danger of bursting from my ribcage, free to skitter across the kitchen floor, where it will sit with us amongst the shards of our marriage.

'You knew? You knew it was me?'

'Yes.'

'So you married me out of guilt? Out of pity? Did you even love me?'

'Kat, I love you. I do.' He reaches for my hand but I snatch mine away.

'It was a lie. It was all a lie.' My head is swimming as I draw in short, sharp breaths through my nose.

'No!'

'How soon did you realise who I was?'

'As soon as I saw you in the high street. I had never been able to forget your face. I waited until you came out of the temping agency and I went straight in and booked you to work for the charity.'

There is a pressure in my skull. A thousand fingers pressing into my temples.

'I never expected to fall in love with you, Kat, but I did. I do love you. At first, I just wanted to make amends somehow. Give you a job. Richard had helped me buy that first investment property, and I'd done so well when the market boomed. It didn't seem right. You needed help too. I wanted to put you back on your feet.'

'You can *never* make amends.'

'I know.' Nick shuffles backwards until he is leaning against the cupboard under the sink. 'I've lived with what I've done every day for the past ten years. But you moving here… It seemed like fate. Written in the stars, almost.'

'Don't you say that.' I lunge at him, beating my fists against his chest. 'Don't you ever say that.' I pummel out my rage until I am spent. Broken. Lying on my back, staring at the spotlights until my vision speckles.

'Why tell me now?' My tone is dull, as though I don't care, but I do. I almost wish I didn't know – knowing can't be undone, can it? After tonight things will never be the same again.

'Him.' Nick nods, and I groan. I'd almost forgotten about him.

'Aaron? How do you know?…'

'That's not Aaron,' Nick says with certainty.

Confused, I roll over, scrambling onto my hands and knees, and turn the head of the figure on the floor. Nick is right. This man is older than us, possibly in his fifties. I take him in: his salt-and-pepper beard. It's the man who has been watching the house.

'Who is he?' I ask.

'My dad.'

I rest back on my heels and, for a moment, all that can be heard is the dripping tap in the silence that stretches under the weight of all my questions.

'Your dad?' I struggle to understand. 'The dad you told me was dead?' I can't tear my eyes away from the figure on the floor. This is my father-in-law? The stench of cheap alcohol forces me to turn my head as I press two fingers to his neck. 'He's alive, at least. We need to call an ambulance, Nick. No matter what he's done he's still your dad. I can't believe you told me he was dead.'

'You didn't tell me the truth about your dad,' he bites back as he hefts his dad into the recovery position.

I moan softly and fold into myself as though I can hide away from what I have done.

'I didn't mean that, Kat. It was an accident. You can't blame yourself.'

But I can. I should. I do.

'Let's wait a bit before we call for help,' Nick says. 'He stinks of booze. I've seen him in this state many, many times before. He's bound to come around.'

'My dad didn't,' I say softly.

As the years had passed it had been easy to pretend it wasn't quite real somehow. That my parents were still living in the same house. That I chose not to see them. Sharing the truth with Nick has turned it into something else. Something worse. I am a murderer. I can't repeat the same mistake now. I won't. The questions I have for Nick that are multiplying in my mind at lightning speed will have to wait.

'We have to call an ambulance. Nick. He may be drunk but he banged his head.'

'He's got a beanie on. That would have cushioned the blow.'

'It didn't sound like it—'

'Shh. I need to think,' Nick says but what he means is, he needs to think of an excuse.

'There's nothing to think about—' I start to rise to my feet but then I remember there *is* a lot to think about.

Lisa is still trapped in the basement.

# CHAPTER FIFTY-FOUR
## Now

'So, is this it?' I can't tear my eyes away from Nick's dad, watching the reassuring rise and fall of his ribcage. 'Or is your mum likely to pop up too?' There is a nastiness in my tone I don't recognise. A blackness swelling beneath the surface.

'Nick,' I say sharply when he doesn't answer. 'Where is your mum?'

'Mum's dead.' Nick drops his head into his hands and the sound of his voice cracking, the sight of him so broken, holds the darkness at bay. Despite him shattering everything I thought was real, and slicing me to the core with the splinters of the truth, I instinctively want to comfort him. But I don't. 'The car accident killed her.'

I am surprised. 'The policeman who interviewed me said only Jake died?'

'She didn't die then. She had a stroke. It's common after head injuries.'

'Hence the charity?' I try to focus on what Nick is saying. 'Stroke Support was for you?'

'Yes.'

'So Richard's grandmother having a stroke? That was *another* lie?' I'm hardly in a position to be judgemental but I can't seem to help it.

'Mum died two weeks ago.'

I feel as though I have been slapped. Out of all the things I have learned tonight it strikes me as odd that this is the one that hurts the most. All this time Nick had a mum who loved him. Who might have loved me. A family. Strangely, I don't blame her. I feel a kinship with her. The other passenger in the crash. She must have felt the same cold, hard terror as me as our cars rushed towards each other. She wasn't the one who lied to me.

'She's been alive all this time? Why didn't you tell me about her? Why haven't I met her?'

'She had brain damage, hadn't been able to speak. Didn't even know who I was. There was little point introducing you.'

'But still…'

'If I had taken you to see her, you'd have wanted some sort of explanation. I didn't want you to hate me.' In his voice is regret and something else. Fear, perhaps.

But I can't reassure him I don't hate him. I don't even know him. He is a stranger to me, this man who I promised to spend the rest of my life with. This man who snatched away my chance to have a child of my own. Bitterness stings my throat, hot and sour.

'So who looked after your mum? Clearly, not you.' I am consumed with the need to know everything about her: the woman who tried to protect her son.

'She's been in a nursing home for years. I've been paying for it every month.'

The bank statements. The regular payments. Not maintenance at all. 'So, Ada's not your daughter?'

'Ada? Of course not. Why would you think that?' Nick shakes his head as though nothing would surprise him.

'But you sent Clare flowers? Your scarf was there. You've been seeing her?'

'She's been helping me arrange your surprise thirtieth party – that's all. She's been doing a great job. Speaking to Lisa, finding out what you'd like. It was going to have a *Desperate Housewives* theme; I've recommended her to clients as a party-planner. She's raking it in, and it's all cash in hand.'

'You've been so distracted. I thought you were having an affair.'

'Why would you think that? I've never given you any reason not to trust me…' Nick covers his mouth with his fingertips and exhales deeply through his nostrils, as though he has realised the ridiculousness of his words.

I don't let it drop. With the rain lashing against the window, the wind howling outside, it is the night for truth. 'You stayed away overnight. Twice.'

'Mum took a turn for the worse on Christmas Day. My Aunt Natasha texted me.'

'Your aunt?' Natasha who had plagued him with texts when we first met. She wasn't his ex-girlfriend at all.

'I went to see Mum. After Lisa had her miscarriage, and you took off, I took the opportunity to go to Farncaster, to the nursing home. I didn't even recognise her. My own mother.' Nick's voice is thick with tears. 'I had to go back to reception to check I had the right room.' He starts to cry again, and my emotions fight inside me as the urge to soothe him is tempered by the knowledge of the irrecoverable damage he has done to me. To us.

'The receipt in the laundry basket,' I say, almost to myself. I knew there was something wrong but I couldn't put my finger on what. The café I went to was called The Coffee House not The Farncaster Bean Café. The receipt was Nick's.

'So the business was never in trouble?'

'No. Sorry. I didn't know what else to say to explain going away.'

'I thought you were having an affair, you know.'

'I would *never* do that to you!' Nick looks so outraged I almost want to laugh. Does he really think sleeping with someone else is the ultimate betrayal?

'I wanted to tell you when Mum died. I needed you with me at the funeral but I didn't know what to say without more lies. I'm so tired of keeping things hidden.'

'The second time you went away? Was that the funeral?'

'Yes. Natasha insisted on arranging it. She wouldn't let me pay either, but it was my responsibility, wasn't it? I left her an envelope of cash.'

'You took the money from the safe?'

'Yes.'

I think of what I found instead of the money I was looking for. 'The teddy? The ring?'

'The bear was mine. Teddy Edward.' A ghost of a smile passes Nick's lips. 'The ring was Mum's. It was my grandmother's first. We can pass it down. If it's a girl. If you still want…' Nick smacks his forehead with his palm. 'Stupid. Of course you won't want me now,' he says, and yet, there is hope in his eyes as he looks at me.

I don't tell him I still want him. I can't.

There's a groan from Nick's dad. A shift in position. I think he's coming round.

'Natasha told *him* about the funeral.' Nick jerks his head towards his dad. 'She said she felt he had a right to know but told him he wasn't welcome to come. He caught me coming out of the office yesterday. Said he left the wreath on our doorstep on the day of the service, thinking I'd take it, but I'd already left. As if a fucking wreath can make up for the years of misery he caused Mum.'

'The wreath was never for me?' All along I'd thought Lisa was out for revenge. Or her parents. Even my mum, after I'd stopped outside my old house and seen the twitch of the curtains. Imagined her behind them. Had I really got everything so wrong?

'Kevin. *Him*.' Nick shoots lasers at his dad. 'Said he's spent years wanting to get in touch, but didn't know how, until Mum took a turn for the worse and someone from the nursing home passed on our landline and our address. He told me he's been ringing here.'

'But he hung up when I answered.' I fill in the gaps.

'He was waiting for me to pick up. He came to the house a few times; probably only when he was drunk and feeling guilty, He was too cowardly to tell you who he was.'

'He must have been the one looking through the window. Watching me sleep.'

'He was hoping to see me.'

'He sent the book? *How to Cope with Death*. I thought it was because of the anniversary of Jake's death, or Dad's death. I thought someone…'

'I ordered that – did it come? I've been struggling.' Nick seems to shrink before my eyes. 'I dream of Mum every night. The way she always read me a bedtime story, no matter how late she came home. Turning the pages with hands red raw with cleaning. Always smelling of bleach. I can't believe she's gone.'

The book was for Nick. The label on the package had been damp with rain and peeling. Only our surname and address visible. I had assumed it was sent to me. I had assumed too much.

Nick rubs his eyes with his sleeve. 'Dad said he was sorry for everything but it's too late, isn't it?' It's a statement not a question. 'He shouldn't have come here. It's all his fault.'

I look at Nick's dad lying prone on the floor and wonder what would have happened if he hadn't hurt his back. Lost his job. The different paths we would all have taken. Jake might still be here. We might be a happy family of three, or four. It's almost incomprehensible how the actions of a complete stranger have shaped my life. The butterfly effect. A flutter is all it takes. So many lives ruined. Mine included.

'Did you ever want a family, Nick, or were you trying to replace what I'd lost?' My throat stings as I swallow my bitterness. 'What you took from me.'

'Of course I do. It was awful seeing you hurt when the adoptions fell through. I felt so powerless. So responsible.'

'If we'd tried to adopt here…' I can't help thinking it would have been different somehow.

'Kat. There was so much red tape adopting from another country but at least it was only Richard filling out the paperwork and us signing it. In the UK, with the face-to-face interviews you have to go through, the home visits, it was inevitable you'd become aware I'd been charged with ABH and, to be honest, after we visited the orphanage that time, and met Dewei, I couldn't imagine not giving a child from that sort of background a home.'

I nod. The first thing I have agreed with. I still feel the weight of Dewei's loss in my heart, his heaviness in my arms. I still remember row upon row of cots cramped into one tiny room. The endless crying. The smell of faeces and despair.

'I was gutted when Dewei went to another family. After Mai… it was almost too much to bear. I decided we'd be better off trying to adopt in the UK after all. I was going to tell you I had a criminal record, but then you suggested surrogacy and it seemed, well, it seemed like the better option and it's working okay, isn't it?'

Ignoring his question, I drift back to our celebratory dinner at The Fox and Hounds. Giddy with champagne and hope. It all seemed so long ago.

'Did Richard sabotage the adoptions?'

'God, no. He fought really hard. He offered some of his own money to try and get Dewei here. He does care about us, you know. He's just always been wary of me being with you, of the past coming back. He'd lied to the police, don't forget, told them he'd lent the car to Mum that night and she was alone.'

The ripples of deceit spread.

'When you told me Lisa was Jake's brother, he was deeply unhappy with the connection. That day we all had lunch, he talked to Lisa in the garden, accused her of being a gold-digger. Ordered her to stay away from us until she went into labour or he'd stop the extra payments. He didn't want… I'm so sorry. I know how much you wanted to be involved with the pregnancy.'

'There is no pregnancy,' I say harshly, and I see the hurt in Nick's eyes and realise how much he wanted this too. 'You'd better come with me.'

'Where?—'

But I don't answer.

Nick trails me into the hall. I open the door of the basement.
It is gloomy. Silent.

'I don't understand?…'

'Shhh,' I say. Fear grips me, and I can't put a finger on why
but I can almost sense something has happened to Lisa. Without
thinking, I hurry down the stairs and must be about halfway down
when I lose my footing and slip. A blood-curdling scream full of
pain fills the air. But my lips are clamped together.

It isn't me who has screamed.

# CHAPTER FIFTY-FIVE
## Now

Everything seems to slow, my hands gripping air as I tumble down the stairs. For a second I see my dad falling, hear the sickening crash as he landed at the bottom of the stairs. There's a searing pain in my knee as I land awkwardly and a strange sensation of floating but I tumble back to reality as it comes again.

The scream.

Lisa is lying on the sofa on her back. Knees bent.

'Lis?' I scramble over to her.

'It's coming.'

'It?' I can't make sense of what she is telling me, and my head is throbbing where it banged against the bannister.

'The fucking baby,' she bellows, and I am suspicious. Elated. Confused.

'There's a baby? You really did it? The surrogacy? God, I'm so sorry, Lis, for doubting you.'

'I'm not ready.' Lisa's distress spreads like ripples in a pond.

I am aware of Nick hovering behind me. I can feel his panic matching mine.

'He shouldn't be coming yet,' I say, as though my words might be able to change things. I can't believe this is happening.

Lisa doesn't speak. Her face hot pink, fringe damp and plastered to her forehead. The whole room stinks of sweat. She pants, and I stroke her hair, let her grip my hand.

There's a baby.

'Call an ambulance, Nick.'

'With the response times somewhere this rural? Last time someone in the village called an ambulance it took a fucking hour. We'd be better off taking her to the hospital in the car. Can you stand, Lisa?' Nick says.

'No. I can feel the head.' Lisa is crying.

'I'm going to have a look,' I say.

Nick turns to the wall as I ease down Lisa's knickers. 'She's right. There's not enough time to go anywhere.'

'Fuck.' Lisa throws her head back and bellows. 'I can't do this. I can't.'

'You can.' I feel a rush of warmth towards her. 'We can. Together. Look at me.'

She turns her head, her eyes full of tears. We are locked together in this moment, in every moment that has come before. School plays where she'd cheer me on, exams I'd help her revise for, bad haircuts, birthday parties, first love, first loss. It has always been together and all of it was leading to this. I am stunned but I can't afford to stand around thinking how I've got her wrong.

'Nick.' I snap to attention. 'Boil some water and fetch some towels, some scissors and something warm to wrap the baby in.'

He hurries up the stairs, and when he's gone Lisa says: 'Kat. There are things I need to tell you… Christ. This hurts.'

The muscles in my back scream as I hunch over her, remembering all the times I'd watched *One Born Every Minute*. My teeth are gritted as I hold the baby's head in my hands, waiting for the next wave of contractions. Lisa can't stop babbling. Shouting. Screaming. And I don't try to guide her. Her body knows what to do, and she will cope with this in any way she can.

It seems like an age before Nick comes back with a scalding kettle full of water but no bowl, and the towels from the bathroom, damp from use, but I don't send him back for more. It's nearly over. Lisa has stopped talking and is wailing and grunting. I tell

Nick to hold her hands, and he shouts out in pain as she squeezes too tightly.

With one last guttural cry, Lisa pushes, and the baby slithers into my arms and, although he is covered in gunk, I have never seen anything more beautiful in my entire life.

But he is still. Silent. Blue.

He's not breathing.

Strangely, I am suddenly calm. I've seen enough births on TV to automatically ease my finger between the umbilical cord and his neck. There's a gasp. A juddering breath. A piercing cry, and I've never heard anything quite so lovely. He is small, but not worryingly so. Perfectly formed.

'It's a boy, Lis.'

Nick hands me scissors and I carefully cut the umbilical cord and wrap the baby in the fleecy lemon blanket with the giraffe in the corner that Nick has fetched from the nursery.

'Lis?'

'I don't feel right, Kat.'

Suddenly there is blood. Too much blood. Lisa's lungs rattle and she is chalk white.

'Nick.' I place the baby gently on the floor. "Fetch some cold water, a flannel and a phone. Hurry.'

'Kat,' she whispers. 'I'm scared.'

'You're going to be fine,' I say, but as I cradle her face between my hands, her eyes start to roll back into her head.

# CHAPTER FIFTY-SIX
## Now

I don't hear Nick come back into the room. I don't know he is here until he touches my shoulder.

'Kat.' He says more than just my name but all I hear is static. I am sobbing so hard I cannot hear. I cannot speak. My head is resting on Lisa's chest but underneath my ear there is no beating of her heart.

'Kat,' Nick says again. This time his hands are under my armpits and he tries to hoist me to my feet, but I grab hold of Lisa's shirt.

'Noooo.' I don't want to let her go. 'Please…'

'Get out the fucking way, Kat,' Nick shouts. There's a whimpering to my side and my eyes are drawn to the baby. My baby. His tiny fingers are flexing. His eyes screwed shut. I scoop him into my arms and step to the side.

Nick tilts Lisa's head back, and despite seeing resuscitation a million times on TV, there is none of the tension I feel when I watch *Casualty*, none of the drama, just a sad resignation it is too late. But still I watch. Two breaths. Thirty chest compressions. I count them in my head. Two breaths. Thirty chest compressions. I wonder if that is the right number. I wonder if it matters.

'Fuck.' Nick sits back on his heels. 'What are we going to do?'

'I don't know.' I am shaking violently with shock. I can't believe what has just happened.

'We have to phone an ambulance. They'll probably call the police.'

'What about the baby?' I draw him closer to my chest. He yawns, wide and gummy.

Nick toes the floor with his shoe and looks at anything but me. 'You think they will take him away?'

'He's not ours, Kat. Lisa has a family. They will want him.'

'He is ours. We had a contract.' Everything is slipping through my fingers. Grains of sand on the beach. The sandcastles me and Lisa used to build crumbling into nothing as if they were never there. But this baby, he is here: real, solid, and I won't let him go.

'The contract isn't legal. Richard warned us. The baby has to live with us for six weeks before a residency order can be granted. Besides…'

'Besides, what?' I try to keep my voice calm as I rock from one foot to another. Gulping back salty tears.

'He can't be ours, can he? I don't know much about babies but, even if he's early, it's still too soon, isn't it?'

'Shut up, shut up, shut up.' I hiss out my words. I am not going to think about the way Lisa had clung to my hand as Nick located towels and boiled water, fetched the blanket from the nursery, telling me how miserable she'd been since Jake died. How her mum seemed disappointed she was the one who was alive. How lonely she had been. It had been easy to get drunk in the pub on what would have been her and Jake's 30th birthday. It had been easy to fall into bed with Aaron at the end of the night, despite the fact they hadn't spoken for nearly ten years.

'I didn't know what to do when I was pregnant,' she had sobbed. 'I didn't plan it. Any of it, I swear. Aaron is married. He doesn't want his wife finding out. He said it was a mistake and he doesn't want anything to do with me or the baby.'

'I thought you'd made the pregnancy up. I thought you were both trying to extort money from me.'

'No! How could you think that?'

Lisa screwed her face up tightly before she carried on. 'I noticed you in that magazine and it said you lived in Craneshill. I just wanted to see you. I've missed you so much. I haven't seen Dad in years. Me and Mum barely speak. I wanted to talk about Jake.' Lisa gabbled as I focused on delivering her baby, and I let her ramble on. 'You know I didn't ever want a baby. I can't be a single mum. Couldn't tell Mum I'd had an affair with a married man, like dad.'

'You were pregnant when we met?' I am strangely calm.

'Yes, but I'd booked an abortion. It seemed like fate you wanted a baby and couldn't have one. I thought I could make everything up to you. There was only a few weeks difference, and I thought if I kept you away from the scans you'd never know how far along I was. I read a newspaper article about that singer who wanted a surrogate and it was easy to pretend I'd done it before.'

Another contraction swept over her and the sounds she was making were like an animal in distress. She was panting hard as she started to speak again.

'I don't see Mum often anyway. I knew I could avoid her for a few months, and by the time he was born and you found out from the date he couldn't possibly be yours, it would be too late. You'd already love him. Want him. Give him the home I never could. I wasn't thinking clearly. I panicked. I'm so sorry.'

'How could you?' There had been no surprise in my voice. Only resignation. I think that part of me had already known.

'My life is a mess, Kat. I've never had a career. I've always suffered with bouts of depression, spending weeks in bed at a time. I've never been able to stick to a job. I made up working in the hospital so you'd respect me. I didn't think there was any harm. I'd get some cash and you'd get the family you wanted.'

My fingers touched the gold cross around my neck as Lisa screwed up her face that was scarlet and slick with sweat. She grunted and I hated her and was glad she was suffering, and yet there was part of me that still cared, even though I knew I shouldn't.

Lisa and Jake and I, we are a tangle of past, present and future. Once her contraction had passed she babbled again.

'I realised how much I had missed you. It felt good to be friends again. New Year, when I came to stay and saw the nursery, saw how much it meant to you, and I met Nick properly, I knew I had to stop. I felt so guilty. It wasn't fair to let you believe the baby was his. Yours.'

'Was it ever twins?' I was desperate for something to be real.

'No. I did slip on the ice. That was true. I pretended to have a miscarriage. Because I cared about you. I felt awful deceiving you both. I was a mess. It was too late to have an abortion and I didn't know what to do. But then you came and found me and it seemed like fate. I didn't want to be without you again. It was easy to carry on lying. I'm so sorry this isn't your baby, Kat. Or Nick's.'

It had been a night for truth but sometimes you can hear so much it's hard to take in, and you look back and wonder whether you ever actually heard it at all. I so desperately wanted this baby to be mine. All along I had believed he was, and sometimes believing is enough. It has to be. Lisa was half out of her mind with pain. She had no idea what she was saying. *It is my baby. It is.*

Nick gently places a blanket over Lisa, covering the face that I used to sprinkle with silver glitter before our school discos. The hard ball in my chest plummets into my gut.

'Let's go upstairs,' he says. 'Make some calls.'

I nod but as we reach the foot of the stairs I turn and hand Nick the baby. Back at Lisa's side I pull down the blanket, lean over to the coffee table and click on the lamp.

'She's scared of the dark,' I say through my choking sobs. I raise her hand to my cheek, linking her fingers through mine, remembering all the times we'd run out into the playground holding hands, eager to reach the hopscotch first. Although I had gone years without her, there's a hollowness inside when I think I will never again hear her laugh. It seems impossible it was only a few months ago we reconnected. I still remember that day. The snow. The taste of frost and hope on my tongue. Lisa will never see another winter, and I feel my heart is breaking. Already, without her, I feel lost. Hopelessly, irretrievably lost.

'Kat.' Nick touches my shoulder.

'I can't…' I can't tear myself away from Lisa. I can't leave her. I won't be able to live with myself. My forehead lowers onto her chest, resting on a ribcage housing lungs that will never again draw in air.

'She's with Jake now,' Nick says and that, at least, is some comfort.

'Goodbye, Lisa.' My fingers shake and it takes several attempts to unfasten the gold cross from my neck and place it around hers.

'I'm sorry too,' I say as I kiss her lips that are already losing their warmth. The kiss of Judas.


I stop in the doorway to the kitchen as I see Nick's dad lying where he fell. I'd forgotten he was here.

Silently I watch as Nick kneels next to him and checks his pulse. His face is ashen as he turns to me. I already know what he is about to say.

'Shit, Kat. He's dead.'

'You killed him.' I shift the weight of the baby in my arms.

'It was an accident,' Nick says but now he has as much to lose as me.

And as much to hide.

# CHAPTER FIFTY-SEVEN
## Now

'You have to go.' Nick is flinging my clothes into a suitcase as I lie rigid on the bed. My cheek sinking into the feather-soft pillow smelling of the husband I should hate, but somehow can't. I'm so very, very tired.

'I'm not leaving you.'

'You must.' Exasperation has again crept into his voice.

'Two people are dead, Nick.'

'Don't you think I know that?' He is shaken. Pale. 'It will be fine.' His blue eyes lock onto mine, and we both know it is as far from fine as it can be. 'I'll sort everything out and then I'll join you.'

'How can you sort it out?' I want to believe him but can't quell my gut feeling telling me this is impossible to sort out.

'Richard.'

The sound of his name tears through me as if I have fallen on barbed wire. Can I trust him to keep me safe, after everything he has done? I am scared. So scared.

There are a million reasons why I shouldn't run away, and one reason why I should. The baby is asleep next to me. Snuffling like a small animal. He is early. A bit small perhaps but I'll get him checked over. I'm going to take very good care of him. There are veins visible beneath his paper-thin eyelids. He is as weak and powerless as I feel but his fragility draws a strength from me that grows with each and every breath he takes.

'I'll go.' I push myself to sitting.

The mattress squeaks and dips as Nick sits on the edge. He smooths my hair away from my temples, cupping my face between his palms. There is nothing quite as painful as knowing something is ending.

'I love you, Kat. I always have.' He rubs his thumb over my cheekbone. I raise my hand and take his in mine. Kiss his palm. Pull him towards me and kiss his lips. The kiss of goodbye.

I don't tell him I love him.

I can't.

Even though I know I'll probably never get the chance again.

# EPILOGUE

There's a sweet scent of freshly cut grass hanging in the breeze that is warming my skin, ruffling my hair. The park is busy, the sunshine drawing out families. It saddens me Nick will never feel this again. Once the bodies were discovered he had handed himself in. Confessed to things he had never done. Confessed to the things he had. I wrote to the prison last week. I do sometimes. But I'm careful to use a different name each time. A different address. Nick may have taken the blame for everything that went on in the house that night – he did owe me – but you can't be too careful, can you? He knew, I think, even as he threw my things into a suitcase, it was all over for him. It was the last thing he could do for me, and I like to think he acted not just out of guilt, but out of love too. Despite everything he told me there is a part of me that misses him. Misses us. The Friday nights spent snuggled on the sofa watching TV in our pyjamas; curry-stained plates stacked on the coffee table.

The police knew, of course, that Lisa had recently given birth but Nick denied all knowledge of a baby over and over until eventually they stopped asking, although I'm sure they haven't stopped looking. Richard defended Nick, as he always had, whether out of loyalty, or out of fear of being discovered for the liar that he is, I do not know. I have never forgiven him for his part in the accident. But we always seek out someone to blame, I suppose. It's human nature. And it's easier to hate him than hate Nick, than hate myself. Still, Richard has at least provided me with a new identity. 'You're a missing person, Kat,' he had said over the phone, his voice cold and hard. 'I've a client who spent time inside for identity theft. Let me make some enquiries.' And weeks later, as we had met on the edge of a pier, the crashing waves spraying salt into my mouth, I had taken the envelope he handed to me and something else wordlessly passed between us as if we both knew this would be the last contact we would ever have. I turned away from the snarling hate in his eyes and stared out at the flat white sky and, despite our strained relationship, I'd felt a pang of loneliness as his shoes clattered against the wooden boards as he walked away from me.

Nick had stuck to his story that I had depression and had left him days before. There were enough people to validate my erratic behaviour. I had watched the live coverage unfold in front of my former home. The reporter sweating in his cheap suit, interviewing the woman with the red hair who lived a few doors down from us. Her eyes shimmered with unshed tears despite the fact we had hardly spoken. Still, everyone wants their fifteen minutes, I suppose. She confirmed that I had rarely been seen in the few months before my alleged disappearance and when I did venture out, I really wasn't myself. Running around without shoes. Even Tamara had cried on the news. She always was the better actress. I'm pleased she got to play Maria in the end; I saw the photos online and she looked stunning. Her dreams came true, at least. The musical ran for two weeks longer than it was supposed to. I'm guessing the attention surrounding my disappearance probably did wonders for ticket sales. Who was it that said there is no such thing as bad publicity?

There were rumours that Nick had killed me. The police had to take those seriously and had dug up our garden, but there was nothing to find. I was distraught as I watched the helicopter reports on TV. Dewei's and Mai's rose bushes wrenched out of the ground as though they were nothing. Over time I was classed as another unsolved murder, another sad statistic. The newspapers interviewed some of our old school friends. Aaron was photographed standing stiffly with his wife. He was quoted as saying he hadn't seen or spoken to me or Lisa in ten years. He always was a liar. But then, we all have things to hide, don't we? Our version of the truth is pliable, we mould our reality to mask our lies, and sometimes it sounds so plausible we even convince ourselves.

There's a mother sitting on the bench opposite me, a baby next to her in a pram. She rocks her with one hand while scanning through her smartphone with the other. The baby gurgles and I see the pale pink soles of her feet rise up as she grabs her toes with her fingers. Her legs are turning red and I think I should go and offer the mother some of the sun cream I carry in my bag. On the patch of grass in front of the benches there's a girl twirling a pink dress, her skirts billowing, and her shiny black bob swishes around her face. For a second, she looks so much like Lisa it snatches my breath away. I miss her. Tears haze my vision as I remember a time when we would link hands and spin until we were dizzy. 'Faster,' she would cry and just when I felt my feet had left the ground and I was soaring high in the brilliant blue sky, she'd unlink her fingers from mine and we'd stagger across the grass before tumbling onto our backs. I would scrunch my eyes against the bright sunflower sun and wait for the dizziness to pass. Once, an inflatable beach ball had landed on her head. 'Hey!' Lisa had sat up and shouted. 'Go and play somewhere else, Jake.' She had thrown the striped ball back and sighed theatrically before flopping back down onto the grass. 'Boys. They are *so* annoying.'

But even then there was something that transfixed me about Jake. It wasn't just his bright green eyes, the way his skin was dotted with freckles. It was more than that. 'Fate,' he called it when we were older and he tilted my chin to kiss me.

I bring two fingers to my mouth as though I can still taste him – Wrigley's Spearmint Gum – and I wonder if it ever fades. The sense of loss. Now Lisa's gone too and my last memory of her springs to mind, as it frequently does. Her black hair fanned out over the chocolate leather sofa, the panic in her eyes, the metallic tang of blood catching in my nose, in the back of my throat.

'Help me,' she had croaked, and I had leaned over and whispered in her ear.

'What have you been hiding for ten years, Lisa?'

'I don't know…'

'I read the texts on your phone. Between you and Aaron. There *is* something.'

Lisa whimpered.

'Tell me and I'll help you.' I stroked her brow.

She began to whisper. 'I told Aaron when I slept with him on my thirtieth birthday. It was a relief to tell someone.'

Lisa's face was as stark white as the wall behind her, and I knew she was slipping away.

'What, Lisa? What did you tell him?' Frustration pricked behind my eyes.

Eventually, reluctantly, she spoke. 'That night at The Three Fishes—'

'What about it?'

Her head had lolled to the side and I had placed my hands on her shoulders and shook her hard. Her eyes snapped open.

'I had a tiny bit of mephedrone left.'

I placed my ear to Lisa's mouth so I could hear her properly. Felt her hot breath.

'Hardly any. I put it in our drinks. Mine and Jake's.'

'How could you?'

A single tear streaked down her cheek. 'I wanted us to have fun. He wasn't supposed to drive.' She drew in a long, juddering breath and closed her eyes as though trying to find the energy to speak again. 'He'd promised me we'd leave the car and get a taxi home. He'd promised…'

Lisa was the one struggling to breathe but the pain tore at my chest.

'I'm so ashamed,' she'd whispered. 'Keeping it a secret has ruined my relationship with Mum. Please don't tell her. She's better off not knowing. Better off without me.'

She had fallen silent but I could still feel warm air against my ear. I remembered Jake feeling dizzy and sick. The way he drove too fast, desperate to get home. I'd thought he was in shock about the baby. But he was drugged. She had drugged him. Would he have been able to avoid the other car if his senses hadn't been dulled? Would he still be alive? Would our baby?

So many lives ruined. So many lives – what was one more?

I can still feel the coolness of the cotton cushion cover in my hand; I can still taste the bile that stung my throat as I held the cushion over Lisa's face. I can feel her struggles growing weaker and weaker. I can still hear the monster in my head laughing as tears poured down my cheeks. I will always carry the weight of my shame as Nick burst back into the room and I told him it was too late. She had died a natural death, and often I try to convince myself that this is true. All that blood. I am sure she had a placental abruption – I'd read about them in my baby bible – being so far from the hospital she'd probably have died anyway. Probably. But I couldn't have taken that risk.

I touch my cheek as though I might still feel the tears that poured from me. My grief was real and raw. The hole inside black and gaping, but it was only right, wasn't it? Only fair. She was the one responsible for Jake crashing. She took him from me, along with my unborn child and my chance of ever being a mother again. How could she do that? Know that? And to stand tall and proud and offer me a lifeline, pretend to be my surrogate and my friend. It could have broken me, it really could.

Sometimes I wonder if it has.

'Mummy.' The word whirlwinds inside me, stirring up loss. Guilt. Hope. But above all love.

'Jacob.' I open my arms wide and my darling, darling boy toddles into them. I bury my face in his black, glossy hair and inhale

Johnson's Shampoo before I tickle his ribs, blowing raspberries on his cheek, tasting the strawberry ice cream we'd had earlier.

He giggles but the sound doesn't drive out the endless screaming that's in my head every time I look at his face and see Lisa's face. Jake's face. All the things I ever did wrong. All the things I ever did right.

'I'm hungry,' he says.

'You're always hungry.' I stand and stretch out my hand, and he places his small one in mine. We swing arms as we walk.

We pass the baby sleeping in the pram, her skin as pink as her vest. I glance around for the mother but she is over the other side of the park, deep in conversation. My fingers twitch with the urge to push the pram away. To slather the baby in sun cream and kisses. She shouldn't have left her here. You can't be too careful nowadays, can you?

I stop.

The baby is crying in my mind. The lost baby. I gaze in the pram and wonder if this is her. The lost baby. My baby. I reach for the handle. Let my fingers rest lightly on the plastic bar.

'Mummy!' Jacob's tugging at my other hand. Across the park the mother still isn't paying attention, but even so, I can't take her daughter. I know what it's like to lose a child. It shifts your reality. You never really get over it.

I allow myself to be pulled away. Jacob chatters as we walk to the wrought iron gates but it's hard to decipher his words over the constant wailing in my head.

We're almost out of the park now. Soon it will be too late to save her.

The lost baby.

I hesitate. Turn. The pram still stands alone.

I'm not a monster.

I'm not.

I just want to silence the crying.

Is that so wrong?

# A LETTER FROM LOUISE

Hello,

I want to say a huge thank you for choosing to read *The Surrogate*.

I'm a little stunned to have finished writing my third book and firstly want to thank everyone who has supported me on my journey so far, both online and offline. With *The Sister* and *The Gift* reaching No. 1, both in the UK and abroad, there was a moment of panic, wondering what I could come up with for another book, until I took a deep breath and remembered the best advice I had ever been given:

*'Write the story you'd love to read.'*

And that's what I've done.

The idea for *The Surrogate* was born after I read a magazine article on surrogacy. All worked out well for the couple involved, they ended up with a beautiful baby, but my writer mind immediately started whirring, pondering all the things that could have gone wrong. There is a huge amount of trust placed in a surrogate and I wondered what would happen if that trust was misplaced, and worse still, what if the surrogate was a friend harbouring a grudge? I do hope you have enjoyed reading this story as much as I have enjoyed writing it.

Thanks so much for generously spending your time with Kat and Lisa. I hope you loved their story, and if you did I would be very grateful if you could write a review for *The Surrogate*. I'd love to hear what you think, and it makes such a difference helping new readers to discover one of my books for the first time.

Hearing from readers really brightens my day. You can find me over at Twitter or Facebook or contact me via my website, where I regularly blog flash fiction.

Speak soon.
Louise x

www.louisejensen.co.uk

@Fab_fiction

fabricatingfiction/

# BOOK CLUB QUESTIONS

1) During the first page of the book we learn that a couple have been murdered. As the book progresses did you find yourself forming theories about the murders and if so, did these theories change as the story evolved?

2) Kat has been lonely since falling out with Lisa many years before and is eager to rebuild their friendship. Do you think it is ever possible to go back and repair past hurt?

3) *'You mustn't tell, Kat.'* When you find out what Kat is supposed to keep quiet about, how did you feel? *'I'm a keeper of secrets, a guardian of the truth.'* Did this change the way you felt about her?

4) Do you think Kat's desperation for a baby has been at the cost of her happiness?

5) Both Nick and Kat are harbouring secrets. Kat says of Nick *'Over time I have stopped asking questions because it's never one-sided, is it? Finding out information. If we have that conversation, sooner or later I'll be the one expected to talk about my parents, my past, and that's the last thing I want to do. Anyway, ultimately, we are all the same, aren't we?'* Do you think this is true?

6) Kat and Nick are both damaged, troubled, characters. How did you feel about them?

7) Throughout the novel did your sense of who could be trusted change?

8) What did you think would be the outcome of Lisa's pregnancy?

9) *'It's almost incomprehensible how the actions of a complete stranger have shaped my life. The butterfly effect. A flutter is all it takes.'* Discuss how different things could have been.

10) What do you think happens after the Epilogue? What would you like to happen?

# ACKNOWLEDGEMENTS

It's often the easy bit, writing the story, but it needs a brilliant team behind a book to bring it to life. A huge thanks to Olly Rhodes and Bookouture, in particular Kim Nash who always seems to be available with marketing wizardry and gin. Lydia Vassar-Smith for being as excited about my initial idea as I was, and Jenny Geras for her editorial insight and enthusiasm. Cath Burke and the fabulous team at Sphere (Little, Brown) for handling my paperbacks, I'm so grateful to have two dynamic publishers on board. Henry Steadman for another stunning cover. My agent, Rory Scarfe, who is forever calm and the source of endless support.

The writing community is amazing and, although I spend far too much time on Twitter, my days are brighter thanks to the wonderful book bloggers, readers and writers I engage with on a daily basis.

Shannon Keating, thanks for sharing your experience of working for a charity. Symon Adamson – your feedback always sounds better coming from the pub. Bekkii Bridges, Karen Appleby, and my mum for always being there. Lucille Grant – it's lovely to have someone I trust so implicitly. Your support means a great deal to me. Mick Wynn, having a good friend who is also a writer is a relationship to treasure. Emma Mitchell – I bloody love you! Hilary Tiney, my oldest friend, always on hand with a listening ear; and Sarah Wade who makes sure I have regular Nando's breaks.

Callum, Kai and Finley, a constant source of joy and pride. Tim: life is ridiculously busy and I'm so glad to have you in my corner.

And always, Ian Hawley.

*Read on for the beginning of*
*Louise Jensen's bestselling novel,* The Gift

Run.

It's dark. So dark. Clouds scud across the charcoal sky, blanketing the moon and stars. Dampness fills my lungs and as I draw a sharp breath nausea crashes over me in sickening waves.

My energy is fading fast. My trainers slap against the concrete and I don't think I can hear footsteps behind me any more, but it's hard to tell over the howling wind.

I steal a glance over my shoulder but my feet stray onto soft earth and I lose my footing and stumble, splaying out my hands to break my fall. The side of my face hits something hard and solid that rips at my skin. My jaw snaps shut and my teeth slice into my tongue flooding my mouth with blood, and as I swallow it down, bile and fear rises in my throat.

Don't make a sound.

I'm scared. So scared.

I lie on my stomach. Still. Silent. Waiting. My palms are stinging. Cheek throbbing. Rotting leaves pervade my nostrils. My stomach roils as I slowly inch forward, digging my elbows into the wet soil for traction. Left. Right. Left. Right.

I'm in the undergrowth now. Thorns pierce my skin and catch on my clothes but I stay low, surrounded by trees, thinking I can't be seen, but the clouds part and in the moonlight I catch sight of the sleeve of my hoodie, which, unbelievably, is white, despite the mud splatters. I curse myself. Stupid. Stupid. Stupid. I yank it off and stuff it under a bush. My teeth clatter together with cold. With fear. To my left twigs snap underfoot and instinctively I push myself up and rock forward onto the balls of my feet like a runner about to sprint. Over my heartbeat pounding in my ears, I hear it.

A cough. Behind me now. Close. Too close.

Run.

I stumble forward. I can do this I tell myself, but it's a lie. I know I can't keep going for much longer.

The clouds roll across the sky again and the blackness is crushing. I momentarily slow, conscious I can't see where I'm putting my feet. The ground is full of potholes and I can't risk spraining my ankle, or worse. What would I do then? How could I get away? The wind gusts and the clouds are swept away and in my peripheral vision a shadow moves. I spin around and scream.

Run.

# CHAPTER ONE
## Now

Every Tuesday, between four and five, I tell lies.

Vanessa, my therapist, nudges tortoiseshell glasses up the bridge of her nose and slides a box of Kleenex towards me, as if today will be the day my guilt spews out, coming to rest, putrid and toxic, on the impossibly polished table between us.

'So, Jenna.' She shuffles through my file. 'It's approaching the six-month anniversary – how do you feel?'

I shrug and pick at a stray thread hanging from my sleeve. The scent from the lavender potpourri irks me, as does the excess of shiny-leaved plants in this carefully created space, but I swallow down my agitation as I shift on the too-soft sofa. I can't keep blaming my medication for my mood swings, can I?

'Fine,' I say, although that couldn't be further from the truth. I have so many emotions waiting to pour out of me, but whenever I'm here, words tie themselves into knots on my tongue, and however much I want to properly open up, I never really do.

'Have you been anywhere this week?'

'I went out with Mum, on Friday.' It's hardly news. I do it every week. Sometimes I can't understand why I see Vanessa at all. I've completed the set number of appointments I was supposed to, yet still I arrive on the dot each week. I guess it's because I don't get out much and I do like my routine, my little bit of normality.

'And socially?'

'No.' I can't remember the last time I had a night out. I'm only thirty but I feel double that, at least. I wasn't up to socialising for ages afterwards and now I prefer to be at home. Alone. Safe.

'Emotionally? Are things settling down?'

I break eye contact. She's referring to my paranoia, and I don't quite know what to say. At almost every hospital appointment the cocktail of drugs I am taking to stop my body rejecting my new heart is adjusted, but anxiety has wrapped itself around me like a second skin, and no matter how hard I try, I can't shake it off.

'The urge to…' she consults her notes, 'run away? Is that still with you?'

'Yes.' Adrenaline pricks my skin and the underarms of my T-shirt grow damp. The sense of danger that often washes over me is so overwhelming it sometimes feels like a premonition.

'It's not unusual to want to escape from your own life when something traumatic has happened that is difficult to process. We have to work together to break the cycle of obsessive thoughts.'

'I don't think it's as simple as that.' The fear is as real and solid as the amber paperweight that rests on Vanessa's desk. 'I've been having more…' I'm not sure I want to tell her but she's looking at me now in that way of hers, as if she can see right through me, '… episodes.'

'Are they the same as before? The overwhelming dizziness?' She lifts her chin slightly as she waits for my answer, and I wish I'd never mentioned it.

'Yes. I don't lose consciousness but my vision tunnels and everything sounds muffled. They're getting more frequent.'

'And how long are these episodes lasting?'

'It's hard to say. Seconds probably. But when it happens I feel so…' I look around the office as though the word I am looking for might be painted on the wall, '… frightened.'

'Feeling out of control is frightening, Jenna, and it's understandable given what you've been through. Have you mentioned these episodes to Dr Kapur?'

'Yes. He says panic attacks aren't unheard of on my medication but if all goes well at my six-month check he can reduce my tablets and that should help.'

'There you go then. And you're due back at work…' she glances at her papers, '… Monday?'

'Yes. Only part-time though. At first.' Linda and John, my bosses, have been more than generous with the time off they have given me. They're friends of Dad's and have known me most of my life, and although Linda said I shouldn't feel obliged to return I've missed my job. I can't imagine starting afresh somewhere new. Somewhere unfamiliar. I'm nervous though. I've been away so long. How will it feel? Being normal again. I'm jittery at the thought of mixing with people. I've got too used to my own company, being at home, filling my time. 'Pottering around,' Mum used to call it; 'hiding myself away,' she says now, but in my flat the jagged unease I carry with me isn't quite so sharp. But life goes on, doesn't it? And if I don't force myself to start living again now I'm afraid I never will.

'How do you feel about going back?'

My shoulders begin their automatic ascent towards my ears but I stop them. 'OK, I think. My parents aren't keen. They've been trying to talk me out of it. I can understand that they're worried it will be too much, but Linda has said I can take it slowly to start with. Leave early if I get too tired and go in late if I've had a bad night.' I've always had a good relationship with Linda, even if she hasn't visited me in the past few months. She doesn't know what to say, I suppose. No one does. The fact I nearly died makes people uncomfortable.

'And the donor's family? Are you still trying to contact them?'

I shift in my seat. Over the past few months I have poured my thanks into letter after letter that was rejected by my transplant co-ordinator. I'd inadvertently revealed too much. A clue about who I was, where I live. But without those details it all seemed so cold and anonymous. Eventually I paid a private investigator to find them and wrote to the family directly. It cost a small fortune just for their address but it was worth it to be able to express how grateful I am and how much their act means to my family, without filtering my words. I wasn't going to bother them again and never expected to hear back but they replied straight away, and seemed genuinely pleased to have heard from me. I know Vanessa won't like what's coming.

My mouth dries and I lean forward to pick up my glass. My hand trembles and ice cubes chink and water sloshes over the side and trickles onto my lap where it soaks into my jeans. I sip my drink, conscious of the tick-tick-tick of Vanessa's clock, discreetly positioned behind me. 'I'm meeting them on Saturday.'

'Oh, Jenna. That's completely unethical. How did you trace them? I'm going to have to report this, you know.'

My face flames as I study my shoes. 'I can't tell you. I'm sorry.'

'You know contact isn't encouraged.' Disapproval drips from every word. 'Especially this early on in the process. It can be incredibly distressing for everyone, and it could set you back several stages. A simple thank you letter would have sufficed but meeting – I just…'

'I know. They've been told exactly the same thing, but they want to meet me. They do. And I need to meet them. Just once. It feels as though someone else is inside of me, and I want to know who it is. I have to know.' My voice cracks.

'It's become almost an obsession and it's not healthy, Jenna. What good will it do you knowing whose heart you have?'

The colours in the painting behind her, something modern and chaotic, swirl together and the gnawing agitation inside me grows.

'It would help me to understand.'

'Understand what?' Vanessa leans towards me like a jockey on a horse, pushing forwards, sensing a breakthrough.

'Why I lived and they died.'

\* \* \*

There's an indent in my chocolate leather couch marking the place I've spent too many hours. There might as well be a sign, GIRL WITH NO LIFE LIVES HERE. I light a berry-scented candle before flopping down in my usual spot. I always feel so drained when I've been to see Vanessa, and I'm never sure whether it's from the emotions that bubble to the surface when I sit in her immaculate office, or the effort of keeping them inside.

From the coffee table, I pick up my sketchbook. Drawing always relaxes me. I stream James Bay through my Bluetooth speaker and as he holds back the river I tap-tap-tap the pencil hard against my knee, staring at the bland walls as I wait for inspiration to hit. I've been meaning to decorate since Sam moved out nearly six months ago. Make the flat my own. Cover up the magnolia with sunshine yellow or rich red: bold colours that Sam hates. It's not like he's coming back although I know he'd like to. He never wanted us to split up but I couldn't stand the look of sympathy in his eyes whenever he looked at me after my surgery, the way he fussed around asking if I was all right every five minutes. I didn't want him to be stuck with someone like me, 'helping me through' as though we're old and there's nothing more to life. Cutting him free was the kindest thing I've ever done, even if my stomach still twists every time I think about him. We're trying to be friends. Texting. Facebooking. But it's not the same, is it? I add decorating to my mental list of things to do that I'll probably never get around to. The days when I had to take it easy have passed but I'm stuck in a rut I can't get out of and, truth be told, I'm scared. Despite the hours of physio and the mountain of leaflets I was sent home with, there's a hesitancy about my movements. An enforced slowness. My body is healing well, my doctor says, but my mind doesn't seem to believe it, and I'm terrified I will push myself too hard. That something will go wrong, and what would I do then? I picture myself lying on the floor. Unable to reach the phone. Unable to move. Who would know? I pretend to Mum I'm fine living alone. I pretend to everyone. Even myself.

What can I draw? I flick through the pages of my pad. Initially there is image after image of Sam, but lately my drawings have become darker. Menacing almost. Forests with twisted tree branches, eyes peering out of the gloom, an owl with beady eyes. I sigh. Perhaps Vanessa is right to be concerned about my mental health.

My mobile beeps. It's a text from Rachel, and I know without opening it she'll be asking what I'm doing later. I'll tell her I'm having a night in and to have a drink for me at the pub. It's our weekly routine, like Punch and Judy. The same every time even though sometimes you itch for a different ending. *I could go*, I think to myself but then I bat the thought away. It seems fruitless to try to fall back into the same habits. I'm not the person I was before, and besides, people treat me differently now, never quite meeting my gaze, not knowing what to say. I'll see Rachel at work on Monday.

Nearly six months ago, someone died so I can live. My world has become so small it sometimes feels as though I can't breathe. Who was it that died for me? I squeeze my eyes tightly closed but the thought still juggernauts towards me and I don't know how to make it stop. I shiver and cross to the window. The breeze blowing in is freezing but I am grateful for the fresh air. I have been home for weeks now but the heavy smell of hospital seems to have embedded itself into my lungs, and whatever the weather I always have the windows cracked open. I peer out of the slatted blinds into the dusk and a chill creeps up my spine. A shadow shifts in the doorway across the road, and the urge to run I told Vanessa about swamps me. My breath quickens but the street is still. Quiet. I slam the window and close the blinds and am cocooned by the dim light in my living room. My world is shrinking; my confidence too.

Back on the sofa, my hands are shaking too much to hold the pencil steady. *I'm safe*, I tell myself. So why don't I feel it?

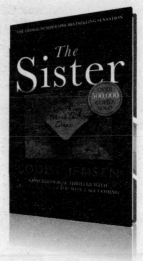

**'I did something terrible Grace. I hope you can forgive me . . .'**

Grace hasn't been the same since the death of her best friend Charlie. She is haunted by Charlie's words the last time she saw her, and in a bid for answers, opens an old memory box of Charlie's. It soon becomes clear that there was a lot she didn't know about her best friend.

When Grace starts a campaign to find Charlie's father, Anna, a girl claiming to be Charlie's sister steps forward. For Grace, finding Anna is like finding a new family and soon Anna has made herself very comfortable in Grace and boyfriend Dan's home.

But something isn't right. Things disappear, Dan's acting strangely and Grace is sure that someone is following her. Is it all in Grace's mind? Or as she gets closer to discovering the truth about both Charlie and Anna, is Grace in terrible danger?

There was nothing she could have done
to save Charlie . . . Or was there?

**Available now**

**The perfect daughter. The perfect girlfriend. The perfect murder?**

Jenna is given another shot at life when she receives a donor heart from a girl called Callie. Eternally grateful to Callie and her family, Jenna gets closer to them, but she soon discovers that Callie's perfect family is hiding some very dark secrets . . .

Callie's parents are grieving, yet Jenna knows they're only telling her half the story. Where is Callie's sister Sophie? She's been 'abroad' since her sister's death but something about her absence doesn't add up. And when Jenna meets Callie's boyfriend Nathan, she makes a shocking discovery.

Jenna knows that Callie didn't die in an accident. But how did she die? Jenna is determined to discover the truth but it could cost her everything; her loved ones, her sanity, even her life.

**Available now**